# ELEMENT OF TRUTH

## BOOK III

## HEATHER SLAWECKI

Jeanne —
Thanks for madis —
literally!

Heath Slawecki

g

Graylyn Press

# ACKNOWLEDGEMENTS

Writing a trilogy in two years wouldn't have been possible without the support of some very special people. I'd like to start by thanking my mother, Carola, and my mother-in-law, Joan, for their involvement, encouragement, and enthusiasm. They read each chapter as I wrote them, helping me build momentum and the determination to cross the finish line.

I would never have been able to juggle so many things if it weren't for my supportive husband, Adam, and our daughter, Lydia. Thank you for sacrificing time without me so I could pursue this goal, and for bringing me breakfast every Saturday and Sunday morning while I worked. I thank both of my parents for their continued support and advice, as well as the love from my entire extended family.

A big thanks to my editing and proofing team: Becky Hamilton, Bill Sorg, Jeff and Liz Cort, and for the most proofs read, Adam Slawecki. I'm grateful for my best friends and cheerleaders who've had my back through this process: Tina, Kim, Steph, Karen, Tammy, Brenda, Tony, Lori, Pammy, Amy, and Tom.

The setting I owe to the beautiful place I still consider home ...

Bucks County. In this series, you'll find true depictions of Lake Nockamixon, Tinicum and Tohickon Creeks, the Delaware River, New Hope, Peddler's Village, Doylestown, Van Sant Historical Airport, Ringing Rocks Park, Fonthill Castle, Mount Gilead, and Lambertville, New Jersey.

This trilogy is dedicated to my Bucks County Classmates from Tinicum Elementary, St. John the Baptist, and Central Bucks East, some are gone but not forgotten. The conclusion of the series is also dedicated to my ΦΣΣ sisters from Widener U.

The many Ford references are in memory of the late and great Gary Buch, who owned McCafferty Ford, Langhorne from 1981 – 1999. The SOOOPER will always hold a special place in my heart, both for being my first feature story, and for being a great friend to our family.

That should cover it! Now, I invite you all to sit back and finish this wild ride.

# 1

## WHERE AM I?

I hear beeps and someone calling my name. My eyes are so heavy. I want to open them, but I physically can't. I give up and feel myself drift back to sleep. "Jenny, try to open your eyes. It's time to wake up." I recognize his voice. It's my ex-husband, John. That means I must be at Johns Hopkins, and I'm in good hands. I drift off again. "Jenny, open your eyes! You can do it." He's relentless. I give it my all just to get him off my back, but it's still not working. Someone with a warm washcloth comes to the rescue. "That's it. That's it. Come on, Jenny. You've got this."

They're open. John is the one above me with the washcloth, gently wiping my lashes. He's blurry, but I see his warm smile. I can see, but I'm unable to speak. A nurse swabs my mouth with a pink wet sponge on a stick, and I become literally unglued.

I'm not sure what I'm supposed to say. Someone else is going to have to start this conversation, because I don't know what everyone knows, or how I got to wherever I am. And all the rousing from John is making me aware of the pain. It hurts everywhere.

"Can you try to speak for me?"

"Where am I?" I manage to say in a very hoarse voice.

"That's it. You're doing great. You're in the critical care wing at Doylestown Hospital in a private room. You've got FBI stationed outside your door. You're safe. Thank God, you're going to be all right, Jenny."

"What happened?" I ask weakly. *I know, but do they?*

"We were kind of hoping you could tell us that," John says. I wince as I lift my head up off the pillow for a closer look at who he means by "us." Everything is still blurry, but I can make out multiple white coats.

"I don't remember anything. Why am I here?"

"Where do I start? Broken hand, severe muscle damage, fractured ribs, a collapsed lung, fractured collar bone, and a large bite wound on your right shoulder. Otherwise, you're the picture of health."

"Did you say a bite wound? How long have I been here?"

"Two weeks. And you've already undergone three surgeries. We thought it would be best to keep you out of it to heal for a bit. No sense in suffering. You almost died though, Jenny. You lost a tremendous amount of blood. Think, hon. You must remember something," John pleads.

"Where was I found?"

"A Special Agent Steven Edwards brought you in. He found you alongside the road near the lake. He said he was searching for you. Thank goodness he found you when he did. He said you went missing after the explosion in the barn. He wasn't sure if you were captured or ran away from the scene. Apparently, you're tough to keep up with." John pauses and looks down.

"I didn't know you bought your old farm. Why would you ...?" He stops himself before getting too intrusive, aware that it's not really his place. But it's tough for him to hide his personal interest, and I can't blame him. "Anyway, your brother called and asked if I'd oversee your care. I wanted them to bring you to Hopkins, but you were too unstable." He looks around the room. "Turns out, this hospital has some of the best surgeons and staff I've ever worked with."

"Thank you, Dr. Keller. It's been a pleasure working with you as well," an unknown voice responds.

I hold out my good hand for him. "Thanks, Johnny." He holds it and takes a seat next to me.

"Was I alone?" *Where the hell is Ryan?*

"Yes. Agent Edwards believes you were attacked by a bear. The marks on your back are fairly conclusive. But the rest of you." He shakes his head and looks me over. "It doesn't add up. You're a mess."

"Maybe I was in a car accident and started walking for help when I was attacked? Was my car nearby?"

"That's been ruled out."

"Has anyone been here to see me? Where's my brother?"

"Yes. Once you were out of intensive care, Danny was able to sleep next to you. He hasn't left your side. He's been terrific. It's a shame I didn't know him sooner."

"I know, John. Where is he? I want to see him."

"He's going to be very excited to hear your voice. Nurse, can you call for him?"

"Of course, Dr. Keller."

"Maybe once you start talking to him, things will come back to you. Once you're off some of the heavier pain meds, things may click again. Sometimes traumatic events take time to recall. You've been through something brutal, again. I'm so sorry." He leans in, kisses my cheek, and heads for the door. "I'll be back to check on you tomorrow, then I'm going to have to get back to my regular schedule. But you're in good hands here." He pauses and turns to look at me. "Unless you want to move back home. You're stable enough. We can move you back to Baltimore. Do you want to come home?"

Home. Where is home? It's an interesting question, one that shouldn't take the average person long to answer. We've been divorced for close to three years, so I assume he simply means back to Baltimore, but it gives me pause. I still have my townhouse with Ryan in Baltimore. But, as a result of some rather stunning revelations, on top of more catastrophic events, Ryan and I now both separately own our family homes in Brandtville. Home? Where do I see myself in the future? Ryan and I aren't even officially together anymore. I'm so complicated.

"Jenny?" John repeats.

"The last thing I want to do is move right now, but I'll see you tomorrow. Thank you so much for everything. You've never let me down. Ever. But me. I really don't deserve your help. You're too good to me."

"Don't be silly. We're good, Jenny. I'll always be here for you if you need me. I promise." He moves back to the bed, kisses my cheek again, and disappears. Now that he's gone, I have a chance to survey what I'm dealing with in this private hospital room. It's a very large suite with living room furniture and a wet bar area. There's a coffee maker and half a dozen mugs sitting on a small granite countertop. There's a faux leather mauve sofa, oak coffee table, and a grey reclining chair. I still have insurance but wonder who's paying for these extras. The Feds or my father?

Danny bursts into the room and rushes to my side. "She's awake? Jenny, hey. How's my girl?"

I reach out my hand for him. It's the most disheveled I've ever seen him in public. He's got greasy hair and the start of a blotchy looking beard. The bags under his eyes look black and blue, and he smells like B.O. "You look like shit."

He laughs. "Well, you should take a look in the mirror. You look like something out of *The Walking Dead*." I laugh and feel a stabbing pain to my right side, followed by a burning sensation, which inadvertently makes me groan. "I'm sorry. I'm sorry," Danny says. "Maybe it's time for her meds." He looks up at a waiting, smiling nurse, who is eager to please.

"No, that's okay. I want to think clearly for a minute. I just woke up," I insist.

Two FBI agents barge into the room. *Already?* They have notepads, looking for information. The real FBI, not Agent Edwards. They start bombarding me with questions. Did I see my father? Was

I put somewhere for punishment? Have I learned more about the cult? *Is it that obvious?*

"My sister just woke up and doesn't remember anything. Could you please leave us alone for a while?"

"You don't remember anything, Ms. Keller? I find that hard to believe."

A challenge. He's challenging me about ten minutes after I rose from the dead. I accept. "What's your name?" I ask. I'm about to mess with this guy to get him out of my face.

"My name is Agent Miller, Ms. Keller. Nice to meet you"

"Were you at the farm? You look familiar. I remember seeing you."

He looks from me to his partner, who's got a raised eyebrow.

"No, ma'am. I'm new to the case."

"You're not telling the truth. I saw you. You had something to do with the fire." I get myself worked up, and Danny attempts to calm me down. My plan works though. I've got one agent shook for the day and one about to ask his buddy some questions.

"We'll leave you alone. Maybe she just needs some more rest," he says. They give me an awkward wave and hightail it out of the room.

"Did you really see him?" Danny asks.

"No, I'm just fucking with him."

"Christ, you're convincing as shit," he says with a laugh.

"Where's Ryan?" I whisper. "Is he here, too? Is he all right?"

"He's fine. He's at the estate. Dr. Braun and another surgeon fixed him up. He's doing well, just very worried about you."

"Why didn't they take me to Dr. Braun? Why am I here?"

"You wouldn't have made it. And apparently, our father wanted better for you. He wanted you here, and he personally asked me to get John involved. He even flew in a plastic surgeon from New York."

"Really? He chose my safety over his system?"

"Yeah. I think you've won his heart, Jenny." I wish it didn't feel so good to hear that. He's still a despicable human being.

"I want to see Ryan."

5

"You can't. Not yet. No visitors. I'm the only one allowed for now. Blood relatives only. Our father, the escaped cult leader, obviously doesn't count. But since you're doing better, maybe they'll let you see him soon."

"Can we call him or send him a text?"

"No. You don't get it. You're under strict surveillance. I'm still trying to figure out who all these guys are, and they're trying to figure us out too. I've been very tight-lipped and very cautious. They take my phone every time I come in."

"Really? That's a bit extreme."

"Obviously, it's not one of my usual phones, but I'm jonesing over here. I hate not having my gear. I'll reach out to him when I step out later. He's gonna be so happy to hear you're awake and improving."

"Have you been in touch with anyone else? Shane and Veronica? And Jack?"

Danny smiles. "Everyone's worried about you and you only. Everyone is fine."

"What about Josh?"

"Well, I haven't spoken to him, but I'll ask for some one-on-one time with him soon. It's possible that he's not allowed to contact us right now. Rules and all."

"He probably hates my guts. I want to talk to him, but I'm nervous. Will you tell Sammy I was asking for him, and to pass it on to Josh? I feel bad for what I said before trial. It was unfair, but I was so angry. I still am. I just don't know who to blame, and I fear I only have myself."

"No, don't do that." Danny gets a serious look on his face and holds my hand close to his face. "I will. He knows you well enough to understand where you were coming from. Listen, Ryan told me everything. Jenny, I can't believe what you've lived through. And I can't believe I let you. I'm a horrible brother. Was all that worth it?"

I break a smirk through very chapped lips. "Yes!" He shakes his head not fully understanding. "I can't explain it, but it was worth it. I almost gave up a few times. If it weren't for Ryan, I would've given up for sure, but I pushed on. And, hey, since I took one for the team, you're back in good graces too, Danny. No trial for you, so, yeah, it was worth it."

Danny kisses me on the forehead. "Sis, I wouldn't have gone through that punishment for all the tea in China. You're amazing and strong and a true survivor. If something would've happened to you, I never would've forgiven myself. Let's hope all of this punishment stuff is over now."

"Wait, I remember something. Right before I blacked out, the Judge granted me permission to initiate into the Order. Shit, what was it? Like United Fraternity or something and I heard Rosae Crucis. Crap, I don't remember."

"Sooner or later, we'll learn it and smother out the flames for good."

"Where's our dear old Dad anyway?" I ask.

"Got me. Hiding again. It'll be Thanksgiving in two days. I'm going to see if they'll let Mom and Nonna in for a few hours."

"Is it really? How long do you think I'm going to be here? Did they have services for Katie yet?"

"Yes, I'm sorry. They had to. But we'll have our own service later if you want. Jack saved some ashes for you and has them in a locket." I close my eyes, disappointed, but I understand.

"That was thoughtful of him," I say teary-eyed.

Danny runs his hand through my hair. "You have months of rehabbing to go, I'm afraid. Once you're able to move around better, you'll need a lot of time to heal. Your injuries are significant. Let's just take it day by day, all right?"

I nod. "Where's Fabrizio?"

"Once he knew you were going to be okay, he went back to Italy. His mother was griping about gout or something. And in the middle of all of this, he landed a side job—like a huge one. Someone's gotta work to maintain his idea of a lifestyle. Such a snob." We both smile. "But he'll be back."

"Good. I miss him already."

"He misses you too, but it's better this way for now. We need to keep things as simple as possible."

"How long are you staying?"

"Through Christmas, or longer if you need me."

I thank him, but I don't want him to leave at all. "I want you to be initiated with me, Danny. You're not going to move back permanently, are you?"

"Please put that talk on hold for now. I'm sorry, but I need to go back. I'll think about it though, okay? You're making me curiously nuts about this cult. But, hell, Fabrizio would break up with me. You know how he feels about this stuff. And after what you went through, he's even more adamant."

I don't want that, but I smile knowing he's thinking about it because I never thought I'd hear that. I feel hopeful that he'll come around and Fabrizio will back him up. I'm really worried about being alone once he leaves.

I start thinking about the love triangle I've created with Ryan and Josh. I was way too spontaneous with Josh. Talk about a rebound. Or, is it possible that I was truly falling in love? I'm not trusting my judgement anymore. The last time I saw Josh was at the start of my punishment ritual. It was intense, and I lashed out. I can still feel the slap he gave me for disrespecting him. It stung in more ways than one, but I'm not angry with him anymore. Still, he has a lot of explaining to do, and I need to know if he turned on his friends for power, or to protect me, or what. And Sal. Thinking of Sal makes me want to go right back to sleep. My heart hurts even more than my ribs. I get a flashback of him and his soon-to-be wife floating face down in the river current. I'll never see my best friend again.

"Question for you. How are you feeling about Kendra? How are you feeling about that?" Danny asks. I almost forgot about that part. I look away. I almost forgot that I'm a murderer. A savage murderer, no less. I get another vivid flashback, this one of me cutting off her hair to bring to my father. I have an out-of-body experience recalling the moment I stabbed her to death with the sharp stalactite from the cave.

I wanted to bring my father proof that I killed her for what reason? Approval? She took her last breath beneath me as I clutched her long black locks.

"Danny?"

"What?"

"I'm going to throw up."

# 2

PETER QUINN

Now that I know what it feels like to vomit with broken bones, I'm determined to never do it again. I ask for nausea and pain meds, down them, and lay still with my buzz. I close my eyes and get lost in flashbacks. I'm thinking of Scott and how disappointing he turned out to be, never telling us what really happened to Katie. But without him and Jacob in the end, Ryan and I wouldn't be alive. And Kendra would. I forgive Scott because Katie loved him. It wasn't his fault what happened to her. He has redeemed himself, for the most part.

I don't regret killing Kendra, but I'll never be the same because of it. I'm certain that taking another human life takes a part of your own soul. I feel hollow inside.

Does her death matter at all? Will anyone mourn her loss? Her journey in life is over, but according to my great-uncle, mine has just begun. My only wish is that her death will restore balance and harmony. My journey will be a lot easier with a little harmony around the time of my initiation. With my injuries, and the winter coming, I wonder how long before I can even begin the process, and if I'll need schooling—or brainwashing—beforehand.

I turn to look at the nurse who enters with another shot of pain relief. "Rest well today. Tomorrow we're going to help you get up. Even if it's just to the chair for a few hours." The effects of the morphine are instant, and I feel warmth and relief. The nurse hands me a breathing spirometer and reminds me that I'm at very high risk for pneumonia. Even with the pain killer, it hurts like hell to use it. I finish, sweating from the seemingly simple exercise, and sink back into the pillow.

Just when I think it's safe to nod off, another nurse enters with a tray. "Liquids first. Can you give broth a try and some juice? The quicker you begin eating and drinking, the better." I sleepily take a spoonful of broth. The cranberry juice quenches my thirst. Danny is smiling, looking happy to see me reach this small milestone in my recovery.

"I'm gonna take a nap, Danny. Make your calls," I slur. "I wanna see Ryan."

"You got it. You good with Mom and Nonna coming for a bit on Thanksgiving?"

"Yes, as long as Nonna brings her mashed potatoes and gravy." And I'm down for the count.

It's dark when I wake up again. I hear people talking from the far end of the room, so I pretend I'm still asleep. "It's not a good idea to move her." *Move me?* They're attempting to whisper, but I can hear them.

"We have doctors at Alpha-MED who can take it from here." I recognize the name. It's a top-secret medical facility in D.C. for people like me. I'd be trapped. "Ms. Keller is a witness to the events from the summer, as well as to the current situation. She cannot disappear again. We need every testimony and every account she has to put some of these people behind bars. The public is demanding justice. Plus, doc, she needs protection too. She's tough and has been invaluable in helping us so far, but look at her. She's been through another punishment ritual with that group. She can't possibly survive another. I don't know if she really doesn't remember, or if she's protecting them. But I want to know exactly who fucking did this to her and where. When she starts talking, I want our people there and no one else. In fact, I don't want her in contact with anyone else from now on. Once she's in D.C., we'll put her back in the Witness Protection Program and get her some therapy. Most of the paperwork is finished on my end. I'll need you to put her medical files under a new name. Dr. Keller is to know none of this for now. We'll tell him later that she's in protection."

"When are you proposing that all of this happen? She just woke up."

"We move her tomorrow, so send the brother packing. No more overnight guests."

"Hold up ..."

"Orders go all the way up to General Jamison."

"I'm not sure how I feel about this, but I'll do what I can to start prepping. Our plan is to get her up tomorrow. If I don't feel like she's ready, you'll need to wait. Doctor's orders. Got it?"

"We'll see. I'll be in touch."

"How's she doing?" Danny enters and asks.

"She's resting comfortably," the doctor replies.

"Great." I hear Danny's footsteps as he walks to my side and can smell his hazelnut coffee. I hear the men exit, then open my eyes and whisper, "Shh!" Danny jumps, spills his coffee, and chokes on the sip in his mouth.

"You scared the hell out of me. I didn't know you were awake. Was I too loud?"

I tell him everything I heard, as quietly as possible. He's pissed. We're at a loss for what to do. I know I need more medical attention than the Brandt's private doctor can handle. *Or not.* Dr. Braun is pretty good, but I want to heal properly. I've seen some of Dr. Braun's patients after his care and they weren't pretty. He practices on the fly and has to use what resources are available to him in the moment. It starts to sink in that we have no choice but to play along until I get better. They don't realize that I'm actually quite safe just where I am. But I can't tell them it's because I'm under the watchful eye of the secret society.

"What if you hadn't overheard? I'd be frantic. Assholes." Danny is pacing when the nurse comes in.

"Everything all right?" she asks.

"Yes. Fine."

"I have Ms. Keller's delicious brothy dinner," she says cheerily. "The doctor also added some toast. Is she awake?"

"She's working on it."

"Ms. Keller? Could you try and eat a bite for me?"

I open my eyes and nod. She adjusts the bed to a more upright position, which makes me cry out in pain. It feels like someone is stabbing me in the ribs and collar bone. I can finally feel the pain in my shoulder too. It's the trifecta of agony. The bite must be deep, so I'm guessing strapless dresses won't be a great option for me in the future. I'm scarred for life, but I knew the risk, and this is what I get for it.

"Oh, I'm sorry. I know it hurts," the nurse empathizes.

"Can I get up *now*? I want to stand." Despite the pain, I need to test myself. "How bad is my leg?"

"It's badly bruised, and the muscle is—how can I put it—a bit shredded. It's going to be very painful to try and put weight on it for quite some time. I don't even know if it's possible yet. We should probably wait until tomorrow."

"No. Let me have the broth, and then I want to stand."

"I'll check with the attending physician. Be right back."

"Oh, boy. She's back. My tough sister. When you make up your mind."

I drink the broth and try to figure out exactly how many things I'm hooked up to in addition to the IV. No catheter. I'm in diapers. *Lovely.* Oxygen mask. Easy enough to take off. I have my usual fight or flight thing happening and need to know if I'll be able to walk on my own if I have to. How do I know I can trust *this* situation? Even if I can, I don't want to be locked up. What if they spoke loudly on purpose, and I'm not really going into a protection program? The more I think about it, the more paranoid I get.

"What's going on in your head? You're panicking. I can see it."

"How do we find out for sure who these people are? The doctor? The Fed? Call Edwards. No, don't. I don't know what to do." Danny sighs.

The attending physician enters with two male nurses. "You really want to try and stand up, Ms. Keller?"

"Yes. Please."

"You're brave. We usually have to force people to get up. Well then, let's give it a try." The nurses surround me. One of the men manages to swivel me so that my legs are dangling off the bed. I wince and almost black out from the sudden movement and pain. I'm weak and start to realize how much weight I've lost through this ordeal. I'm very frail.

Despite the pain, I'm determined to push through it. The female nurse detaches my IV to give me more freedom, a male grabs me a walker. "On three, guys. Take it as gently as possible under her right side. Ms. Keller, try and push off with your good hand and the nurse will pull you up under your left side. Deep breath. Ready?" I nod. Danny is nervously pacing again. "One ... two ... three." I push, they pull, and I'm on my feet. I see stars from the pain shooting through my leg and concentrate hard to maintain my balance. I need to look at my injuries for myself to see how bad I am. "Great job! How are you feeling?"

"A little dizzy."

"Tina, get a check on her blood pressure. I don't want you passing out on me, Ms. Keller."

"She's a little low, but okay."

The doctor, Dr. Fisher, I see from his jacket, hands me a walker. He's young. Younger than me. Decent looking with dark hair, a groomed shadow on his face, and no wedding band. He's the attending. "Who was the other physician? The one who just left?" I ask.

"That would be Dr. Clement."

"Who is he to you and to the hospital?"

"He works under the actual Surgeon General. He works for the government. Not a hometown doctor. You're the most cared-for patient I've ever had. Between your ex-husband, Dr. Rogers from NYU, and Dr. Clement, you're getting the royal treatment."

"Who's the agent he's working with?"

"I have his name, Jenny, relax." Danny pleads. "Just concentrate. You're standing for heaven's sake. I don't want you to fall."

Right. I need to move. My left hand is broken, so it's reasonably useless, but my fingers are exposed enough beyond the cast to get a small grip. My right hand is okay. I give myself a pep talk and start walking. The struggle is real. Both of my legs are weak and shaky, but my right leg feels like it's on fire. I don't like being this much out of control and at the mercy of others. To make matters worse, I can feel my diaper slipping off. I tug at it and tell the female nurse's aide to take it off. She moves in.

"I want to sit on the toilet."

"That's not necessary today," Dr. Fisher announces. It makes me more determined. I know the quicker I'm able to use the restroom on my own, the better. I'm worried about bending my leg, but I think it's okay from the knee down. Dr. Fisher looks like he's breaking into a sweat. I'm challenging *him?* I make it all the way to the bathroom, fighting tears along the way.

"I just want this one with me." I point to the biggest male nurse. "What's your name?"

"Peter. Peter Quinn"

Peter looks nervous, like he doesn't want the responsibility. He's tall and strong-looking and can surely handle someone as scrawny as me. He's got a little extra weight around the waistline, which I can see through his scrubs. He's fair-skinned with a shaved head and round-rimmed, John Lennon style glasses. My kindness radar is reading high. He glances at the doctor for orders, looking apprehensive. "Come on, you two. Don't be such pussies. I'm the one in pain." They both laugh nervously. Danny shakes his head.

"That's my sister."

The doctor gives Peter permission to take me in. I wince all the way and slowly try to sit on the hopper. But there's no slow way down with the pain in my ribs. I sit rather abruptly, which makes me want to scream. I hold it in and wait for it to subside. I did it. I feel like this is a big accomplishment.

I caught a glimpse of myself in the mirror on the way down. Danny is correct. Scary stuff. I feel gross. Sweaty. Grimy. Smelly. Nasty. "Peter, while I'm here how about we get me cleaned up, huh?" I ask for the supplies I want. Soap, for starters. I hear Dr. Clement walk into the room to see what's going on, so I quickly tell Peter to shut the door all the way. I'm all orders, and we get me as hygienic as possible without a full shower. Peter is keeping up. He's a great nurse, confident in his skills, strong but gentle at the same time.

"Peter, John said I had a collapsed lung. Is that okay now?"

"Yes, ma'am. That's fine now. Not to worry."

"I want to see my leg and shoulder. Can you take off the bandages?"

"Not in here. But once I get you back in bed, I'll do a bandage change."

"You can do that on my leg, but I won't be able to see my shoulder from the bed. Just pull the bandage away for a minute. I stand back up by pushing off with my good hand. He's impressed. I'm completely naked, so Peter tries to cover me. I push the robe away. As a nurse, I'm sure he's used to nudity, but not someone lacking in modesty as much as me. I turn in front of the mirror, and he peels the bandage away.

"Holy shit," is all I can say.

"It's going to have to heal from the inside out. You're lucky it doesn't go all the way to the bone," he says. Mentally, it's disturbing and makes me want to cry. Medically, it's going leave a nasty scar, but at least I won't need more surgery, just antibiotic ointment and bandaging for a while. I take a deep breath as he covers the wound again. "You ready for a gown now, Ms. Keller?" I'm still making him uncomfortable, but I hate hospital gowns.

"What other option do I have?"

"What do you mean?

"What else can I wear?"

"This is pretty much it. We need to have access to everything from your shoulder to your leg."

"Am I still on IV antibiotics?"

"No. That treatment is complete."

"Then I don't need the IV or the saline bag. I'm drinking and can use the bathroom on my own. Can you take it off?"

"No way. I can't take it off. Ms. Keller, you just woke up today. You don't need to rush anything."

"Fine. Keep the IV in, but disconnect it. Let's see how I do. You can reconnect it if I'm having trouble. I want underwear, yoga pants, and a T-shirt."

"You don't understand how much it's going to hurt to put on a T-shirt, Ms. Keller."

"You're a big guy. Get me one in your size. We can slip it on and work my right arm in." He's shaking his head but agreeing at the same time.

"I'll have your brother gather some items for you."

"No. My brother doesn't leave my side. Have one of the security guards go out and get them. Something must be open."

"You want them now? Ms. Keller, if you don't mind me asking, what's going on? You're starting to sound like a woman ready to run. Slow down."

"How much do you know about me? Has Dr. Clement mentioned anything about moving me?"

"No. You can't be moved. Although, you're proving me a bit wrong at the moment."

"They want to take me somewhere in the middle of the night

tomorrow. Somewhere unsafe. I have twenty-four hours to come up with a plan to break out of here. I'll have good medical care where I want to go. But I have reason to believe not all of the key players out there have my best interests in mind." Peter is getting stressed out. "I need you to get me ready."

"How?"

# 3

## GAME PLAN

My nurse, Peter, and I are in the bathroom plotting my escape. He's fearful of getting in trouble and losing his job. I don't want that to happen, but selfishly, I won't lose sleep if it does. I need to get out of here. He discloses that he and the nurse's aide, Tina, are in a relationship, so he thinks maybe they'll be able to work together. Apparently, she's a big fan of mine and has followed my story since the summer. She begged for the case when I came in and was thrilled to get it. She's been working double shifts to care for me. He thinks she'll be ecstatic to be part of the action, but he needs to run it by her first. He won't participate without her consent. "That's so sweet," I tell him. "That's the way it should be." I make a mental note to kiss her ass a bit.

"Everything okay in there? It's been an hour." I believe it's the attending physician asking.

"Doing fine. We'll be out in a minute," Peter replies. Now that I'm up, I must admit, I feel a little better. I've got the blood moving. Plus, having a plan makes me feel mentally more in control. I have to run everything by Danny, who will, as usual, have a big role to play. He may need the best of Fabrizio's technology to boot. I can't decide what, if anything, to tell John. He doesn't deserve to be deceived, but he can't know the truth. I just hope that my progress today doesn't rush them into dragging me out of here tonight. I express my fears to Peter before we open the door, and we come up with a backup plan that involves a fake seizure. It would slow them down, and they'd have to order more scans and get results to make sure I'm stable. Peter bundles me up in two gowns for now and puts my sneakers back on for the walk back to bed.

"I hope you know what you're doing, Jenny. Is it all right if I call you that?"

"Oh, God, yes. No more Ms. Keller."

"Okay. Let's roll." He opens the door. My leg hurts, but I know I could make it back to the bed just holding his hand. I need to pretend I'm not that strong and wince and groan as I push the walker all the way back. Peter and the other male nurse pivot me back into a laying position. We all take a deep breath. Phew!

"Ms. Keller, I'm impressed. I've honestly never seen anyone more determined in my life," Dr. Fisher admires.

"You have no idea, doc." Danny says. Peter commends me as well, and I find myself smiling with a little pride. I like this kind of attention. It's encouraging. Dr. Clement enters and looks ecstatic to hear of my walk and hygiene status.

"I understand you want some civilian clothes, huh?"

"What do you mean by civilian? Are you a military physician? I simply want clothing instead of these uncomfortable gowns."

"Actually, I'm a high-ranking military surgeon. Brigadier General." I guess this is where I salute him. I don't know what's wrong with me. This man probably wants what's best for me while helping the Feds protect what I know. I'm wrong to go into hiding. I should be helping these men put the bad guys behind bars, especially my most-wanted father. That's why I want to be initiated in the first place. But I can't get initiated locked up in the Witness Protection Program. They've tied my hands.

"I thank you for your service and your care, sir. I mean that from the bottom of my heart." I truly mean it and second-guess myself and my morals. He thanks me for the acknowledgment.

"Okay, everyone out for a minute. I'd like to have a word with Ms. Keller on my own." He's evaluating me, as I am him. He knows I'm on a mission here. This isn't ordinary go-getter, get-better stuff. He was a little reluctant about releasing me so soon in his chat with the FBI agent. I need to hear him out. With everyone out of the room, he pulls up a chair. "You know, Ms. Keller, I work for the government, but I also took an oath. If there's something you want to tell me, please do." He stares down at me. Even though I want to believe him, he's got his orders. I'm not sure how many times I can get away with this accusation, but I'm giving it another shot.

"I feel like nobody wants to hear the truth."

"I do. Talk to me, Ms. Keller."

"I remember seeing that FBI agent at the farm. He's not new to the case." *I feel so terrible for lying.* "I think he's on the inside, Dr. Clement. He's part of the cult." The doctor can't help but laugh out loud.

"No, Ms. Keller. No. I've known him for years. He can be a jackass, but he's not on the inside." He laughs again.

"That makes me feel better. Maybe I'm just being paranoid. As long as he doesn't suggest I go back into the Witness Protection Program, I'll trust him if you do." I hold my ribs as I say it, then close my eyes and wait for it. He's quiet. But I bet if I were looking at his eyes, they'd be wide.

I reopen my eyes but don't make direct eye contact. "Can I see my leg?" I want to see what's going on there. Did you stitch me up?" He's quiet, deep in thought.

"Excuse me? Sorry. Why would that matter?"

"Well, I just want to see how bad it is."

"No. I mean the Witness Protection Program."

"Before Agent Black died, he told me it was code. He was tipped off that going back into protection would put me in danger."

"How would it put you in danger?"

"Because only the bad guys who put me there will know where I really am. They're not all good guys, Dr. Clement. Anyway, can I see what my leg looks like? How stable am I really, and how many stitches do I have?" He looks like a deer in the headlights. I know how he feels. It's hard to know who to trust. And Agent Black can't back up my story because he's six feet under.

"Sure. Hold on. Let me get Peter. It was a difficult surgery, but you're doing well." I've given him something to think about. "I'll be right back, and we'll all take a look at it together."

Peter and Dr. Clement re-enter. They're both all business. But I can read them. They're equally lost in troubling thoughts, but they've got the lights shining, all the applications they need on a tray table, and blue latex gloves on. "Ready, Jenny?" Peter asks.

"Ready." He pulls the gauze off carefully, exposing an enormous gash, at least twelve inches long and two inches wide. There are staples, stitches, and some kind of glue keeping my leg together. Dr. Clement describes my condition and surgery in more detail. It was very delicate, but thankfully nothing was broken.

Well, I can say goodbye to miniskirts and short shorts. I'm going to look horrifying in a bikini. The sight of this wound is making me feel sorry for myself.

"Ms. Keller, you have no idea how this happened? You must remember something. This is unlike anything I've seen before."

"I'm sorry. I don't. And I'm kind of glad I don't remember. If I do remember though, you'll be the first to know." I'm exhausted and hurting. I ask for Danny to return and for my meds. "Dr. Clement? You won't let anyone release me from here without my full consent, will you? I'd be in danger, but I'm safe here."

"Not a chance. You rest. You've had a long day."

"Will do." I reach out my good hand to him and thank him again. I need him to feel a personal connection with me. He's starting to have that fatherly, protective look in his eyes, which I needed to see. He's got some investigating to do now and looks like he can't get out of the room fast enough. He asks the team and Danny to rejoin me.

I'm alone again with "my" team. "What the hell's going on?" Danny asks. Peter and I smile at each other. Tina has been filled in and can't hide a grin. I can tell she likes adventure, just like me. She's very pretty, likely Italian, with beautiful skin and perfect nails. Her hair is in a ponytail, but I can see it has a natural wave.

"Danny, meet our new teammates."

"I thought you were in the bathroom an awfully long time. What's the plan?"

I give him the parts Peter and Tina will play, then I ask to be alone with Danny. They can't know where I'm going or that I'm actually working toward an initiation. I need them to think I'm going somewhere secret and safe away from the Feds *and* the cult.

Once gone, I give Danny a very long list of things to do and people to contact. First Ryan, who needs to get in touch with our father somehow with the news of the Witness Protection plan. He's not going to like that and will make preparations for my recovery elsewhere. I've had all the surgeries I need, so Dr. Braun can handle my care from here on out. I'll have to wait for my father's orders to know where I'll be. Unfortunately, the Brandt Estate will likely be off limits. But that's really where I want to be. Near Ryan. I'm aching and yearning to see him. The last time we were together, we were being baptized at 2:52 a.m. in the lake. That's a moment that will bind us for life.

# 4

## NO CONSENT

"**G**ood morning, Ms. Keller," a cheerful woman says way too close to my ear. I tossed and turned all friggin night and literally just fell asleep. Who is this annoying person? "My name is Dawn. I'll be your nurse's aide today. Can I get you anything?" she asks while taking my vitals.

"What time is Tina's shift?"

"Oh, they made some changes to the shifts today. She's been reassigned." My eyes pop wide open.

"Where's Peter?"

"Same."

"I want to speak with Dr. Clement immediately." John walks in as I'm shouting orders. *What the hell.* "Could you leave me alone with Dr. Keller, please?" Dawn takes off the blood pressure cuff and exits.

"What's the matter, Jenny?" John asks with a slight smile on his face. "I heard you got up and got yourself into the bathroom. That's remarkable. You're doing awesome."

"Why did they suddenly remove my regular nurses?"

He takes a deep breath before he speaks. "Jenny, the psychiatric team has noted that you've been acting irrational. Paranoid. That's not surprising after everything you've been through." *Psychiatric team?* "I've been briefed, and they're going to place you into the Witness Protection Program, temporarily. I wasn't sure how I felt about it at first, but I'm in favor of it now, especially with this being my last day here. I think now that you're on the mend, it's the perfect place for you. You'll be safe, and they've promised that I will get updates." *Shit! Shit! Shit!* Dr. Clement enters the room.

"Good morning, Ms. Keller. Dr. Keller."

"I took to heart what you told me yesterday, Ms. Keller, and did some thorough digging and vetting. Now listen, there is, in fact, a plan to put you into the program again. But it's all perfectly legit. I looked into it myself. But, keeping to my word, I'll only let them take you with your consent."

"I do not consent. Where's my brother?"

"Ms. Keller, he can't come in today. But everything is going to be just fine. I promise." I begin to well up. I'm losing. My plans are all falling apart. I hope Danny got to our father and that there's a plan I don't know about. I'm fuming.

"Where are the clothes I wanted? I'm still laying here in this disgusting gown."

"Jenny, please," John says. I give him a glare.

"Hold on. Peter did bring you some clothes. I'll grab them." I can't look at John despite everything he's done for me. I push the button on my side rail so that I'm in a sitting position. It hurts but feels a tad better than yesterday.

"Why are you so against the program?"

"Why can't I just stay here?"

"Because, obviously, someone is out to kill you. Jenny, this was no accident. You must sense that much, and they've done this to you twice. You need the protection, and it's becoming a burden to this hospital to operate around you. It's expensive. I know the facility they're taking you to, and it's wonderful. Great doctors and staff. Protecting people like you is all they do. It just makes sense. Plus, I'm not very far from there." *He doesn't get it.* I need to find a way to fake calm down. It's not John's fault. He truly thinks this is for the best.

"I want to get up." Dr. Clement walks back in the room with a plastic bag. I move the handrail down.

"What are you doing? You're not ready to get up on your own," John reprimands.

"Watch me. I have to use the bathroom." Dr. Clement comes to my side. *Ugh.* I don't know if I can do it. I remember the struggles during my trial and try to channel the same strength. I close my eyes and say a small prayer. A tear slides down my cheek as I do. John is getting upset by my reaction. His eyes are watery. He knows I've been through a lot, and he still hurts when I hurt. John had no idea I was in the Witness Protection Program the whole time we were married. Even hearing him call me by my birth name is weird. He's always called me Tricia. My legal name is still Patricia Keller. He knows a lot now, but he still doesn't know me. I use the strength of my good hand and manage to pivot myself at the same time. I'm at the edge of the bed. Both sets of eyes are on me, but I don't want to look at either of them. I push the button to call the nurse.

"What do you need, Jenny? I'm right here," John says. "Come on."

"Can I help you?" A female voice asks over the speaker.

"Yes, could you have Dawn prepare the bathroom? I want to get washed up."

"I'll send her right in, Ms. Keller."

I wait at the edge of the bed in silence. I was kind of hoping at least one doctor would leave, but I can see they both want to witness what I can, or cannot do, on my own. I wipe my tears as I wait and take a big sip of water. This is awkward. No one is saying anything, but I imagine the looks they're giving each other behind my back.

Dawn returns with a smile and prepares the bathroom. "Ready when you are."

"I'm ready. And you can leave."

"Jenny, she's just doing her job," John scolds.

In my head I'm counting. *One ... two ... three.* I push and use my good leg and core muscles to stand. I did it. I did it with no help. I take a deep breath and exhale to release some of the tension from the pain. Dr. Clement tries to take my hand, but I shake him off. *Traitor.*

"Here, I insist you use the walker at least, Ms. Keller."

"No." I push it out of the way so hard that it flips over. I hear John groan as I begin walking, one ginger step at a time. I'm just as surprised as they are to see I'm doing it. My right leg is burning but what muscles I have left are somewhat cooperating. I'm getting a system down and with it, more confidence. I grab the plastic bag Peter left for me with my good hand, walk in the bathroom, and shut the door. *I can't believe I just did that.*

I stay standing at the mirror and watch myself cry. I'm trying not to sob, but I know I'm loud enough to be heard and hope they both feel lousy. I manage to get the gown off and wash myself and brush my teeth. I can't wait for my first shower. I finish and look through the bag. Everything is here like I asked. I really should call the nurse to help me, but I'm too damn ticked and stubborn. I have to lasso my underwear, but I get it up. I sit on the toilet and put on my shirt. Not as difficult as I thought it would be. I grab the yoga pants and feel a tag. I try to pull it off. It's not a tag, it's a note, signed by Peter. Oh, thank God.

*Jenny, it was a pleasure meeting you. Maybe we'll meet again sometime soon. Your friend, Peter.*

I inhale deeply. There's still a plan. It's not me against the world. I still have my team. Maybe all I have to do is just relax and let it all happen. I get the yoga pants on by the grace of God. They were a good call, supporting my leg like an ace bandage. I slide into my sneakers. I can't bend to tie them, but at least they're on. I stand up and look in the mirror. I look tired and need food for strength.

I open the door to find only John left waiting. He's been shedding his own tears and has a tissue in hand. I walk slowly toward the reclining chair and sit.

"I'm sorry, Jenny. You're angry with me. I know you've been through a lot, but this is for the best."

"Go back to Baltimore, John. This is no place for you. Thank you again for everything." He comes to my side, kneels down, and lets a tear fall for me to see.

"What do you want me to do? I just want you to be safe. Don't you understand? Christ, Jenny. I would do anything for you. I would break off my engagement if you wanted me to."

I look at him with surprise and sympathy. "Oh, John." Now I feel guilt. Big time guilt. And his words are having a great effect on me. The offer is so tempting. Normalcy and our old friends sound so appealing, but I'm in love with Ryan. And maybe Josh. I can't destroy John again. He deserves happiness, stability, and faithfulness.

"You know things about me now, John, that you didn't when we were married. But you still don't know me." I take his hand, bring it up for a kiss, and stare at it. It's the hand that once bore a wedding band. "You deserve one-million times better than me." He shakes his head, not wanting to believe it. He wants to believe I have a virtuous side and that I was only misbehaving because of the circumstances. But I haven't changed. I'm worse now. I can add murderer to the list of reasons why I'm horrible for him. "No matter what happens, just remember that you will always have a very special place in my heart. No one will ever be able to replace it, or you." He blows his nose.

"What are you going to do?"

"I'm not consenting. They'll have to force me to go. And, dammit, that's not what the program is all about. But mark my word—they will take me against my will." He's starting to look concerned. Maybe I'm not as paranoid as he thought.

Six agents suddenly burst into the room. "What's going on?" John demands to know. I give him a look that says, *see.*

"Orders. It's time to move." John is on his feet, yelling for Dr. Clement, but an agent backs him up against the wall.

"No sudden movements, doc." A wheelchair is brought into the

28

room for me. John is yelling at the top of his lungs, angrier than I've ever seen him. I need to calm him down a little for his own good.

"Johnny, quiet. It's okay. I'll be okay." He's worked up and having trouble believing his eyes. He attempts to free himself, but the agent is too strong.

"She hasn't signed anything. This is illegal and immoral, you sons of bitches."

I'm being wheeled out of the room backwards and see the brutal, unnecessary force being used on him, and I don't like it. I scream for the agent to let him go. "Get your hands off of him. If you hurt him, I'll see to it that both your fucking arms are broken." *My father's temper is in my voice.*

"Is that a threat, Ms. Keller?"

"No, it's a promise. I'll do it myself if I have to. Now take your fucking hands off of him. You don't know who you're dealing with." The surprised look on John's face fills me with more guilt, but he's realizing what I said is true. He doesn't know me at all. I don't even know me.

# 5

## TEAMWORK

I'm finally getting a good look at the operation they've had in place during my stay. There's a private nursing station with lots of computers and scattered paperwork. Most of the staff moves behind it, giving us room to roll through. Some look surprised by the scene, while others look aware of the plans. There are lots of guards, like they're watching over the Queen of England. The asshole wheeling me is going too fast, seemingly taking pleasure out of my pain as he jostles me around. An elevator opens at the end of the hall and we go up. Why up? We weave in and out of various corridors. A code is used to allow us access to another elevator. It hits me—we're going by helicopter. The reality is that I don't stand a chance. I'm going into the program, and I'll have to come to terms with it. One last exit and we're on the rooftop. The cold air is a shock to my system, and I instantly get the shakes. There's a helicopter waiting and a gurney rolling toward me. I didn't even get a chance to say goodbye to Danny, and tomorrow is Thanksgiving. I'm having a full-blown pity party.

"Ms. Keller? I'll be the nurse handling your care on the chopper."

It's Peter. I look in the distance and see Tina prepping inside. He puts a warm blanket gently around my shoulders.

So, they're the ones who changed shifts, just for this reason. I look around, wondering what else is in store. There must be more to it.

The guards are standing by, looking in every direction. A pilot steps out to introduce himself. There's sudden chaos. The door we exited is blocked from the inside. A dozen men in black scale down from the upper level of the rooftop. Thankfully, there's no shooting, and the men swiftly gain control of the agents. I hear another helicopter in the distance. Peter has me strapped to the gurney and is pushing me toward the helicopter. Every bump hurts, but I grin and bear it, trusting him completely. One of the men in black gets behind the controls, and we take off, barely in enough time for Peter to close the door.

"OMG. Am I happy to see you! What's happening? How did you get *this* shift?"

"Thank Tina. Her mother, Lori, is the staff coordinator. Don't worry, we're both trained for this. In fact, Tina's in med school but couldn't get your assignment without playing an aide."

"There's just something about you, Jenny, that's fascinated me all of these months. I just want to help. When I found out you were in Doylestown, no way was anyone else getting your case. I'm from Brandtville originally and my mother was friends with Denise Brandt. We moved after her death. Kendra, right? Kendra killed Mrs. Brandt."

Oh, boy. Tina is more than commonly aware of what's happening. "Do you have a tattoo by chance?" I ask.

"How'd you know?" She lifts up her sleeve. It's a rose. I'm not sure what to make of it, considering how symbolic they are for Rosicrucians. This is tricky because Tina is a hometown version of me. She wants answers, but she has no idea what it takes to get them.

"It's beautiful. Any significance?"

"I got it when I was pledging as an undergrad. Once a Phi Sigma Sigma, always a Phi Sigma Sigma," she says and laughs. "It was our sorority flower." I crack a smile of relief. I wish I'd have had that experience.

A wave of nausea suddenly overcomes me. I haven't eaten, and the ride is turbulent. Tina sees it on my face and slides a Zofran under my tongue. "Almost there."

"Where are we headed?"

"Van Sant." I know the name well. That's where Scott flies, and where all the air signs learn to fly. It's small but historical. I just hope the FBI doesn't have it surrounded when we land. I hate this kind of suspense, especially in my current medical condition.

"Then where?"

"Unfortunately, that's the end of the tour for us. Take my card. If you ever need anything, give a holler. Maybe we can sit down together sometime when you're better? I would really love to talk to you, Jenny."

"I would like that too. You guys have been wonderful." We're descending. "How will you get away with this? What are you going to do now?" I ask.

"We'll think of something. Not to worry," Tina says. I'm so grateful. They did a lot to get me here and are going way above and beyond. I may owe Tina some details and dinner. Minimal details. They wish me luck as a new team takes over and wheels me toward another aircraft. This one is no helicopter.

"Ready, Jenny? Can you stand?" It's Scott. My morale is soaring. A few men help me get up and into the cockpit. It's a two-seater. No sooner am I buckled in, we're speeding down the grass runway and away we go. The pain is intense, but I'm too fascinated to care. Bucks County is incredibly beautiful from the air, even with no leaves on the trees.

"Scott, is Jacob okay?" I ask, needing to know.

"I'm sorry, Jenny. He didn't make it." Another life I destroyed. If it weren't for me, he'd be alive and well. "I also want to apologize for not trusting you with the truth about Katie. I hope you understand why I couldn't give you all the details at the time. I'm devastated by the loss and the harsh reality of what happened, Jenny. I'll never get over it."

"I understand now, Scott. It must be very painful." I don't have the energy to cry anymore or ask any more questions, especially about Kendra's resting place. I'm too tired. We're not in the air but fifteen minutes when we're landing again.

"Sorry, Jenny. This is going to be a little rough." I try to brace myself but pass out cold from the agony of a very brutal landing.

I'm awake again, in a dark room, in another hospital bed. But I have no idea where.

"Hello?" I call out. I'm hooked up to a monitor, which is taking my vitals, and have a new IV dripping fluid into my arm. I notice some sort of heavy bracelet on my free arm and smell something unusual on my bite wound.

"Jenny, my sweet, Jenny." It's my father. I instantly tense up with fear and jump as he opens a curtain. "There's my girl." He bends down to look me in the eyes and kisses my cheek. "Braun!" My father yells. Dr. Braun rushes to my side.

"How are you feeling? On a scale from one to ten, how bad is your pain?"

"I'm fine. What's this?" I ask, holding up the band.

"A magnet. You're lying on one too."

"What's it for?"

"The energy keeps circulation moving, prevents blood clots, and even reduces pain."

"What's that smell?"

Both Dr. Braun and my father crack a smile. "It's clay. A far superior antibacterial to any over-the-counter cream."

"Okay, well, thank you. I'm hungry. Could I have something to eat?"

"Of course." Dr. Braun shuts off the IV drip and excuses himself.

My father is grinning from ear to ear with every request. "I'm so proud of you, honey. I was worried. How are you feeling?"

"Alive. Where am I, and where's Danny?"

"Everyone's fine. Danny's getting settled."

"Here?"

"Yeah, here." I lift my left eyebrow. That sounds too good to be true. My father asks me what I remember about my trial. I remember almost every detail and give it to him.

"Was that truly a mystery cave, or was it all some kind of mental game?"

"It's mysterious all right. We all knew it landed in the cave where the bears were waiting, but no one has ever gone through the passageway before. You and Michael truly made history there."

"Where's Ryan?"

"You'll see Michael in time. Our goal is to get you better and to celebrate Thanksgiving here as a family tomorrow."

"That reminds me, we were supposed to have Thanksgiving with Mom tomorrow."

"I know it. They're here too. I can't wait to have your grandmother's stuffing. Good stuff. Rest up, love." He taps my nose on the way out. My mouth is hanging wide open when Dr. Braun returns.

"Is he serious? My mother is here? Here?"

"Your father never lies. It's one of the attributes I respect most about him." *Never lies?* This must be a dream. There's no way I'm about to have a full-on Thanksgiving reunion. Dr. Braun helps me sit up and hands me some water. I scarf down some toast, broth, and Jello. I'm determined to see what's really happening. And if there truly is a Thanksgiving dinner to be had, I want to be able to eat it.

# 6

## EMPEDOCLES ORDO ROSAE CRUCIS UNITAS FRATRUM

"How's my favorite sister?" I look up to see Danny making his way over to me. We're both grinning, unable to believe we pulled off my escape from the hospital. I reach my hand out for him to take. He holds it in the air to examine the magnet bracelet.

"Magnet?"

"How'd you know?"

"Well, they're pretty earthy around here, so ..." He smiles. "Get it? Earthy?"

I put my hand over my mouth to keep from cackling. "I get it, my fellow earth element. So, tell me what's going on! Where are we? And is Dad serious about Mom and Nonna being here?"

"Just when you think it can't get wilder! Yes, they're here. They were not brought here willingly, but they're here. They're starting to settle down a little, but it wasn't pretty. It's like time stood still, Mom and Dad going at it again. I was looking for a new place to hide." I can't help but laugh at how truly bizarre this situation is, not to mention the sheer nerve of our father.

"Why does he want them here?"

"Maybe it's some kind of warped peace offering? He knew we were supposed to spend time with them over Thanksgiving, so he made sure it happened? I don't know what makes him tick, Jenny."

"Danny, he's twisted. I wish he'd stop proving to me just how freaking twisted he is. Just when I start giving him a tiny bit of credit."

"I know. Listen, they think you were in an accident. Dad's playing his best hero role. He's acting like they should be thanking him for making sure you're getting the best care. He's made it quite clear that you will heal here." He stops and takes a whiff of me. "What's that smell?"

"Clay. Where is here? Where are we?"

"Clay?"

"Natural antibiotic."

"Sure, it is. We're somewhere within the confines of the Brandt Estate."

"Oh, good. I thought you were going to say we were inside of Kendra's temple. Does Ryan know I'm here? This must be where the tunnel leads. Are we totally underground here?"

"I believe so. I came in behind you, but there must be another tunnel that leads into the house. And, yes, Ryan knows you're here. He's dying to see you." My heart flutters. "Dad's being overly protective though and asked Ryan to wait until tomorrow."

"Oh, come on. That's not fair after everything we went through together."

"I know. Apparently, we're all going to have dinner together tomorrow as one big happy family."

"Please tell me Alicia isn't here."

Danny laughs out loud. "She's not here. Relax. There's no Ryan and Alicia. There's only you and Ryan. Well, and you and Josh."

"Shut up. Oh, God." I close my eyes. "What am I going to do about Josh? I need Fabrizio. *He's* my advisor. No offense."

"I think you just need to take it one day at a time. But you and Ryan do have a history together, and you love each other. Josh is a captivating man, but I don't know if he's right for you. You're the only one who can decide though."

He's right. I got caught up in the excitement that is Josh's world. It will never be mine. I hope he doesn't make it too hard for me to back out, because I could so easily fall right back into his arms. He's sexy, wild, adventurous, affectionate, and fun. Oh, here I go in my head again. Fickle. I'm embarrassed thinking about our romantic interlude and how we professed our love for each other. It felt like a real love spell.

I still care about Josh, and I'm definitely attracted to him. We just need to talk. His dislike for Ryan's family worries me more than any grudge he may have against me. And I killed his mentor, whom he claimed to loathe, but I don't know for sure that's the extent of his feelings. I'm getting a headache thinking about it. I need to focus on Ryan and the here and now.

"Danny, I want better clothes. I know it shouldn't matter, but I want to look good. At least better. And I need makeup. I'm getting a little insecure about all the scarring. I've got surgical scars on my chest and shoulder, my leg is a mangled mess, and my back is gory. Am I still going to be pretty?"

"Jenny, you're beautiful, inside and out. Those scars are a permanent reminder of your character. You're strong. They're your tattoos. Be proud of them. I'm proud of you, and I love you." He lifts my spirits with his words of encouragement. "You just need to wash the feces off your shoulder. Clay my ass." I laugh so hard it hurts again. "I'll figure out a way to get you some clothes. I'm sure Jackie has some stuff here. Looks like you did a good job eating and drinking. Why don't you get some sleep? You're still healing and need the rest."

"Yeah, I am tired and sore. Can you get Dr. Braun? I want a shot of morphine or something. Will you be close by? Can you sleep near me tonight?"

"Dad wants to sleep by your side," he says with a smirk.

"I hope you're kidding."

"I'm not. I'm sorry. I told you, he's being very protective."

"Then tell Dr. Braun I need sleeping pills too. I bet he's just afraid I'm going to run away or something. I wouldn't have the strength."

"I'll go grab him," he says with a chuckle.

Dr. Braun returns with my father, who's tailgating two steps behind.

"You feeling okay, Jenny?" Dr. Braun asks.

"Just sore. I'd like something for the pain and to rest."

"Coming right up," he says and preps something near a table next to my bed.

"How are you feeling about our Thanksgiving plans?" my father asks.

I decide to be straightforward. "Dad, I think you've lost your mind." Before he gets too defensive, I give him what he's after. "I don't know how you did it, but it's very kind of you." *He needs help.* "Tomorrow's going to be a wonderful day. Thank you." He's all smiles. That's the response he wanted. Whoa, whatever Braun gave me is stronger than morphine. Lights out.

I'm awake again. It takes me a few minutes to figure out where I am, which is getting extremely old. Even though I remember the basics, I would love nothing more than to bounce out of bed and investigate. But, back to reality. I've never had to pee so bad in my entire life, and I need help to do it. To my right, my father's asleep in a recliner. I stare at him for a moment, trying to analyze him. I yearn to have a father who isn't a psychopath. Why can't he just be an ordinary father, taking me out to dinner on Sundays or catching a movie. He must have a heart in there somewhere to watch over me like this.

My paternal fantasy world fades as I remind myself that he's put me through two punishment trials. I'm the one losing my mind. He needs to go back to prison and finish however many life sentences they throw at him this time. But only after my initiation. Until then, we're one big happy family.

"Dad," I whisper. He pops right up.

"What is it? Are you all right?" I smile at him.

"Yes. I just have to go to the bathroom."

"Oh, I see. Do you need help?"

"Well, I need to know where it is, for starters."

"Of course," he says with a laugh. "Do you want me to get Dr. Braun?"

"No, you'll work. Let's see how I do getting up here, then you can escort me. If that works for you?"

"Sure, whatever you think, dear."

I'm definitely getting a system down. I swivel myself to the side of the bed, push up, and I'm on my feet.

"I can't believe how well you're doing, Jenny." I smile and hold on to him with my good hand."

"Dad? How do all the members feel about what I did to Kendra? I killed her and brought everyone her hair to prove it. I must've been delirious or having a Samson and Delilah moment. Please tell me I won't need another punishment."

"Hardly," he laughs. "You did the right thing. The Judge accepts the act as well as the symbol. In our culture, cutting off someone's hair removes their power in the afterlife. Somewhere deep down, you knew that, didn't you?"

Oh, Lord, he's freaking me out again. Was that impulse innate or an order given to me through telepathy? Maybe that's why I did it. I take a big gulp.

"Kendra had a dark soul and didn't work for the greater good of anything. Somewhere along the way, she forgot that our life's mission is to celebrate and protect our blessings and talents in unity. Power can get to a person's head, Jenny." *You don't say.* "Anyway, all in the past."

"What about Josh?"

"What about him? He's doing a tremendous job taking over as

39

Grand Master for his segment. I'm quite pleased. Your feelings for him can never go further than respect. Understand?"

"No. But I accept, and I'm eager to simply talk to him and apologize."

"In time. All right, here we go." My father opens the door and leads me to the toilet. "Be careful. Are you going to be okay in here by yourself?"

"I'm fine, thank you." I smile at him as I close the door, but it's gone the second it shuts. What a predicament. Me and my father sleeping next to each other. And another bombshell. My actions may have been mentally prompted. WTF.

The bathroom is pretty spectacular. A large whirlpool tub is the focal point, surrounded by dozens of ornate medieval tiles, each with its own unique symbol. What I wouldn't do to slide into a hot bath right now. That's going to be my next question for Dr. Braun. When can I shower?

I manage to do pretty well by myself and hopefully won't need help from here on out. I'm a little loopy from the drug concoction, but otherwise, I'm pretty steady on my feet. My father ushers me back to the bedroom. While I have him like this, I decide to pry.

"Dad?"

"Yes, dear?"

"When I was getting baptized, I remember my great-uncle telling me the name of the Order I will belong to, but I don't remember it. Can you tell me?"

"I don't see any harm at this point, but you must keep the name a secret because there are quite literally hundreds of Orders who want it. Although, it's really our secrets that come with it that they want. But punishment is harsh for the tongue who reveals it. Understood?"

"Gee, let me think about that?" I joke.

"Okay, ready?" I nod. "Empedocles Ordo Rosae Crucis Unitas Fratrum, or EORCUF as we refer to it. It's pronounced, Ee-or-kuf."

"Does it imply a united fraternity under a Rosicrucian Order?"

"Yes, it does, and if you pull it apart, you'll figure it out. Empedocles was a Greek philosopher, best known for his theory of the four basic elements of water, fire, air, and earth. Later, spirit was added. Plato, and many other philosophers after, completed his work."

"And what does Unitas Fratrum stand for?"

"Unitas Fratrum was the name of the original German Moravian Church, who settled in Pennsylvania. It's Latin for unity of the Brethren."

"We have Moravian roots?"

"Our Order is not technically affiliated with any one religion. But unlike other modern Rosicrucian Orders, we profess Christ. At least our segment does. There are a few who don't want any part of religion. I struggle with that, but we are entitled to certain freedoms. But Christ was the Chosen and is the Holy One. The Bible is one of the least mysterious ancient books we have to base our findings and belief system on. Christ is the Chosen One. It's historical and cannot be disputed," he pronounces.

"On top of that, the early monks who formed the Secret Order of the Rosy Cross would be quite dissatisfied with some of the over-the-top magical-wand-waving bullshit orders out there today. On that note, I must insist that you begin Bible study when you're feeling better. Find the hidden truths, Jenny. They're astounding and they're everywhere."

*Find the hidden truths.* Those were the words written in the Bible that we found in the crawlspace.

"I hope this helps answer some of your questions. I know it must all sound strange to you as a neophyte, but we'll bring you into the light of knowledge. After all, it's already hidden inside you. Anyway, I gave away a pretty big secret tonight, one that comes with a secret handshake. Ready? I'll teach you now."

"Can I teach Danny?"

"Yes. Then have him test it out on me in private. I'll see how you did as an instructor."

"Well then, I better master it, huh?"

He has to go through the handshake many times for it to truly stick. It's silly, but it's also fun to have a secret handshake. I'm a grown woman, overeducated, but there's something about being around my father that makes me feel like a child again. I know I even act like one sometimes.

"I trust you'll be able to keep it to yourself for now?"

"Pinky swear." My father smiles and allows me to conduct the old reliable pinky swear. Then he tucks me into bed, careful not to hurt me. Before falling asleep, he kisses my head and begins a ritual prayer over me. His prayers make my soul weak. A tear streams down my cheek before I drift back to sleep.

# 7

## THANKSGIVING

"Jenny, wake up. Look who's here!" Danny says. I open my eyes wide, expecting to see Ryan, but it's his sister, Jackie. Close enough. She hugs me gently, not wanting to hurt me. We agree this situation is outrageous, but we're so happy to see each other. Ryan and Jackie have formed somewhat of a bond with their own father again. She whispers "temporarily" into my ear. I give her a thumbs-up.

"Ditto!"

"My brother wasn't kidding. You really took the brunt of it. I'm so glad you made it, Jenny. We've all been so worried, and Ryan is beyond excited to see you. He's barely slept. It's been killing him not to sneak in here. To be honest, he's been a real handful. I've been worried about him. So, thank goodness, you're back! I need a break from him." She laughs and roots through a large duffle bag. "I brought you some clothes and makeup. Let's go through them and get you ready, Cinderella."

"Ha ha! That would take a magical fairy Godmother for sure."

"What's that smell?"

We're both laughing as Dr. Braun enters and turns on the bright lights.

"Let's see how we're doing."

"Dr. Braun, can I shower? Please?"

"Actually, yes. I was going to recommend that as a gift to all of us on Thanksgiving."

"Hey!" Jackie and I look at each other and crack up, surprised by his comment.

"Kidding. Believe it or not, I have a sense of humor. We just have to wrap something around your cast, but your injuries are ready to take some water pressure. I'll help you when you need me, and we'll dress those wounds. I'd like you to have a little breakfast first." As he says it, Nonna walks in with a big smile and a plate full of food. She's teary, which starts my waterworks. She hugs me way too tight and hurts me, but I don't want to make her feel bad, so I endure the pain.

"An omelet, bacon, and toast for you, Jenny." She has pride in the meal she prepared, just like she used to. She sets the plate down in front of me and waits for me to dig in. She's such a beautiful woman. I feel so lucky at the moment. I don't know what the future holds, but I'm going to take this day in and treasure it. I just hope my father doesn't ruin it.

I eat almost every bite and wash it down with some freshly squeezed orange juice, which she no doubt processed herself. It's delicious. Everyone, including Dr. Braun, is sitting around smiling at me. I look over at the clock and it's already 10:00 a.m.

"What time are we gathering for dinner? Are you cooking, Nonna?"

"You betta believe I am," she says in her Italian accent.

"Yay! I can't believe this is happening."

"Anche io. Questo è pazzesco," she says and circles her ear with her finger. I laugh so hard that it hurts my ribs again. She's telling me this is crazy. We all seem to know it except my father and Mr. Brandt. "Dinner be ready by a three o'clock. Sound good?"

"Yes, Nonna. Sounds great." She takes my plate and heads back out the door. Dr. Braun is smiling, looking legitimately happy, and I can't help but lose myself in gratitude for this day. I also can't help but wonder how Dr. Braun got involved. He's a smart man and must think this entire scene is utterly preposterous too. But then again, he's probably been brainwashed with the rest of them—or paid a boatload of money to make it all seem normal.

"Ready, Jenny?" he asks. Jackie excuses herself, winks at me, and says she'll be back.

"Yes. Let's do it."

Just when I thought washing my leg was going to hurt the most, Dr. Braun is a little rough on the shoulder. *Jesus.* I know he wants it clean but cut me a break. He finishes up, makes sure I'm steady on my feet, and closes the shower door. As I hear the bathroom door close, I feel some of the stress leave my body. Instead of overthinking, I use the time to let go.

My fingers and toes are wrinkled by the time the water runs cold. I step out carefully, holding on to the railing, and grab my towel. I stare at myself in front of the full-length mirror, completely exposed. The color in my face is back. My ribs are black and blue, my leg is grisly, and the bite mark is repulsive, but I'm here. And Ryan is here somewhere. It motivates me.

Dr. Braun re-enters and carefully dresses my wounds without the stinky clay. He allows Jackie to join us when he's finished, but awkwardly waits for me to get dressed in case I need him. Jackie makes a face behind his back, and I almost lose it. I'm quite punchy, so it's not going to take much to get the giggles. I barely hold it in. But I like Dr. Braun and don't want to hurt his feelings, so I fight to keep a straight face.

"What do you feel like wearing, bones. Jesus, you lost a lot of weight. My clothes are going to hang on you."

"Fine by me. I don't want anything tight. What do you have?" We choose a pair of black stretch pants and a blush-colored cotton sweater. Dr. Braun brings in the chair from the bedroom and tells me to sit once I'm dressed so I don't fall. I let Jackie do my makeup and nails. She blows my hair dry and leaves me with long layers of curls. All covered up, I look like a million bucks. In addition to everything else, today I'm thankful for Jackie. My father is changing my sheets when we return back to the room. I never thought I'd see him doing something like this.

"Well look at you, Jenny," he says, all smiles. Danny knocks and enters, looking smashing. He's got on a pair of jeans, a white dress shirt, and a grey sports jacket. My father looks from him to me with great pride.

"Dad? Have you seen Jenny?" he says, pretending I'm not right in front of him.

"Shut up!" I say with a laugh.

"This is not the same person I saw yesterday. He reaches in and gives me a kiss. His eyes are watery, and then Jackie starts. We all look at each other and laugh through our overly emotional reactions. Dr. Braun checks in to see what the fuss is all about and exaggerates his own response.

"Wow!" he says, holding his hand over his heart. "Breathless." An Elvis Presley imitation. It's so corny that is makes us all laugh again. "Do you need anything for pain?"

"Nothing too strong or I'll be asleep at the table."

"Gotcha! Be right back."

"So, I can go out?" I ask my father. "Can I finally go out and see Ryan and Mom?"

"Yep. Take your medicine and come on out when you're ready." Dr. Braun hands me two pills. I pop them and look at Jackie.

She extends a hand for me, and Danny follows from behind to make sure I don't fall. We take it very slow. The makeshift hospital room is one of many, or at least one of many bedrooms. I count four doors in the hallway. Danny opens the main door, which exits into a large living room. It's hard to believe we're underground. The living room itself is over the top. I guess I should expect nothing less from Mr. Brandt, even if it is a glorified bunker. There are no windows, but he's created an illusion with stained glass and lights shining behind to mimic daylight. There's a faux fireplace, which isn't as nice as the real thing, but it's radiating heat to create a warm and homey atmosphere, nonetheless. The room is similar to the living room in the main home with leather furniture, beautiful accents, family photos, everything it takes to look like home. Apparently, bunkers aren't just for emergencies anymore.

"Jenny." My heart skips, hearing Ryan say my name. I turn to see him holding a dozen long-stemmed red roses, looking more handsome than I've ever seen him. He's got a casual suit on with no tie. His white shirt is partially tucked. I almost forgot how handsome he is. He takes a step before me with just a hint of moisture in his eyes. Jackie takes the flowers and hunts for a vase.

"They're beautiful, Ryan. Thank you."

"You're beautiful. I've been so worried." He gives me a soft, tender kiss. I've waited too long for this moment. "I love you, Jenny."

"I love you too." We're suddenly surrounded by everyone. Mom, Nonna, Jackie, my father, Mr. Brandt, Danny, and even Shane and Veronica. I'm happy to see no Uncle Dennis, but kind of bummed that my Great-Uncle Thomas isn't among us. I don't remember what he looks like from my baptism.

Ryan suddenly drops to his knee. "Jenny, I love you very much. I can't imagine my life without you. You make me crazy sometimes, but I love you. Being away from you has been really, really hard. I never want to be away from you ever again. Will you do me the honor of being my wife?"

I look around the room. They all knew he was going to propose? I'm emotional again. I don't really have to think about it. Maybe I should, I don't know. But right here, right now, I'm convinced more than ever that Ryan is the one for me. "Yes, Ryan, I will marry you." Mr. Brandt clears his throat purposely, as Ryan is not his birth name. He's a junior and wants me to respect him by using it. "I'm sorry. Yes, Michael, I will marry you." I hear laughs. "I would be honored to be your wife, through the better." I pause and smile. "Because, hopefully, we've already been through worse." He laughs and agrees, then

47

stands up and slides a beautiful antique oval diamond ring on my right ring finger. It'll have to do until the cast is off my left hand. The diamond must be at least three carats and is simply stunning. This is the happiest—and weirdest—day of my life.

There's applause and the clinking of glasses. Look at this traditional bunch. If only this was an everyday scenario and not a little glimpse of temporary normalcy. He carefully brings me in close and kisses me. My mother moves in fast. My heart aches to see how puffy her eyes are, like she's been crying for days. My future sister-in-law, Jackie, is pouring wine. Everyone takes turns congratulating us. Shane and Veronica look like a very happy couple themselves. I ask about Jack and get updates on everyone. My father whispers, "No talk about initiations." I hope he has a plan to keep my mother quiet, one that doesn't involve killing her. We spend the rest of the day talking. I even catch my parents chatting a little with each other, without yelling. I find myself wondering if I'm dreaming again. If I wake up, I'm gonna be so pissed.

Nonna makes the best Thanksgiving dinner ever. She's in her element, so to speak. If there were an element for food, she'd be the Grand Master. I'm stuffed and getting sleepy.

"Now what?" I ask out loud. "We can't all be together, so what happens next?" I break the mood, but I need to know. Without hesitation, my father rattles off the plan.

"We'll have to all split up again for safety. You, Dr. Braun, and Michael will stay here until you're completely healed. Your mom and grandmother, back to Jersey. Shane, Veronica, and Jackie, back to Baltimore. Danny will head back to Italy for now with his friend." Danny and I smirk at each other over his lack of effort or ability to use the word, *boyfriend*.

"Veronica's moving to Baltimore?" I say with sass and look at her with a smile. Shane kisses her to embarrass her. I love it. A full blush covers her face from neck to cheeks. "Then what, Dad?"

"If we can pull it off, we'll all be back together for a wedding! Mike and I will find a way to throw you one we'll all remember." Mr.

Brandt nods in agreement, and my father raises his glass for a toast. "Here's to a bright future for Jenny and Michael. They deserve happiness, love, and a family. I, for one, am looking forward to grand-children." I almost can't drink to the last part. Ryan and I shoot each other a raised eyebrow and a grin. My mother looks green.

I look to Ryan and raise my glass. "Here's to the love of my life and to everything we have to look forward to." Everyone can drink to that. As I sip, an image of Josh inadvertently crosses my mind. I try to push it aside, but it's like a skipping record—it keeps coming back. Is Ryan truly the love of my life? Is there such a thing?

I'm not sure how my father's going to get everyone out of here, but I'm in no condition to worry about it. He'll have to figure it out. I'm just glad to know that I'll be here with Ryan. We'll get to spend my recovery together and spend time bonding. That's all that matters for now. I need to let go of any feelings I have for Josh. He's not my future.

# 8

## AN UNHAPPY ENDING

I'm beyond exhausted, so Veronica and Jackie help me into bed. We have quick girl talk, but I have a long line of people waiting to say goodnight. I ask for my mom and grandmother first. They enter with tender loving care. My mom strokes my hair and Nonna makes a fuss with my blankets.

"So, what really happened?" my mom whispers. "Tell me, baby. You weren't in an accident, were you?" My mother is going all-in detective. The woman who brought me into the world is now a hazard to my health. She's the biggest threat I have at the moment, she just doesn't know it. What was my father thinking?

"I honestly don't remember what happened. But as you can see, there was definitely some sort of accident." She's trying to help me, but her maternal instincts are going to screw everything up. I see her hit a button on her phone. I'm very surprised she's allowed to have one. She's recording. Danny enters the room with a big smile.

"I don't want to miss out on this little goodnight," he says. I'm throwing him looks and then looking back at our mother. He gets it immediately, and I see an *oh, shit* look wash over him.

"Hey, Mom. Let me have that, and I'll get a selfie of us all. A

Thanksgiving certainly to remember." He reaches for the phone. She tries to yank it out of his hand, but he wins. She's going back into a controlled hiding after tonight. Maybe our father knew that all along. Danny snaps a picture as my father walks into the room. He looks a little confused at first but puts two and two together.

"Look at this. How lovely. Danny, get in the picture. I'll take one of you all." My mom looks panicked. She's caught with the device, which she planned on using to blow the whistle on this whole operation the minute she got out of here. As I should have expected, my night is going downhill and fast. Danny smiles with the rest of us while my father takes a picture. "Dr. Braun? I need some help," my father yells, while looking through the pictures she took on the phone. He stops every now and then and says, "Good one." My mother looks both worried and irritated, probably wondering if she could take him like she used to during some of their vicious marital battles.

Dr. Braun enters with a smile, which quickly washes away. He sees the phone and checks his back pocket. She took it from Braun. She could have gotten away with it if she wasn't so obvious. Mom and Nonna are wide-eyed, waiting for my father's next move. I close my eyes and pretend I'm somewhere else, knowing I'll have to choose between my mother, who is trying to rescue me, and my father, who is a serial killer. Danny is having the same struggle.

"Sean, I'm so sorry. I didn't realize she took it," Dr. Braun confesses.

"Look through it and see if she was able to place any calls." He practically throws it at him as an expression of his irritation. "Did you, Angela? Did you try to place a call? I invited you to enjoy this moment, to see your daughter as she recovers and gets engaged. This is the thanks I get?"

Her Italian temper is flaring. "You belong in jail." Nonna shushes her.

"You shouldn't have done that, Mom," Danny says. "We could've just all appreciated this time together."

Then my father does the one thing I'm laying here fearing the most. He stops and stares at me for a solution. I wish I couldn't read him so well and hate him for it. I give him a nod to let him know that I approve of whatever he's about to dish out, but my heart is absolutely breaking.

"What did you do? Brainwash my children? Look at them. How can they possibly take your side? They put you in prison just a few months ago. What have you done to my children?" She shrieks and charges my father, shoving him as hard as she can. He was ready for it and barely loses his balance.

She looks from me to Danny. "I'm your mother," she cries out in frustration, both injured and despaired. She doesn't understand, and my father should never have put her in this situation.

"Kids, what are we going to do about this situation?" Oh, God. What does he want us to do? Dr. Braun comes to the rescue, at least temporarily.

"No calls placed, Sean. Just pictures and she started recording. I've deleted that."

"Well, save a few of the good pictures for me and delete the rest. That will be all for now."

"Thank you," Dr. Braun says and exits nervously.

"Guys, what do we do when someone threatens our way of life?"

"You animal!" My mom is screaming again. "You're going to hell for this!"

"Stop it! Just stop it! This is your fault for bringing her here," I yell, pointing at my father. "You find a way to handle it. A safe way to handle it. And Mom, please keep quiet and do as you're told, unless you want us all killed. Keep quiet!" Who the hell am I giving orders? Danny is pacing but quiet. My mother's face is contorted with pain and anguish. My father looks smug and not the least bit angry with me for yelling at him.

"Where, Jenny? She's not good at keeping her mouth shut," my father says.

He's rotten to the core. I wonder if this is another test. Nonna is crying, making me want to cover my face and weep.

"Italy. Get them on a flight to Nonna's hometown in Sicily. Let them both retire there and forget about this place." Danny perks up, knowing Fabrizio can keep an eye on them and protect them from there. "Do you have the resources you need there? To keep them safe and quiet at the same time?"

"Of course."

My mother's in shock. We've finally been reunited, and this is the outcome. Back into hiding. "You're all sick. All of you. You all get what you deserve."

Her words and tone make me snap. "Mother, you don't know what the hell you're talking about, so just shut up. Please get her out of here so I can get some rest."

Yelling at her like that makes me feel like a terrible person, let alone daughter. At some point, I plan to apologize profusely for that remark and try to make her understand that the end goal has always been to get him back behind bars. I look at Danny with shame. He's visibly upset, but his hands are tied too. Two guards enter and usher my mother and grandmother out of the room. I can't bear to look. All I want to do is reach out and hug them and thank Nonna for the delicious dinner.

Danny sits down by my side. "You had no choice. You did the right thing. So help me God though, Jenny, that's the last straw. I'm going to join you. I'll get initiated into his little cult with you and then we'll lock him up."

"What about Fabrizio?"

"I'm not going to tell him. He'll have his work cut out for him watching Mom and working."

"I'll be heartbroken if you break up."

"Let me worry about that."

I'm emotionally drained when our father rejoins us. "What's your plan, Danny? You going to watch your mother when you head back to Italy?"

"I'm not going back."

"What do you mean?"

"I want to be initiated too. I'm moving back home."

"What about your friend?"

He shakes his head. "Maybe I'll find a new friend," Danny says. My father moves in swiftly, shakes Danny's hand, and gives him a big pat on the back.

"I'm proud of you, son. I may know a few lady friends though. Just give it some thought." He walks back out again, glowing with delight. I roll my eyes at Danny. We make a few jokes at my father's expense for comic relief. It's all we can do despite the circumstances.

# 9

## EXIT STRATEGIES

D r. Braun breaks up the sibling banter to give me some morphine, or whatever it is he's giving me. I could probably live without it, but I want it to take me away from this day. I look at my engagement ring and think how this should have been one of the most special days of my life. I've been down the marital road before but have high hopes that this one will stick. The thought of being a two-time divorcee isn't a great one. "Where's Ryan?" I ask Dr. Braun.

"He'll be in shortly."

"I know my mother and grandmother have to sneak out, and obviously my father, but what about Ryan, Jackie, and Shane? Can they come and go?"

"Yes, they can. They still have a full security staff and haven't done anything wrong. The Feds have nothing on them. Don't get me wrong, they'll be watched."

"Dexter and Markus are still in charge, I hope?"

"They're still on the property, but let's be real about who's in charge."

"Understood. Do they have any idea that we're down here?"

"No idea. Their role is above ground."

"Is there another way out of here aside from the entrance up and through the basement?"

"Yes. There are two tunnels. You came in through the first near the Brandt's private airfield, which he leases to a few local pilots and city commuters. That's how most of us enter, although we've been using it too much. Today needs to be the last day, if possible."

"But haven't Dexter and Markus seen Ryan and Jackie, and everyone else for that matter, come in through the basement?"

"No, and they won't. They've been given new orders. Sort of like don't ask, don't tell. Before your trial, Michael moved them to the guest house and they've legally agreed to new terms, with more boundaries and more pay. They're no longer allowed in the main house."

"Is that where he is now?"

"Yes. He's distracting everyone while they escort some of our guests out of town."

"Where should I stay now?" Danny asks.

"I suppose that's up to you. You're welcome to stay here. Or, you own half of Red Rock Farm. Maybe best for you to move in there. Having two missing O'Rourke siblings wouldn't be the best scenario. You've done nothing wrong to raise concern, so you're a free man."

"He's right, Danny. You should move over to the farm, then you can work on it, while acting like you're here to find out where I am. And, listen, you have to find a way to tell John I'm safe too. It was awful at the hospital."

He nods. "That's the plan then."

"Can you trust Dr. Keller?" Dr. Braun asks.

"You have no idea how much he's still in love with my sister. I'll make sure he understands the repercussions of getting careless with information."

"I don't think John would do anything to jeopardize our situation, assuming he knows I'm safe. I can't say for sure if he's worried about me though."

"It's not a good idea. My personal opinion." Dr. Braun shakes his head.

"How's it going in here?" my father asks.

"All good," Danny and I say in unison.

We fill him in on our plan, and he's on board with Danny heading back to the farm. They're starting to rebuild the barn, so he'll be plenty busy. Agent Edwards will be in charge of status updates, and there are still teams at the Twenty-Fifth Acre. They've got trailers scattered about and have basically moved to Brandtville. Some fairly significant arrests have been made. A few of my father's most loyal followers have taken hits for the team, just enough to make the Feds feel good and to ease public fears.

"This is where we say goodbye for now," my father announces.

"What do you mean? Where will you be?" I ask.

"Out of town until late spring. It's safer this way. You and Michael enjoy your time together. I'll be in touch with you about your Bible teachings, studies, and initiation schedule, which will start on June 21. The summer solstice. Continue to focus on getting stronger and staying hidden. The case will get very cold by the spring, and we'll be in a much better position. My team will allude to the fact that you're out of the country. I can make it look like you got on a plane and are secluded in a faraway place. Where do you want to be, hypothetically?"

"Hmm. Bora Bora?"

"Very well. Bora Bora it is," he says with a chuckle.

"Goodbye for now, love." He kisses me on the forehead and taps my nose. I really dislike the sign of affection he's resumed from my childhood and get a shiver every time he does it.

"Wait a minute. Could you break the news to Josh about my engagement? Gently. I don't want to hurt him. Please tell him I still care about him but that I'm in love with Ryan."

"I will. I'm sure Josh will be happy for you." He shakes Danny's hand and just like that, he's out of our lives again.

Now that we're alone, Danny and I discuss our future plans. He's going to keep busy and fix up the farm. Maybe make the barn into a cool living space. I like the sound of that, great for guests. He's plotting some secret spaces too. We can never be sure when we'll need them around Brandtville. He'll be able to come and go freely to visit Ryan at the estate. We'll be able to see each other as often as we want. I'll be the one getting bunker fever, but at the same time, I'm happy to have the privacy and security. And I'm thrilled to have Ryan with me. I'll bet I can sneak upstairs too. With the security team outside, I can be inside and attempt to feel normal from time to time.

"Here he comes. The man of the hour," Danny announces.

"Hello, gorgeous."

"Oh, look. It's my fiancé." He smiles and kisses me on the lips. Danny gets up to give us some space.

"Well, this was one hell of a day, wasn't it? I'm so sorry about your mom and grandmother. I could strangle your dad for that. Everyone told him it would be a disaster, even my father. The truth is, though, your mom had tracked him down. So, he decided to include her before shipping her off again."

"I was starting to wonder if it was something like that." I look up at him. "This all feels like a weird fairytale. I can't believe we're getting married."

"I know. Babe, these past few weeks have been so hard. Not being with you after what we went through. You have no idea how badly I wanted to barge into the hospital. I had a few close moments." He caresses my cheek, looks at me lovingly, and leans in for another kiss. "I need to ask Braun when I can get inside you."

"Shh! Stop it." I laugh. "Pretty sure you're going to have to wait for that."

"Show me. Let me see what's going on with you. I'll show you my injuries if you show me yours." We exchange war wounds. He's got some nasty scars, too, just a little cleaner. He wants to know how I'm dealing with everything emotionally. Especially about killing Kendra. I try to reassure him that I'm handling things as well as can be expected. Ryan discloses that he went back to the entrance of the freakish animal farm and removed all the evidence of our scandalous cheating during punishment. That's another monkey off my back. I ask him if he was able to see what went on at the farm, but he didn't stay long enough to fish around.

Dr. Braun checks in one last time and turns in. Ryan is officially free to sleep by my side, and I'm more than ready to pass out. It's been a long day, full of highs and lows. I try to shut off my brain, but all I can think about is how I'm supposed to have a wedding and a happily ever after with the Feds looking for my testimony. Once initiation is over, will I be able to turn in my father? What will we learn by the end of the initiation? The questions keep coming, but I eventually fall asleep, answers all still unknown.

# 10

## A TIME TO HEAL

Over the next month, I recover slowly but surely. Dr. Braun works endless hours with me, and we begin to grow close. I learn that he and Mr. Brandt were childhood friends and that he is, in fact, a descendant of fire. His father was a physician, like his father before him. He never married but hasn't lost hope, even at the age of sixty-two. But with no children, another linear member will have to take on the position as private EORCUF physician when Dr. Braun passes on. They've got two members in medical school right now showing great promise, including a plastic surgeon. While secret Order physicians do enjoy the benefits of the society, they take a special oath of their own. It's the very first Rule of Conduct established by the original Fraternity of the Rosy Cross. "Heal the sick without charge." I have incredible respect for his sacrifices, which he refers to as his calling.

Dr. Braun has a dry but hilarious sense of humor and has kept me laughing during times when I hurt both inside and out. He's getting paternal with me, and I'm becoming attached to him. He's like a security blanket. I'm not sure how he really feels about my father, so we keep it loose and avoid any deep topics. He's made it clear though that this is his way of life—and he's completely loyal to it. It's his way of warning me that he'll have no choice but to send me back to the wolves if I betray them.

My ribs are getting much better, and it no longer hurts like hell every time I cough or make a sudden movement. He tells me that in another month my leg will feel much better too, and that the bite wound is closing nicely. Today is the day he removes my cast. I'm beyond ready. No more showers with a plastic bag. It's a good day for me. I plan on surprising Ryan later. It'll be nice to finally put my engagement ring on my left hand where it traditionally belongs.

"Ready?"

"Hell, yes!" Dr. Braun smiles and gently removes the cast. "I'm free! I'm free!" I look at him. "Well, sort of." We both laugh. My hand is stiff, and much smaller than my other one. The ring falls right off.

"We'll put some tape around it for now, Jenny. It'll look like the other side soon enough." I smile and watch him wrap it with medical adhesive. "There." He slips it on my finger.

"I'm going to take a nice hot shower. Then can I go up?"

Dr. Braun uses a special line to call Ryan and gives me a thumbs-up of approval from both ends. "He'll be waiting for us in an hour."

It's so nice knowing I no longer have to dress my wounds, and to be free of the cast. Life is good *for now*. I shower, slide on some jeans and a black turtleneck, and apply a little makeup. I look at my ring and smile, feeling hopeful that Ryan and I will be happy together. I'm ready. The walk through the tunnel and toward the basement entrance is eerie. I still don't know how they managed to create such an extensive underground maze. Dr. Braun said there was a natural cavern down here, which they've slowly extended through the years. They completed it when we were all away in boarding school. It's dark, and rodents run freely in some sections. They've kept the tunnel as close to a real cavernous passageway as possible, for good reason. Anything too elaborate would be a dead giveaway. We have to duck under geological formations, climb up and down natural steps, unlock doors. It's a good twenty-minute haul. I'm starting to get it down now. Each time I make the journey, I try to memorize the route so, if I had to, I could do it in my sleep.

We reach the entrance, and Dr. Braun sends Ryan a message. As we wait, he badgers me about getting used to calling Ryan *Michael* because when we marry, I will become Mrs. Michael Brandt III. Mr. Brandt's wishes come first for now. I'm really trying to get used to it, but I can't help but call him Ryan. He doesn't look like a Michael to me. The door opens and we're in the basement. The prison cells have been removed and replaced with an armoire. That's where we enter, like something out of *Narnia*, except we have to crawl under a large TV too.

"Look at you!" Ryan greets me with a huge hug and kiss. I show him the ring, now on the left hand. "Aww. Let's celebrate. Wait. Stay there. I've been working on something. You, too, Dr. Braun. I'll call you up when I'm ready."

We look at each other and smile, surprised that we have surprises waiting for us. While we wait, we talk about the competitive game of Monopoly we're in the middle of playing. "If it's the last thing I do, I'm going to take that Boardwalk," he says.

"Not gonna happen, and I'm coming after Park Place," I taunt.

I haven't watched TV since my arrival. Everyone seems to think I'd be better off not knowing what people are saying about me. They're probably right. My state of mind has been pretty good without the news.

I also haven't started my Bible studies, or anything on my hefty reading list, let alone my introductory Rosicrucian monographs. Dr. Braun has nagged me to death about it all. I promised him that I'll start after the weekend. My first Biblical assignment is to find a passage that speaks to me. I'm urged to use my psychic abilities, which he claims have been passed down to me. I've learned that illnesses, talents, looks, and dispositions are only the beginning of what can be passed down in your DNA. To make it even darker, Dr. Braun related the concept of eugenics to me. Hitler, of course, became the most infamously obsessed, wanting to create a superior

Aryan race—a master-race where inherited diseases, through steril-ization, would cease to exist—one that also met his physical standards in a human being. The analogy darkens my perception of my father's Order even more.

Once I find the hidden truth and my special numbers, they'll be mine, significant to me for the rest of my life. I'm steering clear of the Psalms and 2:52. I wonder how in the world that ever spoke to my father.

"Okay, ready? Come on up," Ryan hollers. Dr. Braun follows me up the stairs and into the family room. Ryan has put up a spectacular Christmas tree—so amazing that even Martha Stewart would be proud. I'm touched by the effort he put forward, knowing this is our first Christmas together.

"I'll leave you two alone," Dr. Braun says, heading back toward the basement.

"No, not yet. Hold on." Ryan reaches for a small wrapped present and hands it to him.

"For me?" I would love to get excited for him, but I have no idea what it is either. He opens it slowly. It's a passport. *I don't like where this is going.* I don't want him to leave. Dr. Braun doesn't seem fond of the idea either. "You're sending me away?" he asks Ryan.

"Oh, my God. Look at the two of you! You're glued at the hip! Just for Christmas. My father has asked you to join him in Egypt for the week. We're all so grateful for everything you've done. You deserve a break, doc." I start to light up for him. Ryan's right. He needs to get out of here for a while. There's nothing technically left for him to do. *Except be my friend and surrogate father.*

He's looking at me for non-verbal permission. "I promise, I'll keep our game just where we left off." I look at Ryan. "He'll be back though, right? I want Dr. Braun to live near us permanently." They both shift uneasily.

"Jenny, this has only been my temporary home. I go when and where I'm needed."

"But ... but ... you're like a dad to me." He turns away. I'm making this worse for him. He doesn't have a family at all, and we've filled a void for each other.

"I'm beyond touched by the sentiment, my dear. It may not be that easy, but I thank you." I'm reassured that he'll be back for a few weeks before his next call to duty. Everything is calm for now, so he can just take the time for himself before moving on to his next assignment.

I look at Ryan. "Well, who's going to be staying with me in that bunker while you're up here? I'm not staying in there alone. No way!" Ryan shrugs.

I suddenly hear a familiar voice coming from the TV. Ryan reaches for the remote, but I get it in time. It's John. But it doesn't look like the John I know. His face is haggard, and his eyes look haunted. His hair is unkempt. He's surrounded by a dozen national reporters. I turn up the volume as the hair rises on my arms. He's asking the public for help in finding me, offering up a six-figure reward. I'm stunned. I assumed Danny told John I was safe, but my father must have forbidden communication. No wonder they didn't want me watching live TV. I feel sick and angry. My face is red, eyes watery, and I don't know who to light up first.

With hands on hips, I turn to look at them both for answers. Before I have the chance to yell at either of them, Ryan attacks and points a finger at me. "What's it going to be, Jenny? You chose this path. You chose it. I followed." Before I can pass the blame back to him, I let his words sink in. He's right. I have no one to blame but myself. I turn off the TV and sit on the sofa. I not only wonder what John has paid financially searching for me but professionally and personally. He doesn't deserve this. I hold back a deep sob but let the tears flow freely.

"Dr. Braun, I'm off the pain meds now. Can I have a drink?" He sits beside me and places a hand gently on my back to console me.

"Yes, in moderation." Ryan gets behind the bar. "My dear, it won't always be so painful. You have a wonderful life ahead of you. Once you're initiated, you can come out of hiding and be you again, just a little wiser and more knowledgeable. It'll get better. I promise. You trust me, don't you?"

"Yes, you're like the only one I trust in the inner circle."

"Really? The only one?" Ryan yells out to me. I ignore him because he missed the point.

"I guess you're right. Only a few more months of waiting and then initiation." It better be worth hurting the people I love the most, John and my mother. I'm disturbed by the image I saw on the television and am going to find a way to tell John, whether they like it or not. And having Ryan yell at me spoils my good mood. I don't like it when he does that, and if it continues, we're going to have problems again.

"What do you want to drink?" Ryan asks in an agitated tone.

"Something strong, like a dirty martini."

"Red or white wine?"

"No vodka behind the bar?"

"Red or white wine?" he snaps. Oh, I see. I'm not allowed to drink a martini. I'm so close to telling him to fuck off. So close. I have anger issues of my own, which were either passed on through these so-called eugenics or learned from my father. I'm making Dr. Braun uncomfortable.

"I'll come back for you in a few hours. Michael is right, not too much to drink. See you in a bit."

"Never mind. Just get me some water," I say, and Ryan groans. "So much for celebrating." I get up, walk into the kitchen, and take a seat in the solarium so I can look out at the property. There are a few inches of snow on the ground. It's beautiful and I can't wait to get outside and feel fresh air again. Ryan joins me and hands me my water.

"Listen, I'm sorry I yelled at you."

"Whatever."

We stare out together. A few deer are grazing on what they can get to.

"Lunch? How about grilled cheese and tomato soup? Feels like that kind of day."

"Sounds good. Thanks. I'll do all the cooking once we get married."

"You bet your ass you will," he says, joking. I try to picture myself married to Ryan. Am I going to be able to go back to work? Will I be stuck in this estate cooking and cleaning? What is he going to be doing? There's no way of knowing until after initiation. I've learned that I will go first. Then we'll go in order by seniority in the following days. Danny, Ryan, Jackie, Shane, then Veronica. Ryan was a bit peeved that he couldn't go with me, or at least right after me. But our generation of earth signs go first, then fire, and then the next generation of earth, which includes only my first cousin Veronica for now. She hasn't told Jessica or Jack of her plans. They know she's fallen in love with Shane and that they live in Baltimore, but nothing else. There will be five separate days of "knowledge" as they call them. Each day focuses on one of the elements, going counterclockwise. Spirit first, then air, earth, fire, and water. Then a Ceremony of Rite. Once we're all initiated and understand the big deal, or no big deal more than likely, we hand it all over to the Feds. That's our plan. I worry about the repercussions of killing another human being, and whether I'll face a prison sentence of my own. It was self-defense but with a very defiant twist that I'm not sure would go over so well with a jury.

"What's got you deep in thought?"

"I guess the unknown. All I do is think. Overthink, or maybe under-think. It's hard to know for sure."

"I know. I do the same."

"Are you happy, Ryan? Do you really want to do this with me? The way you snapped at me concerns me. Are you just going along with this for my sake?" I get another unpleasant thought while I'm questioning him. What if our fathers put him up to it? Like an arranged marriage. I wait for the first answer.

"Of course, I'm happy. We're in this together. Come on. I love you. We're meant to be together." *Meant to be together.* That sounds arranged, and I can't get the eugenics concept out of my head. I wish Dr. Braun never mentioned it. Deep down, I know Ryan loves me, but this is also our destiny, according to this Order. Does it matter as long as we both love each other? Does it matter if our fathers want us married, just as long as we want to be married? What if Ryan doesn't really want to be married?

"What's that look on your face? You questioning me? Us?"

"Were you put up to this? To marrying me?"

He lets out a sigh. "They approached me. Handed me the ring. It was my mother's, Jenny. The rest was me. I didn't even have to think about it. I love you. What's it going to take to prove that to you? I followed you into a punishment. I'm supporting you one hundred and ten percent. It's like never enough." He gets up and removes our dishes.

"Hey, come back here," I say softly. He sits, frustrated. "I'm glad you told me. Thank you. It's a great honor to have your mother's ring, and I know we're in love and that we're truly meant to be together. Our fathers making it seem like they're in charge of it just takes the joy out of it for me. We're in charge. Right?"

"Yes. My God, yes." He lifts my chin and plants a kiss on my lips. It settles me. "Jenny?" I'm still looking into his eyes. "Make love to me. I need you and want you. It's been too long." He's right. We need the closeness. We spend the afternoon getting to know each other on a physical level again and manage to end our day bright and celebrating our love. We talk about marriage and plans for our future. I consider it our best day since he proposed.

Just as I'm about to fall asleep, an image of Josh pops into my mind again. Why? Maybe I just need a little closure.

# 11

## TUNNELS

I spend Dr. Braun's last day before his vacation helping him pack. As I do, it's obvious that I don't need his help anymore. I just like his company, and I'm really going to miss him. He teases me a lot to keep us both from taking his departure too seriously. He'll be back. *I think.* It's around dinner time when he gets the call. They're ready for him.

"Can I walk you out and see what this other exit looks like? That's where I came in right? When I was unconscious? What if I have to use it at some point?" He thinks about it and agrees to let me follow him.

"Don't linger once I'm gone. Just get yourself right back in here. Got it?"

"Got it." I realize I don't even know where the other exit is to the tunnel and the private airfield. Should be interesting.

"Dr. Braun? Please do me one favor when you get to Egypt?"

"What's that?"

"Please call John. Please call him and tell him that I'm fine and that he needs to get off the TV."

"It's time. I'll reach out to him. You have my word."

"Thank you."

"Let's get moving." I pull one of his smaller bags while he pulls a large one. Very large. We end up in the kitchen next to a desk drawer. They should know by now how easy it is to break these thumbprint codes. He pulls out another device and punches in a number code, 7735. I hear mechanical sounds, which I've heard from my room before, but never questioned what they were. The dining room table suddenly splits in the center, the floor opens up, and an elevator magically rises and opens. I'm stunned. He tells me to put my thumb under the table and codes it so I have access. "I assume you saw the code I used for the remote?" I smile and nod. "Good, you should remember it in case of an emergency." He hands it to me, and I follow him into the elevator. There's just enough room for the two of us and no more. We descend what feels like maybe two stories. I ask him what happens if there's no power. "How do I get out?" It makes me nervous.

"Pantry closet. There's a lever under the Frosted Flakes."

"Stop it!" I laugh. "Whose idea was that?"

"Yours truly."

"Goof!"

"Anyway, pull the shelves open. You'll be in another room. There's scuba equipment. Put it on. You remember how that works right?" I nod again. "Open the next door and jump."

"Jump? To where?"

"A spring. Where do you think we get our water supply?" I shrug.

"The passageway is large enough for two. You'll exit up into a private backyard where you'll have to hop the fence. Then run like the wind if you must. But remember, there's no way to re-enter from there. So it's a last resort."

"Got it." We continue walking through a large tunnel. It's open in comparison to the one that leads to the house. I see a few bats hanging above us. They're minding their own business, but I instinctively crouch a bit to make myself less of a target.

As we walk, Dr. Braun enlightens me with some historical information about tunnels and how they became necessary for secret societies such as ours. He relates that esoteric societies, and the search for ancient wisdom, began spreading around 1,200 A.D., during the height of Christianity. Many felt the world was losing sight of ancient philosophies and wisdom, or even the true values set forth by Christ himself.

"Do you recall the Albigensian Crusade or the Cathar Crusade?" I give Dr. Braun a very blank look. "To make a long story short, the Cathars were a neo-Gnostic group in France who rejected the idea of materialism as it related to Christianity and wished, through embracing a state of poverty and humility, to return to Christ's teachings. They felt the Catholic Church was corrupted by power and materialism. Pope Innocent III took offense and waged a twenty-year bloody war against the Albigensians. Many thousands perished in France as a result of that war."

"A war prompted by the orders of a pope?"

"Religious wars have always existed, my dear. I bring it up only because groups like the Knights Templar and Rosicrucians took heed and went into hiding for fear of the same. Secret tunnels, much like this one, were built to protect Orders and their practices. It's a true example of how secret societies evolved through the centuries. Even after the threat had ended, the practice of secrecy has remained. Many Orders are now open and welcoming of new members. But as you already know, ours is not and must be protected."

"I can see another difference, at least with the Albigensians. We're not exactly an Order living a life of poverty, are we?" Dr. Braun smiles.

"Quite the contrary," he agrees. "But in time, you'll understand that those who work toward the greater good are in return granted gifts from above so that they can have the necessary tools to carry forth."

We've walked for a good ten minutes, probably a quarter of a mile, when we're intercepted by two guards. Our guards.

"What's she doing here?"

"Relax, just taking a walk with me. Bring her back upstairs when I'm out, okay? Then call me and put her on the phone so I know she's safe."

"Yes, sir." The guards are young, both tall and strong. I take note of their side holsters, but it's too dark to make out much about their facial features. We walk another quarter mile and begin to climb a steep incline. I lose my breath and have to stop.

"You can turn around now if you'd like."

"No, I'm all right."

"Shh!" One of the guards says, pulling me protectively behind him. The other does the same with Dr. Braun.

I hear voices ahead. Both men draw their weapons in response and order us to retreat back to the bunker.

*Run?* I do my best with Dr. Braun at my side. He hands me a gun just as we hear shots.

"We should go back and help them."

"No. Run, goddam it."

"What's happening?"

"The Feds. The Feds must have found the entrance. I told them we shouldn't be using the airfield to begin with. It's too close to the estate and they've got drones everywhere. So stupid."

Now they're in the tunnel, and I hear more shots ricocheting and echoing through the chambers.

Dr. Braun stops near the entrance. "We can't let them find the entrance to the main quarters. This way!" He pushes a button and a well-camouflaged rock door strains but finally opens. He purposely leaves it ajar just a few yards from the real entrance, which truly looks like a dead-end. He enters a passcode but gets it wrong on the first try. I start to worry someone changed it. Second time is a charm. A small door slides from left to right, and we have to crawl on hands and knees into a much tighter and airier space. We army crawl, making slow progress. My leg begins to hurt so much that I fear I've torn something open. My ribs aren't feeling great either. One more code, and we're up and into a room. Dr. Braun locks the door behind us to buy time.

"Where are we?"

"Guest house."

I'm gasping for air. This is going to be tough to explain to Dexter and Markus, who are living here. "What's the plan?"

"We'll have to make it up as we go." Dr. Braun texts Ryan and gives him the details.

"What's he saying? Let me see." It says, "On my way."

"I think we're going to have to make it look like you've been recovering here, under private protection."

"No way! Then what? They're going to take me into custody and put you in jail. My father will blame you. Think of something else, because that's not happening."

The door opens, and a very confused Dexter and Markus are aiming automatic weapons at us. They lower them as Ryan comes barreling into the room. He informs them that we have zero time to explain. "Here's the deal, you two are going to have to look shocked as balls when the Feds rush in here," Ryan says. Dexter and Markus nod, already in that state anyway.

We move toward the back door but know we can't take a car or we'll be apprehended in minutes. We're going to have to run through the woods and up behind my farm and hope Danny has made progress with his own secret hiding places.

"Michael, we're going to have to go to Kendra's. I have the codes and keys. We'll be safe there until initiation. I'll bag this trip to Egypt and stay with Jenny. We'll arrange ways for you to see each other. You have my word."

"Kendra's? I'm not staying there. Please, there must be some-where else. Why can't we stay at Red Rock Farm with Danny?"

"I'm sorry. Too risky."

"He's right, Jenny. Go! We'll find a way."

"Alert my father. Tell him I followed Dr. Braun out of curiosity and that this is my fault. Make sure Dr. Braun looks good here, please?"

"I will. I'll worry about the details. Now, go. I love you."

"I love you too." We give each other a quick hug and I run. I look back once and immediately worry, seeing his expression. I'm out of his control again. He doesn't do well with that. It's written all over his face.

# 12

## AN UNDESIRABLE SAFE HAVEN

It's cold outside, and in the mad rush, I didn't have time to grab a coat. My sweater was warm enough for a fifty-two-degree tunnel, but not this frosty air. Danny has been forewarned that we need a lift. I hope he finds us fast. Dr. Braun told him to meet us close to the edge of the road. I hear more helicopters, which probably consist of a combination of police and news crews. I feel a sense of dread, wondering what would've happened if I hadn't gone with Dr. Braun. He would have been arrested, maybe killed. I don't have any regrets, despite this less-than-ideal new situation. We make it to the edge of the tree line, duck down on the freezing, snowy ground, and wait as military cars go by and up the driveway. We don't have much time. Another military vehicle is coming our way, a Hummer from the looks of it.

"Yoo-hoo! Here, kitty, kitty." A voice permeates the cold air. Dr. Braun and I look at each other. I smile, knowing it can only be one person—Fabrizio.

"Come on." I have to drag Dr. Braun by the arm because he's convinced it's a trap, but I know Fabrizio's voice and sense of humor. I duck down to the side of the truck and look in. I was right! The door opens for us and Fabrizio is grinning. "I lost my little white kitten. Could you help me find it?" We hop in the back and duck down. "Where are we going, you two troublemakers?" he asks.

"Start driving toward the lake. What are you doing here, Fabrizio?" I ask.

"Nice to see you too."

"You have no idea how nice it is to see you. I've missed you so much."

"I've missed you too. I thought I'd surprise you and Daniel for Christmas. Surprise is on me. Jesus, I just walked in the door like four seconds ago and he sent me back out and on to the road. What's happening?" I fill him in quickly. He has Danny on speaker so he can hear what's going on as well. Danny feels bad for me, knowing I don't want to go to Kendra's mysterious residence. Our immediate plan is for Fabrizio to get us settled and, when the coast is clear, Danny will try and join us. I'm glad he rented a Hummer. We probably looked like part of the force, or we never would have gotten this far.

We're getting closer and closer, and I'm feeling sicker and sicker as we turn on to Lake Drive. Josh told me Kendra lived in an ordinary looking cabin but with a big garage to house her fancy cars. I hope they moved them already, as well as the rest of anything that could remind me of her. Dr. Braun points to a dirt road with no name. We make a right and turn up a steep hill. There are "Private Property" and "Beware of Dog" signs everywhere.

We come to a stop at a wrought iron gate. Dr. Braun gets out and punches in a code. The gate opens for us and we continue traveling on an icy drive about a quarter of a mile more before the house comes into view. It's actually a sizable log cabin and very rustic. There are no other houses in sight, but I know Josh's lake house isn't far from here. We drove the quads over bike paths nearby. I could find it if I had to. We pull in front of the garage, and Dr. Braun opens the door. It's vacant with no sign of fancy cars. All I can do now is hope we don't run into Josh. I need time to mentally prepare for something like that. We close the garage door, and Fabrizio and I take a minute to embrace.

"You keep me worrying. Look, I'm getting grey hairs." Fabrizio points, but I don't see any. "At some point, all of this needs to stop. I mean it." He's whispering. "You and Daniel. You're forgetting what normal is, and it concerns me." I nod to satisfy him.

"Come on. Let's get inside," Dr. Braun says. He opens the door into a large breezeway. There are a few wicker pieces inside, and an indoor/outdoor rug, but not much else. Dr. Braun is working on the lock to the door when someone opens it for him.

"Come on, hurry up." A man waves his hand and tells us to get inside." It's Josh's brother, Sammy. A welcomed surprise.

"I figured if something happened, you'd come here." It's great to see him. "Come on, Jenny." He smiles and takes my hand and ushers us into the kitchen. The inside of the house clashes on every level with the outside. I feel like I just walked into a Mediterranean palace. Ornate tiles line the countertops, and smaller tiles with bright colors create a backsplash. The cabinets are faux-weathered in white, and the walls are as blue as the sea itself. In the distance, I can see a dome ceiling with more tiles, each of them a different shape and size. Dimly lit lanterns, made with colorful stained glass, hang from the ceiling. Horseshoe archways divide each room. It's not exactly my taste, but it's definitely exotic, just like Kendra, and surely filled with mysticism and symbolism.

"We were all so grateful that you survived your trial. Josh told me what he could. I'm sorry about the position you were put in at the finale, and I hope you know that we all support you. You did the right thing for more reasons than you know. It was Kendra's time to cross over and face her punishment in the afterlife, which can only be eternal darkness."

"Thanks, Sammy. I'm still shaken and haven't really come to terms with it yet." I look around. "Being here is kind of hard for me."

"Of course it is," he says, looking down at the ring on my finger. I'm not sure if he meant for me to see the look, but I catch him subtly shaking his head with disapproval. If Sammy disapproves, I wonder what Josh will think. "You're bleeding, Jenny." He points to my leg. *Great!*

"Oh my. Come with me, dear." Dr. Braun leads me out of the kitchen and through a hallway decorated with an explosion of more color and ornate decor. The juxtaposition from cabin to Casablanca is quite surreal. Dr. Braun knows the house well and rushes me into an all-white bedroom. It's still fanciful, but with no color accents. There's a large silk swag canopy over the bed, which is covered in white linens. The dresser and other furniture accents are equally white. Curious.

He opens a drawer and pulls out some first aid supplies while I lower my jeans for a look. I tore some of the fragile skin over my scar on our crawl, but it's not terrible. He cleans and dresses it. "You'll be fine." He looks around with me. "Did you know snow and clouds appear white because almost all of the light from the sun is reflected by water." I look up and notice a faint outline of clouds in the four corners of the room.

"Is that so?" I say, with a hint of sarcasm.

Dr. Braun smiles and leads me back out into the great room, which is beyond great. Purple and turquoise cover handcrafted furniture and one-of-a-kind accents. It's pretty magnificent. Fabrizio and Sammy are each sipping red wine. Sammy hands me a glass, and I guzzle it down as if it were a glass of water. I can't believe this is happening. I had it made at the Brandt Estate. I try to mentally invalidate any suspicion that the ambush could have been a setup for Dr. Braun. I would hate to think anyone within the circle would want to hurt him, especially my father. Sammy has the police scanner going, and his outside sources tell him that they took everyone in for questioning, including Ryan, Dexter, and Markus.

In the meantime, Fabrizio gets a text from Danny alerting him that the Feds are at the door of Red Rock Farm. He'll be questioned, and the farm will be watched again. Under no circumstance are we to return to the estate or the farm. We're stuck. Sammy turns on the television and sure enough, the breaking news is on every channel, revealing to the public that a secret tunnel has been discovered, and two people of interest have escaped. An itinerary was found with a final destination noted in an undisclosed location in Egypt. Several guards inside the tunnel were killed in a struggle. Those were our guards. I'm upset about the loss and plan to seek justice for them when I'm finished with my initiation ... or sooner if possible.

The Feds, on the other hand, are pretty ecstatic about finding the tunnel leading to the Brandt Estate guest house, but unbeknownst to them, they neglected to find the elaborate bunker home. Poor Dexter and Markus. They legitimately have no idea what's happening, which hopefully means they'll pass a lie detector test. I ask Dr. Braun what the odds are of finding the elevator and other tunnel. He's somewhat hopeful that they'll miss those, due to the barriers in place to throw off their equipment. Plus, the surrounding walls inside the rock are layered with thick granite. Unless they decide to use dynamite, it's a tough entry. A similar system is in place in the basement leading to the bunker. He reminds me that they didn't find it over the summer, so hopefully they'll miss it again.

Dr. Braun's phone is ringing. He looks at me and whispers, "Your father." I grab the phone before he can answer it.

"This is all my fault, Dad. I had a hard time saying goodbye to Dr. Braun and I followed him into the tunnel. Thank God I did. I don't think he'd be alive if I hadn't." He's quiet. "But we're okay. We're upstairs at Kendra's house." He advises me not to move but that he'll get Dr. Braun out. *No way.* That's a horrible idea.

"No. I'm bleeding and may have an infection. I really need him with me right now."

"You are? Are you all right?"

"Yes. I'm a klutz. I fell trying to get out of the house. Ryan wanted to show me the Christmas tree he put up, and that tunnel is hard for me to maneuver." He's quiet again. I'm happy, knowing he can't blame Dr. Braun.

"Then you all stay put. Who else is there?"

"Sammy's here. He heard what was happening on the police scanner."

"Perfect. He'll be my eyes and ears. Put him on the phone." I hand Sammy the phone. They talk for a while, and Sammy looks to be agreeing with everything my father says. I try to cut him off before he gives him the Fabrizio Hummer story. Too late. I wish he hadn't done that because I don't necessarily want him to know he's here. Sammy does, however, make Fabrizio sound like a champ, and now my father wants to talk to Fabrizio. They're quick. Fabrizio simply responds with a "You're welcome. I love both of your children and I'd do anything for them." He passes the phone back to me, rolls his eyes, and makes an obscene hand gesture.

"Where are you, Dad? I half expected to find you here."

"No. I'm not even close to home, but the Feds won't find us in Egypt." He laughs like there's a personal joke I'm missing, which makes me worry even more about their plans for Dr. Braun. "But I may move in a little closer to keep an eye on things. This has gotten out of control fast. Until then, Michael stays at the estate. You stay there. I'll have Josh watch out for you. He can get to you from there."

"No, don't do that. I'll have Sammy reach out to Josh if we need him. I have Dr. Braun."

I'm not exactly sure what I said, but it rubs my father the wrong way. I accidentally flipped a switch. I pull the phone away as he rattles off something about obedience and respect. The law of things. Do as I'm told and so on and so forth. I'm not in the mood to listen to it. Even Dr. Braun rolls his eyes.

"Jenny, are you listening to me?"

"I am, Dad. I truly apologize." I need to change the subject. "I wish we could be together for Christmas. I miss you." Everyone in the room stops and stares at me. They're puzzled, but I know what I'm doing.

His switch goes off instantly, and he calms down. "We'll be together next Christmas, pumpkin. I'm sorry we can't be together. I'll have Josh bring you some decorations if you'd like. Would you like that?"

"Oh, that would be nice. Thanks, Dad." He says a prayer for me and tells me he'll be back in touch soon. I've always known my father had a short fuse, but now I wonder if he has split personalities. I've called him crazy and every politically-incorrect word for someone with a mental illness. It doesn't change much about future re-sentencing—perhaps the way they'll treat him later or what facility they'll put him in once he's arrested. Maybe he's ill from his abusive childhood and this anarchic lifestyle. I truly wish I had a solution to help him. But I fear he's too far gone.

# 13

## A TWISTED WEB

We huddle together in front of the TV for hours, afraid they're going to discover the bunker and things *I* don't even know about yet. Dr. Braun insists I keep my leg up and makes a fuss to situate me correctly on a red velvet chaise lounge with lots of dangling fringe. I can't help but think about Kendra and imagine her laying on it, or getting laid on it, or whatever she did here with her free time. Staying here is going to be mental punishment for me, and there's no way I'm sleeping in the white cloud room. I'd rather sleep in the garage.

Every channel has cancelled their regular daytime programming to focus on each angle of the investigation. A news alert breaks about Dexter and Markus. They gave the same statement, saying they saw two people run out of the house, but that it happened so fast they couldn't provide a description, or even determine if the invaders were male or female or one of each. They had no idea there was a secret passageway under the house, or they would have alerted authorities. Agent Edwards backs their story, supporting their testimonies that they've been working very closely with the FBI. They scoured the property, as well as both houses, many times. They're not considered suspects and will be released later this evening. The whole world hopes the invaders were my father and Mr. Brandt, and that this is the beginning of the end of a very long and mysterious story. Some, however, are addicted to the saga and want it to continue, just like they would their favorite soap operas.

Ryan is going to be more heavily scrutinized since he's the bene-factor of the estate. Maybe we should have gone to Baltimore while I healed to avoid something like this. Thinking about Baltimore reminds me that I want to call John. He's probably glued to the television too.

Dr. Braun allows it, telling me he'll deal with my father later about the subject. But I insist on taking the fall if my father finds out. I don't understand why he doesn't want John to know that I'm safe in the first place. John is drawing more attention and even more investi-gation. I suppose his concern is John finding me and having me placed into the Protection Program. Hopefully, the eye-opening scene at the hospital will remind John to put his trust in me instead of the agency for now.

I head back into the wickedly white bedroom for privacy. Recalling the kind of fantastical bedroom Kendra helped Josh create in his private grotto, I suspect that something magnificent lies under the earth beneath us. But, unless we have absolutely no choice, I'm not going down there, and I have no interest in knowing what it looks like. *Well, maybe a little.*

I dial John's office number. I'm nervous. His secretary answers. *Crap.* I hang up and yell for Fabrizio. We dial again. She's nosy, a typical gatekeeper. "What's this concerning, and who should I tell him is calling?"

"Simply tell him that it's a private matter, darling. One that doesn't concern you." Yikes. Not a gentle touch there. But it works. She puts him through. I whisper that she's probably going to be listening in. Fabrizio nods.

"Hello, this is Dr. Keller, who's calling?"

"Dr. Keller. I'm so glad you picked up. I'm going to need you to call me from a private line if you don't mind. Do you have one?" I can't hear what John is saying, but Fabrizio is losing his patience. "A private line will offer you access to private information." That struck a chord. He reads him another number to call. Another burner he'll have to destroy in case his secretary heard and wrote it down. They hang up and Fabrizio hands me another phone. That fast, it's ringing. "All you, baby cakes. I'll close the door behind me."

"John?"

"Jenny?" I can almost feel the pain in his voice. "Is that really you? What's happened to you? I've been going mad."

"I watched TV for the first time yesterday and saw you. I'm so sorry. I wasn't allowed to make any calls that could give away my location, but I'm safe and recovering very well. My cast is off, and I can do everything on my own now. John, please stop the television interviews. Please stop looking for me, and take down that reward."

"Only if I can see you for myself. I need to see for myself that you're okay."

"You can't, John. There are some things I need to do. Some things I need to find out on my own before I come out of hiding. I can't do it in federal custody. Do you understand?"

"No, I don't understand." He pauses. "But I trust you. If I suddenly stop my search for you, they're going to know I've heard from you. I mean, I've been frantic."

"Then keep it going for now and back out slowly. Make it look like you've lost hope. Can you do that? I'll be out of hiding by the summer. I promise you details, and I owe you big. I'm so sorry again that you got involved. How is everything at home and with work? I was worried when I saw you on TV. You look worn out."

"Could be better. I need to get my act together, Jenny. I'm not doing well. I've pushed off patients. I don't trust myself in the OR, and because of my passion and pursuit of you, Deb and I are on the rocks. To tell you the truth, I haven't even cared. All I've thought about is you." He's getting emotional, and I can't blame him. I'm messing up his life again, but this time, so very unintentionally. My father should never have involved him.

"Now that you know I'm okay, maybe you can sort things out with her."

"I've realized over these last weeks that I don't even know how I feel about her. I feel guilty, but I'm too obsessed with what's going on with you. I literally had to be seen by one of our psychiatrists. I've been a nervous wreck. The last words that came out of your mouth deeply affected me. You said, 'You have no idea who you're dealing with,' to the agent. I've agonized over the idea that you're becoming a part of that cult. I want to get you back so you can see someone. Check on your mental state. I want to make sure you're not getting caught up in it."

I laugh out loud to settle any notion he may have of that concept. He's been watching too many conspiracy theories, mostly true. "I promise you, John, I'm doing no such thing, but I am trying to learn more and put an end to it. Not join it." I'm saying too much, but he needs an explanation or he'll never stop looking for me.

"You're going to get yourself killed. How am I supposed to sleep at night knowing you're in danger?"

"Sleep well, John. Sleep well. I'm not in danger, and I'm doing great, thanks to your medical guidance at the hospital. I will only be in danger if I'm found. So please stop probing. I will make all of this up to you somehow. All the worry and anguish. I will do what I can to make it up to you."

"You know. I've had this fantasy. I've had this fantasy that you come home. Home to me where you belong. That we start a new life and have a family."

I take a deep breath. "John, that's never going to happen. You can't fix this, or me. I'm sorry, but you can't. Only I can do that." I hear him sniffle. I need to get off the phone. "I have to go now, and I won't be able to call you again for some time. But I'll have Fabrizio contact you when he can, okay?" He wants to keep me on the phone, but I insist we must hang up. I've said my piece. "You need to take care of yourself now, John. Please do that for me?"

He composes himself. "Okay. You go. I'll be better knowing you're safe. Please be careful. I love you, Jenny."

"I love you too. I always will."

Ugh. He's tough. His attachment and commitment to me are touching but brutal. I feel so guilty that he has maintained such strong emotional feelings. I feel like I owe him the same in return, but love doesn't work that way. The heart wants what it wants, and John isn't even close. The lifestyle he could offer me again would be safe and stable. But as I sit here staring at my engagement ring, I know stability isn't in either my literal or figurative DNA. I could never simply settle down. Fabrizio knocks and enters again. "How'd it go?"

"Rough. But good. He's going to back out slowly, and I told him you'd keep him as up to date as possible until you go back."

"I can handle that. I'm going to have to send that man a special phone, though, and keep close tabs on him. Make sure he's not alerting authorities out of complete hysteria. You cast one hell of a spell on men."

"I don't mean to. Come here. I need a hug." He wraps his arms around me and kisses my forehead. *Maybe I should talk Danny out of initiation.* I fear he'll lose Fabrizio. That would be devastating for us both.

There's another knock on the door. Fabrizio tells whoever it is to come in. My eyes get wide and I feel my heart beat in my throat. Fabrizio stands up and shakes Josh's hand. Gorgeous Josh who probably hates me. The nervous butterflies are fluttering out of control. I'd rather be alone with my father when he's angry than here in this moment. I'm not ready for it. My father must have called him. Why? What is he trying to do to me? And to Josh. He knows our history and, unfortunately, the intimate details of our brief but intense love affair. I don't need a test like this.

"Jenny," Josh says with annoyance. I have no idea how to read him, but it sure looks like I'm not getting a hug. "Your father just called for me to come up. Something about Christmas decorations?"

# 14

A COLD RECEPTION

I throw my hand over my face and shake my head in embarrassment. I can't believe my father disturbed Josh over Christmas decorations.

Fabrizio laughs. "Let me leave the two of you alone to catch up."

"That won't be necessary," Josh says coldly. He looks at the ring on my finger with disgust. I see hurt, resentment, and anger all rolled up into one harsh facial expression. My face feels red, and I start to sweat. He's absolutely not going to make this easy on me.

"Why don't we talk, Josh. Please? We're here. Let's talk," I plead.

"I'm good. Do you actually want fucking Christmas decorations? I'll let you hang a wreath. That's it."

Fabrizio overhears his tone and protectively comes back into the room. "Actually, Josh. We'd like more than a wreath. How about a tree and some Christmas music? Silent Night on a loop perhaps? Listen, don't talk to her that way. That's how you talk to her? After what she's been through?" Josh looks down, but his face remains emotionless, like he's been Botoxed a hundred times over. I'm mad at myself for doing it, but I let a tear roll down my cheek. I can't believe this is our reunion. I expected so much more of him—answers, to begin with. He's hardened overnight. It shouldn't matter to me because I'm planning a future with Ryan, but it does.

"Well, Fabrizio, the last time I saw Jenny, she told me to go to hell in front of my peers during my first punishment ritual ceremony. Way to cut off my balls."

"Right, the ceremony that nearly killed her? *You* poor thing." Fabrizio rolls his eyes at me and sits back down, arms folded and ready for battle.

"And I really appreciated the extra hard backhand to the face, Josh. You're into hitting women now, too? Coward! You know what, why don't you get the fuck out of here!"

"This is my house now, and you will show me respect! You will all show me respect or pay the consequences." His face is blazing with anger and he gives Fabrizio a look that dares him to say another word. It works. Fabrizio is speechless. I've never seen that happen before. *There's no way I'm staying here.* "I'm allowing you to stay only because I've been outvoted by all four other Grand Masters. I don't want you here. Trust me."

"I sure as hell don't want to be here if you're going to treat me this way." I tug at Fabrizio, who's trying to think of a way out of this.

"What's the trouble?" Dr. Braun enters and sits next to me.

"I don't want to be here with him. I don't know who he is anymore." Another tear rolls down my cheek. Dr. Braun rubs my back but offers no solution. I'm trapped. I'm trapped with Josh. I don't know whose side he's on. I don't know if he still has plans to overthrow the leaders and the Order or if he's one of them now. I glance back at him, hoping to get a real read. Hoping he's just letting out some pent-up frustration. I remember him well enough to know what he looks like when he feels bad, but he's stone-cold. He's got zero empathy for me. I stand up in an effort to shake off a huge adrenaline rush, but my leg gives out and I fall to the ground. Now I'm even more humiliated. Fabrizio dives down to the ground to help me, but Josh doesn't even flinch.

"You're bleeding again," Dr. Braun states. "Everyone out." I look at Josh again but get no reaction at all. In fact, I think he's getting sick pleasure out of my pain.

"Don't bleed on the rug or bed, please," Josh says.

That's it! He just pushed my rebellion button. I hop back to my feet and slap him hard across the face. He raises a hand to slap me back, but Sammy grabs him from behind.

"Are you out of your mind? What the hell are you doing?" he yells at Josh.

"You ever do that again, Jenny, and I'll put you through another punishment." He glares at me and walks out the door. Oh my God. Who is he? What is he? I cry the whole time Dr. Braun examines me.

"He's right. Don't do that again. Don't lay a hand on a Grand Master. Promise me?" I nod. "You're going to need a few stitches and maybe some colloidal silver to ward off bacteria. I'll be back. There should still be plenty of medical and holistic supplies here." I sit alone and twirl my ring. It's time to be strong again. The disappointment factor is slowly subsiding. I need to survive in this house somehow, maybe even for months.

"When Dr. Braun is finished with you, we'll need to head downstairs. It's not safe up here. Too many Feds sniffing around. Orders from all the Grand Masters," Sammy informs us. "I'm sorry about Josh."

"What's happened to him? He doesn't even resemble the same person."

"You've been through a lot, Jenny, but so has my brother. More than you know. Not just losing you, but he's lost good friends. Becoming a Grand Master, alongside diseased minds like your father, has been no picnic either. He's in there somewhere, but now's not the time to try to reach him. Keep your distance. This is going to be a huge adjustment for everyone."

"Is this even worth it? I'm struggling. Maybe I need to turn myself in."

"Shh. Don't say things like that out loud. Josh is set. He's in place.

Despite your unpleasant first meeting, trust him. Okay?" I nod, but I'm so tempted to blow the lid off everything. *Again.* I get this feeling four times a day. Everything feels wrong, and I just want to run. Dr. Braun enters with Fabrizio and the medical supplies. Sammy leaves, but I don't have to look to know Josh has quietly edged his way into the doorway. He's spying. I can feel his negative energy. He's going to watch me get stitched up. I pull off my pants in front of everyone. If he really wants to spy, I want to make sure he gets a good look at my leg and see how brutally scarred I am. I want him to feel guilt and shame. Fabrizio starts dry heaving at the sight.

"Jenny, what the fuck!"

"I'm fine. I'm fine." He turns away while I'm poked with numbing needles and stitched and glued back up. I don't flinch or wince. I want to prove to Josh that I'm tough. He's never even been through a punishment, but he's judging me. My skin is raw and tender. I want to cry out, but I keep it together. I squeeze Fabrizio's hand every now and then. He kisses it every time I do.

"Okay. We're done here. You're going to need to rest it for a few days. Let it heal a bit before moving around too much. Here, drink this." He hands me a thimbleful of colloidal silver.

"Fabrizio, could you see what clothes we can get for her? Some comfortable sweats or something—room to the right. Something loose." Josh moves away from the door just in time to avoid being seen. "How're you doing? You were very brave. Are you in any pain?" Dr. Braun questions me.

"Yes. Good Lord!" I laugh. "But I didn't want to give Josh the satisfaction of knowing.

"He watched?" I nod. "I'm not buying what he's selling. He's performing away his hurt and asserting his newly-appointed power and authority at the same time. He'll come around. You're good for now. I'll get you some pain meds and make sure you're comfortable once we get settled downstairs."

Sammy brings me a bright pink sweat suit. I have to wear the woman's clothes now too? This is so warped. Everyone leaves to give me some privacy. It gives me time to gather strength and courage. *Downstairs.* We have to go downstairs. I don't know about this.

# 15

ATLANTIS FOUND

"**I**s everyone ready? Let's go." Josh is shouting orders. "Sammy, it's time to tell Fabrizio."

"Tell Fabrizio what?" I ask, alarmed.

"Hello! I'm right here in the room, you know," Fabrizio utters. "Tell me what?"

"The only reason you're probably still alive, and the only reason you're allowed downstairs."

"Pardon?"

"Have you ever heard of Memphis Misraim or the Grand Orient of Italy?" Sammy asks in a much softer tone.

"I've heard of the Grand Orient. They're basically Freemasons in Italy."

"Correct. What do you know about your grandfather?"

"Which one? What's this about?"

"Your mother's father."

"He was an art history teacher at University."

"Correct. But his knowledge went far beyond the works of Michelangelo and the Sistine Chapel. He was a scholar for the Egyptian Masonry and also specialized in Zoroastrian history."

92

Dr. Braun intercedes. "Fabrizio, you and Danny met by chance, but it was your fate as well. We believe everything happens for a reason. God's will. Your grandfather was a Rosicrucian, a Grand Master of an Order he founded based on his studies."

"This is a joke, right? I'm being pranked. My mother doesn't even believe in God, let alone esoteric societies."

"I'm sure she doesn't know. They are very private and male-exclusive. Anyway, we don't have a whole lot of time to get into it. I just wanted you to be aware that you're a legacy of a secret Sister Order, and that you may enjoy the rights and privileges that come with your stay in this secret location. And this secret location only," Josh forewarns. "Understand?"

"If you say so. But I don't know who this Zoro person is that my grandfather supposedly knew so well."

I bite my lip to keep from laughing.

"Zoroastrianism," Josh snaps, frustrated. "But someone seemingly as bright as you should know they're one of the world's oldest practiced religions. On top of good deeds and good thoughts, they call for the protection of water, fire, earth and air, as do we. They're pre-Islamic, mostly practicing in the Middle East at this time. They seek truth."

"Well, let's have at it then."

Josh looks on the verge of kicking us out. I must admit, I'm boggled by this information. There's so much I don't know. I squeeze Fabrizio's hand, prompting him to tone it down.

"I'm sorry. I just haven't heard of this, and I sure don't know what to make of it. I apologize if I was rude. Are you saying that Daniel and I gravitated toward each other because of our mystical backgrounds? Or that we were even pushed together by some of your people?"

"We don't really know anything other than what you've just been told," Sammy says soothingly.

"I can accept that for now. What exactly is downstairs?" Fabrizio asks.

"In a word, brilliance. It encompasses history, mysticism, magic, and imagination. The privilege of what you're about to see is not to be taken lightly," Dr. Braun warns.

We both nod our heads, trying to wrap our brains around it. I'm starting to get goosebumps and hope all of this talk doesn't disappoint. Fabrizio looks serious for a change, no doubt reeling from the revelation of his ancestry.

"Sam, get the door behind us please," Josh asks, then guides us in front of a huge stone fireplace at the far end of the great room. There are no windows on either side of it. "Jenny?" He turns to look at me like he wants to tell me something. "Never mind." He caught himself about to say something nice, or maybe informative, but switched back to jackass mode. I keep quiet. I'll keep my distance like Sammy told me to do.

"We're going to go through three sets of doors, each of which were significant to Kendra and the Order. Then we'll be in a very large cavern. Keep in mind that this house backs up against Haycock Mountain, and that this cavern is likely one of the largest, probably in the whole country, of its kind.

"Bigger than Crystal Cave?" I can't help but ask. It was one of the caves we talked about the first time we spoke.

Josh laughs. "Um, yeah. Anyway, Kendra's Lenape ancestors can be traced back to the original space. That's why she was put in charge of it. Since she didn't have any kin, I'm the next generation of owners. This is sacred territory and never, ever to be spoken of outside of these doors. Does everyone understand?"

"Yes, we understand," Fabrizio says, losing his patience.

Josh takes a deep breath and lets it out. He begins to chant in a foreign tongue, a mantra he repeats over and over in a hypnotic tone that makes me shiver.

When he finishes, he recites something in Lenape and then maybe something in Latin. It's very confusing. A flame ignites seemingly of its own accord on a pillar candle atop the mantle as he says "ignis." I feel a breeze whoosh through my hair. My body suddenly begins to shake, and my mind flashes to ancient images I don't recognize. Dr. Braun is behind me and whispers, "That's right, Jenny. It's okay to go there." A vision of the sun enters my subconscious mind, so bright that I can't see anything when I physically open my eyes.

"Whatever you're doing to her, stop it," Fabrizio demands.

"Say it, Jenny." I shake my head. I have a word on the tip of my tongue, but that can't be what he wants me to say.

"Say it!" Josh yells again.

"Ra!! Ra!!" I say loudly. My vision returns as I say it, and the fireplace comes alive. Dr. Braun is patting me on the back, and Fabrizio's eyes and mouth are agape. Josh looks both pleased and utterly stunned.

"What does it mean, Sammy?" I ask.

"Ra was the Egyptian god of creation and the sun."

"I saw a symbol."

"Draw it."

Sammy hands me a pen and paper. I draw the eye as I saw it, with an eyebrow and two lines under it.

"The Eye of Ra. It's an ancient symbol intended to protect the pharaoh in the afterlife and to ward off evil. It's a symbol of protection and royal power. Sailors painted the symbol on the bows of their vessels to ensure safe travels at sea."

"It must be incredibly common knowledge then. I must have seen it before. I could have learned about this in grade school." Fabrizio's eyes are wide, but he's aggressively shaking his head in agreement.

"Tell us what else you saw in the vision," Josh coerces. I shake my head, not wanting to do this anymore.

"Tell us now, Jenny!" As he hollers, the flame from the fireplace burns out.

"I saw devastation. People were suffering and perishing from fires and floods."

"Through the gift of clairvoyance, Jenny, you saw the destruction of Atlantis. You're only the second person I know to have ever had the vision," Josh admits.

"Atlantis? As in the Lost City?" Fabrizio belts out with a laugh.

I'm shook. I can't find humor in this moment because it was so real. "Was Kendra the other person?" I ask.

"Only in her dreams," Sammy remarks. "Brother, let's keep moving before we get caught up here and, Jenny, I hope you know how gifted you are."

"Hold on. There's something else." I look specifically at Dr. Braun. "Something else is going through my mind, and I feel like I have to say it."

"What is it, dear?" All eyes are on me.

"The words, 'I am the Lord thy God, which have brought thee out of the land of Egypt, out of the house of bondage. Thou shalt have no other gods before me.'"

Dr. Braun reacts with a huge grin and look of pride. "I dare say, you've given me goosebumps. That's Exodus 20:1-17. That will make your father quite happy. There's only one true God, and no false gods to worship. It's your intuition and perhaps a little Catholic guilt nudging you. The wisdom to understand an ancient culture has nothing to do with true worship. Understand?" Dr. Braun asks. "One God."

Josh has remained stoic and quiet through Dr. Braun's interpretation, but he can't keep his eyes off of me. Sammy calls out his name to snap him out of the trance. He recovers, takes a deep breath, and begins another chant while making the sign of each element in a clockwise manner. As he completes the verse, the fire burns out, leaving no heat behind. The fireplace doors open into the entrance of a cavern. Now I have visible goosebumps all over my body, partially from the excitement and partially from the fear of the unknown. I'm shaken by my vision and unsteady on my feet.

"Please, come in," Josh says. We enter, and Sammy manually closes off the entrance. There are lights shining on another doorway and all around the room. The elements are all represented in beautifully engraved symbols on the walls of the chamber. Above the doorway is the word *Illumination* in bold letters. A poem by Ella Wheeler Wilcox, "The Lost Land," is inscribed on the wall.

*There is a story of a beauteous land,*
*Where fields were fertile and where flowers were bright;*
*Where tall towers glistened in the morning light,*
*Where happy children wandered hand in hand,*
*Where lovers wrote their names upon the sand.*
*They say it vanished from all human sight,*
*The hungry sea devoured it in a night.*

*You doubt the tale? Ah, you will understand;*
*For, as men muse upon that fable old,*
*They give sad credence always at the last,*
*However, they have called at its truth,*
*When with a tear-dimmed vision they behold,*
*Swift sinking in the ocean of the Past,*
*The lovely lost Atlantis of their Youth.*

"Who was Ella Wilcox?" I ask Dr. Braun.

"She was a talented author, poet, and Rosicrucian. I'm not sure how truly passionate she was about Atlantis, but Kendra was obsessed with learning what she could. She investigated every theory, scientific and otherwise."

"Um. Excuse me. Before we go any further with this land of the lost expedition, how are we supposed to get out of here? You know, in case of an emergency, or like when we're just ready to leave?" Fabrizio asks.

"Much easier going out," Sammy whispers. "I got you, Fabrizio."

Josh finishes his tasks and slides the thick wooden door to the side. The path descends steeply from here, so Dr. Braun and Fabrizio move to either side to hold me steady as we go. At the end of the path, we enter a stunning and seductive-looking chamber with reflective purple crystals and cascading waterfalls streaming down each side. Josh avoids looking at me as I take it in, but I catch him out of the corner of my eye a few times. He wants to see my reaction but is too stubborn to show me benevolence.

Above the doorway is inscribed *Wisdom* in the same bold letters as *Illumination*. There's another poem on the wall, this one entitled "Atlantis, Arise," by George Weibert, F.R.C.

*'Twas Plato whose writings we hold dear*
*A tale from Egypt's priests did Solon thus hear*
*Sail the Pillars of Hercules was the course to chart*
*Atlantic Ocean named after King Atlas set lands apart*
*Mysterious metal orichalc bore the light of red*
*Only but gold more precious it was said*
*Yet virtue and friendships were their loftiest might*
*Till time dimmed their divine nature unto mortal plight*
*Fragmented scrolls of the temple's master*
*Impart the tale through final day of disaster*
*Our mystic memories still dimly resonate*
*The Lost Continent did once grandly illuminate*
*Her wisdom safeguarded to places secret from slumbering men*
*The spirit of Atlantis—may she rise again!*

I assume by his title, F.R.C., that he, too, was a Rosicrucian and Atlantis enthusiast. There's one final door to open. Josh looks back at me before he inserts a large golden key. The door opens, and I have a hard time remaining upright. Fabrizio holds me up, but I feel like I'm holding him up too. I blink several times, wondering if I'm getting another vision. But it's real. Before I look too far, behind a pair of ancient-looking Roman pillars, I see the words *PLVS VLTRA* in the center of the enormous gothic archway.

"What does it mean?" I ask whomever is willing to answer.

"More Beyond. It's Latin," Fabrizio says.

"Very fitting," I say, astounded.

It's time to feast my eyes on the wonder before me. It's a simultaneously artistic and philosophical depiction of what the Lost World of Atlantis would look like, complete with the types of animal and plant life that would have existed, however many years ago. I know nothing historical about Atlantis, only the tales, but I had a vision so clear that in my heart I know that the fabled advanced society was real, and that it perished.

I feel like I've stepped back in time and into another world. There are Roman pillars surrounding an enormous saltwater pool. Marble statues of philosophers, most notably Plato, are exhibited museum-style, and ancient story-telling hieroglyphics line the stone walls. I freeze at the sight of the Eye of Ra, along with an entire area dedicated to Egyptian symbolism, including a golden pyramid and sphinx, not unlike some of the items in Josh's lake house master bedroom.

A beautiful bridge crosses over the pool and connects to more open space. There are large natural waterfalls surrounding it, along with both real and faux geological formations. I count five large stalactites and think of the irony. To the far left are mini temples or something. I expand my view and realize this underground wonder actually contains a mini village of sorts. I count seven stone structures, each ascending up a bit higher than the last, like a steep San Francisco street. Above them are more rooms framed by more arches. The cavern's ceiling extends so high that I'll bet it goes almost all the way up the mountain. I hear water flowing in every direction.

This was all Kendra's, and she still wanted more? Despite living a life filled with excitement and mystery, she was empty inside, maybe because she never reached a state of spiritual development that would have made her whole. She could never illuminate her own life because her soul was empty and dark. I wonder if it's the same for my father. Do the roles they've had to play in this Order leave them dead inside, counteracting the goal of a society such as theirs?

Why isn't this creative masterpiece exposed for all the world to enjoy? For all the world to see and experience. The tourism would drive the local economy to new heights. But that's not what they want here. They don't want intruders, for reasons I may never fully understand.

"Sam, take it from here. You know where I'll be if anyone needs me," Josh says and strolls off somewhere to the right without looking back. Sammy leads us to our quarters, which are in fact the mini temple replicas. Along the way, he invites us to use the pool—to purify ourselves. Dr. Braun tells me in a few days the saltwater will be good for me and provide extra healing power. Sammy explains that the original structures were cave-like homes where Lenape families lived. Kendra's ancestors began redesigning them a century ago and have continued to maintain them from local resources, including large creek stones, shale, and granite.

Sammy shows me to my quarters first. The Gothic wood door is arched with geometrical patterns and is heavily varnished to protect it from the humidity. It's templesque on the outside but quite swanky on the inside. Kendra was the master of designer illusion. Diamond-shaped purple tiles cover the floor, and large floral light fixtures grace the corners. The bed is sexy, with plush pillows and a down comforter. A velvet purple blanket is draped across the edge of the bed. I have a love sofa and chair. I hear the faint sound of running water. Sammy flicks a switch, and a turquoise light shines under the glass table, exposing a running stream of water. The base is lined with tiny mosaic tiles in the shapes of dolphins.

"Whoa!" Fabrizio and I say together.

There's a zebra-striped rug defining the seating area and a large air unit dehumidifying and purifying at the same time. Breathing it in feels cool and soothing. Much better than the bunker under the Brandt Estate. I have no idea how it's possible to maintain such a perfect temperature in this environment. Sharper Image special order? I have arched windows to the front overlooking the pool and artificial windows to the back, similar to the Brandt bunker. Above the bed is a lit stained-glass feature. In the center of it is a blue water-fall, surrounded by roses.

"Work for you?" Sammy asks. I enthusiastically nod my head.

"Okay, where's mine?" Fabrizio asks. I tag along behind him, wanting to see more for myself. His quarters are similar but with shades of blue. He's impressed but, nevertheless, can't resist explaining how he'd redecorate the room. I punch him gently on the arm. Two men and a woman join us and introduce themselves as the help. They tell us that whatever we need, we just have to ask. They inform us that dinner will be served at 6:00 p.m. Wine and cheese will be served beforehand in the pentacle room. I'm overly stimulated at the moment.

Another young woman taps me on the shoulder to tell me that she just stocked my room with clothes, toiletries, and mandatory reading. She points at Fabrizio. "You're next!" He, too, has some recommended, but not mandatory, reading. Dr. Braun will be staying in the unit next to mine, which is always reserved for him, stocked with supplies. We'll all be taken care of, and no request is too large. Fabrizio and I skip back to my room to investigate again. There's a mini fridge, sink, and cabinets. Thankfully, it's fully stocked with wine, and he pours us both a glass. We sit in silence, taking it all in, staring down at the stream under the table. It's hard to comprehend, even for him, and the wonder of it all is getting more personal for him.

Just as I was about to say it, he beats me to it. "I wish Ryan and Daniel were here." I couldn't agree more, although that would add to the awkwardness around Josh. "I've worked in some really phenomenal places, Jenny, but this is like the eighth wonder of the world. I have some equipment with me, but I wish I had more. I taped everything Josh was reciting. I'll try to figure out the long-ass code he was punching in and get a copy of that clunky gold key. I want to be able to get back in once we're out if we have to."

I divulge that one of the caverns leads to a spring, which leads to Josh's lake house. I could probably figure it out if I had to. So that's one more option out. Fabrizio starts rambling about the energy resources it must take to run the place. He's guessing solar and wind in addition to electricity. He'll have it all figured out in no time. If I have to be trapped down here with anyone, an M.D. and a tech wizard are the way to go.

Dr. Braun enters and suggests I lay down until dinner. Fabrizio heads off to explore. I happily follow the doctor's orders because whatever happened to me before we came downstairs took a toll on me. I feel utterly weak and tired. There's no TV, which is probably a good thing because I don't want to obsess. I close my eyes and try to focus on Ryan, but my mind keeps wandering to Josh and what I just experienced with him. The mind is a remarkable thing. Under this mystical mountain and in the presence of Josh again, it's hard for me to ache for the one I swore my love to. But that's probably because I'm not in *his* presence. I need to stay strong. I fall asleep praying for guidance from my true Higher Power.

# 16

## A FANCY FEAST

"Jenny, time for dinner." Dr. Braun knocks and wakes me. Oh no, I must have missed cocktail hour. I jump up and look in the mirror. My hair's a mess. I'm a mess. I need a shower, but I'm starving. I throw my hair back in a ponytail and slip on a pair of black stretch pants and a camel-colored turtleneck sweater. I don't care for my shoe options, but I find a pair of flip flops in the middle of the stack that'll work for now. My mandatory reading seems to have grown during my slumber. There are Rosicrucian digests, articles, lesson books, two books on Edgar Cayce, including his holistic medical cures, and a book entitled *Atlantis, The Antediluvian World* by Ignatius Donnelly. There are meditation guides and a few books strategically placed on top about ancient mystery schools and esoteric orders. On my nightstand I find a King James Bible with a bow on top. I have my work cut out for me.

Both Fabrizio and Dr. Braun escort me to the dining area. As we cross over the bridge, I stare down at the pool. It feels like a fantasy world. I half expect extinct animals to appear, or a Sleestak. As if on cue, I see a very large leopard-looking cat cleaning itself near an area of foliage. "That's Mau. He's very friendly, named after the cat in the

Book of Caverns." Fabrizio and I both stare at it bewildered. "It's an important Egyptian netherworld book. It's among both of your readings. Hey, sometimes you have to surround yourself in past cultures to understand them. You should consider that the largest lesson to take from your time down here," Dr. Braun advises.

I can't imagine the work that goes into managing this space, especially with all the mineral water that must leak into it every day. We pass the so-called pentacle spirit room, shaped as such with five corners, each with a mural capturing one of the five elements.

"How was happy hour?" I ask Fabrizio.

"Would have been happier if you were there."

I see where we're headed. There's a brick archway leading to another large cavern. I notice what must be extreme French drains along the way. They've added tile features and special lighting to distract from the mechanics that go into managing the true nature of it all. We step up from the stone ground and onto an airy teak floor that lines the dining room. It's bone dry. The ceiling is lined with copper, slightly pitched to allow any water to drip into small inconspicuous copper features that lead to the drains. The seating for twelve is extravagant. The kitchen is partially open and partially tucked away. The lighting in the dining room reflects crystals off the walls.

I smell something good. Dr. Braun pulls my chair out for me. Sammy enters, along with his wife and children. They're all dressed up like we're at a fancy restaurant. I smile politely as he introduces them. His wife, Kimberly, is attractive, a little preppie with a short bob. Their son, Adam, is eight, and daughter, Lexi, is six. It's been a long time since I've been around children. In fact, I've never really been around them. They're shy upon introduction, both very cute with blonde hair and blue eyes. Lexi has Sammy's natural curly hair.

Just as I'm wondering if Josh will join us, he enters alongside a woman. She's a sight to behold, not as seductive and exotic as Kendra, but quite the head-turner in a stunning black halter dress with a sexy cut-out exposing at least a D-cup's worth of cleavage. Her long golden locks hang both front and back, and her makeup and nails look like she spent the day at a spa. And then there's Josh, who's dressed in his best and groomed from top to bottom. I can smell his cologne from across the table. Within the confines of this room and underground world, he looks like a Roman god. He's undeniably the most handsome man I've ever laid eyes on, and I have to push back the memories of our lovemaking as I look him over. Push them way back.

"Dr. Braun, I kindly remind you that there is a dress code for dinner," Josh reprimands.

"Of course. I apologize, sir. *Sir?*" Cut me a break. He was singing country songs and feeding me chicken salad only a season ago, and now he's a "sir?" Since Josh doesn't introduce us, I turn to his friend. Before I can speak, she goes first.

"Jenny, I've heard a lot about you. My name is Lucia. It's very nice to meet you."

"I've not heard of Lucia, have you, Jenny?" Fabrizio asks sarcastically.

"No, I can't say that I have, but it's very nice to meet you too."

Josh is bothered by Fabrizio's sarcasm but remains quiet during the introduction. Here I was worrying about Josh's broken heart, and he's got himself a trophy girlfriend and a shitty attitude to boot.

Dinner is served. Multiple finely dressed servers place our dishes in front of us and remove the silver dome covers in a grand gesture. We're having pheasant, which I can't say I've had before. I can sense that Fabrizio is about to crack a joke, so I kick him under the table.

I look around and notice everyone is still and silent in prayer. I nudge Fabrizio, who's about to take a forkful. We both make the sign of the cross and wait for them to finish.

Josh grants us permission to begin eating. It's awkward and quiet, but at least the food and wine are delicious. Sammy breaks the ice asking me how my leg is doing. I give him an update, and the room finally livens up a little with small talk and eventually even a few laughs. Josh and Lucia kiss multiple times during dinner. I remember how affectionate and unafraid of public displays of affection he was and can't help but miss that feeling. Ryan's not one for PDA.

"Daddy, can we go swimming?" Lexi asks.

"I'll take you swimming again," Lucia offers. Both children jump up and run out of the room to get their suits on.

"Is this where you're staying now too?" I ask Sammy.

"Technically, we moved into Josh's lake house, but we're here quite a bit. Kids love it. Can you blame them?"

"No, not at all. I mostly only swam in Deep Creek at their age," I say and laugh, thinking of the huge difference.

"Same," he says, and looks at Josh to reminisce. "I wouldn't trade those days for anything. Deep Creek was always an adventure." I agree with him completely.

"You're free to take the kids to Deep Creek now instead, Sam," Josh says defiantly. Sammy takes a deep breath and gives me a look of frustration. He ignores the insult in an effort to avoid a scene. Josh's new attitude is very unbecoming, and I want him to know I don't approve.

"Be a bit cold wouldn't it?" I say to Sammy with a smirk. He smirks back. I was kind of hoping it would lighten Josh up. Instead, he slams his hand on the table.

"You're excused from the table, Jenny." Everyone, including Lucia, stares at me for a response. Each face is saying, *don't do it*. Dr. Braun squeezes my hand under the table, so I decide to take the high road.

"Thank you for dinner, sir. It was delicious." Calling him "sir" was just enough to tick him off but not enough of an excuse to attack me further. I push my seat out and rise. "It was lovely meeting you, Lucia, and great talking to you, Kimberly. I'll see you all again, I assume." Dr. Braun and Fabrizio thank Josh for dinner and follow me out.

"Fuck. That was close. One more outburst out of him, and I would have flipped that Flintstones table upside down," Fabrizio remarks.

"For as long as we're here, I want the two of you to focus on your tempers. I mean it. Do what you have to do later to blow off steam, but don't give him reason to punish you. I tend to meditate after one of them pisses me off. Try it. You've got plenty of books to teach you how."

"Words of wisdom, Dr. Braun. I'll give it a try," I say. He's off to his room for the evening with work to do. Fabrizio follows me back into my room, which is already starting to feel like a cell, despite the pageantry. He fills me in on parts of the day I missed. He snooped and found a security room. There are cameras to at least forty-some houses in the area, all people Kendra was spying on. There's one to the outside of Red Rock Farm and one to the Brant Estate and guest house. Fortunately, none are on the inside. The room is being manned by a security guard. Fabrizio is rambling on and on, and I start to feel sorry for myself.

"What's wrong?" he asks.

"I'm scarred. I can never wear a dress like the one Lucia was wearing ever again. At least not without feeling self-conscious." I well up.

"Stop it. You're one hundred times more beautiful than that hag." I laugh. She's no hag, and he knows it. "And trust me, Josh has you on the mind. I don't care how many times he touches that girl, it's you he desires. She's here to punish you for breaking his heart, nothing more."

"Why's he so mean?"

"I don't know. It must be the title. Or, maybe we both misread him, and he's always been a total asshole. Either way, we stay away from him as much as possible. He's acting like your father."

"That's it, Fabrizio. He's acting like my father. He's mirroring him. My father and Kendra are his role models. He must feel that a cruel disposition comes with the position."

"So, what shall we do for the rest of the evening?" Fabrizio pushes the books aside and goes through the drawers and closets in my room. "Eww. Fashion 911." He pulls out some ugly dresses. I start to laugh and get up to take a closer look.

"Is this a joke? Did he put these in here for me to wear for dinners? They look like something Nonna would wear."

"He's trying to break your spirit. I'll find a way to get you some more attractive dresses, sweetie," he says before cracking up.

"What's so funny?"

"How about if I wear one of these to dinner tomorrow night? How about this little number?" He holds up an ugly green turtleneck dress in front of himself and takes a few dance steps. I flee, trying to make it to the bathroom in time. My bladder is too full for that thought. I hear him laughing in the other room. I dare him to wear it, but in the end, we decide we'd get ourselves in way too much trouble. It's not worth it. But the idea of it, and the belly laugh, were definitely worth it.

# 17

---

333

Fabrizio and I spend our first few days studying in solitude. While I find the books on esoteric societies, ancient Egypt, and certainly, Atlantis, intriguing, I'm focused on finding my special numbers as requested by my father. I try a few games of Bible roulette turning the pages, stopping, and pointing to a passage. But nothing speaks to me, and I'm mentally stuck on knowing there's something about the numbers 333. In fact, at this very moment, I'm looking at the clock and realize that it's 3:33 p.m. I look up passages with the numbers, but the only thing I find from the Bible that comes close to reaching me is John 3:33: *Whoever accepts His testimony has certified that God is truthful.*

I do believe in God, and that He's true, but I think I need some guidance from Dr. Braun. I grab my Bible and stroll up to his room. He opens the door, sees the Bible, and tells me to come and join him.

"Talk to me, Jenny. Any hidden truths?"

"Maybe. But deep down, I know my special numbers are 333."

Dr. Braun places his hand over his heart and takes a seat. I've spooked him for some reason.

"What? Is that bad?" I tell him about John 3:33, but he's silent.

"Dr. Braun, why are numbers important at all? Why such a big deal?"

"Numbers, Jenny, are the one true thing that connects us to the Divine. Man did not make up numbers, but we're slowly beginning to unravel the mysteries of life through them. God loves numbers. Let's not forget that He's the most important architect and engineer of all, having made the whole universe. The number three is extremely significant, Jenny. Tell me about your experience."

"Well, for starters, I see the numbers everywhere. I wake up at 3:33 a.m. nearly every early morning. I see the series of numbers on my car dash, at gas pumps, on license plates, at the end of a grocery bill tab. I mean, I see them almost every day."

"I see. Well, let's dissect them a bit. I'll give a range of history and then tell you what the Order thinks of the numbers." I'm ready. This is the most interested I've been in mysticism yet. "First, the basics. If you do a Google search, you'll find many believe they represent the Trinity—Father, Son, and Holy Spirit. I believe there's truth in that. Or, if you believe in angels, which I do as well, you'll find that mediums believe that seeing the numbers 333 are an indication that your guardian angels are nearby, instructing and supporting you." Dr. Braun takes out his laptop, clicks on a link, and reads verbatim. "This is from a blog I visit from time to time, Joanne Sacred Scribes. They're sacred angel numbers and their messages. I'll read you few paragraphs."

*"The Number 3 is the essence of the Trinity, mind, body, spirit, and is the threefold nature of Divinity. Number 3 symbolizes the principle of 'growth' and signifies that there is a synthesis present – that imagination and an outpouring of energy are in action. Number 3 represents the principle of increase, expansion, growth, and abundance on the physical, emotional, mental, financial, and spiritual levels. Number 3 also resonates with the Ascended Masters.*

*Angel Number 3 3 3 tells you that the Ascended Masters are near you. They have responded to your prayers and wish to help and assist you in your endeavors and with serving your life purpose and soul mission.*

*Angel Number 3 3 3 encourages you to be creative, social, and communicative and use your natural abilities and talents to empower yourself and uplift and enlighten others, as your lightworking abilities and life mission are to be utilized for the good of all. Keep a positive attitude about yourself, others, and the world in general in order to manifest peace, love, and harmony. Have faith in humanity as a whole and the future of our world. Live your truths and express yourself with clarity, purpose, and love, and be a positive light to others."*

"How does that feel to you, Jenny?"

"Wow! It feels spot on, Dr. Braun. Everything you read I can relate to. I feel as though I've been guided toward many missions, at least in finding the truth. I don't know exactly what my mission is for the future, but I believe I have a purpose and that it's for the greater good." I have to stop myself there because I sound like my father. "Tell me what the Order thinks of the numbers."

"First, let me acknowledge that I believe without a doubt that you have been guided. I feel my guardian angels are guiding me all the time and that they have led us to each other."

"Aww," I say, smiling.

"But some Biblical scholars believe the numbers 3 3 3 have a much darker meaning, sort of like an 'End of Days' message from God. And you should know, the numbers 3 3 3 are also seen by many people all over the world. Therefore, our Order feels this strong combination of numbers represents a distress signal, like an SOS that the end of the world is near. I'll give you just a few examples. If you add the numbers three, three, and three, you get nine. Biblically, the number nine represents finality and judgement. Let's see what else ..." He stops and thinks, but I come up with an example of my own.

"Peter denied Jesus three times before the rooster crowed. My father reminded me of that many times as a child," I add. "That's a story of judgment and punishment too, no?"

"Yes. Another good example. One more, and I think that will be enough for one day. Ezekiel 33:3: *He sees the sword coming against the land and blows the trumpet to warn the people.* It speaks of a final warning before end-time tribulations. Evangelicals believe that when you hear the final warning of a trumpet, if you haven't taken Jesus into your heart or established a personal connection to God, you will face the final judgment and be doomed to hell."

"You're scaring the crap out of me. Is that why the trumpet sounds before each punishment ritual?"

"I'm sorry. A trumpet?"

"Don't do that to me. After the drumming, there's always a trumpet sound."

"No, there's not, Jenny. Oh, dear."

"What?" I get up and pace, then look at him again and again, waiting for him to tell me he's kidding, but it never comes.

"Jenny, I dare say, you have found your numbers."

# 18

## MARCO POLO

After spending a full day completely freaked out about my special numbers and the trumpet sound only I could hear, I dive back into my reading. I decide not to tell Fabrizio about my special numbers because he's not taking anything very serious and is antsy as hell to leave.

Right up until today, which is Christmas Eve, I've purposely made myself look awful, which is what Josh must have intended. I've worn every ugly dress hung in the closet for me. No makeup. No hairdo. Fabrizio braided my hair into a Princess Leah look for dinner last night to match a hideous white tunic dress. It looked like a glorified burlap bag. Dr. Braun scolded us for it, but it was worth it.

Lucia has come to the table with one beautiful dress after the next, and I've had to watch her in string bikinis playing with the kids in the pool every day and listen to her teach the kids about space and the stars while Josh dotes all over her. I catch him eying me up every now and then as he does it, looking for a reaction. I've stayed fairly numb, but he's definitely getting under my skin.

I'm excited about today, because I've learned that Danny's been cleared by the FBI and has managed to do some secret shopping. He's bringing me some new clothes, and he'll be staying over for the next few nights. I can't wait to see his expression when he gets a load of this place. To think how brilliant we thought our little crawlspace hide-out was when we were kids. This is going to blow his mind. *Although, I still like ours better.*

I wish Ryan could join us, but that's out of the question. We're able to speak every day, but it's been hard on us. He's jealous that I'm here with Josh, and almost every call ends in an argument. I've made it clear over and over again that I'm not *here with Josh*. It's just an unfortunate arrangement. To make matters worse, Fabrizio will be leaving with Danny. He has to go back to avoid suspicion, not to mention the fact that he can hardly wait to confront his mother and dig up dirt on his family. Josh and Sammy's reveal about his grandfather's own secret society has been eating away at him.

The thought of being without Fabrizio for the remainder of my time here makes me nervous but a little relieved at the same time. I get self-conscious during my studies because he makes me feel stupid and gullible for reading them. It's not that I'm buying everything I'm reading—it's just an important part of ensuring I get initiated. And at least I have Dr. Braun to keep me company and fill in some of the blanks as I study. I had no idea there were so many esoteric fraternities, or how many famous people have taken part over the years. Some well-known Rosicrucians include George Washington, Abraham Lincoln, Ben Franklin, Walt Disney, Victor Hugo, Isaac Newton, Leonardo da Vinci, Thomas Paine and, some say, William Penn, although he never admitted it. I plan on tackling Lenape studies next.

Physically, my leg is much better, but I still haven't gone in the pool because I'm terribly insecure about my scars. The bite scar on my shoulder is almost as grotesque as the scar on my leg. Fabrizio tells me I'm being too hard on myself. I've decided to be brave and bare it all over the next few days, especially if Josh is hanging around. I want to remind him of what he took part in putting me through. He's avoided conversation with me all together, and I've done the same in return.

I'm also excited to see Christmas decorations finally going up. There's a large artificial tree with gold accents in the living room area. There are lots of angel ornaments, which remind me of Ryan's mother and her love of them, as well as my own guardian angels who I'm now convinced are behind me. I've only sat in the living room a few times to catch up on the news. It makes me uncomfortable because it's where Josh and Lucia hang out the most. Well, aside from the master bedroom, which is right above it somewhere. It grosses me out to think of what it must look like, considering Kendra designed it. Plus, how many men Kendra slept with up there, including my own father. And now Josh sleeps in there with Lucia. Gag!

I assume we'll all surround the tree tonight or tomorrow morning when the kids open their presents. How do they think Santa gets in? The help has also strung up lights and garland throughout the space. The pool lights have switched to green and red, a feature I enjoy as much as the kids.

I'm busy writing in my journal, which has become a therapy that I rely on, when I hear a knock. "Come in." It's an ecstatic Fabrizio informing me that Danny's here. I jump up. I haven't seen my brother since Thanksgiving. We decide to greet him as he enters the main chamber so we can see his expression. We've described it to him, but until you see it for yourself, it's hard to imagine. Josh ruins the moment by joining us.

"Danny's on his way?"

"Yes! Thanks for allowing him to stay for Christmas," I say.

"Of course. I like your brother. I'll be initiating him soon enough."

Fabrizio's head snaps in my direction. I shake my head like he's wrong. He looks hugely relieved. *Shut up, Josh.*

Finally, the door opens and Danny makes his entrance. I go in for a hug first, which is basically one-sided as he peers over my shoulder.

"Are you effing kidding me?" Josh lights up, maybe for the first time since I've been here. Josh calls out for his security staff to put Danny's two hefty suitcases in his room. Danny corrects him and tells them that they're for me. "They're clothes. I understand she's been wearing Kendra's grandmother's clothes or something." I bite my lip and Fabrizio laughs out loud. The security guards bring them to my quarters. Josh looks annoyed but doesn't say anything.

"Let me show you around, and then we'll all meet up for drinks."

Danny looks at me for permission. I tell them to go on ahead because I'm dying to see what he brought me anyway. I close the door to my room behind me and open the suitcases laid out for me on the bed. OMG! There are so many amazing outfits. I see a few tags from the shop in Peddler's Village that I liked so much. Casual clothes, bathing suits, undies, pajamas, and seven spectacular formal dresses. There's another bag with accessories and makeup. I love my brother for this! I pull out the classiest dress of the bunch to wear tonight and hang it on the outside of the closet door then put the rest of the clothes away. My morale is rising.

"Miss Jenny. Miss Jenny." I smile. It's Lexi knocking. She's definitely growing on me. I open the door for her and see she's got her bathing suit on. "Will you go swimming with me? Miss Lucia can't. She's packing."

"Packing for where?"

"To go back to school. She leaves in a few days."

"Miss Lucia is still in school?" *Cradle robber.*

"College. She's almost finished. She's going to be an astronaut."

"An astronaut?" That can't be right.

"Yes. She wants to go into outer space." *I like that thought.*

Danny, Fabrizio, and Josh are making their rounds. Danny peeks in. "Nice spread, sis. Dang!" I see Josh smile again. He really likes my brother's approval. Josh introduces him to Lexi as she continues hounding me to go swimming.

"Why don't we all take a dip?" Danny says. "I'd be up for cocktails around the pool. I need to chill. The media and the Feds are exhausting." Lexi starts jumping up and down. Josh looks at me to see what I'm going to do.

"Is it okay with you, Josh?" I'm getting smarter and pander to him, asking for his permission. "Dr. Braun says it'll be good for my leg anyway."

"Of course. I'll get my suit on too, Lex," Josh says, picking her up. She gives him a big kiss on the cheek, and he carries her off with Danny in tow, but Fabrizio lingers behind.

"You got this, girl. Time to get out of this room. Hey, what did Josh mean about initiating Daniel?"

"Nothing. Danny told our father that he would get initiated to get him off his back. He'll be running back to Italy before that happens. Trust me!"

"You sure?"

"Totally sure."

"Okay. Phew! Scared me for a minute. I mean, we'll always be here if you need us, but our home is in Rome. I'm ready to put this madness behind us. No offense."

"I know. None taken."

"Good. I'll meet you at the pool. Be proud of who you are, Jenny." He blows me a kiss and catches up to Danny. I feel bad for fibbing. If I can't talk Danny out of it, I wonder if maybe Fabrizio could get initiated too. After all, his ancestors belong to our Sister Order. I can't wait to learn more about that.

I look back at my new wardrobe. Well, here goes nothing. I have two options. A modest one-piece bathing suit in navy blue, or a classy but sexy red halter-strapped bikini. It's hot. I stand in front of the mirror naked and hold each one up in front of me. Both will show my leg and shoulder scars. The bikini will show the rest, including the incisions from my lung surgery as well as the scars from my broken collar bone. I look like Frankenstein. But my face is still pretty. I'm still me. I put the bikini on and decide to go for it. It's a Christmas color after all. I let my hair down. It has gotten incredibly long, so I give myself a partial up-do and then go through the rest of my accessories. I find some red lipstick. Hell yes! And some red nail polish. Double hell yes! Lexi is knocking again. "Come on, Miss Jenny. Can I come in?" I open the door.

"Wow!" she says with the most adoring expression. "I love your bathing suit! Oh, and nail polish. Can you paint my nails? You have a big boo-boo on your leg. What happened?"

A smile comes across my face for her. "I was in an accident. I've had to have a lot of surgeries. Want to see some more scars? They don't hurt at all anymore." She nods and eyes them up with innocent curiosity.

"I'm going to kiss them all and make them better." The gesture alone makes me misty, but as she follows through, giving each one a kiss, I can barely hold back the tears. I'm in love with this child. "Can you paint my nails now?" I laugh.

"I think I'm going to need permission from your parents for that." I'm amazed by how unfazed Lexi is by my scars. I thought she'd be afraid to come near me, but she doesn't care. I find a long button-down shirt and use it as a cover up. I grab a towel, take a deep breath, and head out the door, Lexi excitedly holding my hand. Fabrizio is already on a natural stone swimming platform sipping a fancy drink. Danny waves to us and hops in the pool. He swims over to Fabrizio, gives him a kiss, and sits down next to him. He takes the drink waiting for him and exaggerates his first sip with a loud *ahhh*.

"What do you want to drink, Jenny?" Josh yells from the far end. *Wow.* He's going to personally get me a drink? For Danny's sake?

"Piña colada," I yell back. He stops and stares at me, remembering. That's the drink I told him I wanted the first time I was invited into his private pool and solarium. Those were much happier times together.

"Watch this, Miss Jenny." Lexi does a cannon ball.

"Yay!" I clap. "Good job, Lexi!" Dr. Braun joins us. I'm trying to time it so that I have to take my cover-up off right in front of Josh. Lexi is whining for me to come in, but I plead with her to give me a moment. I can see Josh coming out of the corner of my eye just as Dr. Braun approaches me. He wants to examine my leg before I go in.

I unbutton my shirt and lay it on a lounge chair at exactly the right moment. I move my hair to the side so that the bite is the first thing Josh sees. "You're good to go. Go in and have fun. It's Christmas Eve," Dr. Braun says. I smile, turn around, and find I'm two feet in front of Josh. He tries to look away but can't.

"Can I have that?" I ask. It takes him a second to understand the question.

"Oh, sorry." He hands me the piña colada and looks me up and down.

"Thanks, Josh. Cheers." We clink glasses. He has a serious look on his face and maybe a hint of sadness. Fabrizio whistles at me for encouragement and support. I feel good, not half as self-conscious as I thought I'd be. "Okay, Lexi, here I come. You know, I can stay under water for two whole minutes." I look back at Josh. He's the one who recorded my time as he prepared me for punishment. His eyes have softened. Mission accomplished. I descend slowly down the main stairs. The water feels amazing, incredibly soothing and warm. I go underwater on a new mission to chase Lexi down. She giggles and squeals as I pick her up and spin her around. The men are all to the side watching, each of them with similar expressions—all smiles. I realize how loved I am and silently count my blessings.

Somehow, Lexi talks me into a game of Marco Polo in the shallow end. I don't think I even played this as a kid, but I find myself getting into it. Adam comes barreling around the corner with his suit on. He's agitated that there's fun going on without him. "Don't play without me! Wait! Come on! Uncle Josh, please play with us like you used to. Please?"

"Oh, I don't know, buddy."

"Please?" We all look at him to see if he has the heart to reject his nephew. He folds and takes off his shirt. *Oh, no.* That body of his. Fabrizio whistles at him too, and Josh can't help but crack a smile. That's the Josh I know, not this way-too-serious dictator of a man.

We play for a while and take turns catching the kids. Josh is Marco now and hears my "Polo." He comes after me, so I let out a squeal of my own and try to get away, but I'm no match. He grabs my shoulder right on the bite area and comes up for air with a huge victory smile. I gasp from the pain because it's still quite tender. He opens his eyes and the smile fades as he sees where he's touched me.

"I'm so sorry, Jenny. Did I hurt you?" He looks from my shoulder directly into my eyes. I don't want to make a big deal, so I reassure him that I'm fine. But I'm ready for a break. I swim over to the ladder and climb out. His eyes follow me all the way. *Damn.* Are those butterflies? The intense butterflies I've only ever gotten with Josh? I towel off and cover myself back up, sensing the need for a little more modesty. I sit at the edge of the pool next to Fabrizio and go to town on my drink.

Fabrizio throws me a look.

"What?"

"Be careful."

# 19

CHRISTMAS

After a few hours of hanging by the pool, I excuse myself to go back to my room. I have nothing to offer anyone for Christmas, and it's kind of bumming me out. It's the first Christmas I've had with Danny since we were kids. He's already given me two suitcases full of things, so I feel the need to do something in return. I peek my head out and yell for Dr. Braun. He looks worried and starts to sprint. I shake my head and tell him not to rush. He slows down, looking curious.

"You all right, dear?" he asks.

"Yes. Come in. I just feel bad that I don't have anything to offer everyone for Christmas."

"I don't think anyone expects anything."

"What about the kids and Danny? I could make something. Do you still have the pictures from Thanksgiving on your phone? Maybe I can print some and frame them. Danny would like that. Although, my father was the one taking the pictures, so make sure we don't look like a bunch of rejects." He doubles over and laughs out loud.

"I haven't heard that word in a while. I think there are actually some good ones. Your mom took quite a few when she was building her case. I'll check with Josh to see if there are any extra toys lying around that the kids haven't seen, okay?"

"Thank you." My eyes get big. "What about Josh? Should I give him something? Can I borrow your laptop and printer?"

"Of course. And I'll download all the pictures so you can decide for yourself." I hop in the shower with the Christmas spirit in mind. I finish and wrap a towel around myself and head into my room. The laptop and printer are already there. I slip on a robe and fire everything up.

"Jenny?" It's Josh, tapping lightly at the door.

"You can come in."

He walks in with a big trash bag, drops it on the floor, and looks around. It's the first time he's entered my room since I've been here. I'm a tad aware that my robe is exposing some decent cleavage, but I'm curious to see if he notices.

"Jenny, cover up. Please." I pretend to be surprised and apologize.

"Here, I bought the kids a bunch of stuff. Why don't you give this to Lexi and give this one to Adam." My face lights up.

"Are you sure? This is an American Girl Doll. Aren't they expensive?"

"Here's a little secret—I'm rich," he says sarcastically.

"Well, la-di-da!" I tease. He breaks a smile and covers his mouth to sort of wipe it away. "When do you open gifts? Tonight? Or tomorrow?"

"Santa comes on Christmas Day. When did he come to your house?"

"I honestly don't remember. But Danny and I played Christmas year-round."

"Oh. Well, we'll be opening gifts tomorrow morning around the tree."

*That buys me time.* Adam is getting an X-Box from me. I'm glad Dr. Braun asked Josh for a little help. This is so great. Josh also brought me some old frames for the pictures I want to print, plus wrapping paper and bows. I can't get the smile off my face. Josh folds his arms and watches me, smirking. There's still a heart in there somewhere.

"I hope you weren't expecting anything from me. I didn't get you anything."

"Yes, you did. You gave me quite a fancy roof over my head, food in my stomach, and a place to celebrate Christmas with my family. That's the best gift ever."

His facial expression gets serious as he looks around the room. I wish he'd come right out with whatever's on his mind so we can have the conversation we desperately need. But he avoids it again. "All right. Well, enjoy the wrapping. I'll see you at dinner." I thank him again as he walks out the door.

My mother took some decent pictures. There are some of Ryan and me from when he proposed. I stare closely at one of them. We look happy but a little apprehensive. It seemed odd at the time, but way stranger now. My whole family is standing around, and he proposed to me with his mother's ring. This is an arranged marriage. But we do love each other, don't we?

Maybe since they don't open presents until tomorrow morning, Dr. Braun can take some good pictures around the tree tonight instead. Then we'll be dressed up and I won't look so sickly. I've come a long way since then. I'm sad that Ryan won't be here and wonder what kind of Christmas he'll be having, and if he misses me. I grab a burner and call him, but there's no answer. I try again and again. He's supposed to pick up. Finally, he answers, three sheets to the wind. I hear loud music and people yelling in the background. "Hello?" he says, stuttering.

"Ryan?"

"Babe, oh babe. How's your day?"

"I'm good. What's going on there? Are you having a party?"

"Why not! May as well. You're probably over there fucking Josh. I'm gonna have me a good time tonight too." I rise to my feet, shocked at what just came out of his mouth.

"Put your sister on the phone right now!" He starts screaming her name. "Jackie. Jackie-O. Phone's for you."

Jackie takes over the call and goes in for damage control. "Jenny, I'm sorry. He's wasted. A few hours ago, he just started inviting everyone he knows over to the house, and he's been drinking all day. He's a fucking handful again. I wish he'd just go back to Baltimore."

Our separation must really be getting to him, and his paranoia about Josh has reached an epic level. But there's nothing I can do about that. I've been as convincing as I can be. I hear him in the background.

"Merry fucking Christmas everyone. I'd like to propose a toast. Here's to my future bride who ain't by my side." A crowd hollers and laughs.

"I'm gonna sober him up. Don't worry." He's back and yelling. I can hear her trying to settle him down.

"Where's Alicia? My best friend. Where are you?"

"What did he just say?"

"Alicia swung by for like two minutes. That's it. She's already got her coat on and is leaving, Jenny. It's not what you think. But shit, this has gotten completely out of control. I'll call you tomorrow morning. Please, try not to worry. He's hurting and drowning his sorrows."

I hang up. Like hell he is. I can't leave him alone for one week? On the one hand, I wish I didn't call him, but on the other, thank God I did. I wonder what the security cameras are showing in front of the estate. I slide on some shorts and a T-shirt and march my way to the security room. There's no one monitoring at the moment, so I take over the controls and find the Brandt Estate. It's excessively lit up for Christmas, and I can see Markus attempting to control traffic. There are cars everywhere. *For the love ...* I think I see a local news crew. He's completely lost control.

"Miss, you can't be in here." The security guard says and tries to pull me out of his seat. Then he sees what I'm seeing.

"Turn that one off. I don't even want it on." He goes in for a closer look, shakes his head, and turns it off. I jump back up and march off to Danny and Fabrizio's room to tell them what I just witnessed. They downplay.

"He's just drunk. He would never do anything to hurt you. He loves you."

"Bullshit!" I'm seeing red and storm back off to my room. How do I calm down? Meditate. I sit on the zebra carpet and give it a try. How dare he! I'm not going to let him ruin my Christmas. What the fuck is he thinking? I'm too irritated to meditate and start wrapping the presents for the kids instead.

I finish and grab the computer for ideas. If I were to give Josh a gift, what could possibly mean something to him? The man has everything. I scour the internet and finally stumble upon a picture of Tohickon Cave before it was submerged by the lake. There's a picture of Henry Mercer, the historical local archaeologist, standing in front of it. He's holding a piece of pottery. It's a pretty clear picture. I plop it into a word document and add the caption "If only he knew." Josh will know what it means. We found much more than pottery in the cave when we went for our dive. I never told a soul about the coins. I take a minute to admire how nice it looks in the frame, then wrap it and lay it with the others. I'm sure his little astronaut will get plenty of gifts. She's not getting anything from me. I clean up the room and start getting ready for dinner.

I'm still aggravated and flushed, but at least I don't look pale. I decide not to wear my engagement ring tonight. It's an insult to his mother after the way he's behaving. I undress and slip on the black sleeveless cocktail dress. I don't know where Danny found it, but it's probably the prettiest thing I've ever worn. It's satin below the waist, with delicate lacy details above it. A skin-toned lining gives the impression of open skin. Embroidered flowers with crystal accents cover the bosom area then wind their way up to the neckline. It's gorgeous, plus it covers almost every single scar. For the first time since I got here, I go full-blown makeup. I almost forgot what I looked like in it. I curl my long hair and leave it down and slip on the stilettos Danny bought, then check myself out in the mirror. Damn! I look hot. I don't feel very well, thanks to Ryan, but I look good. I don't want to bring anyone else down with my blues and vow to keep a happy face.

"Ready, Jenny?" Fabrizio knocks. I step out and Fabrizio pushes me back in the door. "Um. This is going to get you in trouble. Holy shit. Daniel, come here!"

"What's wrong? Oh, my." Danny starts laughing. "You look amazing. Do you like it?"

"I love it."

"You picked this out for her?"

"Yes. Why? What's wrong with it?"

"I'm as gay as the night is long, but I'm getting a woody. What's it going to do to Josh?"

"Who cares. Josh has his young hot girlfriend," I remind him.

"Yeah. Relax, hon. She deserves to look this great."

"You're right. Let's all just go enjoy ourselves in Wonderland. Maybe Alice will show up tonight."

"Thank you. You both look amazing as always. I want to get some pictures of us by the tree. It's our first Christmas together since we were kids, Danny."

"It is. I'm so glad to spend it with my two favorite people, even though we do appear to be in some weird fairytale." He gives me, then Fabrizio, a kiss and ushers us over to Dr. Braun's quarters. Dr. Braun emerges, looking very distinguished in a black suit and red tie. He looks from me to Danny and then right at Fabrizio.

"She's already heard it from me," Fabrizio says. Dr. Braun asks where my ring is. I give him the latest on Ryan. He forces me to put it back on. Reluctantly, I head back to my room and slip it on my right finger instead of my left.

It's been a long time since I walked in heels, so I take extra time going over the bridge. No need to make a literal splash tonight. Josh calls out to us from the pentacle bar room. They're about to make a toast. I enter, and all eyes look from me to Josh, which I find quite embarrassing. Everyone's making a big deal for nothing. Everyone looks good. Not just me. Lucia looks stunning in a red velvet dress, like Julia Roberts in *Pretty Woman*. Kimberly is wearing a longer, very sophisticated black dress. Lexi runs over to me, and I pick her up.

"You look so beautiful," I tell her. She has a gorgeous black and red velvet dress on. Her hair is partially up with a red velvet bow. Curly waves of blonde hair run down her sides and back.

"You look like a princess, Miss Jenny."

"I love this kid." The room laughs, but nervously. "What are we toasting to?" I'm handed a glass of red wine.

"No champagne?"

"No. Sorry," Sammy says.

I finally look at Josh for myself, and he has a look on his face that I've never seen before. Like he's seen a ghost. He's pale and not looking like he's up for celebrating anything.

"Uncle Josh just got engaged." The smile fades from my face. I quickly recover and grab my glass. *A month after us and he's engaged? Well, who am I to judge? So am I*—technically.

"This is exciting news. I'm happy for you both. You make a beautiful couple." Josh's mouth is not moving, so Sammy nudges him.

"Thank you. I'd like to raise a glass in celebration. I'm going to marry the love of ..." he stops. "I'm going to marry my love. Thank you for saying yes, Lucia." We all raise a glass. I think the toast was supposed to be a little meatier. She looks hurt and spends a little too much time looking at me. I go about my business talking to everyone. I pay extra attention to Lexi because she sucks the tension right out of the room. Eventually, I make my way around the bar and give Lucia a half-assed hug. I'm not really sure how to congratulate Josh, so I just extend my hand. He looks at it and shakes it, then notices the ring is now on my right hand. He tilts his head and gives me an inquisitive expression.

"Dinner is served," a voice announces. We make our way to the dining room. Lexi is holding my hand and skipping. My mood is upbeat despite the circumstances. We all sit in silence and pray before eating, even Fabrizio. Danny does a double take, not believing his eyes.

Dinner is delicious. The chef prepared a large, perfectly roasted turkey, with root vegetables and mashed potatoes. Josh's personal chef is incredible. Fabrizio has become his biggest fan, and he's the pickiest eater I know. We all make small talk, but I can't help but notice how unusually quiet Josh is for such an occasion. I need to break the weird silence.

"So, Lexi tells me you're going to be an astronaut, Lucia." Josh chokes a little on his drink.

She smiles. "Well, I don't actually want to go into space. I just study it. I'm finishing my Ph.D. in astrophysics at the University of Iowa. I'm doing my thesis on black matter." *Whoa!*

"That's a hot topic right now. Good for you," Fabrizio says.

"This is probably a stupid question, but what is black matter?" I ask. Lucia looks smug, and I have immediate regrets about asking.

"It's the matter we can't see, but it makes up about eighty-five percent of all the matter in the universe and it's stretching out over time. We call that dark energy. In my lifetime, I want to help solve the mystery of how black matter relates to gravity." I mentally shut her up. She's beautiful and very intelligent. Josh has found his match. I'm happy for him but feel like bursting into tears at the same time. I have to keep it together. Act.

"Where did the two of you meet?"

She looks lovingly at Josh, "I've had a crush on him since I was a little girl. But we finally had our own gravitational pull during my initiation." *She just said that?* "We've kept our relationship quiet, only seeing each other from time to time. But once Kendra was out of the picture, we were able to be out in the open. I have you to thank for that, Jenny." My fork freezes before entering my mouth, and I place it back down.

I'm in mental anguish and start taking noticeably slow breaths. Josh shifts uncomfortably in his chair. Fabrizio can't help himself and drops his fork, which bangs off his plate before hitting the floor. He picks it up and glares at Josh, an obvious sign of disapproval. It doesn't go unnoticed. Josh blushes and looks both ashamed and embarrassed.

I'm out of questions and have completely lost my appetite. I sit and stew and wait while everyone else enjoys the rest of their meal. We're served homemade Christmas cookies before gathering in the family room by the tree. Dr. Braun stops me, takes my right hand, and rubs his index finger over my lifeline. A strange calm envelops me like an invisible hug. Josh sees it and nods to Dr. Braun as if to say thank you. I don't know how, but I feel much better. What an odd experience.

Despite being in a cave, it's still quite homey. The cat is playing with a bow from one of the packages. "What the hell kind of cat is that?" Danny asks. I laugh and explain.

We get lots of pictures, and I even play photographer for Josh and Lucia. But I purposefully take the worst pictures of her that I can. It's not easy, but I get a good one with her eyes shut and mouth open. Josh is uncomfortable with every snap—his smile is anything but genuine. But I can't wait to go back and see how the rest of them turned out so I can frame and wrap them for everyone. Danny even takes one of Dr. Braun and me. I suppose I'm trying to fill the void of never having had a family photo to stare at. I imagine a big wall full of them some day.

Before everyone heads back to their rooms, Lexi asks me to read, "'Twas the Night Before Christmas" aloud. Why not! I read it with enthusiasm, emphasizing every word to help her enjoy the moment. I hope she remembers it as a good one. Her eyes are heavy by the end of the tale, and Kimberly tells the kids it's time to sleep. "Santa will soon be here." She looks at me like, *yeah right*.

I'm tired too. Dr. Braun gives me the camera so I can hook it up to the computer. Danny and Fabrizio want another drink and head to the bar. Lucia is falling all over her fiancé, ready to get laid. I bid everyone good night, and Dr. Braun escorts me back to my room. He asks me if I'm all right. I lie through my teeth and tell him that I'm just fine, and happy for Josh. He gives me a peck on the cheek, and we go our separate ways.

I wash all the makeup off my face, put on a pair of pajamas, and fight the urge to cry. I solemnly look through and find just the right pictures of everyone. Fuck it! I even find one for Lucia. It's been an exhausting day, and despite a very heavy heart, I fall asleep.

I'm awakened by shrieks from the children. "Santa has come! Santa has come! Wake up, Miss Jenny." Lexi is banging on my door. I open it and give her a big hug.

"What's everyone wearing?"

"Just jammies. Come on."

I make her wait until I've brushed my teeth and washed my face, then follow her with my bag of gifts. I feel happy and in the Christmas spirit. Danny hands me some coffee and gives me a kiss. The whole room rises to exchange hugs and personal Christmas greetings as we enter. Even Josh embraces me. Not so subtly, he inhales into my neck as my hair brushes against his cheek. The realization that he's smelling me sends a jolt right down my pants. I sit on the opposite end of the room, alarmed by the effect he's having on me, especially knowing he was with another woman the whole time we were together. I doubt he was ever in love with me at all. Just biding his time, waiting to be with Lucia. I have to force myself to continue smiling every time I think of it, but it's hard to hide the hurt. I catch Josh examining me, more than he's likely even aware, with an expression of guilt. I'm glad he's on that side of it instead of me for a change.

It takes a good hour for the kids to open their presents. There's wrapping paper and toys everywhere, but finally I get to give my presents out too. The kids tear through theirs first and scream and yell with joy. Josh gave me the best gifts to give. I whisper him a "thank you" and hand everyone else their presents simultaneously. There are lots of "awws" and "thank yous." They all love the pictures. Josh hasn't opened his yet, and I'm tempted to take it back. He really doesn't deserve the sentiment.

"Go ahead. Open it, Uncle Josh," Lexi insists.

"Okay, okay." He opens it slowly and fixates on it. He sucks his lower lip into his mouth and bites it as he stares at it. He makes eye contact with me, looking guiltier than ever. "Thank you, Jenny."

"You're welcome," I say, no big deal. Lucia's eyes get wide and she looks at me. "Hal. How ..." Josh cuts her off and puts it aside.

"Did you say Hal?"

She shakes her head, stands, and starts cleaning up. I'm trying to figure out what's got her perplexed and look for a little help from Dr. Braun. He's saved by his phone, which is ringing loudly.

"It's Michael, Jenny."

"I don't want to talk to him." I say it loudly enough that everyone can hear, including Ryan.

"Jenny!" he scolds. I take the phone, hang it up, and hand it back to him. The room gets quiet.

The chef breaks the silence. "Breakfast is served." I stroll calmly into the dining room and take my seat at the table, saving a spot for Lexi. Josh picks through his eggs but looks like he's having trouble swallowing.

We spend the rest of the day relaxing and playing with the kids. I purposely avoid any conversation whatsoever that involves initiation, my feelings, engagements, and everything in between. If I can't physically get away, I at least want a mental escape on Christmas.

I choose a more modest dress and tone my makeup down quite a bit. Lucia toned it all the way up, making sure she's the most beautiful woman in the room. The chef prepared another amazing feast for dinner with lamb chops and a medley of side dishes. I excuse myself from the dinner table early to call Ryan. I can't put it off all day.

I lay down on the bed and dial. He's salty, and neither of us really feels like talking, but we don't feel like fighting either. He doesn't apologize, and by the end of the short conversation, he tells me he wants his mother's ring back. That's when the reality hits me. He's not strong enough to make this work. He never has been. We were never meant to be together, and I make no attempt to argue with him. I slide the ring off and put it in a box on the dresser. I'm finished talking and end the conversation with "Merry Christmas, Ryan." I have no tears left to shed over him.

I'm disappointed in a way but numb at the same time. I decide that I'm through with men for now. I want to focus on getting stronger, studying, and going through with initiation. It's Danny and Fabrizio's last night here. I don't want to hide and ruin it, so I come back out and sit at the bar where the adults have gathered for drinks. Josh's eyes immediately dart to my hand. Everyone's do. I whisper to Danny that he asked for the ring back.

"Fuck him then," he says. "He's acting like a big baby."

"I know. I'm never going back to that." He and Fabrizio support me one hundred and ten percent and pump me up with words of encouragement and love. We spend the rest of the night with happy talk. I don't want any more drama. I don't want to come between Lucia and Josh. I just want to lie low.

I've had enough to drink for one night and thank everyone for a wonderful Christmas. Aside from breaking up with my fiancé and learning that Josh had a girlfriend while we were together, it's been a nice evening. Danny and Fabrizio walk me to my door, and we're all off to slumber.

I fall asleep rather easily but wake up at 3:33 a.m., feeling a sense of doom at the number. I grab my journal, shuffle my pillows, and prepare to let out some pent-up emotions. As I do, I feel something under one of them. I reach to find a small gift. This is a nice surprise, probably from Danny or Fabrizio. I open it up and find two gold coins, which make my heart melt. They're the coins Josh and I found in the underwater cave. There's a small note folded up. It reads, "If only." My chin quivers, and my heart starts to hurt again. There's a quiet knock at my door, and Josh slips in.

"I saw your light on. Did I wake you when I put it under your pillow?" I'm only wearing a very revealing pink tank top and matching panties. Josh sneaks a peek before I cover up.

"Maybe that's what woke me up at 3:33 a.m. Josh, thank you so much. I will always treasure this ... this treasure." We both laugh. He sits at the edge of the bed and asks what's happening between me and Ryan. I tell him the truth, that it's over, but I'm fine being alone and am ready to find myself again. I confess that I'm self-conscious about my scars but acknowledge that I put myself in the position and have no one to blame but myself. He continues to listen, and I continue to jabber. He finally interjects to tell me that I have nothing to be self-conscious about and that my beauty has only deepened with the scarring. It's the first nice thing he's said to me in a long time. I thank him, and even though it kills me, I make sure he knows that I'm happy for him and Lucia.

"We weren't together, Jenny. You know, when you and I were. And I meant what I said. Every word at that time. I need you to believe that. I am ... I was in love with you."

"I really needed to hear that right now." I'm fighting tears. We're both quiet and thinking. He holds my hand and looks me in the eyes. There's not much left to say. I'm happy enough with the explanation. He just really needs to get back up to his bed, the one he shares with Lucia. But the way he's touching my hand arouses me, making it hard for me to control my libido, and I really need to feel close to someone right now.

But I pull my hand away, knowing he probably just made love to his new fiancé. He doesn't back down. Instead, he runs his hand through my hair, then a finger across my lips. He leans in and gives me a soft, gentle kiss. I back away, disturbed by the cruel teasing, and wait for an explanation. He has that look, deep with desire. I don't know if I'm strong enough to resist it. He tests me and leans in again, but I back away again. He doesn't give up, but he's not exactly forceful either. His lips are soft and sensual, and his touch invades my very soul. I almost lose myself completely before getting ahold of myself again—not something I'm good at doing. "What are you trying to do to me, Josh?" I ask.

He stares into my eyes and snaps himself out of this bad idea. "I don't know. I'm sorry, Jenny. I just ..." I pull the covers all the way up to my neck. He deep exhales and runs his hands through his hair. "I just can't wait for this all to be over." He stands up and he retreats quietly out the door. I lay awake the rest of the night overthinking everything. I have five months of this to deal with?

I get myself dressed very early and head into the living room to catch up on the news. A sleepy servant asks me if I want coffee. I tell her to go back to bed, that I'll make it. She's thankful and wanders away. The news is rather quiet until they rerun a clip from the Brandt Estate with Ryan losing it. I see Jackie in the background on the phone and wonder if that's when we were talking. But the timing isn't right, and I start to worry that she's told our fathers.

I shut it off and head into the kitchen to grab a mug of coffee. It's kind of nice being up all by myself, so I decide to snoop a little and see what some of the back rooms look like. I wonder if I can find the spring that leads to Josh's lake house, which is now Sammy's. Not surprisingly, there are a bunch of locked doors, but I put my ear to one and hear water flowing. I startle a guard who was dozing on the job. I apologize for waking him, and he apologizes profusely for being caught. I only get another fifteen minutes before the rest of the house rouses. Lucia has an early flight, and she's right on time, coming down the steps with lots of luggage.

"Boy, you don't travel light, Lucia," I joke.

"I've decided to join Lucia in Iowa until after the new year. Then I'll be back and back to work," Josh informs.

Lucia is even smarter than I thought. No way did she want us alone for the remainder of the holiday season or longer. Unless of course it was Josh's idea. Either way, it's the right thing. Still, I find it hard to hide my disappointment and hard to fake a smile this morning. I grab my coffee, head over to the pool, settle onto a lounge chair, and lose myself in self-pity. Looks like it's just going to be me and Dr. Braun for New Years.

The morning drags on, and I lie low, spending time with Danny and Fabrizio. I'm in their room sadly watching them pack when Josh and Lucia knock. They announce they're off. Dr. Braun joins us and there are thank yous, handshakes, and hugs. I can't look at Josh, not after last night. I don't want to feel anything worse than the gnawing ache that's already there.

"You guys going to be good?" he asks. I still don't make eye contact.

Dr. Braun very enthusiastically blurts, "Yes indeed. I'm gonna kick her ass in Monopoly."

"Jenny, I'm speaking to both of you," he says, forcing me to look up.

"Of course. Happy New Year."

I see him hard swallow. The guilt-trip is eating at him, so I let him off the hook as best I can. "I'm just a little bummed seeing everyone go." Lucia groans and walks ahead, but Josh lingers.

"Jenny, just try to relax. Take care of yourself and take advantage of this space. You deserve it." I almost opened my body up to him and these are his final words until God knows when? He turns to look at my expression one more time as he follows his fiancé out. What was his plan if he had made love to me? Same plan? I'm suddenly really angry and resentful. I feel like punching something as I head back to my room. I lay on the bed and look up at the stained glass and try to find a happy place.

Sammy and his family visit a short time later to announce they're heading home too. I'm going to miss Lexi. She's my one solid picker-upper.

Lastly, I have to say goodbye to Danny and Fabrizio. It's hard for us, but we'll get through it, just like everything else.

"Looks like it's just you and me, Doc!" I say to Dr. Braun.

"Fine with me. Too much company. It's exhausting keeping up with so many strong personalities. You're the easy one."

"Now I know you're full of baloney!" We both chuckle.

I begin the post-holiday by catching up on Lenape Indian history and learning what words I can of their language. Much of what I read, I already learned when I was a child—the peace treaty between William Penn and Chief Tamanend and the three tribes they formed along the Delaware River. Not much of the information is enlightening.

I give it a rest and spend the rest of the week pampering myself with saltwater swims, manicures, meditation, and journal writing. It doesn't *completely* suck.

It's New Year's Eve and I'm in much better spirits, feeling mentally and physically stronger. I should have known the other shoe would drop. Dr. Braun takes a call in the middle of dinner from my father. He, Mr. Brandt, and Ryan are coming over to settle our disagreement. They want us to make up.

## 20

UNWANTED GUESTS

It must have taken a lot of plotting for my father to meet up with Mr. Brandt and Ryan without being caught. I'm less than enthusiastic about seeing any of them, but I'll have to make it look good. They're already on their way, and I'm frazzled. Sammy is even less enthused but makes arrangements to meet them upstairs to go through the rigmarole.

As the staff takes away our plates, all I want to do is hide. Dr. Braun and I have on our New Year's best and were hoping to ring in the New Year playing games.

"You haven't said much, Jenny. Tell me how you're feeling, specifically about Josh. It was difficult to miss your glances, and impossible to miss the way Josh was looking at you. He's still in love with you. I'm a man, maybe an old one, but I know the look of love when I see it. Are you in love with him?"

"Whoa! Dr. Braun." I'm surprised by his candor, but he's waiting for a straight answer.

"Yes. Yes, I'm in love with Josh." I don't even have to think about it. "But I suppose it wasn't meant to be. He's with Lucia, and our families are hell-bent on a Mr. and Mrs. Michael Brandt III. They won't let it go, will they?" He shakes his head.

"I'm afraid not, but it's a shame. You and Michael have been quite good together. I've seen the way you look at each other also. I see mutual admiration and genuine love—maybe not lust, but try to separate the two. Lust doesn't last forever. Michael's been through a lot and has a lot of baggage and resentment, but he loves you. You must know that. He's made mistakes, but he's human. He's also chased you all over God's creation to protect you. You should try."

He speaks the truth, but I fear whatever love Ryan and I have for each other is now out of loyalty more than anything else.

Dr. Braun rises and takes me by the hand. "In case things get chaotic, Happy New Year, dear." He kisses me on the cheek and wraps an arm around me. I thank him for being such a great father figure and make sure he knows that I love him to the moon and back.

"Aww. Thanks, love. And having you as my unofficial daughter has fulfilled me in ways that I didn't know were possible. I'm very proud of you, and I'll always be here for you if you need me."

"Thank you. I've been meaning to talk to you about my biological father's mental state. I think he has split personalities or something. Like real ones. Not just a wicked temper, you know? What do you think?"

"You're a very good observer. Never forget how dangerous and unpredictable he is because of that. Never. You're playing him right. I don't know why, but be careful. If you have ill intentions for him, or our way of life, change course. Most of us are happy. We can suffer through the challenges, knowing we're still quite privileged."

"No, I would never do anything again to jeopardize the society. What about Mr. Brandt? They're very tight. How much of a threat is he to me and my brother? Or Ryan, for that matter?"

"I was quite surprised by his actions over the summer. He's lost his way. It happened after Douglas died. Many things changed at that time. I hope in the not-so-distant future, you, Michael, Josh, and Greg will make it right again. Make it the sacred and special place it's always been. But we'll need to ride out the storm, so to speak. They'll get caught by the Feds eventually. There's nothing you need to do." I inhale deeply.

"Do you think it's possible to help my father? Like through therapy?"

"He would have to admit he has a problem first. That's never going to happen."

"True."

Dr. Braun and I, along with several nervous-looking staff members, make our way to the entrance to provide a proper welcome. I hear sounds behind the large door and try to prepare for the moment. All three emerge, and the staff moves in quick to take their bags. I don't care for how many big bags they have. How long are they staying? Ryan makes brief eye contact with me but looks beyond me and into the space, which is a natural reaction.

"Happy New Year, pumpkin." My father bends down and gives me a hug and kiss. "You look beautiful."

"Thank you. You look very handsome yourself." I look from my father to his partner in crime. "Happy New Year, Mr. Brandt." We exchange pleasantries and watch Ryan as he tries to take it all in. His father clears his throat, bringing Ryan back to my side.

"Sorry. Happy New Year, babe." He kisses my cheek and looks at my hand. I'm not wearing the ring.

"Jenny, why don't you show Michael around, and we'll get settled," my father suggests.

"Settled?"

"Yes. We'll be staying for a few weeks or longer, depending on how safe it is to move again. You and Michael need to be together right now. Jackie is running the estate, and the Feds think Michael is back in Baltimore. Make up! Enough of this nonsense. After initiation, you'll be married." *Is that a fact?* I look at Ryan and I feel nothing.

Jamie, the main caretaker, asks where Ryan's bag should go. I look at my father.

"He'll be sleeping with his future bride, of course." I feel a flush come over my face. Jamie nods and drags his bag into my room. *My goddam room.* I feel completely invaded. Ryan follows her, and I follow him. I don't want him entering my space alone or finding my journal.

"So, this is where you've been. Not too bad. Where's your buddy? Is this where the two of you have been sleeping?"

"You're an idiot! He's not even here. He's in Iowa with his fiancé."

He looks legitimately surprised to hear both tidbits of information —that he's not here and that he has a fiancé. No one told him this? And what's Josh going to think when he finds out he has been invaded by my father and the Brandts? Ryan spots the engagement ring on the dresser. Before he can pick it up, I attempt to walk out.

"Hold on, Jenny. Hold on. Put it on."

"You said you wanted it back. So, take it back."

"I'm sorry. I didn't realize. I'm sorry, okay. Put it back on."

"No."

"Put it the fuck back on now. If not for my sake, for theirs. Do it." He's right. I'm going to have to wear it to avoid a big blowout in front of our fathers. I slip it on, kick my journal inconspicuously under the bed, and walk out. He follows. "I'm ready for my tour." I coldly show him around. He pretends to look unimpressed, but I know him too well. He's in awe, like everyone else who enters. "Where does Josh sleep?" I shrug my shoulders.

"How the hell would I know?"

"Like you don't know." I want to lash out at him something awful.

"Ask my dad. He used to sleep with Kendra in the master bedroom. I would imagine that's where Josh sleeps. If you continue acting like this, I'm going to make a fucking scene, even worse than the one you made on Christmas Eve."

I need a drink. I storm toward the pentacle bar room and plop down next to Sammy, who's having a glass of wine. We give each other looks of mutual annoyance. I order a martini and slurp it down in three gulps, then ask for another. The bartender hands Ryan a beer. He takes it and walks out to check out the pool and do some exploring.

"What the fuck?" Sammy whispers.

"How do we get rid of them?"

"We don't."

"When is Josh supposed to return?"

"Day after tomorrow. He's not going to be pleased. I haven't told him yet."

"Well, tell him this isn't my doing, would you please?"

"I will. This is bullshit. Listen, if things get nasty, tell Jim here. He'll reach out to me and I'll get you out of here. Got it?" The bartender gives me a subtle nod. I return it with one of my own. I feel slightly better having an emergency plan.

There's sudden commotion, and Dr. Braun rushes in to alert me about a situation. There's been an emergency, and he needs to leave. I'm suspicious of the timing and demand to know more. I can't shake the feeling that my father has it in for him. First by the look he gave him after my mother took his phone, then the incident in the tunnel, which landed us here. Plus, it's obvious we've gotten close. I'm worried my father is going to harm him. It's just a bad feeling.

He tells me one of the bears split open a new farmhand. He's going to need emergency surgery. I want proof and make him show me a picture. The man's in bad shape, but I don't want him to go. I feel like I can manage the world without anyone, as long as I have him. We embrace and look into each other's eyes. He looks as worried about me as I do about him. Sammy's on his feet, ready to take him up and out. I want him followed and to be given updates. Sammy agrees to do his best. They're off, and I'm left with my new buddy, Jim, the bartender. I'm on a mission to get bombed and slug down the next martini. Jim tells me to slow down and hands me some water. It's 10:00 p.m. Only two more hours until we ring in the new year.

My father enters and sits down next to me. "How are things?" He lifts up my hand to see the ring. "Excellent. You've already made up.

I knew you would. It's not good to be apart. It'll make you second-guess things unnecessarily."

"Yeah, but why here? This is Josh's territory and home now."

"His home is open to any Grand Master and their family. I admit, we don't have to exchange favors like this very often, but it's safer here than back at the estate." I smile and nod. I can't afford to piss him off. Mr. Brandt and Ryan return. Ryan does what a good fiancé should and puts his arm around me. It makes our fathers happy, but makes me cringe. I can't believe this is happening. I was perfectly content alone with Dr. Braun.

We pass the time listening to my father and Mr. Brandt take a creepy walk down memory lane. They reminisce about the times they spent down here with Kendra over the years. The day they turned the pool water purple for Kendra's fortieth birthday. It makes me uncomfortable for a million reasons. We raise our glasses at midnight for a toast and exchange traditional acts of affection. Ryan's kiss does nothing for me, but I remember the soft kisses Josh gave me on Christmas. Those are the ones I want. I'm no longer confused. And in my heart, I know it's more than lust. Our fathers leave us to be alone. I rub my neck, trying to get the kink out of it. I need to relax.

"Let's go to bed, babe. It's been a long day." He takes me by the hand. I think back to September when his hand was the only one I wanted. So much has changed in such a short time. I rise with him and raise an eyebrow to the bartender. He smirks at me, knowing I'm in hell. We cross over the pool and pause. "Pretty incredible down here." I look around with him.

"It is. Very surreal, I'd say."

"So, you haven't been with Josh?"

"For fuck's sake. No, Ryan. I haven't. We all spent some time together, but the only person I was with is his niece. Turns out, I like children." I light up as I talk about them. "Lexi, she is the cutest, and Adam, oh my God ..." Ryan cuts me off.

"Well, we sure as shit aren't having any."

"No. *We* aren't. I agree completely."

He takes me by the hand and leads me through the door and locks it behind him. I feel trapped. He cuts to the chase. "I know I haven't behaved well. Are you going to be able to get over it? Do you still even want to get married?"

"I can't answer that at this time." I open a drawer and grab some pajamas and head into the bathroom. I wash the makeup off my face, brush my teeth, take a deep breath, and head back into the bedroom. Ryan is sitting on the bed going through Dr. Braun's laptop. He's looking at the pictures from Christmas. I know there isn't a single one of Josh and me, so I have nothing to worry about. I simply stare down at him with my hands folded. He puts it down and looks up at me.

"I'm sorry I didn't believe you. Do you blame me though?"

"No. I don't blame you at all. I was unfaithful to John. You have no reason to trust me. You've made it very obvious. But that's fine. You wanna know why?"

"Why?"

"Because I don't trust you either. Not for one minute. Now move over so I can sleep."

He puts the laptop back down and pulls a few things out of his suitcase. I can hear him getting undressed, but I keep my eyes closed. The sound of him brushing his teeth and using the bathroom makes me shiver. These are all horrible signs.

He slips under the covers, and I feel his bare chest against the back of my arm. I move away from it. He moves closer and puts an arm around me. I try to shrug it off. "Jenny?"

"What?"

"I still want to marry you. But none of this is normal. My whole life has been abnormal." His words are sincere, and I can certainly relate. But I'm not in the mood for a deep conversation.

"Go to sleep. We'll figure it out." I let him give me a quick squeeze, but I never turn back over to look at him.

## 21

### OUT IN THE COLD

I wake up at 3:33 a.m. and dart right out of bed. I'm sweating, and Ryan's still out cold. I open the door for cooler air and head over to the kitchen for a glass of milk, hoping it will help me fall back to sleep. For the first time since I've been here, I'm suddenly really curious about the master bedroom. With everyone passed out, I'm probably safe from getting caught. I tiptoe through the living room and up the stairs. The door is surprisingly unlocked. How daring do I feel? *Very.* I open the door and head up a stone stairway. It's spiraled but very wide. I hold on to the rail until I'm all the way up. Fish tanks are glowing. There are three, each of them tall and round with exotic saltwater species swimming in and out of live coral. I find a light switch and flip it on. *Oh, this is over the top.* It's enormous and very Kendra. But it looks like Josh is doing a makeover. Four monitors and lots of unidentified electronics line one whole wall. A waterfall gently rolls down the opposite wall. The bed is bigger than a King with an enormous purple canopy. I smell chlorine. I open the bathroom door to find another pool. They have their own private pool like something you'd see in a Pocono resort. Heart shaped and all. How tacky. Fabrizio would laugh hysterically at this. I sit down on the bed and think of what could have been.

"Excuse me." I jump up and look around. I thought I was alone. "Pick up the red phone." It's Josh. I'm embarrassed and probably in so much trouble.

"Hello? I'm so sorry, Josh."

He laughs. "Happy New Year, Jenny. Up a little late, aren't you? Or should I say early? Push the green button on the third monitor."

I look awful, but he's seen me for dinners, so I flip it. He's still wearing a tux from whatever formal affair he's attended and looks very handsome.

"You okay?"

"Not really."

"What's happening?"

I fill him in on the unwelcome guests. He's angry. I advise him to call Sammy for more details and apologize for invading the privacy of his bedroom.

He shrugs like he's not bothered. "Why'd you come in my room if Ryan's in your room?"

"Why do you think?"

"Jenny, cut him a break already. The man would die for you."

"Would you?"

"In a heartbeat," he says and changes the subject. "Well, how do you like the room?"

I shrug again. "I think simple is better. This is Kendra's taste, not mine. Maybe something with a little more character than the symbolic white room up in the main house, but this is a bit much."

"It really is, right?" he says with a laugh.

"How was your night? How's Lucia?"

"It was fun, and she's fine. Passed out. Bit of a lightweight. I was about to change and start packing, but I think I'll head back to Main Street now. I'm not coming back there with three loose cannons running around."

"Hey!"

"Not you."

"Your parents' old house on Main Street. That's the kind of house I want to live in some day."

He looks down again and takes a deep breath. "Well, I'm sure Ryan will buy you whatever house you want." I shake my head and get up and pace. "Jenny, you're destined to be with Michael Brandt. I'm going to marry Lucia. Make up. He loves you, and I know you still love him." I shut off the monitor, not wanting to hear any more.

"Jenny. I can still see you." *Damn.*

"Happy New Year, Josh, to you and Lucia. Good night."

I hear him calling my name again, but I run down the stairs and into the living room. I'm still alone. I'm kidding myself with Josh. There will never be a happy ending with us either. I skip the milk and head back to the bar for a drink. A security guard enters and asks if everything's all right. I lift my drink and tell him to join me. He gets behind the bar. "No drinking on the job, ma'am."

"Boring."

"What's going on?" It's my father.

"I'm sorry I woke you. I couldn't sleep."

"Why? What's the problem?"

"Dad, I don't know if I even love Ryan, let alone want to marry him. Can't we just see how things go? Why do we have to force it?" I cry. Mostly over losing Josh forever.

"Did Josh do something? Did he come on to you? I'll kill him. He understands this is the way it must be."

"What? No way. He's very much in love with Lucia. And what do you mean? The way it must be?"

"In good time. Until then, no more of this talk. You love each other. You have for a long time, so stop this silliness, or else."

"Or else what?"

I flipped the switch. My father grabs the drink out of my hand and throws it across the room. I instinctively put my hands over my face to protect myself. The security guard is unsure how to react—

protect me or stay loyal to my father. I stand up to move out of range and excuse the security guard.

"Let's talk about you for a minute. Why did you get married outside of the society?"

"I'm sorry about the way things ended with your mother, Jenny. I know I let you and Danny down. Nothing but your happiness matters to me anymore."

"My happiness matters to you?"

"Very much."

"Then I'm not marrying Ryan." I get up before he can throw something at me, but I'm not quick enough. He grabs me by the hair and shakes me hard. I could stop him. I could play back into his alter ego of loving father, but I don't want to. I'm hurting on the inside, so I may as well hurt on the outside. He turns me toward him, so we're face-to-face. His hand is raised, ready to strike. I'm more than ready for it. His evil contorted facial expression suddenly changes, and he releases me. I can see in his eyes that he has a new and sicker idea.

"Then you will never, ever get initiated. And you will never be part of the Order."

He yells for the security guard. "You will escort my daughter upstairs and out the front door, now."

"Sir, it's snowing. I'll get her a coat."

"No coat. She goes now."

I break free and run. I run toward the underwater passageway to Josh's lake house. I have no time to put on a wetsuit and am wracking my brain to remember the description he gave me. I leap into the cold water. It's a shock to my system. There's no time to spare before hypothermia consumes my body. I use every technique I've learned to remain calm and use mind control to help stabilize my body temperature. Luckily, there are a few lights to guide the way, and my water skills are exceptional, almost effortless. I'm up into the grotto in less than ten minutes and hop in the heated pool to warm my bones.

I hear an alarm go off and clumsily climb out. I run up the stairs and check the master bedroom. It's empty. Slipping and sliding on the stone surface, I rush to the other side and open the door leading up into the basement. Sammy is ready and aiming a gun at me. He retreats seeing that it's me.

"What's happening?"

"I need a phone. And some warm clothes. My father. I've done some damage. I need to run."

"Fuck, Jenny."

"What's happening?" Kimberly looks tired but nervous. Sammy yells for her to get me some clothes.

"You're going to get us all in trouble."

"Tell him you kicked me to the curb. Your loyalty is to my father."

Kimberly hands me some clothes. I undress and dress, give them both a kiss, and run into the early morning air. My feet are cold, but I've been through worse. I almost forgot what freedom feels like. It feels great! The snow looks beautiful, reflecting brightly from the rising sun. I run through the trails Josh uses with the quads. I find a log, sit down, put the boots on, then take off like a bat out of hell. I don't hear any alarming sounds, but I'm mentally ready for anything. I need to run far away from Brandtville. I can't call Danny, and I have no more Sal. I can't even call Jack. I get a thought. My nurses from the hospital, Peter and Tina. I quietly call the hospital, praying one of them is working the holiday, and start heading north toward Doylestown. Tina is available, and an operator transfers me.

"Happy New Year. This is Tina."

"Tina. It's Jenny. I can't explain right now, but do you think you or Peter could pick me up? I need a place to hide."

"Where are you? I'm on my way." I give her the general location. She asks me to wait behind a Lutheran Church somewhat close to where I am. By the time I get there, she'll be there. I still have my little team, and I'm beyond grateful.

I run until my side hurts and break through the woods alongside Route 611. I jog, weaving in and out of the trees until I make it. A Ford Explorer peels into the parking lot. Tina opens the door, still in her scrubs, and shouts, "Get in!" I jump in and she takes off. "Boy, am

I happy to see you. I've wondered where in the hell you've been since I last saw you."

"I'll tell you what I can, Tina, but I can't tell you everything, mostly for your own good. As soon as I have another plan, I'll be out of your hair. I promise."

"Stay as long as you want. I'm happy to help. No one would ever suspect you're with me. You're safe."

I'm not so sure about that. No one is safe when they help me. I spend the rest of the car ride considering what I can and cannot share with her, wondering if I'm really ready to pull the plug on initiation, or even be invited back to have one. Am I scarred for life for nothing? I don't know. But I need to get away from the society for now. I need to think in a normal setting. I really, truly am starting to forget what normal is altogether.

## 22

---

### A NEW IDENTITY

Tina Goodwin describes the scene from her end after I saw her last. Peter and Tina were both questioned but, thankfully, quickly released and haven't been people of interest since they flew me out of the hospital. She's very intuitive about my need for privacy and does most of the talking, which I truly appreciate at this intense moment.

We're literally the only people on the road this early in the morning, during a snowstorm and on New Year's Day. It looks like the end of the world. My SOS numbers of 333 have come to fruition. I imagine the snow being fallout from a nuclear explosion and that we're the only two people alive.

Tina lets me use her cell to call yet another one of Danny's burners. I misdial three times before the number comes back to me. He's groggy at first but jumps to attention. I tell him in very few words, combined with some secret coding, what happened. I give him some solid advice, "Go back to Italy with Fabrizio and put everything on hold." It's time for a reality check and to consider the real consequences of what we've gotten ourselves into.

He's getting another call on another phone. It's Josh. Danny puts it on speaker so I can listen. News travels fast, and my heart skips a beat, knowing he's called so soon. Josh wants to know if I'm all right. "She's shaken but safe," Danny informs him. Then he breaks it to him that we're both out of all things related to the Order and that we've had all the abuse we can handle. He thanks him for the safe haven and hospitality and assures him that the society will remain secret. Josh is quiet at first, trying to digest it.

"Danny, this may sound selfish, but I need your sister. Please reconsider."

"Need her for what?"

"She belongs to the Order and she belongs ..." He stops himself, leaving me on the edge of my seat. Danny doesn't wait for him to complete the sentence, and I can't very well speak up because he doesn't know I'm eavesdropping. *Damn it.* What was he going to say?

"I'll tell her, but I wouldn't hold your breath. Again, thank you, Josh."

He cuts back to me. "I assume you caught most of that?"

"Yes." Hopefully Tina didn't, but I'm all achy again and there's nothing I can do about it. Does he need me because of my legacy or what?

Danny's definitely had enough. He wants to see our mother and try discreetly to make amends. Plus, they have work to do back in Italy. He's also thrilled about all the projects and progress happening on the farm, so he's not afraid to leave it. The construction team is working wonders. He's going to pack, and they'll aim to leave by the end of the week.

Fabrizio interrupts to assure me that we're doing the right thing. "Did you know that some Rosicrucian Orders, including my grandfather's, deride homosexuality, saying that it goes against the Divine Laws of nature? That's why my family didn't introduce me to it. Like I'm some sort of leper. Sister, I was born this way! Laws of nature, my ass."

"I didn't know that. Well, screw them," I say under my breath.

"Damn right, screw them!"

Danny's back on. "I'm leaving Veronica in charge of the farm for now. We'll come and go and check on the projects when we can."

"Sounds good," I agree.

I look up as we pull onto a private dirt road. Before hanging up, I ask Tina for her address and relay the information to Danny. She and Peter live in Erwinna, not far from the Delaware River, in an old converted barn of their own. With the exception of the heavy beams and plumbing, she says they did most of the work themselves. It's rustic and stained a dark reddish-brown, with a large black star on the side of the house. I like the very warm Americana vibe and find it so much more inviting than a giant cave, no matter how luxurious and mystical it may be. I'm nervous and feel a little awkward asking strangers to help me but think how lucky I am to have met Tina. My nonna always said, "God puts the right people in your life at the right time."

The house is isolated, but out of habit, I hunch down until we're in. I'm in love with the refreshing style and compliment every corner as I look around. I've changed my mind. This is what I want some day. The entire middle section is open, with exposed beams angling all the way up to the ceiling. The French country kitchen is over-sized, with a big island and stools. There's a large centerpiece for hanging pots. Most of them are copper, adding even more charm. Peter pours me a cup of coffee and greets me warmly.

"Well, Happy New Year, Jenny. I would've cleaned up the place had I known you were coming."

"I'm sorry to intrude like this."

"Don't be silly. How about some eggs?"

"That would be great. Thank you."

"Come on, I'll show you upstairs," Tina says. The open concept is comforting because there's no place for someone to hide and sneak up on me. "Here, take this one. It's closest to the stairs. I'll be right back." She leads me into a nicely appointed bedroom filled with antique cherry wood furnishings, including a poster bed, dresser, and a desk. I immediately think about my journal and wish I had it. I poured my heart out in that thing. If Ryan or my father finds it, they'll know my true feelings for Josh. I hope the staff finds it first and honors my privacy. I pat my bra and feel for the coins. I've kept them on me since Josh gave them to me. The clothes on my back and two expensive coins—that's all I have to my name at the moment. But I have friends and a roof over my head again. I'm pretty lucky, all things considered.

Tina returns with stacks of clothes. We're the same size. She folds them neatly and puts them in the dresser. "Please let me know if you need anything else."

"You are the best! Thank you." I'm gonna need Danny to send me some money. I'm no mooch.

"Breakfast!" Peter yells.

"Come on. Let's chill and come up with a little short-term plan," Tina says. Peter and Tina spend hours picking my brain. They know, as the whole world knows, that I was put through a punishment. I can't deny it, but I stick with my story that I don't recall the details. They throw each other doubtful looks but don't push. They know I broke up the secret society once, and that my father's still out there. The cult is still in operation. They straight out ask if I'm taking part, but I adamantly deny it. I try to make them understand why I also can't be part of the Witness Protection Program. I'm still searching for answers about my father. They generously offer up their help. I tell them that's exactly what they're doing right now, by giving me a safe and secluded place to stay.

They saw Ryan on TV and ask if it's true. They saw the clip of him on Christmas Eve talking about his fiancé. They ask if we got engaged. I shake my head and tell them that I will never be Mrs. Michael Brandt III, and that it turns out he's not the one for me.

After hours of catching up, Tina stretches and yawns. She pulled a double shift and is ready for some sleep. I've hardly slept myself and am tempted to nap, but I'm also a little wired after the confrontation with my father and the quick action plan that got me here. Peter asks me about my diet, wanting to know if I have any restrictions.

"Nope! I love everything. What are you making?"

"We're on a whole-foods, Mediterranean diet. Wild salmon tonight."

"Everything organic and non-GMO for us," Tina adds.

"Sounds good to me."

I get comfortable on a window seat overlooking the side of the property. The snow is coming down hard, and I get this child-like desire to build a snowman. It feels good to be free and among normal people, with normal jobs. It makes me miss my job working with the doctors at Hopkins. I watch the snow fall and wonder exactly what my future holds.

For now, I want to go into a deep disguise and live as freely as possible. I have plenty of time to adjust and decide whether or not I want to be initiated. Of course, I'll need my father's permission first and wonder how much sucking up would be involved. Even though he gave me the boot, he's going to come unglued not knowing where I am. Banishing me will backfire on him. He wants me to become part of his world way more than I do.

I spend the rest of the day creating an alter ego of my own. I try to invent who I want to be, what my new look will be, and wonder how far I could go without being noticed. I'm suddenly looking forward to the near future.

Tina wakes up in time for dinner, and we toast to the new year. Peter is an amazing cook. I give huge props to the chef and insist on cleaning up before heading right to bed. I pass out relaxed for the first time since I can remember.

I wake up and jump up and down like a child to see two feet of snow on the ground. There's a State of Emergency and no one is allowed on the roads except emergency vehicles. Luckily, neither Peter nor Tina are working today. I beg them to go out and play in the snow with me. They laugh and give me fair warning that Peter has no mercy with a snowball.

After coffee, we put on a mismatch of snow gear and wander outside. True to their word, Peter has mad snowball skills. He makes them and throws them like it's his job. I fall down laughing at him and make a giant snow angel while I'm down.

Before we head back inside, we build a Michelin Man-sized snowman. Tina gives him a red scarf and a Philadelphia Flyers hat. It's the most fun I've had in a long time. We head back inside, and Peter makes us hot chocolate with marshmallows on top. The only person I'm really missing is Danny. I wish he could be here for a sibling snowball battle. In the distance, I hear snowmobiles. It would be so fun to go snowmobiling or skiing—with Josh. Can't get him out of my head.

During lunch, I go over some initial thoughts about a disguise. Peter and Tina are happy to help. They're both due at the hospital tomorrow and can get me everything I need on their way home. I'll take it one step at a time from there.

A new day dawns, and I have the house to myself. I have a new journal and spend some time writing. I need to keep any facts about the society out. As kind as Tina and Peter are, human curiosity will eventually get the best of them, as it definitely would me. I clean and turn on the TV from time to time. My whereabouts are still a mystery, same as my father's. Almost every news channel thinks we're together. Some think he killed me, and none of the locals will talk. There are multiple conspiracy theories as to why. Fear comes up the most, which isn't fake news at all.

"We're home," Peter yells. I get up enthusiastically. "What have you done to the place?" he says with a laugh.

"Just a little cleaning and organizing."

"It looks incredible."

"Well, I have to earn my keep! What'd you get?"

He dumps the bag upside down on the kitchen island. The first thing I notice is a platinum blonde hair kit. Tina hands me colored lenses, which are hazel. On top of that, she found a pair of very trendy non-prescription glasses. They bought new scissors for my soon-to-be, very short haircut, plus a fake nose ring. I don't want a real hole in my nose, but I like the idea of looking artsy for a change. Tina is going to add a pink stripe in my hair, which apparently is the fad.

"What's in the envelope?"

"Someone I never saw before handed it to me at the hospital," Tina says.

I tear it open. It's a note from Josh plus thousands of dollars in cash. It says, "I'm sorry I treated you so terribly while you were here. Be safe, Jenny."

I get a lump in my throat and describe Josh's appearance to see if he personally handed her the envelope. It wasn't, but he knows where I am and who I'm with, which is a little unnerving. I'm thankful for the cash but plan to pay him back.

"Ready, Jenny?" Tina asks.

"Yep! Let's do this."

"I've been watching YouTube videos all day. I don't want to fuck up your hair. My God, look how beautiful it is."

"I trust you. How short are we going?"

"Have you seen Pink lately?"

"Please, not that short!" I say with a laugh.

Over the next hour, I'm completely transformed. I don't even recognize myself. It's strange but exhilarating.

"So, what do you want to do first, Pink?"

"Ski!"

## 23

### SPRING HAS SPRUNG

Weeks turn into months. I've enjoyed every aspect of winter thus far. I took ski lessons at Camelback Mountain in the Poconos and have mastered all of the beginner and intermediate slopes. I'd love nothing more than to feel the rush of a black diamond course, but I have to take it easy. If I fall, I'll be identified because of my unique scars. Tina and I have developed a closeness I've never had before. I love and miss Jackie, but Tina is just what I need in a girlfriend. We laugh about everything. She's a great storyteller, and I look forward to the end of her shifts to hear the details of her day. Inevitably, she has something funny to share.

Neither Tina nor Peter pries like I probably would. I've been protective of my secrets, only relaying information they could have read about. Otherwise, we live in the moment and have established a great routine. They work a lot, and I clean and cook. They love my nonna's eggplant recipe. Peter asks me to make it every Sunday, which makes me feel like I'm contributing.

Every few weeks, more money is funneled my way. I hold on to most of it for now, because it's literally too much for what I need. I've given Peter and Tina enough to finish a few home projects. They're getting ready to build a large greenhouse with access from the house. Peter wants year-round organic fruits and vegetables.

It's March, and I haven't spoken to anyone but Danny. He, however, is bombarded with phone calls from our father, who needs constant assurance that I'm all right. He should've thought about that before kicking me out on my ass. He still wants me to be initiated and wants me back at Josh's. He and Mr. Brandt are back in hiding somewhere far from Brandtville. Danny thinks their mysterious hideout is in Greece this time.

I have no idea what Ryan is up to, and I don't care. I hope he and Alicia ran off to the Justice of the Peace. Danny says that our father has backed off of the arranged marriage concept and has even gone out of his way to ask nice questions about Fabrizio.

Danny and I talk about initiation occasionally, but neither of us is chomping at the bit to follow through. We're both enjoying our ordinary lives at the moment. But I can't stay here forever. I only have two choices: get initiated or come out of hiding and give the Feds what they want. That includes witness testimony, more details about the society, what I've been doing, and who I've been with. It's exhausting to ponder.

Danny phones as I'm folding laundry.

"I have some information to share that you may not care for."

I sit. "Josh and Lucia have set a date. It's soon. Like in six weeks. I'm guessing she insisted on making it before your potential initiation." My heart sinks. I understand why Lucia pressured Josh for such a date. He's told me before that no one gets initiated without him, and there may be close contact during that time. She likely doesn't want to risk us falling for each other in the middle. That's when the two of them fell in love, after all. The news bums me out. I hardly leave my room over the next few weeks, choosing instead to write dark things in my journal.

Tina forces me out of my room on a beautiful late-March day. The temperature is going all the way up to seventy-five degrees, she says. "Come on, sister. You need some fresh air." She takes me by the hand, guides me into the kitchen, and opens a bottle of wine. I follow her out on the back patio and try to lighten up. We make casual conversation until she asks what's eating at me. I decide to tell her a little bit about Josh. That we had a short love affair, that I still have feelings for him, but that he's getting married in a month. She asks if he's a member of the society, but I deny that he has any connection. I have to.

"Jenny, you're not the giving up type. Call him. Tell him how you feel."

"I don't know." I honestly feel like I'm going to jump out of my skin with the need to see him and hear his voice. Maybe he's on the lake today near the dam, either working or playing. Instead of a phone call, I talk Tina into a drive. I put on a heather-gray short-sleeved shirt that hangs ever-so-slightly off my good shoulder, and a pair of denim capris. All of my scars are covered. I go full sexy makeup with pink lipstick to match the streaks in my platinum hair, which I'm letting grow out. I've got a short bob—sophisticated but still very sassy.

It takes us about thirty minutes to get to Lake Nockamixon. It's still off-season, so there aren't any boats in the water, but we're not the only ones out for fresh air. There are dozens of people out enjoying the bright and sunny day, including a few runners, bikers, and a couple walking their dog. We park in a back lot and walk down toward the marina. I recognize the park ranger milling about. He's hanging up a new map of the area for tourists. I stand next to him and look it over. He does a few double takes but doesn't seem to recognize me. I suddenly hear the sound of a motor and look across the lake. I ask the ranger who it is, and he tells me it's the dam engineer looking over the structure.

"Is his name Josh Flannery by chance?"

"Yes, it is." He regards me suspiciously.

"We went to school together."

"Nice try, Jenny." I get wide-eyed at the bust. "Your voice and mannerisms. You should work on an accent or something."

"You're not going to say anything are you?"

"That depends on why you're here." I look out over the lake and try to catch a glimpse of Josh.

"You want me to get him?"

I'm nervous but say yes. I need to see him. I pull the fake ring out of my nose and ask the ranger if I look okay. He laughs and tells me I look great. Different than he's used to seeing me, but just as hot. Good answer.

I look back at Tina and she slips onto a path without my having to say anything. I take a deep breath as the ranger calls Josh on a talkie. I can hear both sides of the conversation. He tells him that there is an engineering student doing some research who would like to ask him some questions about the dam. Josh is annoyed and tells him that he's busy.

"I think you'll want to talk to this one, sir."

"Why?"

"I'll send her out to R-19." I smile. That's where Josh always picked me up. It registers.

"Be there in a few."

I feel butterflies all the way up to my throat. I'm flustered, afraid I'm going to say something stupid. Josh is coming in fast, hardly leaving me enough time to get to the slip before he does. He pulls up, leaves the engine running, and holds on to the dock to steady the boat.

"Get on and get below." I do as he says. It's his private boat, not his County-commissioned boat, so I wonder if he was just getting some air like I was. I take a seat at the table and look up at him as he steers. I wish I had appreciated our times together more when we had them. What was it Dr. Braun told me? Lust fades, and that I should learn to understand the difference. I know in my heart that I'll never lose the feeling of either for him. Maybe the rejection factor increases the intense need for a love lost, but I can't imagine losing feelings for him, ever.

The engine dies, and I hear Josh throw down an anchor. He descends into the cabin and gives me a once-over. "Well, that's an interesting look for you," he says with a smirk. "What're you doing here?"

"It's a nice day. Thought I'd come for a walk at the lake. Then I spotted you."

"I see."

"I heard you've set a wedding date."

"We did." *Now what do I say?* Beg him not to marry Lucia? I'm quiet and look away, but there can't be any mistaking the pain in my expression. "What are *your* plans, Jenny? You've done a good job of disappearing."

"I'll pay you back. Every penny."

"Stop. I don't want it. Are you planning on getting initiated or not? Money stops, if no."

"If you marry Lucia, no. Just stop the money now."

"I'm sorry, Jenny, but I'm going to marry Lucia."

I rise frustrated. "Danny told me that you needed me. For what?"

"You're destined to be part of our inner circle, now more than ever. Yes, I need you and would very much like you to return to your studies. Please, Jenny."

"That's it? You have no feelings for me at all otherwise?"

"Would I be looking out for you if I didn't? Of course I have feelings for you."

"It's my fault I'm in this position, right? And you're punishing me for life over it." I begin to well up and wipe my eyes quickly. As I do, my left contact lens shifts out of position. It stings. I open the small door to the head and look in the mirror. I don't feel like dealing with them and pull the lenses out. My green eyes are back and sparkling.

"Jenny." He pulls me in closer. "That's better. You shouldn't hide those beautiful green eyes." I blush and smile. *Maybe I am getting somewhere.* "I never want you to doubt your beauty. These scars." He pulls down the side of my T-shirt with the bite mark. "They humble me. You're the strongest and most amazing woman I've ever met." He pauses and shakes his head. "But I'm still going to marry Lucia."

"Why?" I see him swallow hard. He tries to move away from me, maybe not trusting what he's feeling. I won't let him. I grab both of his hands hard and force him to look at me again. "Josh, we were just getting started. Can't we try? Can't we just see if ..." He cuts me off.

"Come on, Jenny. Don't do this."

"I'm still in love with you." *Oh, God. I sound like John.* I'm starting to sound pathetic.

He groans and looks away. I keep a firm hold on his hands, but his are limp. With my body weight, I push him back and lean into him. This may be my one and only opportunity to be alone with him. I take one of my hands and gently play with the back of his hair.

"Don't do that." He removes my hand, steps away, and opens the cabinets under the tiny sink and pulls out my journal.

"I found it under your bed."

"Did you read it?"

"Some of it."

"Then you know. You know I still had feelings for you, and you haven't even called." He stares at me but says nothing. "Just say something."

"I don't know what to say." He's a cold-hearted bastard. I give up, but at least I tried. This was truly not meant to be, and I'm humiliated.

"Well, thanks for the money. Like I said, I'll pay you back."

"I won't take it, Jenny. Look, no one wanted us to work out more than I did, but you let me down, and I know you'd do it again. You're complicated as shit, and I don't have the patience for it. Come on, I have things to do today." I feel like a hundred yellow jackets are stinging me. I focus hard to keep my jaw from dropping in utter disbelief. He stops and looks at me before moving, waiting for a rebuttal. All I can think is ... *what about him?* He was hiding a relationship when we were together. I feel like tossing him overboard, but I sulk instead.

I stare into space on the ride back to the dock. Josh ties up but leaves the engine running. "You're clear. Come on up." I can no longer look at him. I just want to run and deal with my emotions and let Tina get me drunk. I refuse his hand to help me off the boat. I leap off and head down the dock toward land without saying goodbye.

"Hey!" I stop in my tracks but don't look back. "Get initiated, Jenny."

I look back only when I hear the boat leave the dock. I watch as he makes his way to the other side, and I'm left to read into his command.

# 24

---

EASTER VOWS

Using one of my new burners, I call the number Danny gave me to reach my father. We haven't spoken since he threw me out in the cold, which left me with internal frostbite. He answers humbly and apologizes for his temper. It's almost unreal to hear the word "sorry" come out of his mouth. I use it as an opportunity to guilt-trip him further by letting him know how disappointed I am for doing that to me after how far we had come. I also suggest that with a little help, maybe there's something we can do to control his anger. He listens to me as I describe his behavior as a reaction to the abuse he endured as a child. With therapy, maybe he can heal and control the rage.

"Therapy? What, from some quack? I can control it on my own. You're crossing the line ..." He stops himself. "Anyway, I apologize and recant. You're a grown woman and can make your own decisions concerning marriage. Initiation is important though, Jenny. It's critical that you're in place in case something happens to me. Will you be following through?"

"Yes."

"That a girl. You're making the right decision. I'm looking at my calendar. You will begin on June 21, the Summer Solstice. Once you finish, your great-uncle will perform your closing ceremony. Will Danny still follow you?"

"I'm not sure. Is it possible for Fabrizio to be initiated?"

He abruptly says, "No."

"Why? Never mind. I don't want to hear anything homophobic."

"I'm not homophobic, not even close. I just want to make sure your brother procreates someday, that's all."

"I'll talk to Danny and see how he feels."

"Good enough. You have a lot to look forward to, honey. You'll see. I'd like you to head back underground until initiation and continue your studies."

I agree to his requests and inquire about Josh's wedding plans. He denies knowing anything about them, but I don't believe him. Dr. Braun is wrong; he lies all the time. In this case, I can't help but wonder if he had anything to do with their accelerated wedding plans. Maybe he figured once they were married, I'd settle for Ryan, but that's not going to happen. We end the call amicably, using nauseating terms of endearment. After everything he's put me through, telling my father that I love him is abhorrent, and I haven't forgotten my real purpose for initiation—the truth, followed by swift action.

I relay the information to Danny, but he's undecided, having much more to fear and lose by following through. We decide it's just me for now, but with full disclosure that I'll tell him everything anyway.

The weeks go by, and I sneak in what studies I can on Tina's iPad, then delete the history and cookies like Fabrizio taught me. I'm burning out on the material because I don't know which of it applies. There's just so much information, and none of it seemingly forms a pattern.

Today is Easter, and the three of us are spending the day at home. I make Tina decorate eggs with me in the morning while Peter works on the greenhouse. We get a bit tipsy over lunch and make each other laugh over absolutely everything. I get the bright idea to call Josh in my altered state of mind. As far as I know, the wedding is still on, but secretly I think he's postponed it until after my initiation. I have a glimmer of hope that he'll wait for me. It's what has kept me going over these past few weeks. But I'm at the point where I need to hear it straight from him, instead of fantasizing about what it will be like when we get back together. Tina and I are still cracking each other up as I dial. She puts on bunny ears and hops around the living room dropping plastic eggs from her ass. I can't take it and can barely breathe by the time Sammy answers the phone.

"Sammy?"

"Jenny. Hey. You all right?"

"I'm well." I laugh again as I look at Tina. "Where's your brother?"

"Have you been drinking?"

"A little. Happy Easter by the way."

"Jenny, don't you know?"

My buzz is interrupted. "Know what?"

"Josh is literally getting married today. Everyone is getting ready, having their pictures taken and shit."

"That's not funny. Seriously, where is he?" Silence. "Sammy, please tell me you're kidding. It's Easter Sunday. Who would get married on Easter Sunday?"

"Actually, a lot of us get married on Easter Sunday. It's a spiritual tradition. Even your father is here."

My father knew this? I'm in a sudden state of panic. Tina stops laughing, seeing the expression on my face.

"Well, where the fuck is my invite, Sammy? You have to stop this. Where are you?"

"I can't tell you where, Jenny. I'm sorry." I demand to talk to Josh. Sammy begs me to calm down, but I warn him of my soon-to-be hellish fury if he doesn't put his brother on the phone. I'm pacing and aching, and almost a hundred percent sure I'm going to vomit. Josh meekly answers the phone.

"Jenny, hey." He exhales deeply. "How'd you find out"

"I didn't. I just so happened to call you today of all days. What the fuck, Josh. Call it off."

"You're going to have to accept this, Jenny."

"Like hell." I start to sob. I'm desperate. His voice cracks as he attempts to console me.

"Everything's going to be okay. You trust me, right?" I can't speak, but I'm listening. I'm trying hard to figure out where they are. I hear water, so if they're not in the cave, where are they? They're somewhere I've never been before. If I found out, what would I do? Crash the wedding? I'm out of tricks. I'm out of ways to try and stop him. I've put my feelings out there, and he's still going to marry her.

I have very vindictive thoughts running through my head. I could narc and tell the Feds. It would be the ultimate wedding crasher. But I did this. I'm the one who said yes to an engagement to Ryan after my punishment before even talking to Josh. I deserve this, but I won't congratulate him either. I end the torment and the call by telling him how horribly disappointed I am with him.

"I will never respect you again, and I'll never be able to look at you the same way ever again."

"Jenny, please. It will ..."

I hang up and run to my room and cry. I cry until my head is throbbing with pain and I can't breathe through my nose. My heart feels like it's permanently broken. I feel broken.

# 25

OPENING CEREMONY

It's Friday, June 21. The first day of summer, or the Summer Solstice, as the Order refers to it. For almost all other Rosicrucian Orders, initiations begin in the spring. Apparently, it's just one of the ways they distinguish themselves, that and the small fact that they have a punishment system. There's nothing barbaric about any other Order that I've studied. On the other hand, I simply refuse to study groups that involve satanism, witchcraft, or wizardry. So there could be more. I'm too superstitious for the dark stuff. My opening ceremony into The Empedocles Ordo Rosae Crucis Unitas Fratrum starts today, and my neophyte days will be over.

Josh has been married for over two months, and I've been bitter and having trouble hiding it ever since. I'm cranky and no fun to be around. Poor Tina and Peter have walked on eggshells, doing their best to just stay out of my way. They haven't deserved being on the receiving end of my misery, but I can't help it. Switching gears from sorrow to anger has helped me cope. I've put Peter's boxing bag in the basement to good use. I thought I broke my hand again the last time I used it and have laid off ever since.

In between intense workouts, I've been secretly packing a small bag, preparing to vanish from their lives after today. They're both at work, making it easier to escape without a verbal explanation, but I have long thank-you letters ready for them, along with some more money and the promise of speaking soon.

It's time to find out why anyone would do the things they do to protect this society. One that's worth punishing and killing people over. I can't help but think it's all a bunch of bullshit and brainwashing.

I received my itinerary early this morning from my father. My first step is to find a way inside Mission Church at noon. It's risky, but most of the federal surveillance is gone. Agent Edwards is left to monitor, and he's on the inside. Once there, all of the Grand Masters, including Josh, will formally decide if I'm worthy of the commitment. Rules will follow and, assuming all goes well, I'll begin my journey at the Lenape Indian reservation, which I'm highly looking forward to.

Danny and Fabrizio have flown in and are staying at the farm for backup, making it look like they're checking in on all the new construction. Secretly, Danny is trying to decide whether or not he wants to go next. Fabrizio is going to pick me up at 11:00 a.m. and drive me over to the church. He rented a truck to fit in with the country crowd and is picking up bales of hay on the way. I'm hoping to stay at the farm in between initiation stages. Danny has prepared a new secret space for me, but just seeing the farm again is what I'm most excited about. I haven't even gotten a picture because they've wanted to surprise me. Shane and Veronica are still living in the house, but the barn has been renovated just for Danny and me. Having a brother as an architect, and his partner a tech genius, I expect to be pleased.

Peter and Tina have finally left, so I rush upstairs into the bathroom to get ready. First step, I dye my hair back to its original color. It's time to be me again. My hair has grown fast and is already hitting my shoulders. It was fun being blonde, but I like being transformed back into a brunette. I decide to throw a few curls in it and probably overdo my makeup a little. But it can't hurt to look good for such an occasion. I put on one of the dresses Tina hung in my closet. It's a sleeveless navy Lilly Pulitzer with gold accents. I look sophisticated, but with my bite scar out for all to see, I'm reminded that there's no such thing as looking perfect anymore. I grab my bag and wait by the front door. Fabrizio's right on time. He pulls up in the red pickup and gets out near the garage. He's got jeans on with cowboy boots and a hat. I get the giggles as I greet him.

"We're in Bucks County, Fabrizio, not Dallas, Texas."

"Well, howdy to you too." We laugh and exchange embraces. He's just what I needed for this ride.

"You ready for this? I'm nervous for you. Here, put it on."

"What is it?"

"Recording device."

"No, not this time. It's just the beginning of the initiation. I'll be fine."

"At least you're only going to be right down the road."

I'm not nervous about initiation, per se, just the Josh factor at the moment. I wish I could squash the sour grapes, but I'm still very salty.

The last time I was in Mission Church was with Danny, when we discovered the cremated remains of murdered children and adults. I wonder what they have in store for me, and where exactly in the building this kick-off will be held.

Agent Edwards is out front waiting to take me inside. In between the trees, I see security watching for unwanted guests, but there are no cars anywhere to raise suspicion. I give Fabrizio a high five and hop out. Agent Edwards is happy to see me and tries not to stare at my scar. "Good luck, Jenny. Enjoy yourself. You look gloomy."

I give him a fake smile. "Just a little nervous, that's all."

"You're going to do great." He ushers me through the front door and into the courtroom area. After the federal scouring, only the pews remain. But the once-secret entrance descending into the very mystic Mission Church basement is open. We descend down and into the memorial room, which apparently the Historical Society convinced the FBI to leave with the remains undisturbed for family members to visit. Seeing the tiny urns on display still gives me the creeps.

Agent Edwards shares the first details. "In this sacred chamber, the Tomb of Silence, which is the abiding place of life and death, you are to stand on the far side of the altar. The Grand Masters will join you soon. Again, good luck. You have my blessing, for what it's worth," he says with a smile.

His blessing is worthless, but I thank him and take my place. I start to shiver, half from the cool basement air and half from anxiety. According to my watch, I still have a few minutes before noon. I say a few *Hail Marys* to calm down.

A woman I've never seen before enters first. She lights two white candles on the altar then several wall sconces around the room. She pays me no mind, acting as though I'm not in the room. She's a plain Jane type, probably in her forties, but older looking. She's got either a perm or naturally curly hair, which is short and old lady like. She's wearing a long-sleeved, very conservative white dress buttoned all the way to the top. She bows in front of the altar and exits.

One by one, all the leaders make their way into the room. They're each wearing a white smock with a different-colored stole, bearing way too many symbols for me to understand. Their obvious element signs are depicted, and I take note of the colors. Earth— green; Water—blue; Fire—red; Air—yellow; and Spirit, oddly, is black, like the black rose on the cross above the altar. The only black rosy cross I've seen. The Lenape Indian's stole consists of unique markings that set him well apart from the rest. He's also wearing authentic Lenape garb, including a headdress. If I weren't getting so used to this kind of scenario, I would have a hard time keeping it together.

They stand on the mosaic pentacle feature on the floor, each on the section they represent. No one formally greets me. The Lenape lights incense and begins with a chant. When he's finished, he places the smoking thurible by the altar and takes his place.

The other members come forward with personalized verbal

addresses. My father recites Psalm 25, which I have memorized at this point. He really needs some new material.

Mr. Brandt follows with one of his own. *"When you go through deep waters, I will be with you. When you go through rivers of difficulty, you will not drown. When you walk through the fire of oppression, you will not be burned up; the flames will not consume you. It's from the book of Isaiah, Jenny. Once you become a member, you will have eternal divine protection."* I nod with appreciation for the sentiment.

Greg Johnson, the element Grand Master of air, is next. Danny and I aren't totally sure what to make of Greg, which automatically translates to—*we don't trust him.* Shane insists he's harmless, having known him for as long as he can remember, but I have a hard time trusting anyone. He doesn't recite a Bible verse but contributes something more philosophical.

"Your journey will delve into the basic elements with me, Jenny. Give thanks for each breath you take of the sacred air that surrounds you here. It will propel you and offer you strength and courage. Only air can lift you higher in life, and only air can connect souls in the afterlife. From this time going forward, each breath you take will be done so for the greater good of the EORCUF Order."

Josh is last. My face is cold, and my eyes are judging him. "Out of every element you've been exposed to thus far, you've embraced and demonstrated extreme talents in the sacred waters that surround us. You've conquered an enemy, survived an extraordinarily dangerous punishment, and have been pre-baptized already by Thomas, our Divine Judge and Imperator. You are deserving and welcomed in our waters and will never be thirsty as one of us." He's smiling at me like I should be overwhelmed with joy, but in an effort to disappoint him, I respond with a look of boredom.

Next, each Grand Master offers a gift for me to take through the five phases of my initiation. My father smiles and hands me a beautiful gold traditional red rosy cross necklace. Mr. Brandt offers me a golden lighter to "light the way." The Native American gives me the same symbolic feather necklace that Josh and Brendan showed me the first time I went to the lake house. I had assumed they received them at the end of initiation, not the beginning. It brings back a nice memory, but I don't want Josh to see it.

Greg gives me a pin with angel's wings, and Josh hands me a chalice from the altar and tells me to drink. I look at his wedding band as I accept it, then judge him again with an indignant look. It makes him uncomfortable, and he purposefully drops his hand to his side. I take a big gulp of water and have instant regret, tasting something between a rusty bowl and rotten eggs. I gag and shudder as I and try to get it down. Everyone laughs at my reaction, which must be a common one.

My father explains, "Well water, Jenny, from the deepest spring in Brandtville. You're tasting the sacredness that fills our waters, along with some sulfur and other minerals." He laughs and hands me some red wine from a gold-plated chalice to chase it down while he says a prayer over me. It helps wash away some of the taste, but the aftertaste keeps coming back.

The same woman who lit the candles gets behind a podium and asks each leader if I have their permission to continue. She asks them each individually if they think I'm worthy of becoming a member and strong enough in character and spirit to become a future Grand Master.

One at a time, each member enthusiastically answers, "Yes." I figure now is the time to look like a glowing, eager pledge. I notice they're all wearing their sacred pledge pins, each with a number indicating which Grand Master they are in line from when the Order was founded. My father's is a three, which would make me a four if I should hypothetically become the next Earth Grand Master. I thank them all for their permission and promise to uphold the society and its culture. I get applause and a hug from everyone. Josh reaches down with a big smile to hug me, but I turn my back. *Too soon.*

Today is Friday. Tomorrow someone will take me to meet Chief Shawtagh at 9:00 a.m. My opening ceremony is over, and the leaders turn to exit in order. Josh is last and lingers. He angrily rushes me, a little too aggressive for my liking.

"It will behoove you to show me some respect." My eyes get squinty. I've got too much bottled-up resentment for his shit. But I force myself to relax my expression because I don't want to rock the boat on my opening day. It will never be possible to muster up the respect he's looking for. The less I say, the better, so I just stand still with a blank look. My lack of response makes him even angrier. He grabs me by the arm and forces me against the wall. "You think this is easy for me?" I instinctively cover my face, assuming he's about to hit me. He looks hurt by the reaction but can't possibly have forgotten the backhand he gave me at the start of my punishment trial. He releases my arm and apologizes. I remain in a defensive stance against the wall, perhaps a little over-dramatically. Josh lets out a huge sound of stress. "Jenny, please."

What does he want me to say? I've been a basket case for months and months, and where has he been in my darkest hours? He's selfish, and I'm not letting him off the hook.

"Coming, Josh?" I hear my father say.

"Be right there."

"Say something, goddam it. I don't want it to be like this."

"There's nothing to say, right? I told you the last time we spoke that I'd never be able to look at you the same way again, and I meant it. But I'll do my best to respect you through the remainder of my initiation. Since that's required."

"Joshua, let's go," my father yells in a very no-nonsense manner. Josh has no choice but to abandon the conversation. But I see something in his eyes as he turns away. He's hurting too. Why? He's married. That's what he wanted, wasn't it?

# 26

## HOME SWEET HOME

I wait alone, aching, until Agent Edwards directs me to come back upstairs and out of Mission Church. The same woman who prepped my ceremony is waiting for me. She finally introduces herself as Emily and hands me a book entitled *An Introduction to the Empedocles Ordo Rosae Crucis Unitas Fratrum.* This is what I've been waiting for, the scoop. She instructs me to read it in its entirety by evening. She's adamant about the privacy of the book and slides it into a leather cover with a zipper and 3-coded lock, much like a diary. She wants me to use my special numbers to open it. I look at her, wondering if we're talking about the same three numbers.

"Excuse me? My numbers, or 252, like my father's?"

"Your numbers, Jenny," she says with a smile.

Can't wait to test that. Agent Edwards holds out an arm for me to grab and escorts me back to my rhinestone cowboy. "Looks like you've got some new bling. Let me guess, each member gave you something? I bet the rosy cross is from your father. What did Josh give you?"

"Heartburn. Let's go. I can't wait to see the farm."

I duck down for the very short trip but peek when we pull into the driveway. Fabrizio enters a code and a gate opens. The property is now completely enclosed by tall, beautiful, black iron fencing. It surrounds the house and barn and extends deep into the meadow. Fabrizio says it keeps the tourists and media out, and it's electric-wired for extra security. One touch, and any intruder will find themselves literally stunned. Unfortunately, the same applies to critters, so Danny built a small shelter in the meadow and waited for a family of deer to show up before closing it off. He didn't want the area to be void of nature. The deer were afraid of the fence and being locked up at first but have gotten quite spoiled.

Apparently, they're eating corn right out of his and Fabrizio's hands now, and the doe is expecting. This news brightens my mood, and I look forward to feeding them for myself. It'll be the next best thing to feeding Miss Mable, Jack and Katie's old goat.

The sight of the new and improved Red Rock Farm literally takes my breath away. The new barn isn't red anymore—it's a greyish-brown color with magnificent windows overlooking the meadow and creek. The house also looks amazing, like the *Better Homes and Gardens* version we had when I was a child. I can't help but get choked up. Fabrizio pulls the car behind the barn and in through the garage. There's nothing behind the house except woods. Danny is waiting with open arms.

"Welcome home, sis. What do you think?"

"Look at me! I have tears of joy. It's amazing!"

"Come on. Let me show you the rest." He takes me by the hand and guides me through a mud room and into a large open space. I see a ladder to a loft at the far end. Otherwise I can't find any doors, except to a bathroom, which is open. There are exposed beams all the way up to the ceiling. The main support beam runs from one end of the house to the other.

I spot the rope swing immediately and gush. It's like the one we had in the barn when we were kids. I drop everything, climb up a built-in ladder next to it, and glide across the living room. "Whee!" I exclaim as I swing back and forth.

"Somehow, I knew you'd like that." He looks at Fabrizio. "See, I told you she'd remember." The kitchen is country French, similar to Tina's, with all the finest appliances and a beautiful black and white marble countertop. It's furnished with the best of everything. A huge cream-colored sectional faces a large fireplace as the focal point of the room. I can't wait until this is all over so I can live here permanently.

Next, we climb up a ladder and into the loft. There's only one bed. I'm surprised and a little disappointed. "Where's everyone sleep?"

"Glad you asked. Ready? Say the magic words." I get a huge smile on my face.

"What's for dinner?" The wall opens into another space. A big space. So big that it confuses me. Danny explains the openness creates the illusion that you're looking at the whole house. Really, it's only about two-thirds of it. There are two more bedrooms and a spiral staircase leading below. "What's down there?"

"Tech room. Check it out."

It's sophisticated, and I don't know what all the equipment does. Fabrizio flips on a few switches, and screens with different views of the property appear. I see the expecting doe with a view of the meadow. "Aww!"

"We've set it up so that we have control over almost everything all the way from Italy. We can even answer if someone buzzes to enter the gate. Someone's always home, as far as anyone knows, so you won't have to worry about feeling alone, Jenny," Fabrizio says. The idea is very reassuring, but I eye up Danny. Until I'm finished with initiation, I won't know where Danny stands. Stay, or go back home with Fabrizio. My vote is whatever makes him happy, and I believe that will always be with Fabrizio.

We head back upstairs, and I'm ushered to my room, which Fabrizio decorated himself. It's sensational. My favorite color, pink, is prominent but tasteful. I have a sleigh bed, trunk, desk, and armoire, as well as a walk-in closet and my own bathroom. I put my book on the desk and tell them I have to spend the day reading. Danny has more to show me first. We make our way back into the garage. Danny punches in a code on a work bench, and another secret panel door opens. This one leads downward.

"Wouldn't be complete without a tunnel. Come on, let's go say hi to Shane and Veronica, have something to eat, and then you can do your weird reading," Danny says.

The tunnel is neat and tasteful, as far as tunnels go. I've seen enough of them to be a critic at this point. Fabrizio took advantage of the county's plethora of granite and covered it from top to bottom. He even included artwork, and benches that magically turn into beds when needed. I'm guessing there's something to the paintings on the walls. I poke at one.

"Lift here." Fabrizio slides the painting up and exposes a safe. Each painting hides a different safe full of all the basics you need in this town. Guns. Money. Food. Medical supplies. As always, he's thought of everything. The tunnel isn't terribly long, maybe half the length of a football field. Danny texts Shane to tell him we're here. Within minutes, another door opens, and a very enthusiastic Shane and Veronica welcome us home.

We spend hours catching up. They're very much in love and oh so happy. They, too, are looking forward to initiation but don't want any spoilers. Ryan officially opted out and has moved back to Baltimore, leaving Jackie in charge of leadership if, more like when, something happens to Mr. Brandt. They don't have to say it, but I'm sure Ryan is with Alicia. I'm relieved. It's better this way. Jackie is running the estate like a pro for now and is also looking forward to initiation. She's gotten close with Dexter, which is good news. He's a great catch, and she's been single for a long time. But she's been keeping secrets from him, especially about getting initiated. And not surprisingly, her father disapproves of the relationship.

"Why? I don't understand."

"It's less about Dex, more to do with our lineage and the fact that he's not from the area itself. We're all apparently tied to the village somehow. If he were a Lenape Indian, it would probably be fine.

We'll see what happens. They're keeping it to themselves for now," Shane says. "Plus, my uncle will be back in jail soon enough, so who cares what he thinks."

Interesting. It makes me think of my father's reaction to Fabrizio becoming a member. Maybe he's not homophobic after all and just wants Danny to marry someone from Brandtville for the bloodline and culture. He brought in a wife from the outside, though. My mom is all Jersey girl, and Nonna, Sicilian. My mother was never going to fit in or be one of them. With limited options, no wonder my father gravitated toward Kendra for a relationship. I can't help but wonder how much potential in-breeding goes on here.

Lastly, I get updates on the village itself. The Twenty-Fifth Acre was taken over and sold by the government. A very wealthy executive from New York City has purchased the property and is making plans to build an estate home of his own. Everyone is trying to get more information about him, but he's not giving anything up. He's very private and very protected. I'm suspicious of his timing and motives. Jodi's old house is empty and up for sale, and the Grover Estate was bought by Greg, naturally, as the new Grand Master of air. He's already torn down the windmill, saying it was a disgrace to use the landmark and symbol in the manner they chose. I agree completely. I plan on making an offer on Jodi's house, for sentimental reasons more than anything else. It's the only thing I have left of her.

Veronica says Jack is holding up in Boston and spending time mending his relationship with Jessica, still grieving the loss of her mom. He blames himself for Katie's murder and forever regrets moving her to Brandtville. He plans on spending a little time this summer at the house he built overlooking the river in hopes of finding some closure. He's aware of Veronica and Shane's love life but is unaware of any initiations. He would most certainly disapprove. I miss Jack and Katie. It hurts to think about their tragic ending as a couple. I'm ready to head back to my quarters. I need to prepare for tomorrow and get through that book. I'm beyond curious. I'm ready for answers.

## 27

AN INTRODUCTION TO EORCUF

I have a cup of hot tea, a stack of pillows behind my head, and the locked leather case. I roll each dial until they form the numbers 333. My numbers. Like literal magic, the case opens and exposes the book. *An Introduction to Empedocles Ordo Rosae Crucis Unitas Fratrum (EORCUF)*. The name is a mouthful, and I'm glad my father has already dissected it for me to some extent.

Empedocles was a Greek philosopher, best known for his theory of the four basic elements of water, fire, air, and earth. He referred to them at the time as "roots" that make up all the structures of the world and the fundamentals of all beings. Plato completed his work in much more depth, and later, the universe, or spirit, was added. Unitas Fratrum was the name of the original German Moravian Church that settled in Pennsylvania. It's Latin for unity of the Brethren. Ordo Rosae Crucis means the society has Rosicrucian roots.

The saddle-stitched book is printed on demand, definitely not something sent to a publishing company or digital source. The cover exposes a much more elaborate presentation of the Fraternity, nothing as simple as the ceremonial version in the basement of

Mission Church. There are seemingly symbols on top of symbols, but I try to decipher their meaning based on my knowledge from months of study.

The center of the page is the unmistakable, all-encompassing Rosy Cross. It's layered in symbolism, with each arm of the cross bearing a pentacle and the element symbols.

The alchemical symbols of sulfur, mercury, lead, and salt are present. There's a hexagram representing the Star of David, along with the letters INRI shining in the background, like those on the Catholic crucifix.

But that's just one aspect of the elaborate drawing that's depicted on the cover. There's more symbolism to interpret, including a burning building. If I didn't know better, I'd say it represented Atlantis. But the scene surrounding it doesn't look ancient at all.

Archangels Gabriel, Michael, and Raphael are depicted looking down at the cross. There's an X, dotted behind the Rosy Cross, leaving four open areas filled with more symbolism. Swords represent the symbol for air, wands for fire, pentacles for earth, and the cup for water, all a nod to the Tarot, which my father refuses to take seriously.

Lenape Indian and Egyptian symbols, including letters and words, are sprinkled about, but what catches my eye are the words PLVS VLTRA written boldly at the bottom. The letters are surrounded by a mosaic tile background with Roman pillars and a cryptic design. "More Beyond." I already know what it means. Perhaps it's the key to bringing this explosion of symbolism together, and I wonder if the volume of tile used within the society may have a significance beyond a mere design element.

I open the book and get the answer I've been looking for. I finally know who the founder is of our Order. There's a picture of Henry Chapman Mercer in his youth, very handsome, groomed and looking like a member of high society, which he was from birth to death. Not in a million years did I foresee that a local, early twentieth century Renaissance Man would have been the founder of my father's seemingly unorganized society. The first chapter is exclusively about Mercer's childhood and life leading up to his role as Founding Imperator.

Henry Mercer was born in Doylestown, Pennsylvania, in 1856 to wealthy, prominent parents on both sides. His grandfather on the Chapman side was a state senator and judge for both Bucks and Montgomery counties and was an influence academically. Henry was worldly and traveled to Europe for the first time when he was just fourteen years old. He attended Harvard University and studied law at the University of Pennsylvania. The same year, he became a founding member of the Bucks County Historical Society. Despite passing the bar, he never practiced law.

I stop and think about that for a moment. It sounds strangely similar to my background. And my father quit practicing law very early in his career. I read on. From 1881 to 1889, he traveled the world, studied castles, and spent time in Egypt, Israel, and the Mediterranean, learning everything he could. Later, he became consumed with the mysterious rise of esotericism. He met with members of the Ancient Mystical Order Rosae Crucis (AMORC), including Harvey Spencer Lewis himself, who was born close by in Frenchtown, New Jersey, as well as members of the Golden Dawn in both England and the United States. In an effort to acquire their mystery school knowledge, he was initiated into both Orders.

In addition to studying secret societies, mostly as a way of understanding them, Henry devoted himself to archeology both in the east and west. He collected artifacts as old as 2,000 BC and took up philosophy, science, history, and math. He learned to speak six languages before eventually being enthralled by the American Arts and Crafts Movement. He felt a call to preserve history through the arts and began using tiles to not only decorate, but to tell stories. He built his business and architecturally phenomenal castle out of his imagination.

The book goes on to explain that he built the Moravian Tile Works as an adaptation of the California Mission Church, partly chosen because Mercer believed good art came from religious faith. The Moravian Tile Works as it stands today is the second, constructed after the first was destroyed by fire. *That's what the fire was about.* He created all three of his architectural masterpieces—his museum, his textile business, and his home, Fonthill—using concrete as a base.

His mind brimming with talents, knowledge, and passions, Henry enlisted the services of renowned clairvoyant Edgar Cayce to help him synthesize his ideas into a Master Secret Society that would allow him to accomplish his life's work and give credit to God, nature, history, and creativity alike. He spent months with Cayce coming up with his society. Cayce claimed Henry had the most extraordinary mind he had ever analyzed.

Under hypnosis, Henry was able to give the location of hidden treasure, speak in ancient languages, tell native American folklore, and even expose truths that contradicted modern-day historical "fact." Despite these revelations though, he never wavered that the Bible was the true word of God.

"How's it going?" Danny asks. I jump up, spilling my tea.

"I have to tell you, I'm incredibly surprised so far. It's nothing like I envisioned."

"Give me the short version?"

"I can't. Not because of our father, out of respect for the founder. Make sense?"

"Seriously?"

"I'm sorry. Who am I kidding? I'll tell you later." He laughs at me.

"Doesn't matter. Press on. I just wanted to check in on you."

"Thanks, Danny."

"Can I get you a snack to go with your tea? Or a napkin?"

I shake my head and dive back in. Danny leaves probably as confused as I am about my reaction to this introduction. I flip to the next chapter. Cayce and Mercer narrowed the Order down into six categories.

**I. God the Almighty is to be praised above all else.** However, members of each sect may choose the faith that speaks to them.

**II. Politics outside of the Order are never to be discussed**, as they are no longer relevant. No one may vote in elections outside of the Order.

**III. Monographs include experiments and exercises from five Rosicrucian Orders.** Aspects of each will be taught, and grade levels must be earned to achieve full EORCUF status.

**IV. Lenape indoctrination was, and is, a necessary aspect of the Order.** A psychic reading revealed that without the sacred traditions of the Lenape, all wisdom will die. Original land occupants must partake in all rituals in order for them to be considered legitimate.

**V. Harsh punishment must be strictly enforced as a deterrent against secret-exposure.** Punishments must fit the crime and will be handed down from the societal council alone.

**VI. Eugenics are encouraged** to ensure the Order increases in intelligence, health, psychic ability, and talents for future generations.

Even though I know that the concept of eugenics predates Hitler, the last category is a tough one to swallow. The Holocaust is a fateful reminder of what can happen when such an idea enters the wrong mind. In my reading, I learned that Plato initiated a state-run program of mating in an effort to strengthen the guardian class in his Republic. Galton, a cousin of Darwin, was also interested in the concept in order to create better humans. Seemingly well-intended scientists and policymakers in the early part of the 20th Century supported eugenics in the United States, Britain, and Scandinavia to encourage people of good health to reproduce and create "good births."

It gives me pause about my mother. Why did my father choose her? Were Danny and I an exception, or am I missing something? At least all the talk about bloodlines makes a little more sense now. It's disturbing, but it's coming together.

The next chapter lists the original five chosen Grand Masters and defines their roles as they relate philosophically to the elements. Assigned disciplines and job descriptions fall under each. I'm not surprised to see that, as a descendent of the element of earth, our bloodline handles council and punishment—runs right down the line. In addition, it includes creative fields in writing, art, landscaping, and architecture. "Spy" is on the list too.

The next chapter covers marriage. *Here we go!* It describes who can marry whom. They actually encourage Grand Masters and their members to marry into elements other than their own. But once they marry, they must convert into their alpha sub-sect. That's what Scott was trying to explain to me about him and Katie. They were going to have to go through some sort of other ritual since Katie was a descendent of the earth segment and Scott of air. That's probably why there isn't a bunch of inbreeding.

The next section describes marriage to anyone outside of the pentacle. It's not completely forbidden, but the spouse must never know of the society. How would that ever work? I think again of my parents. *It doesn't work.* Fabrizio knows about the society already, at least what we know up to this point, and has kept quiet. I hope he's not in danger. What happens if the partners and spouses do find out about everything? And what's the big deal, as long as they don't say anything? I guess the logic is to keep the knowledge as limited as possible, and to trust no one outside the circle.

Next, there's a section about who active Grand Masters can marry. Two leaders may only marry if their signs are adjacent. Earth is next to fire and air only. That means I could never marry Josh. This is why my father is so adamant that I marry Ryan. I can never marry Josh according to the laws of EORCUF—well, not if I become a Grand Master anyway. It makes me wonder why they didn't interfere when I married John. Maybe they knew it wouldn't work. Ugh.

I suddenly remember what Sammy said after my horrible first encounter with Josh again. *"He's in place. Despite your unpleasant first meeting, trust him."*

There's a notation that Imperators can never marry. I guess that means Henry never married, or my great-uncle either. I find that kind of crappy, too, but that's not something I ever need to worry about. In fact, I don't have to worry about any of this because I'm not really going to become part of this Order at all. I'm going to hand over its evil leaders. After reading all of this though, I think I'll respect much of the privacy.

There's an extensive list of current members that follows, approximately one hundred bloodline members and hundreds more on the payroll. They're able to study and reach minimal levels of knowledge, enough to satisfy the truly curious, under a different and simple name, The Hermatic Philosophy Organization (HPO). This is the first I'm hearing of this shell organization.

The next chapter is about The Extremum Dextrae Initiation, the final rite in which I'm about to partake. I can see for certain that the Order is fast-tracking me. Most members are introduced very slowly, then initiated in steps. There are many steps, stages, and ranks. It's a lifelong commitment.

The next section deals with food. *Food?* The Order has similar restrictions to those I saw at Tina and Peter's house. I just assumed they were health conscious, but now I have to wonder. I read on.

"Food helps nourish the mind, body, and spirit and helps us be our best selves. Only non-processed, chemical-free plant-based foods and uncontaminated seafood, eggs, and poultry are allowed."

I dart up into a sitting position as I read the next titled section. NO ALCOHOL. *Excuse me?* There's one exception—blessed wines can be consumed in small quantities. Prayer must accompany each drink. Wait. Josh and I had mixed drinks. No, I had one. He was drinking wine. They were all drinking wine and nothing else. *Totally didn't pick up on that.*

The page before the back cover concludes with the following: "By agreeing to the terms in the pages of this book, you take an eternal vow to protect the Empedocles Ordo Rosae Crucis Unitus Fratrum, to abide by its rules, and to pass on its traditions to only those with linear rights." There's even some fine print. "No part of this book may be reproduced, scanned, photographed or otherwise copied." *Eyeroll.*

There's a dotted line for me to sign and legally solidify my commitment. I sign it then pore through the list of names a few more times trying to memorize some of the member names. That's when I realize I missed a section of names on the "watch out" list. They're specific people from other Rosicrucian Orders and fraternities who have tried to infiltrate the society. There's a list of about fifty or more. One name stands out, Lori Stuart. I think that's Tina's mother. I found an anniversary album with a family tree when I was snooping one day. She's a member of the Knights of the Rosy Cross, which has a lodge in lower Bucks County. That's too freaking close for comfort, and I can't believe I wasn't forewarned about it.

I remember now that Tina's mother and Mrs. Brandt were good friends. Perhaps that's when Lori was put on the "Watch Out" list. I should've looked into that more, but surely Josh knew and trusted Tina. Or maybe he just trusted me. Perhaps it was even a test to see if I could keep a secret, which would be incredibly risky, based on my history.

The red rose tattoo on Tina's arm had nothing to do with a sorority. She lied to me. Her presence at the hospital and interest in me and my life—way too coincidental. I fell right into her hands after being kicked out of Kendra's underground fantasy world.

She tested me often to see what I'd be willing to spill to outsiders, or maybe just to her. I know I passed that test with flying colors. Peter's name is nowhere to be found. My stomach turns as I realize I don't know anything about the people who took me in for so long.

## 28

DIFFICULT DECISIONS

I yell for Fabrizio as I tear through the Lilly Pulitzer dress I hung back in the closet. It's Tina's dress, the one I wore to my ceremony.

"What's the matter?" Fabrizio asks, Danny on his tail. Using sign language, I tell him to check the dress for bugs. He rolls his eyes like, *here we go.* I'm starting to shake, praying she didn't get me on some sort of speaker as I kicked off my initiation ceremony. While Danny holds my hand to comfort me, Fabrizio breaks into *You Don't Bring me Flowers* by Barbara Streisand as he searches. He's got what he calls his bug killer out and shakes his head. He hasn't found one, but he finds something sewn into the gold accents on the dress.

"It's a tracker. She's been tracking you. Or someone's been tracking her." I grab my duffel bag, which is full of the clothes she laid out for me and dump the contents on the bed. We go through all of them. Each piece of clothing has a tracker attached. Now I'm really perturbed.

"What should I do? Because of these, how many people know I'm here now?"

"I'll disable them," Fabrizio says. "For fuck's sake, I can't wait

189

until this is all over, everyone's in jail, this town is exposed, and we can go home." Danny and I throw each other a look. I have no idea what's going through his mind. Stay or go. Get initiated with me or not.

With all the trackers removed from the clothing, it's time to calm down and have a drink. Fabrizio pours me a glass of white wine. All I can think is, *this is not blessed wine*. Danny prepares us a delicious dinner. Lamb chops, blue cheese mashed potatoes, and grilled asparagus. Everything is scrumptious. As we eat, we try guessing what my first day under the element of spirit is going to involve. Fabrizio pokes fun at me, saying I'll probably come home in a headdress.

I hightail it upstairs, hearing someone at the door. It's Agent Edwards barking orders at a few men behind him. I rush back downstairs to see what all fuss is about. He calls for me.

"Jenny, the next Five Days of Knowledge are sacred, and therefore, you must do them alone. No one can be waiting for you at the end of each day. I know the three of you are very close, but initiation is secret. So secret that I don't even know half of it," he mutters. "If even one aspect of your journey is revealed, there will be severe consequences." He looks down and then at Fabrizio. "Consequences of no return, if you catch my drift."

I gulp because it's decision time for Danny. Either they both go, or Fabrizio must go. "Jenny, I'll need the book back now with your signature. Danny, you may stay, but only if you're going to be initiated. Your initiation ceremony is set to begin tomorrow. Each day, the five of you will go in status order, and by the end of ten days, you'll all be finished.

Agent Edwards looks at me for a response. I quickly reply, "I understand." Danny's mouth isn't moving, let alone his legs. He's in a serious pickle, one he didn't expect tonight. Fabrizio is already heading upstairs to grab his things and calls down to Danny on his way up.

"Come on, Daniel. Time for us to go. Where are we going anyway? Are these guys taking us somewhere or what?"

"No. They're just here to make sure you go. You can go wherever you please."

"Oh, good. Let's head over to New Hope, babe. Maybe do some dancing?"

Danny has lead feet.

"Come on. Don't be so overprotective. She'll be fine," Fabrizio prompts.

"I'm staying. I'm going to go after Jenny and start tomorrow."

Oh, God. Here we go. Danny needs my support, and fast. "It'll be okay, Fabrizio. I promise." He must know we'll tell him everything, but he looks betrayed, nonetheless.

"It'll be fine, hon. It's just something I have to do. Please understand. I love you, but I have to do this," Danny negotiates. Fabrizio continues to walk slowly up the stairs in a state of shock. I nudge Danny to follow him, but he shakes his head. Fabrizio descends a few moments later with a bag and an attitude.

"It's not okay, Daniel! You lied to me. It's not okay."

Danny's promise to never join has broken their trust. I plead with Danny to go with Fabrizio, telling him it's not worth it. But he stands his ground. They argue for the next ten minutes. It's excruciating to watch. I shed tears for them both. How will this ever work out from here? Without saying goodbye, Fabrizio is led out the door. I'm sure he'll be followed from now on to make sure he doesn't become a so-called enemy. I spend the remainder of the evening trying to console Danny and wondering what we're doing and why it's so important.

# 29

SPIRIT

I wake up in a cold sweat after dreaming that Fabrizio was burned alive in the old incinerator near the Brandt Estate. I need to hear his voice right now. I jump out of bed, splash some cold water on my face, and make my way down into the tech room to see if I can reach him through some of the equipment. It's useless. Before he stormed off, he must have turned everything off. I can't even be sure if the electric security fence is working. I feel sick to my stomach and look for Danny. He's already up, or maybe he never went to bed. I find him staring out of the kitchen window and into the woods, looking like something the cat dragged in.

"Danny?" I softly call out to him. In a semi-trance, he looks in my direction and holds his arms out, needing a hug. We embrace, and I rub his back and give him words of encouragement like he's done for me so many times. Unlike me, his love life has been honest and stable. Mine has been like a game of chess. I tell him if Day One is a disappointment, there will be no Day Two. We'll find Fabrizio, get the hell out of here, and face the consequences. End of story. He nods sorrowfully. We sit in silence and stare out the front window together, watching the sun rise while scanning the grounds for anyone who shouldn't be there.

I finally hop in the shower around 7:00 a.m. and return to Danny's side, still not knowing exactly what I'm doing today or what I need to bring.

A few minutes later, there's a knock at the door. Danny opens it a crack and a man with a deep voice introduces himself as David. "May I come in? I'm here to give Jenny a tour of the reservation." Danny steps aside and allows the man in. He doesn't look very Native American, but his mixed bloodlines could explain why. Oh, how I hate to think in those terms. He's tall, about six feet two inches, with a short ponytail. He has high cheekbones, kind eyes, and a sincere smile. He's roughly my age and wearing a wedding band. He catches me staring at it.

"My bride is a descendant of water, in case you're wondering." We both awkwardly smile and nod. "My name is David Rawtom, Jr., I believe you met my bewildered father last summer. You guys locked him in a safe or something?"

Danny and I look at each other, surprised. "Yes! I connected immediately with your father. He's such a nice man and was even more confused than I was at the time. I don't understand." He smiles. "And you put my brother in prison for life."

"I'm sorry. We're not off to a great start, are we?"

"It's okay. He was a total dipshit and deserved it." I'm beyond relieved to hear that, but a bit shook. "My dad, on the other hand, let's just say we're still having some deep family discussions. It's not pretty, and he's under strict surveillance. My mother is in the doghouse, yada, yada, yada. This is her side of the family. My father is just your ordinary Lenape Native American she 'just so happened' to marry." He uses air quotes for that part. "So anyway, how about if I sit down with you both for a pre-session speech. I've got quite a week ahead of me, apparently."

"Please. Come and sit down," I say, leading him to the kitchen table. Danny pulls a mug out of the cabinet and pours him a cup of coffee.

"I'll start here. You're both my third cousins. It's a disturbing kind of tale, one you can't really prepare to hear, but here it goes. You may already know this part. Your great-great-grandmother was dear friends with Henry C. Mercer and became the first Grand Master for the segment of earth."

"Hold up!" I say. "My great-great-grandmother?"

"It wasn't our great-great-grandfather?"

"What are you guys talking about?" Danny is confused, so I advise him to take a close look as he reads this evening. I apparently missed this important detail, that a woman on my side was a first Grand Master on Henry's list.

"It's true. And my mother's grandfather was the first Grand Master for the root element they call spirit. I'm going to cut to the chase here. Basically, they were asked to fornicate, outside of wedlock, to produce within the circle and begin building our united bloodlines."

"What the fuck. What?" Danny asks.

David laughs at Danny's response. "I know. But if it makes you feel better, your great-great-grandmother remained married to her husband. Just handed the son over to Chief Shawtagh, Sr., my great-great-grandfather, who is a confirmed ancestor of Chief Tamanend himself."

"Oh, my God, why?"

"You'll read more about that later today, bro."

"With that introduction out of the way, ready to learn more, Jenny?" As strange as this news is, Danny is pacing and showing some heightened enthusiasm. He needs to know first-hand too.

"I'm ready," I say. "Do I need to bring anything?"

"Just yourself and a hat to catch all the bits of brain when your mind is blown."

Danny and I look at each other, not particularly amused. "Sorry. What you have on is perfect." Yoga pants, a blue T-shirt, and sneaks it is. David isn't moving, and I don't understand why. "Your gifts, Jenny." I put my hand over my face. Oops!

"Be right back." I run upstairs and grab everything. Two necklaces, a lighter, and an angel pin. Got it.

Danny rushes to my side and grabs me. Insecurity and vulnerability written across his face. I reassure him over and over. "I'll be all right." David doubles the reassurance. "I'd be more worried about tomorrow and those crazy air elements."

On the way to his truck, I look over at the farmhouse and catch Veronica and Shane staring out the window. I smile and give them a wave. Here we go. My first Day of Knowledge.

On the way over, I get a little history about the reservation. A rather large tribe of Lenape Indians originally occupied the region. He asks me how much I know about the Lenni-Lenape Indians from the area, and I give him what I know. That they occupied the areas up and down the Delaware River, and that William Penn crafted a peace treaty with Chief Tamanend. From what I understand, they lived in harmony for quite some time before they were forced to move out west to Oklahoma.

"That's it?"

"Well, I read about the customs, culture, and general way of life. I know that the grounds were, and still are, considered sacred, especially the waters."

"Okay, better. Let me give you a little more detail before you come face-to-face with Chief Shawtagh, some that aren't so pretty."

"Please do." The car ride is so short that we have to sit in the truck while he gives me a history lesson. While everything I learned is somewhat historically accurate, there's a lot of darkness that I wasn't fully aware of. William Penn was able to keep the peace and his squatting rights with the Lenape Indians through bartering. They were indeed friendly, and celebrated at times with gatherings, just as I've seen depicted. But when Penn died, his sons took over and a much more sinister treaty formed, known as the Walking Purchase. I've heard of it, of course, but I look to David for more insight.

"John and Thomas Penn abandoned many of the original fair practices that earned the trust of the Lenape Indians. In 1736, years after Penn's death, his sons sought to claim more land and produced a deed dating back to 1686 by which the Lenape promised to sell the land through a walking pact. It was to begin at the junction of the upper Delaware River and extend as far west as a man could walk in a day and a half. The Lenape Indians were rightfully suspicious. To satisfy them, land officers produced a map, but it incorrectly represented the farther Lehigh River as our closer Tohickon Creek." That's the creek right by the farm. "It included a dotted line showing a reasonable path that walkers would take. Satisfied, they signed the agreement.

The Indians held their end of the bargain, but the new settlers cheated, clearing a direct path and riding horses instead of walking through tangled woods. As a result, they gained 1.2 million acres of land instead of the mere forty miles that the Lenape Indians had anticipated. They were friends no more, but to avoid bloodshed, most Lenape simply continued to push west."

"Horrible. I learned about this in school and from my father."

"Yes, it is. And it turned some of the once docile and peaceful natives into revenge-seekers. Ever hear of the Penn's Creek Massacre?"

"I'm embarrassed to say, I know very little about that."

"Name sort of implies the act. Lenape were tired of being taken advantage of and took out their aggression quite savagely. One night in October of 1755, they raided a group of twenty-five new settlers—just an innocent family—and massacred them. They skinned them alive before brutally murdering them. Raids like that continued through the years. Real cowboys and Indians stuff. Relations have suffered ever since. As you know by now, Henry Mercer was incredibly intrigued by, and respectful of, Native American history and culture. He had a very soft spot for them and their way of life. If you've ever been to his museum, you'll find many relics, arrowheads, and pottery that he himself found on the very ground beneath us.

With all of his inherited wealth, he decided to give something back. He invited and paid for a group of twelve documented ancestors to come back and settle here. He purchased the land from the Brandt family and opened it up to them. He paid for everything and continues to pay to this day through the fund he gave to the Historical Society to manage for them."

"I like where this is going, but how did they end up agreeing to things like punishment trials and Henry's secret society?"

"Henry was adamant about keeping their culture alive and insisted on knowing everything he could about their tribal life. He got a little more than expected." David chuckles. "Sure, he learned how they made pottery from the clay in the area, about their celebrations, and hunting and gathering techniques, but he also learned how they punished their own."

I smile at him. "Well, it can't possibly be the way this Order does it. Do tell."

"It's evolved, but that's definitely where it began, Jenny. The tribe members he gathered told Henry that if one of their own was caught lying or deceiving the clan, they'd banish them."

"Okay, well, that's not so bad."

"Not quite there yet. They'd banish them straight into areas where known wolf packs roamed, or into hibernating bear caves, or into regions where poisonous snakes nested. If they passed through unharmed, they might get the chance to come back."

I'm shocked and quiet because I don't know how my father turned this primitive ritual into a Biblical, mystical mess. David reads my mind.

"Once the Order was formed, Chief Shawtagh was asked to incorporate the punishment into our culture. It has evolved a little, but honestly not very much. Wolves and bears must still be a part of the ritual. Of course, we need to bring them here, as they are mostly extinct from the region now."

"What about guns? I've seen people savagely murdered with no respect to a punishment trial at all."

"The toughest crimes call for the toughest punishments. It's allowed because some enemies who threaten our way of life don't deserve a chance at all."

I take a deep breath. There's that talk again. And I disagree with it.

"Hopefully I've given you some insight into the punishment culture."

I nod, but I'm still blown away, just like he said I'd be. I would never have guessed it all originated there. I thought it was some bull-shit my father made up from an interpretation of his favorite Bible passage. But still, I believe he found his idea of a hidden truth within the Bible, which gave extra credence to the ritual.

We both open our doors, and for the first time in my life, I'm standing in front of the reservation. There is a lot of land surrounding a visitor building. I can see the old wolf pens off to my right. Small wigwam homes rise in the distance, I assume for educational purposes, as the reservation used to be open to school children.

The building is as described by Danny, the media and everyone else who has seen it at this point. Most of the structure is a log cabin, but creek stones have made their mark on certain aspects of the building as well. David opens the door for me and Chief Shawtagh is waiting in the center of a display area. He's simply wearing a pair of jeans and a Jack Daniels T-shirt, which makes me smile.

"Well, Jenny. It's about time we were able to speak outside of rituals, don't you think?"

"Definitely." We shake hands, and he invites me to look around. Pottery and other relics encased in glass are displayed throughout the room. He tells me a little about each and the loca-tions nearby where they were found. Another room displays tradi-tional garb dating back to before Penn showed up with his treaties. I have to fake excitement because aside from the facts David just told me, none of the relics are very enlightening, and I hope this isn't it.

"Jenny, if you've done your required reading, you'll have read the book entitled, *The Lenape Stone*, by none other than H. C. Mercer himself."

"Yes. I have. I read it was a controversial find by a farmer. There are some doubts about the origins, but Henry kept an open mind and made a case for its credibility. It was a piece of slate with Indian art, depicting a mammoth and people. Right?"

"I'm glad you read it. Follow me."

I follow Chief Shawtagh and David into a locked room. On the wall is a large 3-D mural of the markings that were on the Lenape Stone.

"Is this ivory?" I ask, touching the tusks of the mammoth.

"Likely." They're both looking at me and smiling.

"What?"

"They're the tusks of the remains of an actual mammoth Henry himself found. He used them rather artistically to tell the story, don't you think?"

"Um, yes. But wouldn't the world of science and archaeology prefer them at like the Museum of Natural History? He destroyed them by placing them in this piece."

"He did indeed. But Henry was insistent that they be preserved here in Bucks County where they were found, to remain on this sacred ground, a secret just for us to keep. Any other questions, Jenny?"

"Well, I guess I have hundreds of questions, but you've both done a great job of filling in the blanks when it comes to your role within the Order and the Henry connection. I guess I'm obsessing a little about punishments though. Maybe because I lived through two."

"And you should be proud of that. You're blessed."

"Thank you, Chief. Since we're on the topic, would it be possible for me to see the animals that you bring to initiation?"

"You're one step ahead of us. David will be escorting you to Henry's private farm. You're aware of some of the grounds, seeing as you survived your final punishment and landed on them, but I think it's time for you to see the whole picture."

# 30

COYWOLVES

David and I talk about a multitude of topics on the way over to Henry Mercer's mystery farm. He discloses immediately that he's aware and approves of the plan to overthrow the current two most evil Grand Masters, my father and Mr. Brandt. Like the others, he believes I was a blessing sent to straighten it all out again and restore balance among the elements. They're all giving me too much credit. My only plan is to get the FBI involved again and then get out.

But the more I learn, the more my moral struggle deepens about deciding how much intel I'll offer the Feds. I'd be screwing with an over century-old lifestyle with a thousand perfectly happy members. Most of them are indirect members, but still. They're able to run up certain ranks to make them feel part of the society and protective of it. Most would die for the Order, that's how well they've been brainwashed. Many of their instructors are trained psychiatrists who practice the art of hypnosis to gather hidden knowledge as well as to implant information into their subconscious.

Speaking of subconscious—I haven't been hypnotized, but I feel like I have knowledge that I wasn't directly told.

"You'd like to know about the Kendra hair thing, wouldn't you? Why you did it without knowing you were supposed to?"

"Oh, boy. You know about that?"

He laughs. "Of course, I do. It astonished us all. You had a remarkable ability to infiltrate our society on a mental level—though your physical ability is quite remarkable as well," he says with a wink.

"Your grandfather. It was his job to infiltrate other Orders in case they knew something we didn't, then bring back anything relevant to us. Henry's obsession for knowledge was all-consuming. Even though he wanted to narrow down his belief systems, he could not. He was like a walking Encyclopedia Britannica. So, he assigned some of his strongest and most reliable members to infiltrate deep into other sects, cults, and orders."

"He was a spy."

"Yes, that was your grandfather's assigned position. Our society took what we felt was relevant from other secret societies and tossed out the rest. Your grandfather did his job too well, and eventually got in too deep with some dark sects. They messed him way up. He wasn't always a bad person."

"Really?"

"That's a tale for your father to tell. I'm overstepping. So, what were we talking about?"

"Why did I cut off Kendra's hair?"

"You cut off her hair to remove her power once she crossed over into the next world. And in doing so, you also made sure she could never come back."

"What do you mean come back?"

"How much do you know about the Bible?"

"Learning more every day, David."

"Samson was the weakest strongest person in the Bible. Out of love, he gave up the secret of his strength, his long hair. So, one night as he slept, his love, Delilah, cut his hair and called the Philistines. They gouged out his eyes and took him to prison. But they made the mistake of not killing him. His hair grew back, and he pushed down the whole temple, killing himself and others in the process. But God forgave Samson, and God forgives you, too, for what you had to do."

"David, this story is not apples to apples. I don't get it."

"You're right. I apologize. The short of it, so to speak, is that we symbolically cut off the hair of our wickedest enemies who don't make it through a punishment alive. We do this just before they take their last breath to ensure any special powers that they could take with them are lost. Many of us believe in reincarnation, including me, and without her power, you ensured she could not return back to earthly flesh."

I roll down the window for air. "This whole hair cutting thing was not Henry's idea," I say.

"No. Henry knew nothing of it and never witnessed a trial. It was a superstitious practice incorporated by the original council. They were very Biblical, including your great-grandparents."

"So I've heard. What if the person didn't have hair?"

"We're here." Thank God. I don't want to talk about this anymore.

A gate opens for us near the spring where Ryan and I emerged on the night of our punishment. I get a horrible flashback of my murderous attack. It will haunt me for the rest of my life, and I vow to never put myself in a position like that again. No one should play God—or Mother Nature—or whatever else they may believe in.

We're greeted by special rangers, definitely not county. They're in fatigues, looking more like the National Guard. They're on talkies and give us the go-ahead. They're protectors. I see the way they move. I've lived with these types for twenty-odd years.

We pass through an average-looking farm area with horses, ponies, sheep, and goats grazing. We cross a creek, quite literally going through it, and then drive through a mini tunnel elaborately decorated in Mercer's famous Moravian Tiles. Over the entrance are the same Latin letters that were on the cover of my intro book, PLVS VLTRA. I inquire immediately.

"It was Henry's motto. There was always more beyond with him."

"I see."

A guard opens the door for me. "This way." We follow him down a trail that leads to another building. I spot several men looking into the sky with guns drawn.

"Drones, Jenny. They shoot them down to keep them from spying. The struggle is quite real. Our Order is one of the most desired by secret society enthusiasts. But we have the ultimate weapon to keep them from infiltrating."

"What's that?"

"Blood. No match, no entrance."

Ingenious, I must admit, for a secret society. We enter through a side building, and I immediately smell zoo. A man emerges from a side door and describes his title, which is, in fact, zookeeper.

"You're probably wondering why Henry would want a private zoo?" I nod. "Well, it's actually quite simple and pure. Henry loved nature and worried about the possibility of extinction of even the simplest life forms. He was right about wolves, moose, and a large variety of other mammals and amphibians, which are extinct from Bucks County. So he insisted on bringing some back to keep them protected just in case. We have full permission by the state, which is well-funded by Henry's juicy trust fund, but under the agreement that only a select few may visit. This of course is his highest-ranking members. Even then, it's only under circumstances such as these. Come have a look."

He guides me through an area that resembles something more like Noah's ark. There are two of everything that once roamed the area, many of which still do. Species of snakes, especially the copper-heads, intrigue me. There are basic deer, rabbits, skunks, opossum, and water mammals including otters and beavers. This man was paranoid and passionate. I respect him for it but can't help but wonder how exhausted he must have been with a mind that worked and worried like this.

Finally, we descend down into a new level with the more fero-
cious animals they use for punishments. I count five black bears and
try to make out which one left me with a giant scar on my shoulder.
They don't look thrilled to be locked up, and I can't help but wonder
if this is what Henry would really have wanted.

Next are grey and red fox, followed by real-deal wolves. This
section of the zoo makes me very uncomfortable, and they sense my
fear, letting out deep growls. I've seen enough for one day and walk
faster toward another set of stairs that lead up and out, I assume.

"Hold on, Ms. O'Rourke. Let me first tell you about another
species. It occurred quite by accident. I'm not sure if you heard, but
there are stories in the area of a hybrid animal roaming the area
known as coywolves."

"Yes! I've definitely heard that. I Googled them when I heard the
sound of wolves while I was farmsitting for Jack and Katie."

"Well, truth is, one of our coyotes and one of our wolves managed
to get loose and breed. The female gave birth to a large litter and
disappeared. The rumors are true about coywolves, and ever since,
we've bred others because we don't believe in coincidences. We feel
this breed was meant to happen. More good news, they're very docile
and surprisingly gentle. As a gift from us to you, we'd like you to have
a pup from one of our recent litters. We feel it would be a splendid
addition to your land, but you're welcome to use one as a pet in the
house if you prefer."

He opens the door and we step into the most precious sight I've
ever seen, four coywolf pups nursing from their mother. They're all a
beautiful greyish red color. I'm instantly enamored and enthusiastically accept the gift.

"Is this legal?"

"Yes. You'll have an official license once you're able to move
home again. They're too young to leave with you now, of course."

I think of all the warm memories I have of Sonny and Cher,
Jack's golden retrievers. I can't wait to have one. He allows me to hold

them one at a time, so I can pick just the right one for me. I choose one with a marking above its mouth that looks almost like a mustache.

"Very well. Would you like to claim a name for her?"

"It's a girl? Aww. Yes." Without thinking, I name her Sallie, after Sal.

"Very well. You may pick her up in a few weeks."

I'm ecstatic. I'm going to have an exotic pet to call my own. I wish I could take her now.

"It's time to head home, Jenny," David announces. "Your brother is finished with his initiation ceremony. I'm sure the two of you have things to discuss."

"Is Danny going to get one too?"

"Of course. They'll need to continue breeding, after all. But he'll pick one from another litter so they're not too genetically close." *Just like me. Ugh.* I get a huge smile. Wait until he hears about this.

I'm escorted back to the truck and we make our way home. David asks how I enjoyed Day One. I must admit, it was full of surprises and insight that I needed to know. I enjoyed it very much. He tells me to buckle up for tomorrow. It's a new day with even more knowledge to gain and, best of all, filled with a fun little adventure.

# 31

---

AIR

**D**anny greets me with book in hand. "You read all of this?"

"Yes. Crazy, right?"

"You know I've always been a huge fan of Henry Mercer. I fell in love with architecture after seeing his castle when I was a boy. That wasn't a coincidence. My mind is playing weird tricks on me."

"Danny, what were your numbers? Did you have special numbers to unlock the book?"

"Yes! I was just going to tell you about that. How could they have known that my numbers are 333? I've been seeing them since I was young."

"Me too."

"That's right. You mentioned that before. Wow!"

"I had a long talk with Dr. Braun about them." I give Danny the full scoop about them, and about the trumpet. He's utterly shocked. He also heard the sound of a trumpet. But unlike me, and my prior knowledge of them, he just instinctually punched in the numbers, not knowing why. He also hasn't done half the reading I have, not really caring much until now. We spend the rest of the day in discussion, but he spends the night cramming. I give him a kiss goodnight before retiring early because it's going to be an early one. He pries on my way out of his room, but I don't give him all the details of my day with David. He's in this now. Time for him to learn as he goes too.

I'm ready to go at 6:30 a.m. as requested. Danny is already up, reading *The Lenape Stone.* I smirk as I grab my coffee. The only thing I know is that I'll be with Greg for Day Two of Knowledge starting at Van Sant Historical Airport.

A knock at the door comes in a series of threes, startling us both. It's Edwards being not funny. Clearly, he knows both Danny and I share the same special numbers. I open the door with a not-so-amused expression. "What are your numbers, Edwards?" I ask.

"Not the same as yours." He hands me a bag with some gear in it. "Bring it with you. I'll fill you in on the way to Van Sant."

"Okay. We're leaving now?"

"Yep. Get a move on."

Danny stands up and gives me a hug and basically threatens Edwards. "If anything happens to her, I'm gonna fuck you up three times over."

"Relax, Danny boy. She'll be fine."

It takes about fifteen minutes to get to the airport. I allow my guard to come down ever-so-slightly as we pull into the drive next to the grassy runway. It's incredibly peaceful atop a high hill with views of rolling farmlands in the distance. There's a hazy mist from the start of the day weaving in and out of trees and covering the whole runway. I eye up the hangers filled with historical old Navy single-engine planes and a few recreational aircraft I wouldn't know a thing about. There are two planes out on display, one a bright shade of yellow and one red. This scene would be perfect as a painting.

Van Sant was once a private airfield but was sold and purchased by the Bucks County park system and made a historical landmark, but few know of its existence—coincidence or not. It's a true glimpse into the past, with no commercial takeoffs or landings. It has remained a local hangout for aviation enthusiasts, local families, and bikers. Lunch is served in the summer, and special events take place, including movies under the stars, airshows, and antique car shows. Not one hundred feet away from me, a plane and glider take off. The pilot waves down to me. I enthusiastically wave back. I have goosebumps and am getting pretty pumped up. How wonderful the adventure must be! Maybe I'm going to get a ride and get to check out the view of the towns and get a history lesson from the air. Greg pops out of the office and calls for me to come in.

"Am I going for a glider ride?"

He smiles. "No glider ride. Power paragliding with a twist."

"What the heck is that?"

"You'll see. I have to teach you how to fly before your actual task. No time to waste."

I'm getting nervous. I head into the bathroom with my bag and pull out the light flight suit. It's long-sleeved, bottom and top. I think I have it on correctly and head back into the office to find the room has filled in with people. I'm asked to stand in the center of their circle. Scott is among the group, smiling at me. They all hold hands and bow for a prayer. I bow too.

"Angel of mercy and light, we pray that Jenny will be graced with your sight." Together they say, "We thank you for your everlasting love and guidance. Take Jenny under your wings as you have taken us all." Each member has a candle. They all light them one at a time around the circle, clockwise. Scott hands me one of my own.

Greg speaks again. "Jenny, only until you hear what I'm going to tell you, and accept it without doubt, will your candle be lit. You must have faith to take this journey. If there is any doubt in your mind, we cannot continue. Understand?" I nod and say, "I do."

"Then let's begin. I'll try to ease you into this so that you're not as wigged out as we all were in the beginning." The members laugh and nod. "Have you ever looked in the sky and seen the shape of an animal or other object?"

"Yes. All the time. I saw an angel as clear as can be over the river the day before my punishment. It was magnificent." The members mumble to each other and utter sounds.

"What?" I ask.

"That was an even greater sign than you could have imagined at the time. Jenny, above the Delaware River, in the same spot, almost every day at the same time, the shape of an angel appears in the clouds. Weather permitting." They laugh. "We're going to fly to her, assuming she makes an appearance." I immediately get the chills. How can this be?

"There's more, but that's all you need to know for now. How are you feeling? Ready to fly?"

"Nervous. Excited. I don't know. But, yeah! I'm ready."

"Do you feel like you have enough information for us to light your candle? You must have faith. Not everyone has it in the beginning. Do you? You have to be sure."

I take a few deep breaths and close my eyes. If an angel appears in the clouds every day at the same time, I believe. I've seen one with my own eyes, so with confidence I nod, and Greg lights my candle. The members blow out their candles and take their seats. I have to admit, I'm really into this.

"When it comes to this segment of the Order, air members are a bit progressive about religion. Of course, we don't advertise that. Most of us are Christians, but some, like me, are simply spiritual. But at the end of the day, we still all fall under one Order. Your journey will end with an official initiation into that Order. For now, you must leverage the faith that's already deep within you. Over the next few days, you're going to see things that science can't explain. That we can't explain. You're also going to see things that can be explained but can never be exposed. They're to stay with us and only us. Not to be shared. Understand?" I nod.

"Once the elements are aligned again, there will be peace, and we can never take it for granted ever again. Horrible acts of violence have plagued our communities for over two decades."

"My father."

"Yes. But soul-devouring evil started before him, then spread like cancer. Your great-grandparents did what they could to regain control. Hell, they even performed their own exorcisms, but the force was too strong. Our Divine Laws were broken, and so were we."

"This is all about my grandfather. I've learned that he murdered my grandmother and forced my father and uncle to bury her here. He must have succumbed to black magic or satanism to do what he did. He had his own children bury their mother. What kind of animal did he become? But it was this very town, and his very own parents who forced my father to defend him. To try and get him out of jail and bring him back here for punishment. Why would they want to bring him back here if their methods didn't work to begin with? He deserved the punishment he got in prison, don't you think?"

The members shift uncomfortably at the question. It seems like a simple question to me, based on the facts. "Blood runs deep and we, I should say your great-grandparents, never gave up on him. Many think they should have. Your father, along with his legal partner, worked hard to free him. Billy was a homegrown bad influence, and working in the city made it worse. He succumbed to common ways. Sins of the city filled his head with filth, and as a result, he created fierce enemies. You know the rest. He killed and brought killers here. Billy's dead body poisoned our sacred baptismal waters at Deep Creek. Then one of our own was killed. Chuck was one of the finest men I knew. Immediately upon the news of his death, your family was banished. You and Danny were sent away at our request, as well as Michael and Jackie. We, as a society, commanded it, and your father abided. The Witness Protection Program made it easier for your father to accept. He had no choice, but the government had reason to protect you too. Organized crime blended with your father's dark side. I'm so sorry for the years you've lost.

"Your mother had no idea what was happening but accepted the remainder of your schooling away to keep you safe. At the time, we wanted the Engel family line to be broken off permanently from the Order. Your house stood vacant, purposefully, but your father still lurked. He lurked, went through punishment, and repositioned himself through tyranny and fear as Grand Master. And it continues right up to this day. He's powerful, and people are afraid of him, so they follow, or at least stay out of his way.

"We, the good people of the EORCUF Order, have waited for God to send an angel to help mend us. Who knew it would be from the very bloodline we wanted to abolish? With Jill Grover dead and her husband behind bars, you have nothing but friends here under the element of air. We are whole. We cannot say the same for the members under fire and earth.

"Your father and Mr. Brandt are tight. Be careful. They aligned after Douglas Brandt was murdered. It was a terrible tragedy, deemed punishable according to our judicial system.

"But that's when Michael Brandt stepped up punishment to include hunting for prospects. It wasn't enough to find them among ourselves. They sought them, even creating a foundation to help others find them. So fucking twisted! You put an end to that already, Jenny. We're incredibly proud of you. Murderers from our town were not cast out to be placed in government facilities. They lived or died here by our laws."

"How often did this happen before my father's enemies arrived?" I ask.

"Once in a blue moon, really. Like I said, our villages ran smoothly. Then mayhem. A few members escaped in hopes of just living normal lives. They were found in such a way that no one dared try again. We believe you've been sent back to us to cleanse our society and restore us."

I'm starting to feel pressure again. "How many people have been initiated since the summer, aside from Lucia?" I roll my eyes as I say her name, making Greg smirk.

"Just she, and one who tried. A reporter who managed to dig

himself into deep shit. They and the FBI are chipping away at us. It has to stop now."

"Where's the reporter?"

"He's locked up and considered a missing person. Your father will likely order you to do the sentencing once you're initiated, as your first task under his leadership."

"Well, I will be fair if that's true. The man was just doing his job. There will be no harsh punishment like I went through. No bears, that's for sure." Everyone looks around the room, seemingly reading each other's thoughts. Do they think I'd be too lenient? I'm forgetting that this punishment ritual dates way back.

"I know you'll do the right thing, Jenny," Scott says.

"All right, let's get going. You can ask me more questions along the way. That's what initiation is all about. Knowledge. Hopefully, I don't have to tell you that the later part of this discussion is between us, or you'll be punishing me next," Greg says with a smile, then begins barking orders to a few members. He asks me to follow him to the bottom of the grass runway.

It's a beautiful day, not a cloud in the sky. I hope this angel appears, or I'll feel like a total failure. Greg has my full attention as fan motors attached to what looks like a parachute are brought out to the runway. I get a demonstration from a few experts. They make it look so fun and easy. They're way up in the sky in no time at all, gliding back and forth above our heads. Greg lays out my "wings" as he calls them. It looks like a big kite to me. He explains the lines. The A lines, which are red, will lift the wings and expose the air cells to the wind. His feet come right off the ground as he demonstrates. Next, he goes over the brake lines, steering braces and the method to go right and left. I pay very close attention to the method it takes to go up and down. Squeeze the throttle to go up, release the throttle to go down. He spends a lot of time on the proper way to land. For the time being, we have plenty of landing space. But not for long, he says. I practice using the lines for a good hour before the engine is strapped to my back.

"Ready?"

"I can't believe I'm about to do this."

"Run into the wind, Jenny. Let's go. Stay calm and focused."

I run with a huge grin on my face but have a failure to launch on my first try. It makes me more determined the next time. Greg gives me a thumbs-up and I run like I'm being chased. I do everything just as he's described, and I find my feet off the ground. I use the throttle to go higher. My heart is racing, and I feel so alive. I'm soaring high above the runway, circling near my takeoff point. It's breathtaking. A herd of deer graze in a field below me. I spot two covered bridges. I'm flying. This is how a bird must feel—minus the sound of an engine and the smell of fuel.

I go up and down three more times before Greg tells me I'm ready for my mission. He officially declares me a pilot and pins me with a special set of wings. I'm still wearing the angel pin he gave me from my opening ceremony, on top of wearing and carrying every-thing else that was given to me.

We have to head over to the river and look near an area of rapids for the angel to appear. In that area, the spray from the water under the sun creates a perpetual rainbow. That's where we'll be looking. The ever-so-slight skeptic in me can't help but wonder if the forma-tion has something to do with the water and sun above the rapids. But I can't wait to see for myself.

"When you see the angel, Jenny, go through her. Stay in control. Then rise above and follow me. Got it?"

"Got it."

Greg gets up in the air first, and I follow his lead. I look down at all the air members. They're waving. Some are taking pictures of me. Even if this were my only task, I'd say, kinda worth the hype. We head to the east. I spot the river in no time at all. I see farms and beautiful homes along the way that I didn't know existed. The river looks amazing from the air. There are small islands and camp-grounds, which I didn't know existed either. There are some pretty high cliffs on the Jersey side too, one with fairly even ground at the top. I make a mental note that I could land there in an emergency situation.

I look at my watch. It's 3:30 p.m. The sudden realization that the angel appears at 3:33 p.m. shakes me to my core. I know now that in three minutes I'll be either incredibly blessed or incredibly disappointed. Clouds have formed in the sky above. I look for shapes but see nothing out of the ordinary. Greg points and I shift to face south. I see the rainbow, as he described. He lowers, and I follow. It's exactly 3:33 p.m. when I spot her. There's no mistaking the shape of an angel. Her arms are open as if to accept us. Tears stream down both of my cheeks. I try to stop them for fear of blurring my vision, but they keep coming.

Greg is all the way through, and it's my turn. As I glide toward her, my goosebumps disappear, and I feel something pierce my soul. It tickles one minute, feels warm the next. I laugh. I cry. I feel caressed. I feel loved. I have to remember to concentrate on what I'm doing because the only thing I want at this moment is to be taken away with her. There's no drug, glass of wine, or prayer that can bring about this feeling, and it's over way too soon. I'm desperate to feel it again and try to turn back, but she's gone. Throttle. I need to throttle. I'm coming in too low.

# 32

## THE EAGLES

My boots touch the water, but I manage to pull up before plunging all the way in. My stomach still tickles, and my eyes are still watery from the angel in the clouds. I wonder if this is something I'll be allowed to do on my own, any time I want in the future, or if this is a job only meant for air elements. I've never had a spiritual experience like this before and I don't want it to end.

I look in the distance and see that Greg has landed on the flat area above the cliff that I was eyeing up earlier. He's waving me in and putting his wings away to give me room to land. I maneuver my way over to see what I'm in for. I only have about one hundred feet to land but know I can give it some gas and turn around for more tries if I have to. I come in low and slow and somehow manage a perfect landing. Greg smiles, rushes to my side, and puts an arm around my shoulder. He wipes a tear from one of my cheeks.

"I thought you were going right into the drink there for a minute. Nice landing. Well?"

"I feel like I died and went to heaven. For real."

"I'm so glad she appeared for you. Tell me what you felt."

"I felt drugged. I felt warmth, love, and a tickling sensation."

"Wow! Pretty intense first experience. Some have described the same kind of sensations and believe they were filled with the Holy Spirit."

"Really? Filled with the Holy Spirit? I've never thought about such a thing. But if it's a thing, maybe that's what I experienced." I say a silent prayer of thanks while Greg helps me off with the equipment.

"What do you feel when you go through her, Greg?"

"I just feel a sense of peace mostly. Gratitude." I nod, understanding. I feel much lighter without the equipment and stretch out my back as we take in the view. It's tranquil and peaceful. I spot hawks soaring to and fro above the river.

"Ready for the twist?"

"That wasn't the twist?"

"Nope. Follow me. Leave the gear here, and someone will come and grab it in a few."

We edge over to a flat rock and sit down with legs dangling. Greg pulls out two thick gloves, slides one on his right arm, and helps me on with the other one.

"Put your arm out as I do. Stay still and as steady as possible when they land. Understand?"

"What kind of birds? You better be talking about doves or something, and not those hawks. I'm actually a little afraid of birds. Well, mostly afraid of chickens."

"Chickens?" He laughs out loud. "You'll be fine."

Greg makes a bird calling sound, and within moments two large bald eagles fly toward us. They're so intimidating that I'm tempted to drop my arm and back away. But I channel my bravery, close my eyes, and stay as steady as possible. I hold in a squeal as one lands on my arm. Its wings flutter, slapping my face a few times before resting steadily on my arm. I slowly open my eyes and stare at the eagle. I turn my head very slowly toward Greg. He's gently petting his bird from the top of its head down its wings. As he does, he says, "Good girl."

"Can I pet mine?" My arm is starting to shake from the weight as I ask.

"Sure. The one on your arm is Isabelle."

"Is she going to bite me?"

"Try to relax, and she'll relax more." I concentrate hard, slowly raise my free arm, and give her head a stroke. "You're doing great. She likes you. Twenty-five pounds of awesome, don't you think?"

"Only twenty-five?" Greg pulls something raunchy from his pocket and hand-feeds them. "Okay, on three, we're going to push up and let them go. One, two, three." We both lift and watch them soar high in the sky. Yet another beautiful moment I could never have imagined.

"Jenny, the lesson with the eagles is one of freedom. In our society, we live a life of freedom that is unknown to the outside world. Sure, as Americans, we live in the land of the free, but that's becoming more and more an archaic concept. This Order allows us to live as we please, free of the complications that come with the burden of government. Of division. Of right and left. If we don't agree, we work it out. One person ensures that ... well, is supposed to anyway."

"The Judge. My great-uncle, the Imperator?"

"His position is to be kind of like a glorified parent. When his people disagree, he weighs in with rational, unemotional wisdom and helps solve the problem. But he's been partial with your father. The family tree has clouded his judgement. You'll be the one to reset the course someday. You're wise already."

I'm understanding, but pressure, pressure, pressure. I did feel an undeniable connection to him when he baptized me. And, ironically, I always felt like our government needed that one person. Kind of like a father or mother figure who said, *okay, okay, enough. I've heard both sides, but here's what's going to happen ... and the solution is fair.* That's been the role of Imperator, a mighty big task with many layers and responsibilities. Members who've never met him are under the impression that he's to be feared, but quite the contrary. Because he's 'invisible,' his presence and role are simply misunderstood.

"Did he ever practice law?"

"Indeed! Retired as an honorable U.S. District Court Judge here in Pennsylvania in the 1970s, under the name of Judge Henry Thomas. He's still high profile and can't risk exposing himself as a member of our Order, or even trust the members not to expose him to the government. He's always played it very safe. Josh and I have only just learned his identity as we were initiated as Grand Masters."

"Wow! That's remarkable."

"It is, isn't it? You know, he's almost ninety-two years old. When he dies, we don't know who will take his place. Your father was once a great candidate, but not so much anymore—even he knows that. But you have dual law degrees, a good heart, and the bloodline. You'll take his place."

"Whoa. Slow down."

"What? Too much for you?" He elbows me and laughs. "Sorry. Getting way ahead of myself."

"Yeah, and excuse me, but I'd like to marry again someday."

"Fair enough. Let's come back to the here and now. The feather on your necklace that Chief Shawtagh gave you. Remember this place and think of the sculpture you've seen of Chief Tamanend. Remember his ability to keep peace and bring people together. You've seen the sculpture, correct?"

"Not in person yet."

"The eagle on his shoulder represents a message from the great spirit and symbolizes friendship. In his case, he formed a friendship with the Quakers, both Ben Franklin and William Penn. And hey, it's how Philly scored the Eagles as their mascot." He eyes me up, and I smile at him but have nothing to contribute, as I'm not exactly a football fan. "Kidding."

"Josh told me that Chief Tamanend is known as a Patron Saint of America. He was a distant relative of Kendra's and lived in the cave at one time, correct?"

"Yes. But the descendants that matter, those who care about their history, won't go into that cave, even though they could have rightful ownership. Only Kendra positioned herself to occupy the mammoth space. The rest gave it up to the element of water."

"Why?"

"They feel the cave symbolizes a depression of their freedom. It's a hiding place. They hid enough and never want to do it again. This is their rightful land. The last bit of knowledge I get the honor of offering you today is a few more facts about the Lenape Indians who abandoned it. Before Kendra and her family decided to turn it into their idea of Atlantis." He laughs. "Don't get me started."

"Not a fan of Atlantis?" I inquire.

"No. Anyway, the cave was discovered and maintained by Henry. It was used as a very large Underground Railroad station. You've heard of the Underground Railroad, I hope? I swear I'll toss you off this cliff if you ask me if it's a real railroad."

Now I laugh out loud. "I know what they were, but I had no idea that there were stations in this area."

"Plenty of them, but no one but us knows of that enormous one. It once protected hundreds of slaves." I'm letting this information sink in. What an incredible piece of historical knowledge. "There were other stations in Bucks County, but none as large as the cave we secretly refer to as Mercy station, taking the name from Mercer and adding the spiritual twist."

"Greg?"

"Yes? Let me guess, you have a ton of questions," he says with a smile.

"Were like the Masons part of this group at one time? I understand three Freemasons founded the Golden Dawn, one of the Rosicrucian Orders I will be studying."

"Good question, but no. Neither the Mercer nor the Chapman families were ever a part of the Masons, despite the architectural work they did. EORCUF was formed instead, and here we sit today." He gives me time to look around at the scenery to appreciate it again.

"Jenny, the FBI isn't the only group who wants to break us up. There are hundreds of other Orders who want to know our secrets. They feel they're entitled to whatever we have."

"What do 'we' have? Where does all the money come from? All archaeological findings from Henry Mercer and his inherited wealth?"

"Not all. It's getting late. You'll know by the end of the week. I'm impressed though. You've followed very well. Listen, you've officially passed your "air" test, so you can ask me most questions at any time. But if they cross into another element, you'll have to wait. More big reveals to come. Feel enlightened enough for your second day?"

"Yes, I do." I look around. "How are we supposed to get down without the power paragliders?"

"Well, in addition to loving my new job as the Grand Master of air, I still have some hobbies as an extreme sports enthusiast. You're going to tandem jump with me."

"Excuse me?" I watch Greg as he gets into a wingsuit. This is nuts. People jump from much higher places to do things like this, and they still die.

"Have no fear. I invented this little gizmo myself." He grabs a section off of his paragliding gear and attaches it to his back. "Trust me?" I nod. "Then let's fly." He straps me into a harness beneath him and tells me he'll do all of the work. Before I can back out, he leaps off the cliff with wings spread wide. I can barely hear this "gizmo" of a motor, but we're flying. We're really flying. We follow the river up and I relax, feeling safe beneath Greg. I take in the scenes along the river, trying to memorize every detail.

I look up in time to see the runway and my new friends at the airport waiting for me. Greg lands us as gracefully as possible, but we don't quite stick the landing. Instead, we get tangled and tumble over each other. We're both laughing at what must have been quite the scene.

"I haven't totally mastered that part yet, Jenny. In fact, you're the first I've tried that little stunt with. At least in tandem."

"Are you serious?" He cracks himself up, and I punch him on the shoulder. "As if I haven't taken enough risks!"

"Dead serious. I'm pumped that it worked, aren't you?"

"Don't you dare kill my brother tomorrow doing this."

"I promise."

I get greetings, embraces, and congratulations from all. They're thrilled to hear that my trip was a success. A few members said they had the same exact feeling with the angel. Some looked bummed they didn't feel as much, but they're all overjoyed for me. I see Agent Edwards waiting for me in the distance. He's waving to be sure I see him. I pull Greg aside to ask more about him. "Whose side is this man really on?" It certainly isn't the U.S. Government.

"Not the Order entirely, the way it should be. He's loyal to your father and is paid very well. It's destroyed his sense of honor altogether. There's no real redemption for him as far as I'm concerned. He's nothing but a messenger, and I suspect your father will kill him off eventually." I'm not totally surprised by the answer, having suspected that he's just been a puppet all along.

He walks toward us, so we cut the chat. "Jenny! How'd it go?" he asks.

"It was incredible."

"That's fantastic news. Just wait until tomorrow. You'll be spending the day with your father and a few others. You need rest, because it's going to be another early start." I look at Greg and lift an eyebrow.

"Best of luck tomorrow, Jenny. Take good care of her, Edwards."

"You know it," he replies.

I thank Greg for everything and wave to everyone else as we head out the drive. Agent Edwards asks me a few questions about my day. Enthusiastically, I give him a few tidbits. I know he's about to report to my father, so I allow myself to show real emotion to share with him. He's pleased with my responses.

We pull into Red Rock Farm, behind the renovated barn and into the garage. Danny's waiting for me and is no-nonsense, just staring, seemingly into my soul. He basically shuts the garage door in Edwards' face.

"What's up? Did something happen today? Don't want a baby coywolf?" He leads me into the tunnel he and Fabrizio created, knowing it may be the safest place to talk.

"Well? Was Day Two worth it?" he asks. My answer is very simple and followed by streams of tears.

"Yes, Danny, it's worth it."

He grabs me and holds me close. I feel some of the tension leave his body, but then he transitions into uncontrollable shudders. He's feeling the loss of Fabrizio. He's mourning, but I see hope and relief in his eyes. It's not all for nothing.

I wipe his tears and tell him I love him. We go over the details of his day, but I refuse to tell him much about mine. I pray his experience isn't disappointing, because I'm probably more spiritual than he is, but he has faith. If he didn't, he wouldn't be here with me right now.

Then he breaks the news to me that Ryan has decided to follow through. His initiation ceremony is today or tomorrow. We're not sure what it means, but it leaves us both uneasy. Ryan is unstable and ready to rip this Order apart. I hope the Grand Masters are prepared for potential disaster.

## 33

---

EARTH

"Rise and shine, Jenny," Danny prompts. Why's he up so early? His day doesn't start for another few hours. "Come on, I couldn't sleep and made us some breakfast."

"What time is it?"

"5:30 a.m. Your ride will be here soon. Assuming I get Edwards. I wonder who's coming to get you."

"Okay, okay. I'm getting up."

Wear something comfortable—those were my only orders for today. I showered late last night, so I just wash my face and brush my teeth. I slide on yoga pants again and the Van Sant T-shirt Greg gave me on my way out. I grab all of my initiation gifts and meet Danny downstairs. "Yum! Cheese omelets." Danny's leg is jumping up and down the way it always does when he's anxious.

"You're going to do great, bro. Keep the faith, got it?"

"Got it. How are you feeling about being with Dad?"

"What choice do I have? I wonder why we have to leave so freaking early."

A knock at the door makes us both jump. Danny makes sure it's legitimately my ride before opening the door. "Oh, boy. Your ride's here."

"Who is it?"

"Come in, Uncle Dennis." *Oh, Lord.* My father's militia-happy little brother. The one who was forced to bury his own mother by my father's side. And the bastard who shot Jodi before my father finished her off like some kind of savage beast. I'm raging on the inside and feel no guilt for shooting him in the shoulder myself that day. I do not like this man. He's another one who's going to jail when this is over.

"How's my favorite niece this morning?" he asks. Not even remotely funny.

"I'm terrific! Great to see you," I say with snark and sarcasm.

"You ready? Truck's still running." I nod and look at Danny. He grabs a sweatshirt, places it around my shoulder, and gives me a kiss. "Wish I would've had the opportunity to be friends with my sister like you two."

He means Katie. It's unfortunate to think that my father and Dennis never had the chance to form a relationship with her. My grandmother did the right thing by giving her up for adoption, and yet she's the one dead. It's ironic in the most awful way possible.

"I wish so too. Katie was a beautiful lady." He lets out a sigh, humanizing him slightly, and opens the door for me. We hop in Dennis' truck just before the sun comes up.

"Why so early?"

"We're heading over to Ringing Rocks. Heard of it?"

"The place with a big boulder field. Kids bring hammers and listen to the sounds they make. We had a class trip there."

"Well, that's the basics. Let me offer you some knowledge. Ringing Rocks, to this day, is a geological mystery much like Stonehenge. Same type of rock. Different shape, size, and design. If kids were allowed to climb atop Stonehenge with a hammer, they'd hear the same thing."

"You're shitting me?"

He laughs. "Not shitting you. Here's the deal. Stones don't usually ring, but these do. They vibrate and make sound sorta like a bell. Christ, people have been coming here for ages, even putting on concerts with the sounds they make. Stupid. But anyway, they consist of diabase, the same type of rock that makes up most of the earth's crust.

"Even though all of the rocks are made of all the same material, mostly iron and hard minerals, only about one-third of 'em ring. Rocks that ring are called 'live' rocks. Rocks that don't, 'dead' rocks. That'll be important when you get there.

"More knowledge for you. No vegetation, animal, insect, or reptile life inhabits the boulder field. Birds don't even fly above it. Ever. There are lots of theories as to why, but only ours is the correct one. The rocks give off magnetic energy and electromagnetic activity. It's instinctual for them to steer clear of it. Thanks to the hard work of our own members, we've discovered the connection between black matter and black energy, and how they help create the phenomenon you're about to witness. We have to get there early before all the kids come scrambling out of camps and shit and grab their hammers and make me nuts. Rangers have it blocked off until 9:00 a.m. Any questions?"

"You said the earth's crust. Our family reins over the element of earth, is there a connection?"

"There's a big connection. Our land—your land legally as of now —contains the same rock. But it goes deeper into the earth. While Danny is out flying today, take a hike behind the barn and into the woods. There's a small cave opening between two large rocks. Have yourself a good old time exploring."

"You mean the rocks where my father claimed copperheads lived? Danny and I were terrified of that spot." Dennis chuckles.

"No snakes or anything in there. Your old man just wanted to scare you away from that area. Make sure you didn't fall down or discover it and open your big mouths to your mother. Punch in the code 252 when you find the lock. Stick your arm all the way down to the right and behind a pointy rock. You'll feel it."

"Seriously?"

"Yep. Feds didn't find that one," he mocks.

Neither did Danny and I and there's been construction there for months.

"By the way, my shoulder still fucking hurts where you shot me."

"Yeah, well, the bite on the back of my shoulder hurts too. What kind of tough guy are you?" We exchange evil eyes. He doesn't scare me anymore.

"We're here." Two rangers check out the truck and wave us through. Dennis parks the car alongside a public restroom where two more rangers are standing guard. One opens the door for me, and my father appears out from behind the restroom shed. I jump and hold my heart.

"Sorry if I scared you, pumpkin," he says with a laugh. "Give her the background on the rocks, Dennis?"

"Yup."

Another figure appears from the trail leading to the boulder field. It's Lucia. Of all people. I should have put it together. Her studies with black matter and energy and the particles all around us we can't see.

"Good morning, Jenny. Nice to see you."

"Great to see you too, Lucia." She shakes my hand and tells me to follow her. *Wait, she's a fire element, not an earth element.* How is she part of this? My father looks like he's reading my mind.

"Lucia's mother, Lacey, was my second cousin. She comes from earth roots, in case you're trying to make the connection. Lacey worked for NASA and married a member under the element of fire. She converted but never stopped working for the greater good. That's what we do, Jenny. We all work together. Lacey passed down her knowledge, and Lucia has carried on her amazing work. God rest her soul."

"Sorry to hear that, Lucia."

"Father too. They both died experimenting here," my father says, matter-of-factly.

"Oh, geez. I'm so sorry," I repeat sincerely. She thanks me for the condolences.

"Unfortunately, they found out the hard way what negative particles do to the area when magnetic energy is released. But you're going to find out what happens when we counter it with positive charges. Don't worry, you won't be tested on this. It's for Lucia and the other scientists within our society to continue to master."

Three other members emerge holding metallic instruments. Another man straps something around my waist.

"That's a magnet, Jenny. We're all wearing them." He lifts his shirt to show me. "The instruments being used are made of platinum and uranium." I'm trying my hardest to figure out what's going to happen, but I wasn't great in chemistry or physics. It went in one ear and out the other. "Follow me," one of the men says.

They guide me to the center of the boulder field, which is not the easiest task in the world. But after about twenty minutes of balancing and hopping from one to the next, I'm steady and ready. My father, Lucia, and the three other men position themselves into a pentacle-like formation. They look at each other and begin. The sound doesn't sound like a bell at all, more like a loud vibration, which I can feel through my shoes. I lean down to steady myself on the rock and realize it's heating up. That's when it happens. I begin to rise, not far off the ground, maybe six inches. It takes some doing to balance myself. It's a magnetic field, and it creates a feeling of weightlessness. I wonder if this is what it feels like on the moon. I look around and see Lucia do a front handspring from one rock to the next. It was an awkward and sloppy one, but she did it. This must be a dream. How ridiculous. Lucia just did a handspring over giant boulders. I hold my stomach and laugh. My father brings me back to reality. I'm not dreaming.

"We've released enough magnetic energy to last about thirty minutes, Jenny. Enjoy the feeling. Experiment with it. See what you can do. The live rocks, like the one you're standing on will give you the experience. You'll know it when you hit a dead rock because you'll come back to earth, so to speak."

For the second day in a row, something I can't explain makes me a little emotional. I know the magnet around my waist has something to do with this situation, but I don't understand how this is happening. I decide to lie down, thinking of battery charges. The feeling around the center of my body near the magnet is super intense, and I wonder if I'm getting radiation from it. I come about two feet off the ground and lie suspended in the air like Superman. I can't go higher. It's where the force field stops. I float over the rocks in that position, pushing myself with my hands. Every now and then, I strike a dead rock and lose height. I bang my knee hard once before finding another live rock. The hair is standing straight up on my arms, and I can feel static electricity making my hair go in different directions. The other men have the same look. I can't help but giggle. Lucia came prepared with a tight bun. I float over to where my father is standing. He's smiling at me.

"What do you think?"

"It's like a weird dream. Come and walk with me." I take my father by the hand. I'm playful now and do a semi-split in the air from one rock to the next. "You do it, Dad."

"Jenny, even under these circumstances, I'd pull a groin muscle if I tried that." He takes a simple leap instead and almost loses his balance.

For the next twenty minutes, my father and I go over almost every inch of the rock field. I start to feel heavier and know we're getting close to the end of this experience, so I push off and manage one forward flip and consider it my last stunt for the day. Day Three of knowledge doesn't disappoint. It makes me wonder how the next two days could ever compete.

Once the weightless feeling has disappeared altogether, we're able to take off our magnetic belts. One of the men collects all the instruments and everyone disperses except my father and me.

"Come with me. You and I are heading to the waterfall."

"There's a waterfall?"

"Yes. It's where we'll go over the rest, and you'll have time to ask me all the questions you want."

I've waited a long time to hear that.

## 34

---

### THIRTY-THREE

My father leads the way very carefully, using a walking stick to navigate around more large boulders. There's a path, but it's still hard to maneuver, especially for him. We make it to the edge of a cliff overlooking a medium-sized water-fall. The rock bed is on a slant, causing the water to spill to one side. It's underwhelming in size, but there's something simplistically beautiful about it. We press on down a narrow path to the base of the falls. My father is on a mission to get to the water running over the edge. I follow. Both of our feet are soaked by the time we reach it. He asks me to bend my head backwards for a prayer. The water is cold, but I've certainly been through colder.

"*Saint Michael, the Archangel, defend us in battle. Be our safe-guard against the wickedness and snares of the devil; May God rebuke him, we humbly pray and do thou, O Prince of the heavenly host, by the power of God, thrust into hell Satan and all the evil spirts who wander through the world for the ruin of souls. Amen, Amen, Amen.*"

I return with an "Amen" of my own and squeeze some of the water from my hair and wipe my eyes with my T-shirt. He guides me over to a large flat rock where we can both sit down.

"That's a pretty intense prayer, Dad."

"A prayer to St. Michael. It is indeed. My mother would recite it to us before we went to bed each night to protect us from evil. To protect us from whatever evil spirit had taken control of my father." He looks down, saddened by memories. "It gave my brother and me a little hope."

This is the exact topic I want to explore. "Please tell me what happened. David Shawtagh said your father was a good man at one time."

"He was a very good man. We had some good times together as a family. Took us to Deep Creek to swim, the whole nine yards."

"Really?"

He nods. "It's one of the fondest memories I have of him."

"I understand he was a spy?"

"It was his job to infiltrate other secret societies, everything from Scientology to Freemasonry, and at least four or five reputable Rosicrucian Orders. He brought back invaluable information that we still use to this day. His work took him away quite a bit. He'd be gone for months at a time while he studied, deep under cover. When the Order felt he'd learned what he could, he was asked to infiltrate satanic cults to understand why anyone would worship the devil and to learn what kinds of rituals they performed and so on. From what Uncle Thomas told me, he joked about much of it in the beginning. They drank goat's blood and snuck around in dark robes. He thought they were a bunch of misfits at first. He made the mistake of allowing himself to believe. They cast dark spells over him and summoned the devil through a special Ouija Board. Promise me you'll never play with one of those."

"I promised you that as a child, if you recall. I still promise. They freak me out."

"Good. They should. Anyway, for whatever reason, he stayed. I would have run, for the sake of my family. Eventually, he participated in rituals, including a human sacrifice, honey. My grandparents believe a demon attached itself to him at that point."

"This is terrifying."

"It was very scary for two little kids. My father became very abusive, especially if we brought up Christianity. If he heard my mother pray to God, he'd beat her mercilessly. She finally called the authorities and filed a restraining order. He got help, and she allowed him back in the home. Everything seemed normal for a while. Then one night, my mother woke up to my father hovering above her. He had a large crucifix in his hands and was about to stab her with it. She swore she saw the figure of a horned monster behind him, ordering him to kill her. She kept a hammer under her pillow and got to him first, knocking him out. She was able to slide out from under him. Then she whisked us off to Red Rock Farm, pleading with his family to help."

"Your mother wasn't part of EORCUF?"

"Nope. Just a regular sweet young schoolfriend of my father's. He swore it was love at first sight in the sixth grade. I'm sure it was her green eyes that captivated him. They were just like yours," he says and looks into mine. "At the time, there wasn't a linear match within the circle, so he was granted permission to marry her. My father was an extremely good secret keeper. My brother and I had no idea about the society or why he became mad. And my poor mother never knew. She thought he worked undercover for the CIA," he smiles. "One day, my mother disappeared on us. We thought she abandoned us, but it turns out she was trying to protect her unborn. I wish I had known. It would have made a big difference in my life."

I'm getting so depressed by these stories because they're peppered with history repeating itself. My father is a bad man. I'm not sure if he's filled with the devil, or maybe thinks he's acting out in warfare against the devil, or what. And here I am infiltrating my own inherited society. It's really screwed up.

"How did he finally snap, and why did he kill the cult leaders?"

"Unfortunately, you know the story of what happened after my mother came home. It ended tragically for all of us." My father pauses, finding it hard to speak. I instinctively grab his hand and hold it. "My grandparents took charge of him from there. After months of attempted rehabbing somewhere in Brandtville, they invited an exorcist. It worked. But with the knowledge of what he'd done and that he was going to face a punishment trial, with virtually no way of surviving, he lashed out. He killed cult leaders from every satanic cult he could, as well as other religious cults."

"The Scientologist? I read about him."

"Yes. It's how my father was finally taken out. The Church of Scientology has protectors too—their security is top notch. He was arrested by their team and turned over to the police, then sentenced to death. But the death penalty is extremely slow for some, especially in liberal states. As we got older, Billy and I were ordered to go into law, appeal his case, and try to bring him home. Never got the chance."

"How exactly did you escape prison?"

"I got people, and now you do too," he says and winks.

"It's a lot to take in, in just a few days. That's why we generally do things slow around here. You can imagine how difficult it was for me too."

"So, what about my mother?"

"I met your mother in the city. She was waiting on my table. She was chosen for me though, Jenny. It's a pretty wild story."

"Wilder than what you've already told me?"

"Yes! Your nonno was close friends with the late Pope John Paul I."

"You're pulling my leg. That cannot be true! I would have heard about it from Mom."

"It's the truth."

"He was friends with an actual pope? The one who came to the shrine in Doylestown?" I'm trying to put it together before he tells me.

"No, that was John Paul II. I'm talking about the Italian-born priest who was his predecessor. The one who died thirty-three days after his election."

"Did you say, thirty-three days?" My numbers again. "Tell me, please."

"Your grandfather and Albino, the pope's birth name, were both Freemasons at the same lodge in Sicily, which is forbidden by Church law. None of this is substantiated of course, except by us. But if you go online and Google it, the way you kids do these days, you'll find plenty of conspiracy theories."

"You bet I'm gonna jump on that!"

"Be my guest," he says with a laugh. "Long before Albino became a pope, he was a very skilled writer and researcher, extremely well read. The day of his death, he was found with a book in his hand, so they say. We believe he was found with information in his hand about the Church, a dark secret he was about to expose. But we'll never know the truth. Too many cover-ups." My mouth is so wide that I almost forget to swallow. I'm three seconds from drooling.

"Our Order has always studied the practices of the Roman Catholic Church. Historically, they're the most documented, and don't forget, they were the first Christian church."

"The one true church as Nonna always said. But wait, Nonna said my grandfather was a journalist."

"Giuseppe Ricci was a gifted journalist, specializing in Roman Catholic affairs, scandals and sects. He was a living testament to very secret and very sacred information. Our Order sniffed him out and wanted him here. They paid him substantially to settle his family in Manhattan. He was able to provide the Order with great knowledge, particularly about the Knights Templar and Opus Dei, stuff so off record even the Cardinals don't know about it." He pauses and looks me in the eyes. "Before I forget, you must continue to align yourself with the Catholic Church, Jenny. My path remains outside it, under non-denominational sects. Together, we divide and conquer all the mysteries of faith. That's why we're given religious freedoms, to learn from one another."

"Makes sense. Well, what happened to my grandfather? Nonna couldn't possibly have known any of this."

"She did not and will not. Neither will your mother. He had a heart attack exactly thirty-three days after they moved here."

"Stop it. Stop it!" I stand up and start pacing but my father continues.

"Mind you, this was years before the pope's death, but I assume you see a pattern. The number three doubled. The first three represents faith in the Trinity. The second three, symbolizes a lack of perceived loyalty to it."

"What about Danny and me? Our special numbers are 3 threes."

"Different all together. You're blessed by the angels, but it also means your life in faith will be turbulent." I sigh a little with relief.

"Back to Danny. How did he end up in Rome?"

"Everything happens for a reason, Jenny. Isn't that what Christianity preaches?" My head is reeling from all of this information, but I keep at it.

"Did you love my mother?"

"Yes, I did. She was a handful, but I loved her in a special way. Things went terribly wrong. They weren't supposed to. I was committed to our family."

After this information dump, I know that I'll never turn my back on my home again. There's no going back to Baltimore. This is where I belong, and even if tortured again, I won't give up my family's secrets. I look back at my father, aching with sadness. If he wasn't so damaged and deranged, we'd be here together for the remainder of his life. I have one last question in me.

"The children who learn things so early, like Adam and Lexi. How do they keep from blabbing to other school children?"

"Great question. I chose not to introduce you and Danny to any aspect of our Order early on, mostly because we were nestled in New Jersey and your mother was not a member. Once we moved here, it was for your own good until I could figure things out."

"Right. Because of our enemies."

"You know, honey, after what happened to my mother, I wasn't sure if I was ever going to teach you our ways. I really just wanted you and Danny to have normal lives. But I gave in to the pressure of the responsibility and tradition of our culture. And here you are. When you marry someday, you can decide what your own children know and don't know. If you start them early, they should be home-schooled and only play with children in the society. No television. Lots of repetitive teachings."

"Brainwashing?"

"Well, you need a certain mindset, combined with a fear factor. Children need to know the consequences early about breaking the rules. That's how they fall in line. I think that's enough for now, but you have almost a full day ahead of you to do some exploring. Did your uncle tell you about the code near the mouth of the cave behind the barn?" He chuckles to himself. "You know, the one I told you was filled with copperheads to scare you and Danny."

"Yes, he told me."

"Truth is, it always scared me a little. I've only been in there a few times. Check out the formation. I always thought it looked like the mouth of evil, like a serpent. I've said many prayers over it. You could say I'm just a little superstitious. Explore, but be careful. If you sense evil, leave immediately. My grandmother used to tell me there was a force down there so powerful, it could make or break you, for good or evil."

"Well, holy shit, Dad! I'm not sure I want to go down there now. At least not alone. Can I wait for Danny?"

"No. That's not how this is going to work. The remainder of your day ends in the cavern. You got this. Let's get a move on. I hear children. I don't want them recognizing either one of us."

On the way back to the truck, I ask my father if any scientific experiments were ever conducted in the cave underneath Red Rock Farm.

"No. The rock is the same, but the air is much different and enclosed. Too much could go wrong," he says.

I can buy that, knowing what happened to Lucia's parents. He adds that no one but Danny and I is to have access to the area, with the exception of Veronica if she wants it. But that's it. It offers some mental relief because I wouldn't want future initiates roaming the property. It's mine now, and I'm more protective than ever.

# 35

### INTO THE SERPENT'S MOUTH

The wine does the trick. I'm ready to face the cave. I've still got all the gifts the Grand Masters gave me during my opening ceremony, including the necklaces, pins, and weird lighter Mr. Brandt gave me. I've tried to turn it on multiple times, but nothing happens. I have to assume it's simply symbolic of fire. I'm also bringing a super bright LED flashlight and a hammer to listen for the tones that make the rocks so mysterious. And as always, I'm carrying the coins Josh gave me on Christmas, half for luck and half because I like them close to my heart, even though it breaks a bit every time I think of him.

As I approach the cave, I notice what I haven't before. My father is dead-on. The opening really does look like a serpent's mouth. There's a bulging section of rock that looks like an eyeball and a pointy part that looks like a fang. If there were two fangs, I wouldn't go in without Danny. No way in hell.

I have the full-on heebie-jeebies as I put my hand inside the opening of the mouth. I need to brush away twigs and leaves to find the secret panel with the code. I'm still convinced there could be copperheads lurking inside. I find it, take a deep breath, and punch in the code. I guess I was expecting something to open up in front of me but instead a small door opens downward, bringing a large layer of debris with it.

I scan the property to make sure Shane, Veronica, or the FBI aren't watching before heading down. There aren't any stairs, just layers of natural rock descending into the cavern. I'm trying to decide whether or not to close the door. If I do, how will I get out? I decide to leave it open and venture down with the flashlight on. Once down, I'm struck by the marvel of what's before me. The subterranean boulder field isn't as large as the one at Ringing Rocks, but it's impressive. Above me is flat shale rock, but everything on the ground is diabase rock. I use the hammer to test a few. They all ring, even louder than the exposed boulder field due to the echoing effects of the chamber. Nothing scurries, which offers me a little relief that I don't have to dodge bats, rats, or snakes. But the air is heavy and eerie. I feel like I've already seen enough and am tempted to get out, but I know there's much more to it than rocks. *Explore,* my father said. What am I supposed to find?

I'm mentally plotting my strategy when I hear a loud bam followed by darkness. No way! I get the jitters followed by the goosebumps. I'm locked in. "What the fuck!" I scream and pound up at the door for someone to let me out. I can't be certain if someone locked me in or if the door was set to automatically close. I wait until the shakes die down and try to rationalize the situation. If worse comes to worst, I'll be found when Danny comes home. He'll have to reach out to my father, and they'll find me. I decide to press on, clutching the hammer for dear life. I quickly learn it's virtually impossible to hold the hammer and flashlight without falling, so I take a good look around and slip the hammer into the side of my yoga pants.

I decide to give this test my all. Find anything I can to make the Grand Masters proud of me. I make my way deeper and deeper into the underground boulder field, looking for something grandiose.

Every so often, I take out the hammer and give the rocks a ring. They're all live. I hear the very faint sound of water to my right and follow it. I lose my balance a few times trying to jump dry rocks, but each time manage to catch myself before doing any physical damage. The last thing I need is to seriously injure myself down here. I shine the flashlight to the right and see moisture on the rocks above. I move in that direction. The cave is well-endowed with geological formations, including large stalagmites, stalactites, and crystals. It must be very old. The internal boulder field ends at the edge of an underwater stream. I have a hunch that if I follow it to the left, it'll take me right to the creek, perhaps up and through another cave entrance.

Now I know how some of the men may have entered our property in the middle of the night, seemingly out of nowhere. They probably used this passageway to gain access to the property and then right up and into the barn. They one-upped me on a few occasions over the summer too. It's probably how someone snuck onto the property and locked Jodi in the chicken coop. The memory is vivid, and I have to suppress the urge to cry.

My father must assume I'll follow the creek bed all the way to the end and up and out. I loosen up a bit, knowing there's most definitely another way out. Something about the sound of the water is soothing. It's very shallow and clean. I could head right out, but I still have plenty of time, so I decide to explore the opposite end. It's tighter, and I have to duck under a jagged rock ceiling and walk through deeper water, but something is calling to me and I'm not good at ignoring my inner voices.

Was this underground anomaly simply a passageway for members, or is there more to it? The answer comes quick as I hit a dead end. I point the flashlight in every nook to make sure I'm not missing anything, but I only spot a small section where water is slowly trickling in through a small sliver. So much for this! I turn around and shine the light along the rock wall to my left and spot a narrow opening in the shale rock above me. There's no obvious or easy way to get up without a ladder. But there's a jagged rock wall on the opposite side where I may be able to climb to get a better look.

I take off my sopping wet sneakers and look for grooves to climb in my bare feet. I slip on the first one, lose my balance, and wind up right back where I started. The flashlight has become a burden. I memorize the sections I'm aiming for and tuck the flashlight in my pants too. I'm going to have to go at this blind, feeling my way instead. It forces me to concentrate. When I max out of headroom, I steady myself with one hand and shine the flashlight toward the opening. It's a decent-sized opening. I could totally crawl through it if only it were possible to get up there. I squint to zero in on what looks like scratch marks near the opening. The scratches are too big to be from a flying or crawling rodent species. I put the flashlight back down my pants and stop to think. I have all the gifts for luck on me, but none are going to help me hop over there. I pull out the bizarre lighter Mr. Brandt gave me and give it a flick. A mysterious blue flame ignites, which is not something I saw in the light of day or in the house. I turn off the flashlight altogether and try again. The cavern is suddenly luminescent and aglow. The scratches are actually cave drawings, and they're everywhere. I make out symbols and stories, men with spears, and even a few woolly mammoths. I'm in awe. More history is revealing itself, this time right on my own property.

If archaeologists knew about this cave, it would be worth millions, but even better, it may unlock important historical facts. But my property, which sits aside a vast meadow, a babbling creek, and our beautiful home would be history too. I'm about to ease my way down when another marking catches my eye near the opening I was hoping to reach. It's written on an angle, but clear as day, I see the word, "help."

A chill runs down my spine, wondering when it was written and by whom. It's amplified my interest, so there's no abandoning it now. I'm determined to find a way over there. I scale back down and search for anything to help me climb up the smooth rock to gain access. I've got the lighter, the flashlight, and my brain at work. Combined, they help me faintly see several areas that look patchy. I run my hand over a spot that feels more like clay than rock. It's similar to the clay we found in the cave under Lake Nockamixon. It shatters like pottery. I smash three more and expose what was once a natural ladder, one that's been used over the years then hidden.

I put all of my gear back down my yoga pants and climb up to a flat platform. I sit and shine my new inanimate best friend, the lighter. There are a few more Indian drawings on the outside, but none on the inside. I'm going in.

I go at it, tummy down in a crab crawl, dragging the flashlight along with me. I feel a breeze and smell an overwhelming metallic odor, like rotten eggs. It's sulfur. I'm feeling my way and using all of my senses to try and anticipate what may be ahead. I'm a good twenty feet inside the rocky slit when my hand is free and into a larger open space. I position myself head-first through the opening with feet trailing behind and shine the flashlight. It opens into a very large cavern with a flat rock ceiling and huge geological formations to either side. But below is nothing but abyss. I wish I had glow sticks to see how far down it may go. I've worked too hard at this to go back. *Think.*

I shine my light from side to side. It's risky, but I see a ledge that I could possibly drop onto to my right. The problem is, I may not get back up and there's about a twenty percent chance I'll fall. Where to, I don't know. Who would write the word, "help," and what if the person is still down here? "Hello?" I call out. The only answer is my own voice echoing back to me.

I decide to go for it and crouch down, ready to take a big leap, but feel something at my fingertips. I shine the light for confirmation. It's a rope, the same kind of rope Danny and I swung from in the barn. Maybe it's from the same spool. Perfect! I start pulling it up and hear a clanking. There's something attached to it. I use my arm to measure how long the rope is and count about thirty feet before I pull up a bucket. For access to spring water? That's a bit extreme. I shine my light inside the bucket and get a sick feeling. The contents include a bowl and a thermos. This is what Katie found in the barn when she moved in. Someone was jailed and fed down here. For what reason? For punishment? For protection? There's really only one way for me to know for sure. I'm going down.

## 36

HELL ON EARTH

I figure if the rope with the bucket goes down thirty feet, the bucket must be within reaching distance of its intended target. Maybe there're another six feet from the top. I yank on the rope to see how secure it is and how much weight it could withstand. It's tightly fastened with hardware drilled into one of the rocks, making it plenty sturdy. I put the flashlight back in my pants and check to make sure I haven't lost anything on the way. I've got all of my gifts and the hammer. *Here goes nothing.* I remove the bucket, throw the rope back down, and form a loop for a good grip. I climb down as fast as I can, knowing my strength won't last long at a slow pace. I hear water below and all around me. It's unsurprisingly chilly and I regret not wearing a sweatshirt. But I couldn't have foreseen this little detour.

Just as my arms begin to shake, I feel the end of the rope, as well as an opening with my legs. I hang on with one arm and shine the flashlight with the other. Yep! There's a cavern entrance at my feet and I have a plan to get in, but no time for a plan to get out. I kick off the wall, swing like Tarzan and release in time to fall flat on my ass into the cavern. I turn on the flashlight to find old tattered blankets and pillows, plus a notepad and Bible. There are notches on the wall going in fives. I count enough to make out eight months and three days. *Holy mother of God.* Someone was down here for that long? Who? My father couldn't have known about this cavern when he sent me down here. I bet my grandfather was locked up down here. When his parents couldn't keep him in the crawlspace Danny and I found, they may have resorted to this space for punishment, or even to hide him from the rest of the members.

A very eerie feeling overcomes me again. My great-grandparents must have tried everything to avoid resorting to something as disturbing as this. I open the Bible; It's musty and moldy but otherwise intact. Then I open the notepad, see what's on the first page, and drop it like it's on fire. I caught the glimpse of a sketched demon with red eyes and a grotesque face. A drawing inspired by imagination or from memory? I take a deep breath and feel the air thicken all around me. I pick it back up again and leaf through. There are images of evil, hell, demons, sacrifices, and bloody bodies. I feel bile rise in the back of my throat. I don't want to be here anymore. I try to drum up the feelings I had as I glided through the cloud angel. I feel like I've experienced both heaven and hell in the span of two days. I turn the notepad over to find a message in cursive, *If you want to worship the devil, you will live like one. Repent or face the consequences.*

Okay, I've had enough. Still assuming this was my grandfather's underground prison, he would have gone mad down here if he weren't already. Who has answers for this? Uncle Thomas, the Imperator? There's no way my father could know, or he wouldn't have sent me down here. *Would he?* I have to remember there's no rhyme or reason for what he does. Maybe he knows about it and covered up the natural grooves himself with pottery clay, hoping to hide it forever.

I need an escape plan out of here, and fast. I flick the lighter again, hoping to reveal something of relevance. There are no Lenape cave drawings to discover here. I crawl to the edge of the prison cavern and look down. There's water, but I have no idea how deep it is. If it's deep, it's survivable, assuming I don't break every bone in my body on the way down. I see more dry rock beyond it. But whoever was in here couldn't get out. Or maybe someone told him he couldn't, and he believed it.

It's decision time. Grab the rope, climb up, and follow the course my father is likely expecting me to take out, or explore some more. Sometimes, I wish I would just take the safe route. For certain, I can't risk losing the flashlight, so I take off my shirt and wrap it tightly around it, hoping to pop up quickly and ward off any water damage. I second-guess my decision a hundred times before taking the plunge.

The cold water knocks the breath out of me, but it's nice and deep. I didn't come close to hitting the bottom, but I did get a mouthful of very metallic tasting water. Now that I know the pool is very deep and that the water is completely still, I'm reasonably sure I'm screwed. There's no water way out. The taste wouldn't have been so strong if it were a moving spring. I swim over to dry rock and put my drenched shirt back on. I'm shivering and know this isn't good. I hold my breath as I test the flashlight. Phew! It still works. I shine it around the cavern, which is quite large. Water is actively dripping in several places from the rock ceiling, down the walls and into the water hole. I'm racking my brain and cursing myself out. I don't want Danny and my father to be the ones to find me, and I may freeze to death before then anyway.

I have to keep moving. I grab a rock and begin marking the area with it so I can find my way back. I make it through spaces only a petite woman like myself could shimmy through. That is ... until I'm stuck. I'm stuck in a space that looks like it will get me into a much larger cavern. The rock above me is jagged and digging into my chest. I can't flip. I can't do anything. Inch by inch, I back out. *Bloody hell!* I examine the space again. This is it. It's this way or go back and wait until I'm found. I try the opening again, this time on my stomach. I feel the scratches on my back but keep inching. My head is out, but I can't reach the flashlight. I have to reshape parts of my body like a cat trying to squeeze through a fence. But at last, I'm free.

I take in deep breaths to replenish the oxygen I lost holding it in and shine the light. Something very unique gets my attention. If my eyes aren't deceiving me, it looks like a pyramid ahead. I steady myself on slippery rocks and slowly edge my way toward it. It's more than just a resemblance, it is a pyramid. A perfect pyramid like the shape of the giant incinerator we discovered last summer where they cremated people. This one is much smaller, coming up to my chin but quite solid. There are no other loose stones. Whoever did this placed the stones here purposefully and permanently. I flick the lighter Mr. Brandt gave me, hoping it will reveal secret clues, but it doesn't. I circle the pyramid looking for anything to enlighten me, but there's nothing written, English or other.

I'm freezing and jump up and down for warmth. After my fairly extensive Rosicrucian research, I believe this is the final resting place for at least one person.

I move beyond it, ducking down to get into the deepest corner beyond the pyramid. As I do, I see an opening to yet another cavern. How far am I going to take this? I'm lost and getting really nervous. I still have images of demons dancing around in my head. Images my grandfather might have drawn. I'm starting to hear things. Whispers. I sense danger. I'm freezing and sweating from adrenaline at the same time.

I shine the light in front of me and see markings of a different sort. A Rosicrucian Rosy Cross is the largest, followed by elaborate pentacles, geographical lines, the planets and constellations.

I'm busy studying when I hear my name. "Jenny!"

I freeze. The voice is familiar, but I'm paranoid that I'm imagining things. I hold my breath and listen.

"Jenny, it's Jack. Are you there?"

"Jack?" Now I'm thoroughly confused but call out for him. "I'm here."

He reaches me and takes me in for a giant bear hug. "You're freezing." He opens his North Face jacket and pulls me in. The warmth is just in the nick of time. Jack Dorcy, who I haven't seen since the day of my punishment trial, is geared up for exploration, looking like something out of an Eddie Bauer magazine. He's got some questions to answer.

"How'd you know I was down here?"

"I saw you go into an opening in the rocks behind the barn."

"From where?"

"I didn't know there was an entrance there. I found an entrance much further away and always had a hunch they met but never found a way. It's a good thing I came down when I did." He rubs my back. "How did you get in here? I've been here at least a dozen times, but always hit a dead end."

I don't answer the question because he hasn't really answered mine. "Jack, where the hell were you when you saw me go in?"

I hear a throat clear. "Excuse me, Jack. Aren't you going to introduce me to the much-acclaimed, Jennifer O'Rourke?"

I look at Jack for an explanation as a tall figure steps out from the shadows. He looks to be in his sixties, dressed simply in a pair of blue jeans, a purple polo, goose down black vest, and hiking boots. His grey beard needs some manscaping.

"Of course. Jenny, this is Dean Banos. He's the Grand Master of the largest Rosicrucian Order in the United States. But it was a local chapter in Bensalem, Knights of the Rosy Cross, who called upon him to investigate your father's Order."

I let the Grand Master part go in one ear and out the next. "Again, how did you know I was here and where've you been, Jack? Have you been spying? You haven't been in Boston at all have you?"

"Protecting you more like it, Jenny. I wouldn't call it spying."

"And which Rosicrucian Order, Dean?"

"The Ancient and Mystical Order Rosae Crucis."

"AMORC."

"You've heard of us?"

"Of course. Your Order is like my father's, same kind of esoteric formula."

"It's not the same!" I make Dean intentionally mad and watch his face get red by the insult. "Punishment is up to the universe, not mankind. Gifts found in nature are meant to be shared, not stolen or hidden. I'm quite sure that's just the beginning of our differences."

"Listen, I don't have time for this," I say impatiently. "Why are you here, and what do you want from me?"

"Dean is establishing himself on the property at the Twenty-Fifth Acre. His chapter has purchased the land."

"So, you're the one. There's been a lot of speculation about who you are and what you're up to. What are you up to?" I'm suddenly not appreciating this ambush, but at the same time, I walked into some important intel.

"Don't worry, it's all good, Ms. O'Rourke," he laughs. "The new location will certainly be an illuminating improvement over the darkness that was there. We're building a beautiful chapel, memorial gardens, and the proper school to teach children about ancient mystical truths versus what they've endured over the years. Your father's Order, what's it called again?"

"Wasn't aware it had a name." *Nice try, asshole.*

"Well, whatever it may be, it needs transmutation, or you could call it a transformation. No more barbaric punishments. And historical findings, such as this cave, will be revealed for others to appreciate and study. Authentic Rosicrucians do not hide like this. We are not a secret Order in the sense that only a small few are privy to the information, only the commitment to it. We believe in being as transparent as possible about our culture."

*This guy is as good as dead.* Even though busting up my father's Order is what I've wanted, I'm not a fan of someone else doing it. "How many people are privy to this location or are spying on my father's fraternity, Mr. Banos?"

He laughs. "Fraternity you're calling it, are you? Well, despite how abundant in numbers we are, I'm taking this on as my own personal project. Too dangerous to move the whole flock so to speak."

"I'd be careful if I were you. You're going to get yourself, and maybe your whole flock, killed. And I'm personally and officially warning you that you're on private property. And what makes you so sure this particular flock wants transmutation, and what business is it of yours?"

Jack shifts uncomfortably. "This is the perfect solution, Jenny. Dean can help bring about order without a big deal from the Feds. He can work with the villagers to regain peace and safety. Something's changed about you, and it's concerning."

"Without a big deal? You're kidding me, right? You've met my father, no? Thanks to you, Jack, this land is now mine and I'll decide who sees it and when." My head is starting to hurt, and I need to move forward with my day. They must be aware that I'm in the middle of an initiation. "Jack, how exactly did you get involved and when?"

"I've known about this cavern and the pyramid since Katie and I moved to the farm. But like I said, I didn't know there was another entrance. The one you went through is new to me but it sure as shit was right in front of my face, huh?" He scratches his head.

"Why did you keep this information from me?"

"Research. Sorry, Jenny. I'm a hopeless journalist just trying to make sense of it all. That's how I met Dean. We've been working together since the summer. I'm following the AMORC teachings now. I've learned so much and it's helped get me through Katie's death." He looks at me for approval, but I'm annoyed and consider the lack of details a lack of loyalty. "I'm helping fund Dean's project as well as helping him build the new lodge. Now that you know, will you help us?" Jack asks.

"Help you how?"

"I assume you're in the middle of initiation? When you're finished, find us. Tell us what you know so we can make this right."

"I'm not committed to any religion or Order. I'm here for my own closure, Jack. You know this."

"We're not a religion," Dean interjects.

"Cult then," I snap.

"Jenny, chill out," Jack says.

I'm contemplating what to do here. I need Danny's opinion, and maybe even Veronica's. I don't know how to deal with this situation on my own. If I tell my father, he'll kill them both and wreak havoc on Dean's AMORC chapter. I wouldn't want that either.

"Where are you staying for now, Dean?"

"I'm on the property. I can't say much else, but I've got a close watch on the farm at all times." *Not for long.*

"Here's my advice to you both. Actually, it's not advice. Let's call it Jenny's Order. Stay off my property. Stay out of my way starting now, understand? I work alone. If you get too close to me again, I'll spill it to the leaders, and there'll be a holy war. This thing your people have about karma, it's gonna bite you in the ass if you interfere. Got it? Now show me your way out, please."

"Ms. O'Rourke, I understand the position we've put you in. Just think about it. I know you'll do the right thing. We know that transformation will take time, and the last thing we want is for someone to get hurt."

I follow them through more caverns. Jack stops abruptly to let me know the property line ends where we're standing.

"Who owns the property from here on out?"

"I do, Jenny. I purchased it from an ex-member of the group whom I helped flee. It once belonged to Christopher Brandt though. Interesting, don't you think? The house on the river isn't the only house I built with the money I made."

Spying, lying traitor. No wonder it was so easy for him to just turn the deed of the house over to me. He wasn't really going anywhere. I grab a loose stone and draw a line. "Then after today, you stay on your side and I'll stay on mine. Got it? Now let's see that exit."

## 37

IS THAT A THREAT?

Jack literally built a small cabin on top of an exit out of the hidden caverns on my property. Danny and I are going to have to seal it off somehow. At least he admitted that he hasn't yet found a way up into the creepy punishment cavern or into the internal magnetic boulder field with all the Lenape drawings. He thinks his big find was the pyramid and Rosicrucian markings. The same goes for the EORCUF side. I have to assume my father and friends aren't aware of this route. Or maybe they're just unaware that the two caves connect.

Jack said Christopher Brandt, Shane's incarcerated father, used to own the property up above Red Rock Farm. It surprises me, and I wonder if Shane's aware. If so, he's never said anything, which is peculiar. Their family home is off of Deep Creek Road and currently vacant. He said he'd rather be here because the house depresses him, and he prefers being with Veronica. Hell, we invited him to stay here, so I can't accuse him of any wrongdoing, but I suddenly realize how little I know about Shane's immediate family. He's always just tagged along with his cousins, Ryan and Jackie. What if Shane locked me in the cave? He could've easily seen me go in. I'm on high alert and am not fucking around. I decide to exit right out of Jack's little cabin and storm back to get some answers.

Before leaving, Dean invites me to attend a special service at the local chapter in Bensalem where he is guest-speaking. I decline and am a bit taken aback by his nerve. He'd better hope I don't come, or I'll bring anarchy with me.

I agree to protect what I know about Jack's cabin and my new neighbor, although I think they underestimate my father and the others. Even Josh must know who has really moved into the village. The Historical Society has a way of snooping. They all know by now. What they plan on doing about it, I'll know soon enough on this fast track to membership. I have my father's words running through my head. "What do we do if someone threatens our way of life?" I'm a little concerned about the well-being of this new AMORC chapter and irritated that they're putting themselves in this dangerous situation.

On my way out the door, Jack makes a surprising move. He pulls me aside and threatens *me*. He threatens to give me up if I say anything. He tells me I'll go down first if I say a word to my father or any of the others. "It's time to bring the bad people down, take the village down to its rafters, and rebuild something truly special." I think about what he's saying carefully. Had he started the conversation more carefully, leading with the idea of bringing down the bad people, and not with the personal threat, I may have taken it better.

But Jack didn't choose his words wisely, and I've been through too much to let a little pissant like him bring down my Order. Something very protective stirs inside me again. I suppress the urge to verbally threaten him in return but give him a glare that says it all.

"It was good seeing you, Jack. Shall I tell Veronica of your whereabouts, or does she already know what her father's up to?"

"Glad you brought that up. How is she? Is Shane treating her well? I hope she's happy."

He has no idea. Not a clue that she's about to start her initiation ceremony in a few days. "Very happy."

"I'll leave it up to you what to tell her."

"Fine." I turn to Jack's new pal. "Nice meeting you, Dean." I open the door and step into the woods for the trek back to the farm. I know I'm a bit northwest of the house from here. I check my watch and am surprised to see it's only 4:00 p.m. Danny will be home by dinner, and we can sort this out.

The farmhouse is in sight, but so is something unwelcome. Police cars. State police and the FBI are in the driveway. They're in the house, and Agent Edwards is in handcuffs. It was only a matter of time before he was discovered by his own agency, but this is trouble. I make out Shane and Veronica in the driveway. Veronica has her hand over her mouth like she's utterly shocked. The Feds nabbed Edwards only. Thankfully, he was the only target today and won't give anything up. He's way too loyal to my father. Now what? I'm still a missing and very wanted person, so I can't get near the house. They're going to find women's clothing inside. They'll know I've been back unless Veronica is fast on her feet.

I suddenly get the most unwelcome thought. What if Shane and Veronica are responsible for this? What if they're working with Jack to spill the rest of the big story for him? Whose side are they on? I have to stop and listen to myself. Whose side am I on? My heart is with Josh and with the people I've learned to love in the Order. I desperately need to talk to Josh for counsel.

I sit hidden and wait. Edwards was Danny's ride home from Van Sant. At least he was my ride home after Day Two. When he doesn't show, the internal alarm system will go off. Me without a damn phone. Finally, I see a car pull into the driveway and Danny jumps out. Two federal agents approach him. Scott was driving and is asked to exit the car. Danny's very animated and walks up to the car where they have Edwards. He's screaming, "Where's my sister!" Oh, no. This is bad.

I have no choice but to turn around and ask Jack for help. I don't have to go far. It appears he's been hidden behind me the whole time. Just watching. Spying. Jack was once like family to me. Now, I don't trust him. He's dangerous. But he'll have to do for now. I need him to go down there and stop the bleeding.

Jack and I huddle together and make a quick plan. He darts off, but I have no choice but to wait and watch. Danny is scanning the property looking for me. I'm so frustrated.

As planned, Jack rolls into the driveway. He's frisked and questioned before being allowed to embrace his daughter. I wish I could see their expressions, because it's too hard to read them from here. How much does Jack know? Veronica and Shane were to keep the secret aspects of the house private, even from Jack. That includes the tunnel stretching from the barn to the house. I'm fearful those details may be breached.

Finally, Jack makes his way to Danny, gives him a hug, and pats him reassuringly on the back. He must be whispering something in his ear. Danny tries to look casual, but he looks up in my direction. He knows I'm safe, so that leaves me able to move. I decide to explore the perimeters of the property to pass the time. I wish I had Fabrizio with me to help me locate any kind of spy system Jack set up and destroy it. Think like a hunter, I tell myself. Check for tracks, broken branches, anything that could resemble an area that's been tampered.

At this point, my father, the Feds, Fabrizio, possibly Josh, and now Jack could have monitoring systems around the house. It's like a spy fest, and I realize it probably hasn't been a good idea for me to be here. I decide to head over to Douglas's memorial which should still stand at the border of our property and the Brandts,' minus his remains, which are in the Catholic cemetery now. I climb up the tree stand I've used so many times in the past. It reminds me of Sal and fills me with sadness. The memorial is still there, with fresh flowers in front. I see movement beyond it. It's Ryan, Alicia, and Markus. They're armed and ready for action, pointing in separate directions toward my house.

"Ryan!" I call out. I need to put a stop to whatever the hell this is.

I meet the three of them at the base of the tree. "Where've you been? I got a call from Shane that you're missing."

"When?"

"About three hours ago. Then I got a call that Edwards' identity is blown."

Boom! It hits me like a brick. Shane's been one of them all along. He's already been initiated. My evolving theory is that he's worked by Ryan's side for all of these years to look after him mostly. He loves his cousin, but he's known more all of this time. Damn, he's almost too good! But it adds up. Ryan's always been somewhat unstable and hasn't been ready. Same with Jackie. They were sent away while our fathers built up their weird empire. Mr. Brandt probably couldn't deal with children after losing a wife and son. They would've gotten in his way during his idea of healing. Revenge healing. But I'd bet a million bucks that Shane never went anywhere. That's why he knows so many more people, including Greg, so well.

I can probably cross Shane off my list as someone working with Jack. He's here to protect the Order. But he knows new secrets, including our plan to overthrow the system and hasn't said anything. Somewhere along the way, he's taken our side. Maybe he's truly in love with Veronica and wants a fresher, healthier start. It also means he's hid a lot from Ryan. Shane's been a resource of information for my father and Mr. Brandt, clearly not accurate information or we'd all be dead or in some sort of homegrown jail.

As I'm trying to put it all together, the three of them are staring at me.

"What?" I ask.

"Jenny, we know you well enough. Please say what's on your mind."

I decide to throw it out there. "Shane's already a member."

"Not possible," Ryan refutes. "We tell each other everything. I mean, look what we've all been through together. He was shot, remember? No way."

"Yep. I remember. I sewed him back together. But I'd check into that boarding school he said he went to. I never asked, but where's Shane's mother?"

"She died during childbirth."

"Where's she buried?"

"How would I know?" Ryan starts to think and pace.

I'll bet it's Shane's mother whose remains are buried under the pyramid. While I have Ryan in front of me, I probe.

"Why did you decide to get initiated all of a sudden? I thought you wanted a normal life."

"It's time to blow this shit open, Jenny. Only then can I get on with my life. This is insanity. This whole system is insane, and you freaking know it more than anyone. That's still your plan, right? To blow it open? After next week, this is done. We see first-hand what all the bullshit is about, and then we're out. You. Me. Alicia. Shane and Veronica. Out. Got it?"

"Michael's right," Alicia says. "It's time to let this go and move on."

"Michael?" I look at Ryan and roll my eyes. "How long have the two of you actually known each other anyway?"

"We met in Baltimore, Jenny. She didn't know any of this. That's what I wanted and needed back then. Someone I could trust who wasn't connected to Brandtville."

I look back at Alicia and point my finger at her. "Then, you don't get a voice here." I point it back at Ryan. "And she still shouldn't know any of this. You're putting her in danger. It's not her problem, it's ours."

"Knock it off. My problem is her problem. That's how a good relationship works."

"Seriously? You're lecturing me about a good relationship?" Ryan backs down knowing I'm about to light him up. "We take it out when I say, *Michael*. That's the deal. Got it?" I say, heated.

"As long as it all ends next week, got it," he replies. This is getting us nowhere. We sound like the couple, not Ryan and Alicia. I look at my watch and realize this was Ryan's Day One, so I ask him how it went.

"Since I procrastinated, Jackie went first. Fuck, I have to get to my Initiation Ceremony by 5:00 p.m. What time is it?"

"Um, time to run. I need to talk to you first."

Alicia doesn't care for the request, but Ryan dismisses her with a wave. We stand near a large oak tree that's just starting to bloom.

"What? Make it quick." I toss aside my internal Ryan baggage and rationally ask him to wait until he's finished with his initiation before doing anything rash. He mocks me like I'm crazy to think anything's going to change his mind. I can't help but wonder if his horrible attitude will destroy his initiation experience. I grab his arm before he can walk away "We're both a little bit fucked up right now, Ryan. Don't fuck this up. Take the next five days as serious as I am. You're gonna learn a lot. Please, keep an open mind or you won't get it. You deserve to get it."

"Get what? What am I in for here?"

"Please?" He looks beyond me. "And when you do get it, don't share it. Not even with her for now." He looks from me to Alicia. "I mean it, Ryan." Maybe there's something about the way I'm touching him that settles or confuses him. I still have a gentle grip on his arm. He looks at my hand and into my eyes. He's lost. He's so lost that it makes my eyes water. I see a glaze come over his eyes too. I don't like to see him hurt.

"For you, Jenny, I'll still do anything. Happy? I'll go in with an open mind." He releases himself from my grip. I'm a good part of the reason he's so fucked up. Tears flow freely now from both my eyes. He looks back and sees me wipe them away. His gait shifts and he's racing to get home in time. He's off to see the wizards.

# 38

DEVIL INSIDE

Ryan is off for initiation and Alicia storms off toward the estate. Markus stays behind to escort me to wherever I want to go. I have to admit, it's great seeing him. He was by far my favorite of Ryan's security advisors. At my request, he calls Danny to reassure him that I'm safe, then hands me a water bottle and a power bar. We sit and talk for a few minutes. He confirms what I'm fearing. Ryan is coming unglued. He's on the verge of a nervous breakdown and has it in his head that when this over, everything will be better. Markus and Alicia have had a lot of late-night talks without Ryan knowing. She's confided in him how difficult Ryan's been and admitted there's been non-stop fighting. He doesn't sleep and he's still obsessed with me, even though he denies it. How couldn't he be after everything we've been through? I warn Markus that he should probably bail as part of the security team now, because he knows too much. But he wants to see Ryan through this.

"It's like a bad accident. You know you should keep moving, but you need to see just how bad it is for yourself," he says,

I think back to a time not so long ago when I only thought my life was complicated. Back when I had protectors in Baltimore. Ryan

259

being my number one. He was so solid and so sure of himself. I felt safe around him, and I was so in love with him. I shake off the guilt and sentimentality because that time is gone.

It's time to move. With all the Grand Masters in one place for Ryan's opening ceremony and the cops at my door, I actually have an enormous window of opportunity. I'm headed to Shane's childhood home on Deep Creek Road. I want a glimpse into Shane's upbringing, hoping the walls can speak just a little. Markus and I stay close to the forest line and make our way to the creek. We have to go deeper as we near the meadow and the electric fence. The doe looks close to fawning. The rest of the herd is listening. Their ears flip front to back, trying to hone in on a noise. All eyes and ears freeze at a sound in front of them, one that wasn't heard or made by us. We stop and listen. Could be another animal, could be the Feds, could be a journalist. Could be anything. I try not to get too paranoid.

We reach the end of the property and stop at the creek. I need to go it alone from here. It's much more open and we're making too much noise together. Plus, Markus is a big guy and way too easy to spot. We part friendly ways, complete with a fist bump. I can always make my way back to the Brandt Estate if I get desperate. But I'd have to really be desperate to spend the night with Ryan and Alicia.

I cross the creek and make my way up a very steep rocky slope. I stop and listen every now and then, but I appear to be alone. I make it to the top, exhausted and out of breath. I can see the top of Mission Church in the distance. It's just me and my senses moving slowly through the brush as the sun begins to set.

I've gone a good half mile when the house comes into view. The old stone farmhouse is dark and eerie and buried in overgrowth. It's much smaller than my childhood home, about the size of Michael Brandt's guest house. How did Shane's father inherit so little compared to Ryan's father? Maybe he just played the role of a modest police officer, not wanting to draw attention with a mansion. I still have my flashlight, the hammer, and all the initiation gifts on me from my very long day. My feet are wet and cold from the creek, and I'm shivering. But I'm ready. I circle the house looking for access. All the windows are boarded. The hammer is going to come in very handy. I aim for a window that's almost entirely covered by a large shrub. I flip over a rusty old wheelbarrow, balance myself on it, and start tearing out nails with the claw. I leave the last nail in and flip the board to the side. The widow itself is unlocked but not budging. The old wooden frame takes what's left of my strength to finally open. I take a quick look behind me and slip in.

I land in a small office. There are plaques and pictures on the wall of Christopher Brandt winning various law enforcement awards. Now that he's in prison, we can add his mugshot. I'm mostly interested in Shane's old room and find the stairs. There are footprints in the dust so Shane must check on the house, at least from time to time. I investigate all three bedrooms, but they leave nothing to the imagination. There are no pictures on the wall. Just stripped beds and empty closets. I decide to give the basement a quick look before coming up with a plan to crash for the night. I have Day Four ahead of me and it stands to be exciting. I'll be with Mr. Michael Brandt himself at the Fonthill Mansion, home of the founder of the EORCUF Order.

The basement door is unlocked. Despite being extra quiet and careful going down the stairs, I'm leaving wet footprints everywhere. I reach the bottom of a basement with an earth floor. The smell of dirt and mold fills my nasal passageways. At the far end is a raised platform where the water heater and washer and dryer sit. I would hate to haul laundry down here. These walls aren't giving away much of a story.

I decide to investigate a coal shoot before heading back upstairs. There isn't a breeze coming through the semi-grated iron door, which means it's blocked. I shine the light and am surprised by how deep the space appears to go. I take the claw of the hammer and yank the door open. I crawl through to the end which leads to more stairs.

There's police tape scattered about, which means the Feds found whatever it is I'm about to find. But no one ever talked to me about Shane's family. Not even Ted, my dear and trusted FBI friend.

I take a deep breath. What's my sixth sense telling me? It's telling me to leave. I ignore it and descend. The stairs are in better shape than the stairs in the house. I end up in a meeting room of sorts. The floor is tiled and there's a French drain surrounding the room. Curiously enough, the ceiling is made of strong wood beams and thick wood supporting the earth floor above. A good disguise, but not good enough. There's a large chalkboard and conference table in the room. There are two doors. One to a bathroom. The second door opens into a large storage room. I sit on a wooden trunk and open another beside it. Nothing could have prepared me for what I find.

It's full of items only a devil worshipper would keep. There are old books and pictures of demons, similar to the sketches on the notepad I found in the cave. I hop off the box I'm sitting on and open it. It, too, is full of devil worshipping and cult-like gear, including dark masks and upside-down crosses, amidst pentagrams. I open a box and find old photos of a young Shane sitting in the middle of a pentagram. His hands are tied and he's crying. The pentagram contains the numbers 666, certainly not the elements that this Order represents. I'm in utter disbelief and wonder why the bureau didn't take all of this as evidence. It must have been moved and replaced after their investigation. *Freaking why?*

I jump and simultaneously scream at the sound of hearing my name.

"Jenny," Shane says sternly.

I'm on my feet with the hammer in front of me. "Don't come any closer. What the hell is all of this?"

"I can explain. And don't look at me like that. You know me."

"Do I? It was you. You were the one sent into the underground prison for punishment."

Shane takes a deep breath and sits on one of the conference room chairs. I follow him to the opposite side of the table, remaining on my feet.

"You're so right about that, Jenny. So right." He's having flash-backs and covers his face with both hands. He begins rocking back and forth while searching for words.

"Tell me what happened, Shane. That stuff in there. That's devil worshipping stuff. What happened?"

"I found it all down here one day. I snuck down after my father had one of his meetings. Your father wasn't the only one to host them you know. I was about fifteen. I didn't really understand what it was, but it intrigued me. I was rebellious at the time. My father was strict, and I was tired of all the rules."

"Whose stuff was it to begin with?"

"It was your grandfather's."

"I was afraid you were going to say that."

"It was confiscated a very long time ago. They stored it here, my maternal grandparent's original home."

"What happened?"

"Like I said, I was rebellious and looking for trouble. I had no mother, and Jackie and Ryan were sent away. I started playing with this stuff. I went around town drawing the numbers 666 on every-one's sacred pentacles. Lord." He puts his hand over his face again. "So stupid of me. I was mostly just entertaining myself, but I got caught and was sentenced by the members to be punished. I followed in your grandfather's footsteps down in the ground. His old blankets were still there. It was absolutely terrifying. Despite repenting imme-diately, I remained down there for the full two hundred and fifty-two days."

I jump up, take Shane in my arms and let him weep. I'm sickened thinking of a teenaged boy locked in a hellish underground prison, alone for so long.

"It fucked me up. But I persevered. I could've even escaped, just like you did down there, but I stayed. I stayed because I was afraid of what they'd do next, and deep down, I wanted to be accepted again. This was and is still my home."

"Shane, why didn't you tell Ryan?"

"Wasn't allowed. Once I was free, they performed all kinds of rituals on me. I was brainwashed for months. Years really. I became the poster boy of redemption. When Michael came home, it was my job to watch over him as he watched over you. I've never stopped. You've been a total pain in my ass, but I've learned to love you like a sister. Never had one you know."

"Aww, Shane. And I love you like a brother." I give him another hug. "Where exactly do you stand with this group? You've heard everything. You know there's a plan to overthrow my father and your uncle. You say this is your home, but you know there's a plan to end this."

"I know it. I stand with you. I want my own revenge for what they did to me. I'm healed in some ways, Jenny, but an eye for an eye. We say it all the time as part of our code. I want to see the people who really deserve it, eat it. But ..."

"What?"

"When it's over, we must follow the rules of the Order once again. It must be preserved because there's none other like it. Our blessings are abundant, Jenny."

We sit and talk for another hour. Shane does his best to sell me on the many attributes that come with the Order. But he doesn't have to try hard, because I already know in my heart that this is where I belong too. I tell him about Jack and his new friend, Dean. Shane's aware, and the others are too. They've been spying on them as much as they've been spying on us. It's one of the reasons he's staying at the farm. It's put him in a rough spot with Veronica though, who's unaware.

One thing's for certain, Shane's surprised me with his backstory. There's so much more wisdom and depth to him. I look forward to being part of his life for a very long time.

# 39

## THE GLUE

I help Shane spruce up the place a bit and watch him as he works, breaking up the cobwebs and scrubbing the kitchen. I realize he's been the glue keeping it together all of this time. Letting us figure everything out on our own and interfering as little as possible while keeping the Grand Masters happy with the progress we've been making. He's been the one to reassure them that our commitment is real. And they've believed him. Hats off to him for successfully wearing so many himself.

We decide I'll be safest staying with Scott, at least for tonight. I was secretly hoping I could stay with Josh, even though I realize I'd be setting my heart up for more punishment. Now that I know Shane is practically spilling over with inside scoop, I probe him about Josh's relationship with Lucia. I see a look wash over him like he wants to tell me something but can't. He shakes his head and tells me he looks forward to a day when I find true love again. I fear I've had a piece of it a few times but keep letting it go.

A sudden knock at the door makes us both scramble. I dart toward the basement door to take cover if need be. It's Ryan. His initiation ceremony is over, and he came to find out if what I told him was true. If Shane was already initiated. He's angry and confrontational, so I come out of my hiding place to join Shane for moral support.

My presence riles him up even more and it takes all I've got to settle him down to simply listen. The truth is hard on him. He's rightfully upset and feels deceived. I tell him to look at it from Shane's perspective. We may have been sent far away, but he was held prisoner. He had it far worse than we did. An hour of explaining comes and goes. I'm tired and starving and ready to crash.

I call Danny from one of Ryan's burners, and he vehemently advises me to stay away from the farm. I give him the game plan for now. It would take too long to tell him about my full day and all the findings and admissions happening here, but I do warn him about Jack and our new neighbor on the hill. He's surprised and less than thrilled.

I'm dying to know what kind of experience he had with the cloud angel. He said the day was fun and intriguing but thinks I'm naïve to believe the cloud angel was a real phenomenon. Danny dismissed it as a man-made smoke-and-mirror facade. The falls can hide something manufactured that could produce such a mirage using water right from the river. I'm so disappointed and don't want to believe him. Even if it were a man-made production, I left filled with a sense that there's a true Higher Power. That was real. I'm hoping tomorrow will be a more impactful day for him. Science is real to him.

It's late as hell and time to go. Shane and Ryan give each other a brotherly embrace. Things between them are going to be just fine. I slip into the darkness with Ryan, then under a blanket in the back of his new Mercedes SUV. He's gone on a spending spree with his father's money. A man's retail therapy he calls it. We make our way to Scott's cabin, which is tucked away on the top of the hill close to Van Sant Airport. The garage door opens and closes, and I hop out of the SUV. I'm covered in dirt from my long day and stink to the high heavens. I need a shower. Ryan pulls me aside before he leaves.

"This is getting out of control again, Jenny. Nothing good is going to come of this."

"Read tonight. Read and learn. Once you're initiated, we'll have time to come up with a plan. Please? Let's ride this out the rest of the way."

He lets out a big sigh. "I knew you were going to say that, but I don't want any regrets later for not asking. This is fucked up, you know? Living like this."

"I know. But it's going to be better soon. I can feel it."

"I hope you're right."

"Read the book."

"Okay, okay. I'll read the book. See you on the other side then, huh?"

I smile and hold out a hand for him. "I'll always be on your side, Ryan." I lean in and kiss him on the cheek like I would a big brother. He smiles. We're connecting again on a new level. I feel gratitude knowing we're still in this together, even if we're not together.

"All right. Let's get 'er done. I love you, Jenny."

"I love you back. Now go."

I push through the door and into Scott's kitchen. I no longer fear that Ryan will bail before his full initiation. I worry a little about Alicia, but I think Ryan will be tight-lipped after tomorrow.

I'm spoiled with a hot bath, a hot meal, and pajamas. I don't ask if they're Katie's or his late wife's. It doesn't matter. Scott gives me the master bedroom and before you know it, I'm dead to the world.

It's Monday. I rub my eyes and look around and remember that I'm already more than halfway through my initiation. There's a picture of Scott and Katie on his dresser. It makes me ache. She was so innocent in all of this. I can't help but poke around a little as I get dressed and ready to go downstairs. He's got aviation images and certificates on the wall. He's very organized. I open his top dresser drawer to find his socks all lined up by color. Scott has OCD. That's the only thing I've learned.

I head downstairs wondering what my orders are for the day. I have no idea who's picking me up and what time. Breakfast is spread out for me next to a note on the table. Scott is at the airfield with Jackie for her Day Two. He tells me to help myself and that my ride will be here at 1:00 p.m. I'm to dress any way I like, as long as I'm comfortable. He said to go through the spare closet and take what I want. I push back a plaid kitchen curtain and peek out the window just in time to see Jackie learning to fly with Greg. I grin. She's doing pretty well. I hope she has a better experience than Danny.

I pick at my eggs and toast and wonder what my own day will bring. I'm a little intimidated by the thought of being alone with Mr. Brandt. Aside from his obvious evildoings, one thing has stuck with me. The accusation that he's a thief. I remember Josh telling me that he stole from his parents. That they found things but had to give them to Mr. Brandt. Maybe I'll get to see what some of those finding were today. Mostly, I'm just looking forward to a tour of Fonthill, the iconic cement castle, home of Henry Chapman Mercer, the founder of our Order. People from all over the world tour the home, but whatever it is they learn, I'm sure they don't know the beginning of it.

I get dressed and pace. I snoop a little again, trying to learn more about Scott. There's an old family portrait on the wall in the living room. I recognize his daughter, Tracy. She's one of the few school friends I remember from my childhood. When Scott was being interrogated by Fabrizio, he told us she moved to California. I wonder why. Didn't like the lifestyle? Had a fallout? Was never initiated?

It's almost 1:00 p.m. I put on a pair of sneakers and toss a light sweater around my shoulders. The garage door opens, and I feel my heart begin to race. Here we go. My mystery driver is none other than Amy, the nervous young woman who handed me the note about Scott while we were investigating Katie's death. We were staying at the Lambertville Station at the time.

"Good afternoon, Jenny. It's nice to see you again."

"Well, it's nice to see you too."

"Just so you know, I have no affiliation with the society. I'm simply doing Scott another favor by giving you a ride today. I'm not going to ask any questions, and please don't tell me anything. I don't want to know anything to ensure I can pass a polygraph if need be. They need people like me too. I'm paid well for the services I do."

"Fair enough."

"I'm to take you to the cemetery next to the castle. I have directions to a headstone where you're to place a rose on a grave." She hands me one. "Someone will lead you from there. I have no idea where you'll go after that. This is my only assignment. I'll be doing the same tomorrow for Danny, and so on."

"Okay. Let's roll."

I duck down as usual so as not to be seen. This is getting old. The quarters are tight in Amy's Ford Focus. I come up for air once we're back on Route 611. The twenty-minute drive to Doylestown is pleasant. It's another beautiful early summer day. The tulips and daffodils are blooming. Landscapers and a few stay-at-home mom types are milling about, planting annuals and throwing down mulch. It reminds me again of what normal people do. I look forward to a day when gardening is at the top of my priority list.

We pass Fonthill Castle and make a right on Court Street just beyond. The gate to the Doylestown Cemetery is open. It's quite lovely as far as cemeteries go and very well kept. It's peaceful. Amy parks the car and points in the direction I'm to go. I'm to meet a woman in front of General William Watts Hart Davis' headstone. That's the only thing she knows.

"Easy enough." I barely have the door closed before she backs out of the drive and takes off out through gate. Can't blame her.

I head toward an older section of the cemetery. The headstones are difficult to read. This isn't going to be easy. I spot a woman attending to a plot in the general direction I'm aiming for. I walk slowly toward her, desperately trying to read the stones along the way. She's a matronly middle-aged woman with a long grey braid running down her back. She's not wearing makeup and is dressed like a woman from the Civil War era. She's wearing a late 19th century dress with a small floral pattern. What gives?

"Ms. O'Rourke?"

Guess she's my escort. I nod and stand beside her. "My name is Catherine Davis Harrington. This is my great-uncle's grave. You may pay him tribute now." I place the rose in front of the grave and eye her up. "He was a courageous man. A general. In his later years, he was a writer and historian. He founded the Bucks County Historical Society and kept impeccable local genealogical records. One of his protégés was Henry Chapman Mercer. Hal was in his early twenties when he worked with my uncle."

"Hal?"

"Yes, that's what his closest friends and family called Henry."

"Ah." That's what Lucia said when I gave Josh the picture. She said, "Hal." No wonder they both looked surprised by my gift.

"Recordkeeping has been passed down in our family. I took over for mom last year." She looks at me and taps her head. "Dementia. Anyway, I keep records for the Brandtville Historical Society as well as for the Order. You've read some of my work I assume?"

"I have. You've certainly kept very good records. But I fear you're missing a few names on your 'watch out' list."

"Oh?"

I tell her quickly about Tina, Peter, Jack, and Dean. She thanks me and jots down the names on a small notepad. "If you don't mind me asking, what's with your attire?"

She laughs and looks down. "I give historical tours here at the cemetery. I like to get into character to help create a realistic presentation of the era. I have a tour coming at 3:00."

"Oh, I'm a little relieved to hear that." Catherine smiles and proceeds to clip a few thorny, dead branches from the rose bush aside his grave. I don't need to ask to know General Davis was likely a big influence on a much younger Hal, as she refers to him. The roses are symbolic. But this cemetery is not. There aren't any pyramids to be seen. But there sure are a lot of Davis headstones, including a familiar name, General John Davis. Catherine catches me eying up his stone. "John was William's father. The village of Davisville, just to our southeast, was named after him. Are you ready for Day Four of Knowledge, Ms. O'Rourke?" She eyes me up. "Today will be a good one."

"I'm ready, Catherine."

"Very well. Follow me and I'll contact Mr. Brandt when we get close."

She grabs her long braid and brings it forward, playing with it in a childlike manner. She's an odd one. We zigzag through the large cemetery. She can't help but point out a few notable eternal residents. A famous author, an actress, and a judge. I pause at a black granite stone which catches my eye. There's a depiction of Christ praying during the *Agony in the Garden*. I think of how scared Christ must have been in his hour of death, but he trusted and accepted what must be done. It's a solid reminder for me to stay strong and keep the faith, no matter what.

"Ms. O'Rourke, hurry along. We can't read them all."

"Right. Sorry."

We cross a street and take a trail through a wooded area leading to the castle. As we come up behind the majestic building, I see tourists photographing it at every angle. The large red gothic doors and windows catch my attention first.

"Hal was afraid of fire you know."

"Is that right?" How ironic, considering I'm about to embark on my initiation journey into the element of fire.

"That's one of the reasons he built his estate, museum, and business out of cement. Fireproof. He never wanted to worry about a fire burning down his house and all the treasures inside it. The original tile factory burned down though. The one you'll be entering is the second iteration."

"I know a thing or two about fires myself. We aren't headed for the castle?"

"No, ma'am." I stop and stare at the castle again. "There are forty-four rooms, eighteen fireplaces and two hundred windows, all of them different in every way. You'll be staying here tonight in the forty-fifth room." She looks at me and smiles.

"A secret room? I'll be staying here?"

She nods and smiles.

"Awesome!"

"I thought you might like that. Not all initiates are invited to do so. Only those destined to become Grand Masters. I'll have clothes for you. You're a tiny thing. I used to be like you."

"Thank you, Catherine. Question for you, I understand Henry, or Hal, was a lawyer but never practiced?" *Just like me.*

"Yes. No need for lawyers when you have your own judicial system." Catherine gets the giggles. "When he wasn't traveling or searching the area for relics, he was creating. He wanted to preserve history through his work, just like the Indians did with their cave drawings. A legacy where people would remember him and his time. Kind of like a thumbprint. Hal was also very protective of Indian culture."

"I've heard."

"He's got a whole room dedicated to the travels of Christopher Columbus. No one is totally sure why the obsession, but he contrived alternative stories about Columbus' discoveries. Or, maybe they weren't stories at all but actual facts. He liked to invent fiction among non-fiction."

She pauses and points across the street. "James Michener lived across the street there. He was Hal's paperboy."

"Really?" That's an interesting fact.

Catherine gets on a phone and announces my arrival. She replies with a "Yes, sir" multiple times through her short conversation. I stare back at the castle while I wait. A dark figure in a tower window catches my eye. I'm being watched. I'm spending the night in Henry Mercer's castle, but who else will be?

# 40

---

FIRE

Catherine gives me verbal directions to the entrance of the Tile Works. I thank her and head toward another architectural marvel. For people with secrets, they're not very discreet. The building is one of a kind. I can appreciate my brother's fascination. It's like something out of a storybook. Everything is Gothic and medieval looking with gables and irregular shapes. The Tile Works is built in a U-shape with a large, inviting manicured garden. There are a few families picnicking and a couple admiring tiles they just purchased.

There are too many chimneys to count, all irregular in nature. It looks like one giant DIY project to me with no solid blueprint. I enter the first door and am immediately ushered by a nervous-looking older gentlemen down a flight of concrete steps. He closes off the section to the public, much to the dismay of a few waiting tourists. Tiles adorn the walls, ceiling, and floors. It's a working museum.

He doesn't introduce himself but leaves me standing in the middle of a dozen old kilns. Out of nowhere, Mr. Brandt emerges with one of his charming smiles. He reaches out a hand for me. "Good afternoon, Jenny. How are you doing so far?"

"Very well. Thank you."

"We can't stay here long, so I won't waste time. You're standing amongst the ovens that once set Henry Mercer's original tiles. The Tile Works building itself is an adaptation of the California Mission Church."

"Is that how Mission Church got its name? Up on Church Road"

"Yes, indeed. The Missions of California were established by the Catholic Church in the 1700s to evangelize Native Americans. Henry was passionate about Indians, protective of their traditions and rights. He was also curious about religions and their customs, always searching for answers. He studied and learned what he could from them all, and eventually committed to Episcopalian, liking the feeling of unity. His headstone is close by at the Episcopal Church within a family plot, but I assure you, his body is not. Henry sought to combine his knowledge into one Order and focus and perfect it for generations. I know you've read much of this already, but quite ingenious, don't you think?"

"Yes, very much so," I agree.

"Henry was also fascinated with fire. He feared it, worked with it, and thought of it as a gift in every way. He wanted to use it for as many great purposes as possible. Rosicrucianism taught him how to use ancient wisdom to develop his talents and gifts. He had so many.

He concluded that his artistic talents and lifegoals would not be possible without all of the elements, and so it became the soul center of our Order. Think about it. The clay he chose to mold the tiles still comes from Mother Earth. Our part of the earth. To this day, only red clay that comes from our village lakes has the acceptable formula. Lake Towhee provides us with just the right concentration. Which brings us to water. Our springs, creeks, and lakes are an abundant source for so many reasons. I'll save that speech for Josh. The air is not just what we breathe. It's the element that cooled Mercer's tile craft. We've expanded our talents to use windmills for power and energy, and flight is part of our daily lives as you have witnessed. It's true freedom.

"Finally, spirituality is most important. Without faith, it wouldn't be possible to develop our skills at all. You'll soon be initiated, Jenny, but that doesn't mean you're finished learning. Learning the values and culture of the EORCUF Order takes a lifetime of dedication. You'll need to constantly work to master your skills and talents." I nod along, but it sounds exhausting.

"Back to our founder. Henry Mercer had no formal background in architecture. But he wanted to build something truly unique and special. He consulted with an engineer about building with cement but wouldn't allow anyone but his own loyal men to help him build. He relied on faith, inner guidance, and disciplined creativity to construct his architectural masterpieces. The men and women who helped him build his castle were the chosen ones he assigned to the branches of the Order. Earth went to your ancestors. Fire mine. Water originally Kendra's family, but we won't go there. Air, Ben Grover's ancestors. And, finally, Spirit to the Lenape Indians. So, you see, our Order is complex, but it's perfect. Henry, with all the money he inherited from his aunt on top of his wealth from treasures and revenue from his businesses, built an amazing empire and legacy.

"Henry also purchased the land that became the home for his Order and gave it to his original Grand Masters. That's us. He wanted to establish the all-encompassing pentacle in the small village of Brandtville for its private and isolated location. Doylestown was getting too big. He assigned job titles, rituals, and so on, to make us what we are today. Following?"

"I am. Brandtville became the headquarters so to speak, correct?"

"Correct."

"How much of our current traditions were approved by Mercer?" I've stumped him now. He knows Mercer wouldn't approve of their evolution.

"Well, all Orders evolve, Jenny."

That answers that. Henry Mercer would never have approved of most of the things they do now.

"Do you understand enough to move forward? What you are

about to witness is so strictly private that even your own father would snap your neck if you told another soul outside the society."

My first threat of the day. How nice. Maybe I'll snap his neck when he least expects it. "Yes. I already took my oath, and I will always honor it. You can trust me, Mr. Brandt."

"All right then. Jenny, do you know what alchemy is?"

My jaw drops. As part of my homework, I was asked to read two books. One was about spiritual alchemy and one was the history of alchemy as a science. I'm not sure which one he's referring to, but I suspect he's referring to chemical alchemy.

"Isn't it like converting base metals into gold or something like that?"

"You did your reading. Good for you. I hope Michael has at least skimmed a few chapters, or it's going to be a long day for me." I can't help but laugh at that. I'm sure Ryan hasn't done any reading. "Anyway, during one of Henry's travels, he asked to meet with five of the most known alchemist researchers and scientists from Italy, Czechoslovakia, Russia, Germany, and France. Together, they almost figured out the formula to create pure gold. Almost. Today it's considered a pseudoscience by most. Failed attempts to master the art are plentiful. Henry figured it out, but he kept it to himself. Maybe selfish, maybe protective. Call it what you wish. The tile factory didn't catch on fire creating tiles from these kilns. It caught on fire experimenting."

My heart is beating with anticipation and excitement at this unbelievable reveal.

"I can see you're ready," he smiles at me. "Let's head inside."

Mr. Brandt ushers me through door after door, past tours and old kilns. We head into what he refers to as the clay room, where they store the clay to be used for the tile making. It's all the way down as far as you can go in the building, very musty and damp. Bags full of clay are stacked in the corner. There's only one door left in the room, and he stops beside it.

"You're about to see alchemy in action. The chemistry behind it is very dangerous work. We work with lead here, among other very toxic elements to create twenty-four karat pure gold. That requires a lot of protection."

He punches in the code and we enter into a large walk-in closet. He hands me radioactive hazmat protective gear. *Jesus.* After a quick lesson on how to put it on, we proceed. He checks over the seams, straps, and respirator. Satisfied, we move to the opposite end of the closet and toward a solid metal door. He punches in another code, deliberately covering it with his other hand so I can't see it. We enter a hallway covered in artistic tiles. Each with a story to tell, perhaps from Henry's travels and meetings with the scientists. We have to enter two more protected corridors before entering a large lab. We only have access to a small section, but thick windows allow us to view the production. There are scientists in special gear that looks lighter and easier to work with than what we're wearing. But they're covered from head to toe. I'm waiting for more details about what they're doing, but Mr. Brandt doesn't offer any. I'm left to my own logic to understand what's happening. There are large basins and pots, as well as sophisticated equipment. I can't see the end result of whatever it is they're doing.

That's when another door opens in front of us, even thicker than the last, and we enter into a brightly lit gold chamber. Gold tiles line the floors, instead of ceramic. There are gold arches, gold fixtures, gold everything. Mr. Brandt flicks a button to a vent and takes off his respirator.

"Impressed?"

I take off my respirator and instinctively take a sniff. It's metallic smelling, but I assume safe to breathe. The smokestacks above the building are probably part of an intricate ventilation system to protect the workers and environment, which I know Henry would have insisted upon.

"All gold? Alchemy is real?"

"Yes. It's the real deal and absolutely vital to keep safe from public consumption. Imagine this process getting into the wrong hands."

It's difficult to avoid thinking of the irony of that statement. But the secret gives me pause, because I wouldn't want anyone else knowing it.

"Come on. We're not finished."

Through another chamber we go. I cover my mouth in disbelief once again. The enormous chamber is sectioned off by gold products. I'm a woman after all, so my eyes dart off to the jewels. Mr. Brandt asks me which one I like the best. I point to a rather simple rope chain.

"Then it's yours. That's one of the benefits of membership, Jenny." He pulls it out and places it in my hand. "Now choose a charm that best suits your personality."

I see what's happening here. This is a test. There are trays of gold charms in the shape of relics and symbols. I need to pick something that makes me look like I belong. I decide to go with a simple rose. I flip it over to see a tiny pawprint—the same print on the back of Mr. Brandt's pin."

"It's a nod to Henry's dog, Rollo. That's what the print represents. You'll see his paw prints throughout the house as well, permanently set in cement."

I'll take Mr. Brandt's smile as an indication that he's happy with my choice. He places it through the loop and then around my neck. I've got quite the collection of jewelry at this point.

"It's beautiful. Thank you so much."

"You're welcome. Before I forget, I have a few details for you about Billy Weber, your father's law partner, and member of our Order. Not only was he an attorney, he sold some of our gold in a small, but very lucrative store in Manhattan. You already know Billy was defending Dominick D'Angelo on the Alderman case, but Billy's real assignment was always to sell a portion of our gold creations. His own wife designed most of the pieces, including the one you chose."

"Really?" I touch it again. This would have been great to know.

"Yes. Billy got mixed up with Dominick during his case. They exchanged a few favors without us knowing, and the next thing we knew, the D'Angelo family stole an enormous amount of gold from a secret location. That's when the deadly feud began. That's why we're extra careful about who we trust and why the punishment for defying us must be so extreme." *Billy really did fuck up.* "We never expected it to get so out of control. It was a valuable lesson for us all."

"This makes so much more sense now. I never really understood the entire connection."

I move to another section, this one containing gold bars. I get a sick feeling about them, as this is surely illegal tender. "In case you're wondering. Yes, we do trade in this level of gold to bring in money for the Order. We need to do this ever-so carefully as you can imagine. We trade with Greece and other international countries mostly. I must know if you have a problem with that."

"Of course not. It's what makes us so special." *Wing it.*

"Yes."

Now I know how Mr. Brandt gets some of his money. I wonder if he skims a little extra for himself. I would do amazing things with the profits. Feed the poor, take care of the sick, and house the homeless.

"It's been said that Henry Mercer died from complications from malaria. But he really died from complications of long-term lead exposure. Some of the men and women in there will too. They're sacrificing for the greater good. You have to be willing to do the same at all times." He looks at me for a response.

"Well, hopefully, I've proven that I'm good for that so far."

"You have. But obedience in the Order includes marriage. There will come a time soon, when you must marry my son. You see why there was a push now, don't you?"

"Yes, I do. But I don't understand. Michael—*I have to force his birth name out of my mouth*—is already quite married, with your approval, from what I understand."

"You've heard. My son has been acting like a childish fool. I blame myself. I got sidetracked after Douglas' death and didn't spend the time with him and Jackie like I should have. The delay has been costly for us all, but we're back on track and Michael will see things the way you do. It's all going to fall into place." Before I can guess what that means exactly, I get an answer. "Don't worry, Jenny. Alicia is being taken care of as we speak. She no longer serves a purpose here or poses a threat."

# 41

FONTHILL CASTLE

Alicia is being taken care of as we speak. What does that mean? Maybe the less I know, the better. Maybe they've just sent her away and nothing else. Ryan is going to be frantic though and act out. Then he's going to be my freaking handful again.

"Any questions I can answer, Jenny?"

"What part does cremation play? I mean, last summer I thought the cremation site was only for criminals. But that's how we dispose of the deceased as well, correct?"

"Yes. I'm glad you mentioned that. Dating all the way back to Egyptian times, our belief is that the Soul cannot be entirely free from the body until it's returned to earthly elements. "Dust to dust. Except the Pharaohs, of course, who were preserved to ready themselves for the afterlife."

"What about pyramids?"

"Have you seen pyramids?"

"Well, the incinerator you used was shaped like one."

"Oh, of course. Well, there's more to it than that. For many, we do memorialize our members under sacred traditional pyramids. Otherwise, rose bushes are sufficient to scatter their ashes. That's why I was so pleased when you chose a rose as your symbol."

I play with my new rose necklace and smile.

"It's not on topic, really, but what about other Orders who spy and seek our knowledge?"

"Very good question. They'll stop at nothing to learn our secrets. You must use extreme caution and learn to discipline yourself. When you went on your tirade last summer, you left us vulnerable. Two different Rosicrucian Orders got way too close. That can never happen again."

"Then why was I allowed to stay with Tina Goodwin?"

"She kept you tucked away for selfish reasons. We let you stay for our own purposes—to test your ability to keep a secret, and you kept an eye on them too, whether you knew it or not. You passed, as far as I know. Anything you want to tell me now? Did you give away anything you shouldn't have?"

"I didn't tell her anything that she didn't already know." I didn't realize just how important that was until now. I'm bummed to think that Peter and Tina are technically not allies. They helped me, but only in an effort to learn more. And the whole time I thought I had a secret hiding place, I really didn't. They'll find me anywhere. It wasn't just Josh who knew.

"If that's all, the last tour is ending now. You ready to spend the night in Fonthill? It's everyone's favorite part of initiation. I warn you it gets a bit spooky in there at night, even for an old timer like me," he says with a smile. "But it's a time to reflect and draw from the energy that radiates throughout the house. Its vibrations will stay with you forever."

"I'm looking forward to it a great deal, Mr. Brandt."

"Someone as nosy as you, I'm not surprised," he chuckles.

As pleasant of a man as I've found him today, I can't forget that Mr. Brandt was and is a dangerous man. No matter how charismatic and spiritual he portrays himself, protecting these prolific secrets is what he does best, with no regard for human life. I wonder what he was like at my age, before death and darkness seized his character. My mind is racing, as usual, as I put my protective equipment back on.

We journey back out the way we came. Mr. Brandt has an alternative route, but I will be heading back out through the main entrance. Catherine is waiting in regular attire, wearing a pair of mom jeans way too high up her belly and a floral blouse. The same grey braid is hanging between her shoulder blades.

A "Closed" sign now hangs on the door, but a few tourists and photographers remain gawking outside. Catherine hands me a camera to help me blend in. We'll be entering through the garage, which is now a visitor center, and down through a hidden passageway into the house. There's a shock! A secret passageway. Henry Mercer was probably the inspiration behind all the secret passageways in the villages.

"This part here is what's left of the original barn, which he replaced with the garage. Hal wanted to preserve what he could of the original farm. He actually built a house on top of a house. You'll be staying in the master bedroom from the original farmhouse. It's the only room in the house off limits to tourists and kept secret just for us. First, I'll give you a quick tour of the castle, so you'll get an understanding of the layout, which is very purposefully complicated."

We head down cement stairs covered with his infamous tiles. We reach a door that says, "Restroom Out of Order." She unlocks it and we descend again. The tunnel is well-constructed, with a tiled floor, but lacking in design otherwise. We're soon up and into the main building. We pop up through a hidden bookcase entrance. *Cool!* Old fashioned, but classic and fun. I like his style already and know Danny is going to love this tour.

"This was Hal's library. He spent a great deal of time here."

Very old books line the shelves. She informs me that there are over four thousand books in total throughout the house. There's a balcony above our heads leading to more books, accessible only by a staircase hidden behind the fireplace.

The fireplace itself is designed with large three-dimensional tiles running lengthwise, depicting the story of Christopher Columbus' discovery of the New World. The words PLVS VLTRA are dead center. I'm beginning to understand his motto more and more.

"This way."

Catherine guides me through a maze of rooms leading to a central area. Every so often I see Rollo's pawprints set in the cement floors. *He must have loved that dog.* She closes a heavy gothic doorway, which exposes where all the keys to all the rooms are kept. She points out that Henry left signs above each doorway to describe the rooms. The one above me reads "West Room."

"Henry studied castles for ten years but built his own in five. He wanted the castle to look medieval, so he brought in gothic doors from all over the world. There are seven stories in all." I feel like I should leave breadcrumbs to find my way out if I have to. I try my best to memorize details, but each entranceway and nook is mysteriously unique yet difficult to distinguish. None of the arches are symmetrical, and the floors aren't level.

"What's this?" I ask Catherine, pointing to a bell of some kind.

"Servant bells. There's one in every room."

"Henry had servants?"

"Ten of them. With all the research and work he did, he needed them to run the castle. Couldn't very well do it on his own." She points to a dumbwaiter where food or supplies could be brought to him on every level.

"Tomorrow you're welcome once again to explore the grounds. We just ask that you stay away from the little house in the woods for now." Telling me to stay away from something is a bad move. I know exactly what she's talking about. The little house in the woods is where the temporary new prison is located. How do they hide prisoners there amidst all the tourists?

"Is it open to the public?"

"Good heavens, no. But little assholes from town have done a number on it. Graffiti and so forth. Each time we refurbish it, they come back. May have to teach them a lesson one of these days. What they can't see, the Order has access to and uses."

"For what?" I want her to tell me herself.

"Meetings mostly, I believe."

"Where's the building?"

"Don't get any ideas. You couldn't get in even if you tried. It's off limits."

"Do you have a key?" I'm determined to know how many prisoners are in there. I know there's at least one—the journalist who got too close. I can't exactly set him free or he'll tell his story to the whole world, but I would like to know what kind of condition he's in.

"Catherine, you are aware that I'll soon be a Grand Master, right? You know it will be my job to punish and hopefully redeem those who threaten our way of life. As part of my initiation journey, don't you think the little house in the woods would be something, I, of all people, should have access to?"

"I'd have to ask."

"Catherine, if you don't hand me over the key, I'm going to put you in there as early as next week for disobeying me."

"I'm not allowed to have a key, Ms. O'Rourke, and it's not as simple as a key to gain access. The building is very dilapidated."

"Details, Catherine."

"Okay, please don't tell anyone." She's between a rock and a hard place. Get punished now or be punished later. "There's a springhouse next to the castle. That's where Henry came up with the name. Font ... as in fountain. We're atop a large spring." *Ugh, more springs.*

"Let me guess, you need to swim to get into the building?"

"Heavens, no. Henry had passageways for everything. Inside the springhouse is a tunnel that leads to the little house. There's a hidden door inside. But the key to open it is in the attic dumbwaiter, all the way upstairs. I've never gone myself and it's heavily guarded.

"Thank you for the details. I likely won't either, but I think part of my Day of Knowledge here should be complete, don't you? I'm ready to see my room now. And, of course, we never had this conversation. Now, let's talk about that person who was peering out at me earlier. Does he come with this program? And I'm going to need a phone."

# 42

NIGHT TERRORS

Fonthill comes with security. My father's team. They're on constant lookout from the tower of the castle, and worse, there are hidden cameras. The good news is that Catherine caved easily and told me where they're positioned, so I know how to work around them. The front door will be tricky, however, because an alarm is sure to blare, which pretty much makes me a captive. I'm going to have to work extra hard at this.

Catherine escorts me to my room. It doesn't disappoint. The tiles tell the story of our entire Order. At least how it stood before Henry passed. They're so ornate and beautiful that I get the chills. Art has always had that effect on me. I want to take the time and study and try to interpret every single one. I suppose that's the point. Left for me on a desk is my dinner, which reminds me of how absolutely starving I am. I also have my own working shower and restroom. There are clean clothes piled on the bed for me. Nice and warm ones, although the old radiator is working just fine.

I dismiss Catherine for the evening and go to town on my dinner. Roasted chicken and rice never tasted so good. I wish the lighting was a little better, but the Historical Society wanted to preserve even that in most of the rooms. The museum has electricity, but the bulbs are only twenty-five watts and very dim. They left a few candles for me, so I get a few going and spend the first hour just looking around the room. It's incredible. All the elements are represented beautifully with different stories of how each is used in nature. There are artifacts in the room as well. Some look very ancient and some Native American. The vibe in the room is mysterious. I lie down on the bed and try to imagine what Henry's life was like. He had a beautiful mind indeed.

I suddenly feel a chill come out of nowhere. There are no windows in this interior room or even a chimney. Perhaps the spirit of Hal, as Catherine calls him, is present. I shake off that thought because I have to sleep in here. I step back to the desk and polish off the rest of my water. I pick up an antique phone not expecting a dial tone, but I get one. It's probably bugged, but I can still call Danny.

He picks up on the first ring. Before he can ask or say a word, I tell him that I just got bit by a bug to keep the conversation basic. I ask him about his day, and as I'd hoped, he's very impressed by Day Three. He rants on and on about black matter and the live rocks.

"Wait until tomorrow, brother. You're going to love Day Four." He hasn't mentioned anything about the underground boulder field, so I try and find a way to ask in code. "You find any copperheads out there?"

"No. Jenny, no life there at all." He doesn't get it. I listen to him tell me how there's no wildlife in the magnetic fields.

"How about at home, Danny?" Now he pauses.

"No. Nothing. But thanks for checking on me. You know how much I'm afraid of them."

We both laugh awkwardly for the sake of our unknown audience of listeners.

"Well, I love you, brother. I'm going to bed soon. I'm exhausted. I can't wait to catch up again tomorrow if we can. Sleep tight. Don't let the bed bugs bite."

"I love you too. Sleep well."

I put him on edge. I didn't really mean to, but now he knows I've discovered something he didn't, and where. But with the Feds roaming around again, he'll have to wait to investigate. At least it will keep Jack and his new AMORC friend away too.

I change into some warm sweats and sit in a meditative position on the bed, hoping the energy from this house is on my side. I need the key and to see what's in the little house in the woods. It's time to learn my way around this big old cement house. I go room to room memorizing details about each and how they connect. It's not an easy task. I get lost more than once but enjoy the challenge of finding my way. I spot the cameras Catherine was describing. But I'm only doing what I'm supposed to be doing—exploring. I continue examining the antiques, artwork, and photographs, while trying to interpret as many tiles as possible.

It's difficult to see without a flashlight. I take it even slower, after I bump my head and miss a few stairs going in and out of the passageways. I find my way up into the attic and spot the dumbwaiter. There's a camera directly across from it, so I come up with a quick and believable plan. Pretending to lose my footing, I fall up against the lens and hear a crack. Perfect! No time to waste, I open the door and grab the key. It sets off an alarm. *Crap!* I close the door back up and sit and wait, rubbing my ankle as I do.

As expected, two armed security guards rush to my side and ask me what happened. One attempts to fix the lens before eying up the dumbwaiter door.

"I fell and need some ice."

One nods to the other and is off.

"Did you open the dumbwaiter door?"

"What's a dumbwaiter door?"

Let the head games begin. As he explains what the door is, I tell him I simply fell back and hit it. I told him I did hear a clanking. He curses under his breath, convinced the key fell down the shaft. Trying to find it will keep them busy for hours.

The other man returns with the ice. They inspect my ankle,

looking for obvious breaks. One man lays the ice gently on the side where I tell him it hurts the most.

"Just a twist. Happens all the time. Let's get you back to your room."

"I'm feeling a little claustrophobic. Is there a place where I can get some fresh air? Can I come and go, out the front or back door?" I ask.

"No, I'm sorry. You'll be seen, and you'll set off a high-level alarm." They look at each other while I pretend to hyperventilate. "Let's get her to the West Terrace balcony."

I hop along as they guide me to a large outdoor patio. There's no alarm on the door, or at least it's not on right now, as far as I can tell.

"Much better. Wow! Look at that moon. Thank you so much for your help. I just need a few minutes."

They doublecheck to see if I'm all right and head back to search for the key. I start looking for a way down. If only I had a rope, or hair like Rapunzel. There's no way down without actually breaking something, but the moon is glowing, giving me great light. I search in the direction of the little house and see movement. I duck back inside, not wanting to be seen, and peek out the window. The person moves into plain sight, with arms outstretched in a *what gives* gesture. It's Danny. I give him the one-minute sign and try to come up with a plan. He knew I was up to something tonight and snuck out. Now what? I can't tell him about the underground boulder field, but I can guide him to check out the little house. There's no way I can leave the building, but I can throw him the key. I walk back out to the end of the balcony and wave at him to see if he can come closer. He dodges a few trees and I hold up the key. Using sign language, I point to the springhouse, then into the woods. He nods his head, knowing exactly what to do. I aim and throw the key. He runs for it, grabs it, and darts behind the springhouse. He peeks out to give me a thumbs up.

"Are you feeling better, Ms. O'Rourke?"

I jump and hold my heart. "Jesus Christ. You scared the shit out of me."

"My apologies. We should get you into bed. You shouldn't be seen."

"I'm starting to feel better. Thank you. What's your name?"

"I'm Phil. My partner's name is Sean. His mother named him after your father."

"Isn't that something." I try not to roll my eyes.

I let Phil take me back to my room, while I pretend to have an absolute nervous breakdown. "I've been through a lot, Phil, and I get claustrophobic easily. I understand why I can't be seen, but is there at least a window I can look out as needed?" He nervously inhales but gives in.

"Sure, follow me. I'll shut off the alarm to the window so you can open it as needed."

"I can't thank you enough. I think I'll sit here for a bit."

"Here, take this and call me if you need me." He hands me a talkie, which I wish I could use to call Danny instead. I thank him for being so accommodating and promise to reach out if I need him. Now for the waiting and praying Danny doesn't get caught. Maybe this wasn't the best idea.

# 43

---

## THE LITTLE HOUSE IN THE WOODS

wo hours have come and gone with no sign of Danny. I'm getting angry at myself, worried that I could blow our entire initiation being so impatient and careless. I'm pacing and walking in and out of the building and onto the third-floor terrace. The castle security team offers me wine as a solution to calm my nerves. They look genuinely concerned, thinking I'm claustrophobic and suffering from panic attacks. I'm anxious as hell, but not for the reasons they think. They must think I'm a real shitshow.

Finally, I see a shadow emerge from the woods and a wave of relief washes over me. It's Danny's turn to throw me back the key. He waves it in the air, and I notice something attached to it. A note. There's no way in hell he can chance a miss if he's written me a note. I'm nervous again. I decide to distract the security team but point to a camera blind spot so Danny can move in for a closer aim. I move back inside and ask Phil, over the talkie, for some wine and maybe a snack in the kitchen.

He's more than happy to oblige. I follow him back through a maze of rooms and sit at the old dining room table. It's cold but the wine warms me up. We engage in a thirty-minute session of chitchat, while

I guzzle cabernet and nibble on some sharp cheddar. He's doing most of the talking and behaving more and more flirty. I have my master's degree in this game and have him eating out of my hands in no time. I'm sure in his heightened testosterone state, he's thinking I'd be a great notch on his belt. Having sex with a Grand Master's daughter would elevate an average Joe's internal rank and ego. It's a dangerous game for Phil. My father would knock him off for such an act.

I use his recklessness to my advantage in case I need the card to play. With a little coercing, I get him to drink on the job. I dick tease him with a little inappropriate touching, and he leans in for a kiss. I decide to give him one. I'm pent up anyway, and he's not terrible looking. I'd take him right to bed for a quick release if I wasn't fearful of the repercussions. There's something erotic about the castle and having sex in it would be magical ... *with the right person.* I think of kissing Josh as I return Phil's kiss, then back off and put my glass down. I apologize for my advances and tell Phil I'm drunk. He goes from looking like he won the lottery to looking like I kicked him in the nuts.

"I'd best be off for a little fresh air and then back to bed."

"My pleasure. Please let me know if you need company again, Jenny," he says with a flirty smirk.

"That's Ms. O'Rourke to you. Thank you, Phil." My sudden chill is emasculating. I let Phil escort me back to the terrace in silence and request to be alone again. He shakes his head but leaves me to it. I pace the balcony scouring the ground with my eyes. I spot the key and note under a wrought iron garden chair. *Perfect.* I plop down, swipe it up, and head back to my room.

My hand goes over my mouth as I read. The journalist wasn't locked in the prison, but Dr. Braun is there. He's being punished for getting too close to me. He has broken bones but insisted Danny leave him for now. Danny made a key and is going to come up with something. "Don't worry," he says. "I'll deal with it tomorrow." I'm trembling with rage. Phil is going to have to take one for the team here. Tomorrow is too late. I call him to my room again.

Phil enters with a smile on his face. I give him the bad news. Not only is he not having sex but he's about to break a few rules. If he doesn't help me, I'll tell my father he made advances and drank on the job. If he helps me, he could get caught and put in punishment. Either way, he's fucked. His assignment from me is to help me get out of the castle and to the little house in the woods without detection. He pisses and moans that it can't be done. It's time to show Phil who's in charge. I attack and push him against the cement wall. He bangs his head and rubs it. The poor guy has been through the full range of emotions with me, but this one is particularly alarming for him.

"We go now. Tell Sean Junior to turn the backdoor security system off, including the cameras."

"Jenny, you don't understand. I'll be banished if I'm caught."

"Again, it's Ms. O'Rourke, Phil. Listen, if you do as I ask, I will do what I can to protect you. You have my word."

Phil looks close to tears as he picks up the talkie. I take it out of his hands. Whatever pussy story he's about to tell him is costing me time. "Sean, it's Ms. O'Rourke. For your own good, you're dismissed for the evening. Understand? First, shut off the backdoor security system and cameras. Can you do that without triggering more alarms and security?"

"What's going on?"

"It's kind of like one of those things, Sean. If I tell you, someone may kill you. Do we have a deal or no?"

"Yes, ma'am."

"Keep the talkie handy and I'll give you follow-up orders. I appreciate the favor, Sean. If all goes well, you'll have a spot on my personal security force once I become a Grand Master."

"Thank you very much, Ms. O'Rourke. I'll do what I can to help."

I look at Phil. "Now that's a good attitude, don't you think?" He nods and looks at the tile floor. "Off we go. Your part is a bit more dangerous. Don't worry, I'll take that into consideration."

Down through the maze we go and out the back door. Phil shuts off the back lights to give us more cover, but the moon is very bright. We hustle into the springhouse, open the tunnel door, and make our way to the little house. "Once we're inside, is there a code to get into the prison?"

"Prison?"

"Don't be an ass, Phil."

"Seriously, I don't know anything about a prison."

I could call Danny, but he'd force me to abort the mission. He got in, and so can I. I decide to bring Phil with me all the way. Thankfully, the key to the springhouse also opens the main door into the basement. We enter into a dark and dingy room. There are three more doors, all of which are locked. But only one door is made of steel. That's going to be the one. We're suddenly surrounded by two other armed men. I was naïve to think there'd be no security here. Phil is in a panic and attempts to explain. All three of us tell him to shut up at the same time.

The taller man speaks. "Josh feared you'd come. Your brother is going to take care of this, Jenny. Just be patient."

"No way. Danny said he had broken bones. Open the door."

"Who has broken bones?" Phil asks.

One of the guards backs him against the wall. "Don't say a fucking word."

"I'm not saying anything."

"Then put a lid on it, Spanky."

My new friend, the security guard, opens the door and ushers me in, while the other stays with Phil. It's an intricate space, with multiple half-finished hallways and more doors. Finally, we're in the prison section, and I lay eyes on Dr. Braun. He's less than happy to see me back.

"Jenny, you shouldn't be here," Dr. Braun says weakly.

I feel physical pain looking at him. He's in horrible shape. Tears and rage cover my cheeks seeing him in this condition. This is the nail on the coffin for my father. I don't know how I'll fake another emotion for him ever again.

"I'm not leaving you here like this. You could die." The guard opens the cell, and I rush to his side and carefully take him into my arms. We weep together, half from the predicament and half from just seeing each other again. There's only one plan I can think of that may work.

"I have an idea. Let Phil take you to safety and then call Dr. Clement. He can get you safely to Alpha-MED for treatment and then provide you with protection. When this whole ordeal is straightened out, you'll be back with me."

"Who's Phil?" Dr. Braun asks.

"My bitch right now," I say and smile. Dr. Braun shames me with a look.

"Watch your mouth, or I'll wash it out with soap." We both laugh, and he winces.

"That's something only a father would say." He looks at me and nods. "I love you, Dr. Braun. Let's get out of here."

"Let me take over from here, Ms. O'Rourke, and I'll go into hiding myself until this is all over. I'm going to be held responsible for this when your father finds out. Take Phil back into the house and keep his ass quiet," my new friend the security guard says.

"Are you sure?"

"Quite sure. I'll have my partner tell the Grand Masters that I rushed him off because he was flatlining. Your father didn't want him dead. Not yet anyway."

"What do you mean, not yet?"

"Finishing him off was going to be your first Council Leadership Sentence."

I'm shocked and appalled for the last time. "Is he telling the truth, Dr. Braun?"

"I'm afraid so, dear." If he was expecting me to pass a test like this, he set me up to fail big time. Now I have to wonder what Josh had to do to make it all the way to Grand Master.

"It's a plan then? Your name?"

"Jax Underwood."

"I can trust you, Jax?"

"Completely. Josh assigned me to this station for a reason. We didn't know how bad he was, though. I swear."

We attempt to help Dr. Braun up, but he can't put weight on his broken ankle. With broken ribs too, Jax only has one option, to cradle him like a baby. We head back through the tunnel, out of the spring-house door, and into the night. It's very early. Close to 2:00 a.m. now. Security guard number two decides to stay and deal with the repercussions. He's scared, but I won't let anything happen to him if I can help it. I say a final goodbye to Jax and Dr. Braun and watch them disappear into the woods toward the cemetery.

Phil and I make our way back to the castle and in through the back door. I yank the talkie out of his hands and tell Sean it's time to return to home base. He's back in a hurry and sweating from the fear of punishment that may transpire from this unexpected jailbreak. As a team, we lock everything back up, and I move back to my room and into bed. Waiting for what's to come is the hardest part, and I just want to get it over with.

I don't have to wait long. About twenty minutes goes by, and there's a knock at the door. It's Mr. Brandt, and he's pissed.

## 44

ONE FOR THE TEAM

I hear Phil adamantly denying that anyone has left the castle. I open the door and allow Mr. Brandt to enter, rubbing my eyes for good measure. He walks up to the bed and touches it, feeling for warmth. My stomach flip-flops, but I pass the test.

"What's happening, Mr. Brandt? You're scaring me. Did something happen to Danny?"

"How stupid do you think I am?" He slaps me hard across the face. I've had enough of the physical abuse. Phil is wide-eyed, and Sean looks like he's about to cry. I revolt and slap Mr. Brandt, a Grand Master, even harder than he slapped me.

"Don't you ever, ever lay a hand on me again. What's the meaning of all of this?"

Mr. Brandt is taken aback by my hard return and looks like he's contemplating his next move. I don't wait for it.

"Phil, call my father immediately."

"Yes, ma'am."

"Hold on. Hold on." Mr. Brandt backs down. He knows damn well a slap on my face, without his approval, will land him in hot water.

"A prisoner is missing."

"The journalist?" I ask.

He looks torn about believing me. Not knowing what I know, he can't very well spill the beans about my father figure being beaten and locked in a prison for no good reason.

"My father told me a journalist, posing as a member, was imprisoned. Has he escaped?"

Mr. Brandt, shakes his head, takes a deep breath, and without warning, pulls out a knife and plunges it into Phil's chest. I'll never forget the look of fear in Phil's eyes as he falls to the ground. But it's time to show Mr. Brandt that even this despicable move won't break me. I don't flinch as Phil falls to the ground. His head lands on my left bare foot. For some shock value of my own, I kick his head off my foot with no sign of empathy whatsoever. Mr. Brandt's eyes are bewildered, as he tries to think. He's determined to rattle me one way or another and turns his attention to Sean. I remain calm and play with the necklace I picked out with Mr. Brandt earlier in the day. It doesn't go unnoticed.

"If you're through, I'm quite tired." I point to Phil. "I assume this one had it coming to him." Then I point to Sean. "But this one's been with me on and off all night." I stop and look back at Mr. Brandt. "You know he was named after my father, don't you?" I continue. "Sean, could you kindly find another room for me to sleep in? And we're going to need to clean up this mess. Will there be anything else this evening, Mr. Brandt?"

He stares me down then looks back at Sean, considering his options.

"Do as your told," he barks to Sean.

He points a finger in my face and says, "Watch yourself, Jenny. You don't want to get on my bad side."

"I intend to stay on your good side. You'll be my father-in-law, after all." He curses under his breath and exits to manage damage control. Sean is back with towels and bags. We kneel down together to assess Phil's condition. It's too late. Phil's gone. Sean's lip is quivering. I rub his shoulder to comfort him.

"Sean, as promised, you'll be part of my team as early as next week. Are you strong enough to handle this situation?" I challenge. "And I'm so sorry for your loss."

"Yes. I am, Ms. O'Rourke."

"I promise better days ahead. Now let's get Phil out of here and cremated, shall we?"

It's daybreak. I'm sad and exhausted but have my final day to look forward to today. And with Josh, no less. Catherine arrives bright and early to escort me back to the cemetery where Amy is waiting to pick me back up. We drive back to Scott's house in silence, but I'm thinking so hard I fear I can be heard out loud. I've now witnessed the other side of Mr. Brandt first-hand. And I've witnessed yet another murder I could have prevented. I wonder what Mr. Brandt told my father, and what my father believes to be true. I'm skating on thin ice. But I'm prepared to murder him in cold blood, even before my initiation, for what he did to Dr. Braun.

Scott welcomes me back into his home and lays out breakfast. He's quiet. The rumor mill must already be churning. Phil's death is another loss for the good guys.

"You have a few hours to nap, Jenny. Sammy is going to pick you up around noon. I'm off. It's Michael's turn today, and Veronica's tomorrow. No offense, but I'm ready for this cycle to be over. I understand you've learned that Shane is already a member."

"I have."

"I'm glad that's out in the open now." He pauses and looks at his feet. "I'm not going to ask any questions about last night. I trust you."

"Thanks, Scott. I trust you as well. See you tonight."

I eat what I can, but I'm not terribly hungry thinking about last night. I suddenly remember Alicia. What kind of method does Mr.

Brandt have for getting rid of her? I call Danny before attempting to nap. He hadn't heard about the fallout from last night and is very upset with me. But what's done is done. I give him full disclosure and ask him to keep a close watch on Sean to make sure he's not cracking and tell him to sleep with one eye open around Mr. Brandt.

My anxiety level is a ten. I toss and turn until I can't try anymore. I get up, pace for a bit, and finally hop in the shower. I barely have the towel back around me when Scott bangs at the door.

"Jenny? Change of plans. Sammy's been taken into custody by the Feds. They're working their rounds. I'm going to take you to Josh. We'll be parachuting."

I open the door holding the towel in place. "Parachuting?"

"In tandem. I got you. Here, put this on over your clothes."

He hands me a safari green jumpsuit and tells me to hurry. Like Scott, I'm ready for this all to be over. It's way too stressful.

Scott checks all the windows for unwanted visitors and directs me to meet him around the back of the main hanger. We'll take a golf cart down the runway to our plane. I have the shakes as I make my way outside and through a wooded area. I'm startled at first to see I'm not alone but realize they're my "air" lookouts. They wave me through as I go, giving me the all-clear every ten yards or so. I look up and see Ryan and Greg getting ready for their journey. I have a good feeling about this day for him. Knowing how much his mother adored the angels, I think it's going to be a powerful experience.

The cart is ready. I hop on and we putter alongside the runway. The grassy field slopes downward, placing us out of sight from the main stretch. Scott yells a few quick directions at me but tells me not to worry, because he'll be doing all the work. We'll be jumping out of Greg's private Cessna C208B. The engine is on, and a pilot is waiting for us.

"Welcome, Jenny." He holds out a hand for me to hold as I clamber in. Scott is behind me and working the equipment. I've got straps and more straps, a full helmet, the works.

"I'm nervous."

"Keep the faith, Jenny."

I take a deep breath to channel some. He buckles me to a seat for takeoff, and the plane turns and heads down the grass runway. There are waves from a few friends below as we pass overhead. Scott and I both see the black federal SUVs pulling into the drive at the same time.

"Man! That was close. They're really gaining traction."

"You think we're okay?"

"We'll be just fine." Scott looks up. "Ready?"

"Already?" I unbuckle and let Scott attach us. He gives me directions on what to do and where to pull, in case something happens. We inch awkwardly toward the door. I'm clinging to a handrail as he opens the door, feeling nauseous and geographically lost.

I get no warning at all. No "on three." No nothing. We take a flying leap and drop so fast that my stomach is left far above me in the clouds.

# 45

---

## WATER

U nlike the cliff dive I took with Greg, we're up high and dropping fast. The louder I scream, the louder Scott laughs. He's got our arms and legs spread out like I've seen them do on TV, except I'm not enjoying it very much. Skydiving was never on my bucket list of things to do some day, so I'm glad I didn't know this was going to happen. I'm pleading for him to pull the parachute. He taps my shoulder and points. I see where we're headed, and there's not a lot of room for error.

He pulls the chute, and we're forcefully yanked up into the sky. By the grace of God, it opens, so I try to calm down. Scott gives me a pat on the back. I reopen my eyes to take in the view. It's a beautiful clear day. Ryan should have no trouble seeing the cloud angel, whether it's real or not. I have so many mixed emotions about spending the day with Josh. Do I continue to torture him for marrying Lucia, or let it go? I decide to let it go. Maybe I should even apologize.

The trees are getting closer and closer. I've lost track of the field that is our target. I close my eyes and let Scott do the work. He's working the steering elements.

"Legs up, Jenny, now!"

I open my eyes and lift just in time for landing. We slide ass-down across the grass and topple over each other.

"Holy shit!" I exclaim as we unbuckle and rise.

"What'd you think?"

"I think once is enough." Scott laughs and helps me off with my helmet and the rest of my gear. He gets to work packing the chute.

"We have to move quickly. Out of sight. This way." He takes my hand and pulls me into a wooded area.

"Where are we?"

"Close to Buckingham Mountain. Ever hear of Gravity Hill?"

"No."

"Oh, come on. You've been out of the area too long. The local legend first—there's an old Church at the top of the hill called Mount Gilead. It's been empty for decades. But it's been preserved as of late, and access is given upon request. Anyway, legend has it that the church is haunted. A lot of people believe devil worshipping once took place in the church. The road is eerie, especially at night."

"Why is it called Gravity Hill?"

"There's a phenomenon that happens on the road near the church. Instead of cars going down the hill, they'll roll backwards, defying gravity. Some experts think they've figured it out. Say the road really inclines the other way for that stretch. But it doesn't. Truth is there are more live rocks under the road, but even more magnetic than Ringing Rocks. The more metal on a car, the more mysterious the trip." Scott laughs. "Engines die. Dashboard components flash. Kids scare themselves half to death."

"That's hysterical. What's with the church?"

"Mount Gilead was the first black church in Bucks County, built in 1809. They called themselves the Society of Colored Methodists. It became a refuge for the Underground Railroad. There's even a movie about it. Very rich in history."

"I'd love to see it. I didn't realize Bucks County had so many Underground Railroad stations."

"Yes, slaves were dependent on the kindness of strangers to give them shelter. As you've learned, there was no bigger station than the one you lived in temporarily. Hundreds hid in Mercy Station, thanks to the Mercer and Chapman families. Once they left, they never gave away the location. Took it to their graves. It's not exactly on the Underground Railroad tour."

"Fascinating."

"Okay, we're behind it." Scott sends a text.

"I have a ride coming shortly. You can go into the church now."

"In?"

"Yes, Josh is waiting."

"Then where?"

"That's so secretive, even I don't know. My water initiation was in a spring in Solebury. It was amazing, but I'm guessing you're going somewhere even more incredible. A place only future royalty goes."

"Shut up." I push him gently.

"Anyway. Best of luck to you, Jenny."

"Thank, Scott. And thanks for not killing me up there."

"I'll never let anything happen again to someone I love."

I give him a squeeze and a peck on the cheek. He's getting emotional, thinking of Katie.

"Okay, I'm off. Later, gator." I break into a jog and head for the front of the church. I check my surroundings before opening the door. All seems quiet.

Josh is sitting on a pew near the altar. We're alone. It's awkward, and I still feel butterflies. He rises as I walk slowly toward him. He looks incredibly handsome as usual, wearing a simple pair of blue jeans, hiking boots, and a camo T-shirt.

"Before we begin, I just wanted to apologize. I'm sorry for my behavior. For lashing out at you. It's not your fault. Lucia is beautiful, and you make a great couple. I just want you to be happy."

"I want you to be happy too." His smile is boyish, like he's hiding something.

"What?"

"Nothing. You're beautiful." He bends down and plants a tender kiss on my lips. What the hell is he trying to do to me? And despite my past flings, I don't like the idea of Josh being a big cheater. He's better than that. I pull away and stare him down. No ring.

"Josh?"

"Come on. We have a fun day ahead of us, and I have so much to tell you."

He takes me by the hand and leads me toward the door. He looks out the window and moves out of sight again.

"What?"

"Kids. They're testing Gravity Hill. Cops will chase 'em away in a minute. Yep. There's always a cruiser stationed down the hill."

"Really?"

"Yeah, once he heads back to his spot, we're gonna cross the street and head down the mountain on an angle. We're headed about a mile away." He looks at me and smiles. "I've waited so long to show you this, Jenny." He peeks out the window again. "Okay, let's go." He takes me by the hand, and we cross a narrow but paved road and head into the woods. I'm starting to feel excited and have to admit, I love holding Josh's hand, even if it's not mine.

We work our way through the just-bloomed greens. Sticker bushes and dead winter branches scratch my hands. I hear the sound of a babbling creek. We're nearing water. Out of the corner of my eye I see a building. No, it's a bridge. It's an old covered bridge. I pause, knowing in my heart this is where Denise Brandt found herself the day she was threatened. It's just as she described in her letter to Ryan and Jackie. The mysterious place only a select few know about. Even Mr. Brandt's own wife wasn't allowed near it.

"You okay?"

"What bridge is that?"

"Mercer Covered Bridge. Abandoned now. Keep moving."

We make our way around boulders and crawl under branches until we reach a mystical cove. A waterfall trickles down the side of rocks. It's surrounded by the same type of ringing rocks I've seen so much of lately. Josh points to the mouth of a cave. This is what Denise never got to see. We're greeted by two park rangers. EORCUF guards in disguise.

"Good afternoon, Mr. Flannery and Ms. O'Rourke."

"Afternoon, gentlemen. Supplies ready?"

"Yes, sir."

"Ready, Jenny?"

"Very."

"Watch your head on the way in. Then we're going to crawl."

I get on my hands and knees and follow Josh through the opening. It's tight, but I've gotten quite experienced at cavern and cave exploring. I hear the sound of water and smell the earth below me. It's pitch-black.

"You can stand now."

Josh helps me to my feet and flips on six battery-operated lights. He pushes a button, which locks off the cave from the outside world. We've arrived in a large cavern with seemingly shallow water covering most of the pebble floor.

"It's deceiving. See that spot there? Goes down maybe a mile, who knows. We'll be free diving, Jenny. There are quite a few air pockets along the way if you need to breathe. Then we'll have to dive down into another channel where there aren't any. Still have a good two minutes in those lungs if you need them?"

"Damn right."

"Along the way, stop at the first large air pocket."

"Okay." Josh has the most adoring look on his face. I can't help but stare and think how much I love him. He smiles and looks down bashfully. Oh no, my telepathic vibes are back, and I wish I hadn't thought it. It makes me feel vulnerable.

He reaches behind a rock and pulls out some gear. We'll have full wetsuits, head gear, and flippers. He turns his back like a gentleman as I get undressed and into my suit. I do the same but sneak a peek at his ass. He catches me.

"Sorry. I thought you were finished."

"See anything you like?" I shake my head but smirk. This is the flirty Josh I fell in love with. "Okay. Ready?"

"Yep."

"Follow me," he says and turns on his underwater flashlight. I follow him and we descend. The shallow end drops off sharply into the abyss and we doggie paddle in place for a moment. Josh looks at me, holds his breath, and kicks off the underwater rock ledge. I follow his lead. I'm getting more and more excited about my final day of knowledge. Maybe we're about to find the motherload of more coins or ancient relics.

A few more strokes, and Josh taps my shoulder. He rises and I follow. We end up in a large, cavernous air pocket. No sooner am I up, he moves me over to a ledge where I can sit.

"I can't tell you how good it feels to finally be able to tell you the truth."

# 46

---

## BETTER HALF

I stare at what I can see of Josh in the tiny space. "What truth?"

"My parents discovered this cave when Sam and I were in our teens. They were half on a diving adventure and half looking for potential waterways to build another dam. Between this spring and the creeks that run through it, they saw a lot of potential. They were looking for an opportunity to build another lake, smaller than Nockamixon, but one for the area to enjoy. As EORCUF members, they had to report their findings. They presented it to Michael Brandt first. He thanked them and shunned them. He wouldn't allow them or anyone but the Grand Masters to go near it."

"Josh, what did they find that was so relevant?"

"The largest yellow diamonds, possibly in the world."

"Diamonds?"

"They're everywhere. It's where most of our wealth comes from. They trade in Greece, Egypt, parts of Africa, Asia, and even India. Black market mostly—we have to make it look like the diamonds are actually imported internationally. It's a whole thing. And, of course, we keep a few for ourselves."

"Kendra's ring? She was wearing a large yellow diamond."

309

Josh nods. "Yeah, she had more than one, that's for sure. Used to really get my goat."

"I thought diamond mines *were* in faraway places, like Africa."

"They are mostly. In fact, there are no working diamond mines at all in the U.S. right now. And that's how we want to keep it. Even I, who'd love to show the whole world what my parents discovered, want to keep it to ourselves. Imagine the invasion on our peaceful society here. And these diamonds give us the ability to contain our own wealth and continue to govern our own. I plan on using much of my cut helping others. Sammy and I have two big projects we're working on. The money we earn goes so far in places like Haiti, where the government takes what comes in. We can do it privately and build. We have a responsibility to use our assets for the greater good, not just in our villages, but where we can. But we can't let them get into the wrong hands."

"That's one of the most selfless reasons I've heard for keeping the society secret. Whose property are we on? Do the owners know about it?"

"Mine, babe. I was barely eighteen when I purchased the property, shortly after the incident with my parents and the Brandts. I wanted to protect it as best I could. I outsmarted them on that front, and there was nothing your father or Mr. Brandt could do about it. But they're still going to pay for what they did."

"Tell me what happened."

"After watching their fortune slip through their hands, my parents confronted Michael Brandt in private. They thought they were dealing with a rational human being, unfortunately." He pauses, lost in a memory but smiles. "My parents were joined at the hip. They were almost always together. If they weren't, people would ask, 'Hey, where's your better half?'" Josh's smile transforms into a frown.

"What did he do?"

"He dismembered them. Their better halves. You know the old expression, 'I feel like I'm missing my right arm?'" I nod but am afraid

310

of where this is going. "Well, that's what both of my parents are missing. Their right arms."

"No." I shake my head in disbelief.

"Oh, yes, indeed."

"Please tell me Dr. Braun didn't have anything to do with it?"

"No. He sewed them back up and took care of them until they were well enough to run."

"You didn't go with them?"

"No. Sam and I have worked hard to convince the Order that our loyalty is with them. That my parents were wrong. We've spent years building their trust. Being patient. Waiting for the right time to take them all out. Then you showed up on my doorstep. An early morning angel. One that already raised holy hell in the village," he says and smiles again.

"I don't know what to say, except that I'm so sorry." I reach out and bring him in for a hug. He squeezes me hard. "Are you telling me here because it's safe? No chance of cameras or audio?"

"Yes. It's safe here from eyes and ears."

"Well, let's go see those diamonds."

"There's something else, Jenny. Forgive me for all the lies, but I'm not married to Lucia. The ceremony was a farce for the sake of the Grand Masters."

"What? But on the boat and my phone call on your wedding day. You were adamant. And I saw the chemistry. No way." I'm not buying it.

"It fell into the plan, Jenny. Forgive me for being unable to tell you sooner."

"Josh, please. You were beyond convincing. Those outfits you had me wear. Kissing in front of me. A big wedding?"

"Had to be done. And I'd say Lucia has a competitive side. She got a little too into the role with the outfits. But it's why everyone bought it so easily."

"Are you sure you didn't buy it? You looked in love to me."

"It's always been you, Jenny. I love you."

"You're going to have to give me a minute on that one, Josh. I mean, Jesus. You hurt me so bad in the process. So bad."

"I know. I'm so sorry. I'll make it up to you. I promise. If you'll have me back, of course. I never want to hurt you ever again or see that look of disappointment in your face."

This is what I've wanted, but I definitely need a hot minute to think about it. I switch topics and tell him everything that happened yesterday. He takes it all in, organizing the information and trying to figure out what to do about some of it. The part about Jack is disturbing, on top of everything else. To my surprise, he already knew of Shane's punishment cavern, but only as of late. He and Shane have gotten close working together, both victims of the evil aspects of the society.

"We'll figure it out later. We have to keep this day moving. There's one more air pocket before the channel. Remember what I taught you about your breathing?"

I nod, except my breathing has changed. I'm getting waves of hope for love and a future with Josh. He dips down and dolphin kicks his way to the next air pocket. I follow behind again.

We take some deep breaths getting ready for the next phase. "Here we go. On three. One, two, three."

I take a deep breath of air and follow Josh through a narrow channel. I've been through much tighter and rather effortlessly make it to our next destination.

"Wow, I'm impressed. You did great."

"You should have seen me in the Mystery Cavern."

"I knew you'd survive that too, Jenny, or I would've found a way to stop you. I am sorry that you were so injured though. My guilt will last forever."

"Good!" I say with a smile. But he still looks sad. "I forgive you, Josh. It's all on me." I stop the chat and look around. "Is this it?" I grab the flashlight. We're in a small cavern.

"Almost." We swim to the far end of the cavern and onto solid ground. I see an opening and walk toward it and look back at Josh who's smiling again. "Go ahead. Ladies first."

I slip through easily and into a much larger space. Josh flips a few switches and the whole room lights up. This room is full of outside electricity. Mining materials are scattered around. Maybe I thought the room would light up and sparkle, but I don't see anything.

"This wall." I walk over and stare. I see it now. There are flecks and bigger stones.

"Is this what they look like in the rough?"

"Yes." He laughs at me. "You look disappointed. Diamonds are composed of carbon atoms. When they're composed of pure carbon, they're colorless. These contain traces of nitrogen which give it the yellow color. When we clean 'em, they're spectacular. The geological gifts bestowed upon us by Mother Nature are a blessing. Sometimes a curse, but hopefully that will change."

I'm overcome with a feeling of joy. Of being in this moment with Josh. I reach for him. The look on his face has the desire I wish to consume, but he shakes his head and nonchalantly looks up. I get it. Cameras everywhere.

"Now what?"

"We head back. If you need to, remember to use the air pocket on the way out." I smile.

"I will."

We head back out of the diamond chamber, through the next tunnel and dive into the narrow channel out. I emerge alongside Josh up into the air pocket. He plops me on the ledge and kisses me with such intensity that I can't help but let out groans. We go at it hard, both of us pent up. But it's too damn cold to make love in the water without our wetsuits, so it'll have to wait.

"Save some of this energy. You're going to need it when I get ahold of you again."

Josh reaches into his suit and pulls out a yellow diamond. "This is the one I want to plant on your hand someday. Will you take it?"

"Are you asking me to marry you?"

"Well, we'd have to change the rule book about marriage."

"Oh hell, yes. That book needs rewriting. And yes. I would take it. I would say yes." Josh kisses a fresh tear off my cheek and tells me how much he loves me and will forever. This day, my last day of knowledge, has been my favorite. I'm so in love. "You still have a plan, Josh? To make all of this possible?"

"I do. I actually have a new plan. It's much better than my original. I was about to destroy the villages if I had to. Open up the dams and flood them all. But luckily, that's not going to be necessary. You have nothing to do but wait."

## 47

THE B&B

We make it back to the final chamber before our exit and get changed back into our clothes. There's nothing sexy about getting out of a full wetsuit, or I would tease Josh a little. Of course, I almost forgot, we're under the watch of big brother. Or, in this case, my father. Josh turns off all the lights and whispers for me to be quiet. "Cameras aren't infrared." I know where he's going with this, and I immediately start throbbing in places only he can sooth. I'm still down to my undies when he picks me up. I wrap my legs tightly around his waist as he carries me up against a cold rock. I'm as quiet as I can be, but it's not easy. Josh gently covers my mouth with one hand and kisses my neck. We make love until we're both weak and shaky.

The union of body and soul is broken by the sound of Josh's phone ringing and pinging. Josh's annoyance takes on a more somber tone as he answers. On his end, I hear an "oh boy" followed by "fuck." This can't be good and, as usual, I worry something's happened to Danny. Josh flicks on one of the lights and I look at him for an explanation. "We'll figure it out," he says and hangs up.

"What's going on?"

"You can't go back to Scott's. Feds have moved in and are claiming it as a stakeout. They've taken over the airfield. Copters coming and going."

"What about Veronica's air day?"

"We'll get her up somewhere else. Fortunately, Ryan is almost finished. They'll just need to land elsewhere."

"Now I need to figure out what to do with you."

"Josh, I'm so tired of running. It's exhausting."

"I know. It'll be over soon, babe."

"I hope so." My morale was soaring and now it's heading south. I wonder what they'll do with me. "What if I'm locked up for aiding and abetting, or worse?"

"I won't let that happen."

Josh's phone rings again. This time Josh curses under his breath and asks, "Is she alive?"

"Who?" I tug on him.

He tersely holds up an index finger. "See what you can do. Did anyone tell Michael yet?"

"Who?" I demand.

"Alicia."

I hold my hand over my mouth and feel a pang of guilt for not saying something sooner. Ryan will never forgive me if he finds out. I walk away and let Josh finish his conversation.

He hangs up and takes me by the hand. "Here's the deal. I think we can finish the rest of the initiations right up to me. But then you'll all complete your final ceremony together."

"Sounds good. What happened to Alicia?"

"Found her in the river. They don't think she's going to make it. Michael can't know for now, or he'll lose his shit."

"Josh, you have no idea. This is going to destroy him. Where will I stay? I have almost a week to get through on my own."

"It'll be all right." Josh starts feverishly texting while I look around at what could be my residency for the next week.

"We're good."

"We are?"

"There's a bed and breakfast about two miles from here. I own it. But it's in another name. Friends of my parents. No one knows except Sam. And now you. You have to make it there without being caught. The manager is preparing you a large suite overlooking the property. It's elegant and private and all of your meals will be delivered," he says with a hint of snobbery, as if I'm high maintenance. Quite frankly, I'm feeling a little high maintenance at the moment.

"I can't deal with any more underground bunkers."

"You'll like this one. I'd join you if I could, but we can't risk it. No leaving. Got it?"

"Got it."

"I'm dead serious, Jenny," Josh whispers. "You have a habit of snooping. Don't do it unless I tell you to move."

"What should I do if the Feds show up?"

"Run. Head back up the main road and to the church. But, hopefully, that won't happen. We're in the homestretch, babe. You in this for the long haul?"

"With you by my side. Yes!"

Josh shuts off the light again and gives me a kiss. I cling to him for dear life, so worried. So many things can go wrong from here. He pushes the button, and our escape route opens again. Back on hands and knees we inch our way toward the light. We're just about out when we hear voices.

"What can we do for you, agent?" *Oh, no.* They're here.

"What are you guys doing way up here? This isn't park land."

"Trust me?" Josh asks.

"Yes, of course. Why?"

Josh wiggles his way out of the space. "They're helping me. Hi. I'm Josh Flannery. I engineer the dams in our parks."

"We know who you are. What are you doing here? A little far from the lake, aren't you?"

"Checking the water. Bacteria is high in the creeks. It affects the lakes. We're trying to figure out where it's coming from. Can't kill off all the fish or endanger the residents."

"What's in there?" a man asks.

"A spring. But it's clear. I have about four more to check. What's going on?"

*Oh, come on, Josh.* They're gonna want to check. As quietly as I can, I back into the space again. Do I hide behind a rock, or make my way back to the air pocket? Ever so faintly, I hear one of the men tell Josh they're gonna need to take a look. "Be my guest. Watch your head." I grab both wet suits, sink into the deep hole, kick off, and make my way to the air pocket. It's cold as heck, and I'm irritated by the intrusion. I lay Josh's wetsuit on the ledge then hop up and put mine on as quickly as I can to stop shaking. I can't hear anything. How am I supposed to know if they're gone?

I can't tell if Josh is a genius for letting them in the cave or not, but I have to give him the benefit of the doubt. He couldn't very well kill them, and the agents won't be prepared to dive, so hopefully Josh's story will keep them away. But this is way, way too close for comfort in front of our biggest secrets as an Order. I wait a good thirty minutes before I brave it and come up slowly into the cavern. It's dark, and I don't hear any voices. I slowly rise, find my way to a light, and turn it on. Much to my amazement, close to the rock where we just made love, lies a plastic container with water samples. Josh has prepared wisely for this.

I'm absolutely sopping wet and decide to leave the wetsuit on. My sneakers are soaked, but I need them. How am I supposed to walk into a bed and breakfast like this? The other guests will recognize me, one of the most acclaimed missing persons of all times, roaming around in a wetsuit. I shimmy on my belly again toward the exit. It's quiet. I hop out and look in the direction I'm supposed to go just in time to see a fully armed Mr. Brandt. He's got a team of security with him. They're here to protect the diamond mine 'til the death, if need be, or to take me. I'm in full fight or flight again.

I crawl through thick brush around the opposite side of the mouth of the cave. They'll be too distracted to look my way for a little while. It's taking every ounce of discipline I have left to not jump up and just make a mad dash for it. But I have to be patient until I'm completely out of sight. I weave around boulders, trees, and giant forest ferns, then take a look back. All but one appears to have gone inside. I wait until he turns the other way and bolt. About a mile in, I feel the blisters forming on my feet and a stabbing pain in my side. I stop for a break to catch my breath. I dodge behind a tree, hearing a helicopter hovering above. Great! I stay close to the tree line but won't have it for cover for very long. I have to make my way through an open field, the corn barely sprouted. But it's the only thing separating me from my shelter.

"Pssst," a voice says.

I gasp and swing around in a defensive position. An older gentleman is standing in front of me with a smile on his face. He's completely grey but has a good head of hair. His cheeks are red, either from the sun or his heritage. He's wearing a very beat up pair of denim jeans and buttoned-down shirt, which is partially concealing an undershirt and suspenders. A farmer? He looks familiar, but I can't place him at the moment. I look around, wondering where he came from.

"Here. Give me your suit and put this on. He hands me a pair of denim coveralls. I don't bother to ask questions. He turns his back and I strip and get dressed.

"Here."

"What's this?" He hands me a key. "What's it for?"

"See that tractor over there? Know how to drive one?"

"Um. No. I have no idea how to drive a tractor."

"Time to learn."

I get the world's fastest lesson, and it gives me a pounding headache. But I think I have it down.

"Okay, good luck, kiddo. Drive it along the edge so you don't disturb the crops. It'll take you right to the B&B. You'll look a lot less out of place too." He laughs and looks at the wetsuit.

"Who are you?"

"I was wondering if you were going to ask. I'm Josh's father. I'm Henry Flannery. Nice to finally meet you again, Jenny." That's when I look at his right arm and realize he's got a prosthetic.

## 48

HENRY FLANNERY

Josh's father is kind and promises me better times to come. "Keep the faith," he says. I thank him profusely for coming to my rescue and take off toward the tractor. I have to laugh at my new predicament. I come up next to the blue Ford tractor with an eight-speed transmission. Who would need so many speeds? There are two sticks. I make sure the right one, the high and low range something or other, is in neutral. I climb up on the seat and hear a chopper overhead. I need to make it look like I know what I'm doing here. I place my foot on the brake and turn the key. It doesn't turn over. Now what?

I look into the woods for Mr. Flannery. He's using hand motions to tell me to do it again. I try again. It turns over. I look back and smile, then release the brake and put the transmission in first gear, which is exactly where I plan on leaving it until I get there. I release the clutch and it stalls. *Dang it.* I go through the whole process again but release my foot much more slowly. I did it! I'm moving. I give a subtle wave to Mr. Flannery and drive my first tractor. It's sort of fun. I wonder if Lexi and Adam have been for tractor rides with their grandfather. I miss them terribly and can't wait to see them again. I smile, thinking that maybe someday they'll call me Aunt Jenny.

The B&B is in sight. It's a huge old farmhouse with additions, including a tennis court and pool. The barn's been renovated into guest rooms. I spot another building that looks more like a big garage and make my way over and park. A few guests are looking at me from a large deck. I give them a warm smile which they return, probably thinking how cute it is to be in the country. Now what? There's a young woman with a ponytail heading my way. I pretend to look over the tractor.

"Ms. O'Rourke, please follow me."

I follow her through a side door into a laundry area. The dryers are running, and the room smells like soap and dryer sheets. We step up into a large, well-appointed sitting area. It's definitely high-end with Victorian furniture, heirloom accents in rich cherry, and expensive custom window treatments. The whole back wall is lined with windows overlooking hundreds of open acres and the pool area. The pool is filled and open for the season, but no one is in it just yet.

I continue to follow the ponytail up a flight of stairs and to a room. "You have our largest suite. My name is Stephanie. Just ring the front desk if you need anything." I barely have time to thank her as she runs off to her duties. She's not hiding her fear of me or what trouble I could bring here. I'm going to follow Josh's advice and stay out of sight.

The room does not disappoint. I have a king-sized canopy bed, sitting area with a fireplace, and a desk with a window that overlooks the property. The bathroom is lined with Italian marble. And I have a large jetted tub. I can handle this for the next five days or so. I have a stocked wet bar with wine, cheese, and something for dinner. I'm about to take a bite when my room phone rings. I pick it up but don't say anything.

"Jenny?" It's Josh.

"Yes."

"You made it. You did great in the cave. I just dragged the agents to two other springs to check water samples. They got bored and left. I think we officially threw them off. Sam is home too and off the hook."

"Fantastic." I tell Josh about Mr. Brandt and his goons showing up to the cave. He's already aware, and they're already gone. They closed it off completely for now, and Mr. Brandt is back at Fonthill to finish Danny's tour and Day Four of Wisdom. I should be safe from the FBI and all harm.

"Where does my father think I am?"

"Unfortunately, I had to tell him where you are, but he doesn't have a clue that I own it. Please make sure no one knows that my parents are here. How did you like my dad?"

"I loved him. Both of your parents are here?"

"They help me manage the B&B. The Grand Masters never go there. Too much exposure and out of the way of Brandtville."

"Like your room?"

"I love it. I'm going to eat and get in the tub. Are there extra clothes?"

"Kimberly is going to bring you some later."

"What a freaking three-ring circus," I say. We both laugh. He tells me not to worry and that we'll be back together again soon.

I'm finished eating what's left of my meal when I hear a knock at the door. It's Kimberly with my clothes, followed by an older woman. I can tell by her prosthetic arm that it's Josh's mother. They both bring me in for a big hug. Josh's mother is very pretty. A little weathered, but attractive. She's got a short blonde bob, perfect teeth, and character lines. She's thin and looks very preppy in her Ralph Lauren pink paisley shirt and khakis. She came to wish me luck and to share her concerns as a mother. She knows what the Grand Masters are capable of and proves it by taking off her prosthetic. I pull down the back of my shirt and show her my bite scar to reassure her, as best as I can, that Josh has a plan and that I trust him completely.

"I hope you're right. I'm so proud of him and worried at the same time. Amazing, isn't he?"

"Truly amazing. Must have good parents," I say with a smile. The conversation makes me think of my mom and grandmother. They must be so worried too, and I wonder how they're coping. And how Fabrizio is doing. I hope it's possible to get them all back and back to a normal life.

It's dark outside when we say our final goodbyes. Mrs. Flannery promises good meals every day while I'm here and tells me to rest up. I fully intend to try. I watch them as they head down the hall and down the staircase. I close the door to my room and lock it.

It's an odd feeling having nothing to do for awhile. I look out the window and realize the helicopters have stopped flying, hopefully for the rest of the night. I grab my wine, fill the tub with hot water, turn on the jets, and sink into the closest thing I've had to relaxation in a long time.

# 49

CLOSING CEREMONIES

T his is it ... the day of my initiation, which will begin at the traditional high noon. I tossed and turned for most of the night. My stay at Josh's B&B has been so wonderfully uneventful that it made me forget at times that this day could get ugly.

Josh called late last night to tell me The Imperator has ordered us all, including the Grand Masters, to join him at the Mystery Cavern instead of Deep Creek where most people have their final ceremony and baptism.

"Oh, hell no! I'm not going back to that place." My post-traumatic stress is flaring. Josh reassures me that it's going to be all right. It's just the only place that isn't surrounded. I express my fears that they'll put me back in for my third punishment for saving Dr. Braun, or that all of us will have to go in. I'll never survive it again. I don't have the mental or physical strength for it, and I doubt Ryan does either. I'm scared, and contemplate telling the bureau now, or maybe even running far away. But I could never do that to the others or to Josh. He continues to reassure me.

It's 7:00 a.m. when Stephanie delivers me a white dress and

informs me that a driver will come and get me at 10:30 a.m. She wishes me luck and takes off like a bat out of hell, just like she's been doing all week. I hold up the dress to get a better look. Well, it's official. I'm going to be a cult member soon. The dress proves it. It's old and lacy and creepy. I'm definitely not the first to wear it, but I can't help but wonder if I'll be the last. I lay it on the bed and step into the bathroom. My stomach is queasy. Something isn't sitting well with me, and it has nothing to do with food.

I shower, towel off, and get ready. The dress is a little big, but good enough. God forbid I'm seen wearing this on the way out. I look ghastly. They'd think for sure the place was haunted.

I stare out the window at the beautiful sunny summer day. Everything is peaceful. There's a couple playing on the tennis court, blissfully unaware of the darkness I'm about to step into.

There's a knock on my door. It's time. "Ready, Ms. O'Rourke?" It's the same driver who took me to my punishment trial.

"I suppose."

He hands me a trench coat to put over my dress. "This way."

We head out through the laundry area and over to a black Lincoln Navigator with very dark windows. There's no way to see in. He opens and closes the door for me, and I immediately start praying. "Hail Mary, full of grace." I say it over and over as we back out of the drive and onto the main road.

"Music?" he asks.

"No. Please. I need to think."

"I understand. I wish you the best today. You're going to do great."

"How was your initiation?"

"Mine? Pretty easy. A few prayers were said, and I got dunked in Deep Creek. Yours? I'm sensing something a bit more intricate. But I will be waiting for you. I'm not going anywhere, so if you get scared, or if something doesn't go well, head back to the parking lot. I'll be there."

"That's reassuring. Thank you." *Hail Mary, full of grace ...*"

I stare out the window as the villages go by. One after another, all named after the original settlers and Postmen. We pass Brandtville and Ottsville. I see the sign for Kintnersville, and my leg starts bouncing up and down like Danny's does when he's nervous.

I see the Mystery Cavern ahead, and a sudden feeling of peace spreads throughout me. I realize I'm ready for whatever is about to take place. There are a few cars in the lot. A parking attendant lines us up to the far right of the entrance.

"Should I get out?"

"Not yet. They're gonna shut the road off altogether so you can all go in safely, without being noticed. The Grand Masters and guests are already there."

"Oh." It's ten minutes until noon.

"Here they come." I turn around to see huge construction vehicles clog up the lanes in both directions. Then another further up the road. Cars are honking.

"They're ready for you." I can see that the front door is open. "You go in first, Ms. O'Rourke. Good luck."

"Thank you." I open the door and head into the lobby. Emily, who led my opening ceremony, tells me to wait by the entrance of the cave. Danny, Ryan, Jackie, and Veronica enter in order and stand behind me. I'm so happy to see everyone. Danny and Ryan have white smocks over their clothes. Jackie and Veronica are wearing the same white dress I have on. We look ridiculous. Fabrizio would have had a field day with this. We attempt a hug but are told, "No touching."

At noon, a bell chimes and the door to the cavern opens. We're led down the drafty cold tunnel and into the large chamber with the giant cross. My great-uncle, The Judge and Imperator, is standing next to the altar. He's wearing a purple robe and holding a pamphlet. In order around a hand-drawn pentacle stand all the disciples—Chief Shawtagh, Greg, my father, Mr. Brandt, and Josh. They all have blank looks on their faces like they don't know what's happening, except Josh. He looks somewhat relaxed in comparison to the rest.

There's a small audience above us. I see Shane and Dennis among the crowd. Emily hands us candles, and my great-uncle begins the ceremony.

"It is with great pride and honor that we welcome our family of new members today." He recites all of our names aloud as Emily lights our candles."

"Jenny, please come forward." I do as I'm told. My great-uncle looks frail, much thinner and older than I recall. "Will you accept the responsibilities given to you as required by the Empedocles Ordo Rosae Crucis Unitas Fratrum?"

"I will."

He continues, calling up the others and asking them the same question. Next, we are each baptized with the water that trickles down the side of the cave behind the small altar. The words of blessing my great-uncle uses give me the goosebumps.

"At this time, I'd like to call Dennis Engel down to join us as well." The Grand Masters look perplexed. "You may stand behind your brother." I wonder if he's about to remove my father and make Dennis the new Grand Master. Ugh. "Would you kindly hand out the wine so that we may all celebrate this momentous occasion."

Danny and I look at each other, like *is this it?* After everything we went through, this is it? Each Grand Master has a unique chalice. New ones were made for us as well. Mine not only has my symbolic element plus the rosy cross, like the others, but it's also fully inscribed with a depiction of Lady Justice. I take note that my great-uncle's bears a similar resemblance, and it doesn't go unnoticed by the others either.

The other chalices are full of symbolism, but none looks like mine. My father is getting red in the face, which makes me nervous. "Please drink to the new members of EORCUF." My Uncle Thomas holds up his wine and drinks. Everyone in the room follows, including the guests. They clap, then recite a passage from the pamphlets they were given. I'm looking at my father, who doesn't seem to recognize the verse and is shifting nervously, not liking being taken off guard.

"Now, I have some important news to share with you all," my great-uncle announces. "I have been an Imperator for almost fifty years. As you all know, the original Order was established to create a higher path for its members. A heightened level of knowledge, intelligence, faith, discipline, and above all else, peace. A perfect Order that could separate us from the evil ways of the rest of society.

"Well, I must confess and beg for forgiveness, because I have let you down. This Order has been permanently scarred by my own family. Sean, you disgrace me the most. You've been given chances upon chances, and you continue to prove that you're nothing more than a ruthless dictator. But I'm the one who gave you those chances, and for that I'm guilty. Our founding members would never have approved of hurting our own or punishing them to the point of disfigurement. Michael Brandt, the same applies to you. You will both be stepping down as Grand Masters, effective immediately. Emily, please remove their sacred allegiance pins at once." Emily's hands shake as she approaches them.

There's a rumble, followed by whispers from the crowd above us. My father begrudgingly asks what his responsibilities will be going forward. My great-uncle tells him to keep quiet, and that he'll be getting to that part. Mr. Brandt looks ready to pounce. With their pins off, he asks Danny to come forward and honors him as the new Grand Master of the symbol of Earth. My father looks proud, pissed, and confused all at the same time. Next, he honors Jackie as the Grand Master of Fire. Ryan was the next in line theoretically, but I'd say my uncle made the right choice. He smiles proudly at his sister while she graciously accepts.

"I've saved the best for last. Jenny, please come forward." My great-uncle removes his symbolic pin and places it on the collar of my dress. "When I die, which I assure you will be soon enough, you will be the third Imperator of the Empedocles Ordo Rosae Crucis Unitas Fratrum." I'm completely stunned. "All orders of business, all discipline, all amendments to our Order will first be approved by you." My father's eyes are wide. I see a vein throbbing on the side of his head. Clearly, in his mind, this honor was to be his when the day came. He was grooming me for Grand Master, but certainly not to advance before him.

With that enormous bombshell, Mr. Brandt lunges forward and grabs my uncle by the throat. There are screams and gasps. My father attempts an act of mutiny by going after Josh. He knows, as well as I do, that Josh had something to do with this new and shocking plan. But Josh is too strong and has my father in a chokehold. Shane takes immediate control of Mr. Brandt while Danny eyes up Uncle Dennis, practically begging him to make a move. He stands down.

I'm just standing here hoping my great-uncle has a damn good plan for what to do from here. Simply handing us leadership is like handing us a death sentence. The Judge looks up at his guests. "My cherished Fratres and Sorores, will you uphold and respect the authority I have bestowed upon your new leaders?"

"They all answer loudly, "We will."

"Shane Brandt, you will now head up security, with all other deputies and private security officers reporting directly to you. Jenny, you will help Shane uphold the laws and agree upon terms together. Understand?" We both agree completely and smirk at one another.

"My beloved fellowship, you may now leave in peace. Thank you for your trust over the years, and remember to continue to do the right thing for the greater good. God bless you."

One by one, the guests file out of the cavern and back to their homes and lives. Not without much gossip though, I'm sure. Today is most likely a historical one for the Order, giving new hope to live life without fear. When the last one is out, my great-uncle turns to my father.

"Sean, you asked what your responsibilities would be from here."

My father nods. I'm secretly praying he doesn't ask me to come up with them. My father looks lost and broken. He's been in control for so long. I wish I could feel sorry for him, but I can't anymore. He's gone way too far, for way too long. He's sick. And as he once said about my friend, Jodi, he's like a rabid animal that needs to be put down. I just hope I'm not asked to do the honors.

"I would be happy to grant all three of you with new responsibilities. Important ones, under one condition."

"What's that Imperator?" Mr. Brandt asks.

"Pass through your punishment unharmed."

There's panic on the faces of the aging leaders. "We'll never make it, Uncle. Jenny and Michael were in their prime of health and fitness," my father defends.

"Your punishment ceremony begins now." Chief Shawtagh, obviously in the know, begins the traditional drumming. Danny grabs me and pulls me toward the door, not knowing what could happen. Ryan grabs Jackie, Shane, and Veronica, and we huddle together.

"What should we do? We have to stop this. That's my father," Ryan says. Jackie agrees.

"Cousin, you need to know something. Alicia is very sick. She was dragged out of the river on the brink of death just a few days ago. Your father's doing." Shane breaks the news.

Ryan's face contorts to anger, the last straw for him too. Jackie steps away, letting him make the final decision for them both. "Then let nature take its course, whatever that may be."

"Jenny, please come closer." I heed the Imperator's request and take small steps toward them, everyone else behind me. "You found your way through the hardest part of this Mystery Cave. But there's one more zone, one that's quite daunting." My father closes his eyes, perhaps getting a small glimmer of hope that his punishment will be easier. "What is it that you and Daniel were afraid of as children? Copperheads?"

Four beefy security guards rush in and cuff the masterminds of the past together. I'm getting emotional despite myself. The snakes are symbolic for many reasons. It's sick and twisted, and I wonder if I could stop it even if I wanted to. Danny reads me and shakes his head.

"It's time to end it," he says through watery eyes.

"Gentlemen, follow me," my great-uncle says coldly.

"Wait!" I scream and run up behind them. I'm thinking to myself, maybe if he survives, he'll be a better person for it. Maybe there's a way after all. I try to give him some encouragement because even though he doesn't deserve it, I want him to feel loved before he goes. "If anyone can do this, you can, Dad. Please try your hardest, and we'll help you repent." He's touched and smiles at me.

"Not this time, pumpkin. Do what you think is right. I love you."

We all put our hands over our ears to tune out the blood-curdling screams that shortly follow. Their pain and fear echoes through the caverns. I fall to the ground and weep, my father's death killing me inside. Veronica is afraid and looking frantically around for a way out, but Shane swoops her up into his arms. Danny joins me, close to hysterics. Josh leans down and embraces us both.

"What do you think of this, Josh?" I ask him. It's not his immediate family so he can't possibly know what this feels like. His parents are dismembered, but they're alive.

"It's not over yet. I need everyone to leave except Jenny. Now!" Josh orders.

"No, way. I'm not leaving my sister here." Ryan and Danny take a stand and put themselves between me and Josh.

"You have to trust me."

"Just go. Do it," I tell them shaking

"I won't let anything happen to her, Danny. We'll all be together again soon. Go home. Look and act normal, because they'll be coming."

"Who?"

"The law."

Chief Shawtagh gathers his things with the help of Emily and leaves. Shane takes a shivering and close-to-shock Veronica by the arm and leads her out. Greg tells Ryan he'll take him to Alicia. Danny takes Jackie by the hand to lead her out but checks on me first.

"I'll be okay," I tell him. "Go."

Josh wipes my tears and kisses my cheek. "It's going to be okay."

"Come sit, child," my great-uncle orders.

Josh has rope. "Trust me, right?" I nod at him. The screams are dying down, and I only hear an occasional moan. I can't believe I allowed this inhumane torture. Josh ties me to the chair. For a moment I feel panic, but in my heart, I know Josh would never hurt me.

"My dear, I'm very old and very sick. I don't have but a few more weeks to live. Not even some of our best home remedies can cure my disease. I'm ready to go. I'm also ready to give the outside government something they can feel proud of, enough that they can close this case and leave our people in peace."

"Your missing person status is finally going to be closed, babe." I think I'm starting to get it.

"They're going to find me tied up and them dead. They'll find my original punishment cavern and the bears. Problem is, I look awfully good for a woman who's been tied up for how long?"

"Here, drink this."

"Wine? I'm trying to trust you, Josh, but I don't know. Your plan has holes in it." I take a gulp. And that's the last thing I remember about that day.

# 50

## A NEW ERA

G rand Master Dean Banos rambles on and on while I think back to five years ago. So much has happened. The FBI finally got their big break. The case of the Brandtville cult killers was closed and I was rescued. That's the short of how the tale is currently told. After all the legal fights and public interviews, we all moved home and joined Dean's AMORC chapter, right up the hill from the farm. It was meant to be. The large lodge sits right at the center of the old Twenty-Fifth Acre. I thought hard about destroying the lodge at first. But after studying and attending services a few times, I realized it was the kind of spiritual healing we all needed. Their mystical practices and traditions put us back on the right path to becoming happier. I never miss a service and even lead several initiatives for the fellowship, traveling quite a bit to other chapters, sharing my personal story and gaining more knowledge.

Professionally, I'm back to work using my law degrees as Assistant District Attorney in Bucks County. I inherited my father's old law office in Doylestown. Turns out there was a lot more to that office than I knew, but what's left of his secrets are safe with me. I feel fulfilled on almost every level, but sometimes I miss my father and feel like I failed him.

I look at my watch to check the time. "Stop making it so obvious that you want to leave," Josh whispers. I smile and roll my eyes. "I can't help it. I still haven't finished the potato salad for the party. And this one wants some food." I rub my growing belly. I'm six months pregnant today. It's Josh and my first child together. I'm beyond excited but a little nervous too. I pray every night that I have what it takes to be a good mother.

After much debating, Josh and I decided to settle into his lake house. It's where we fell in love and where we feel closest as a couple. We finished decorating the baby's room this week in shades of yellow and green. Since we don't know what we're having, we kept it neutral and hope to be blessed with more than one.

Danny and Fabrizio have been amazing parents to an adopted little boy. I keep thinking, if they can do it, we can do it. Today we're celebrating their son's first birthday back at the farm where they permanently live. They adopted Celestino in Italy, but Danny convinced Fabrizio to move back, to be part of our bigger family back in Brandtville. I was so relieved when he caved. It took a good year of sucking up for Danny to woo Fabrizio, let alone adopt a baby. But his love finally won him over.

Dean wraps up services and wishes us all Peace Profound. I catch Tina staring at me on the way out and give her a wave. She and Peter left their Rosicrucian Order to join Dean's. We've been friendly, but nowhere near as close as we once were. We have some trust issues, to say the least.

Josh and I bolt out the back door and make our way on foot back to the farm. There are a few stragglers following us, including Alicia and Ryan. Alicia still has to take it easy but has mostly recovered from the brain damage she incurred during her near-drowning. It's been a long road to recovery. Ryan never left her side through it all. His love and devotion to his bride are inspiring, and I'm so proud of him.

The farm is decorated beautifully. There are pony rides, a bouncy house, a juggling clown, you name it. Fabrizio pulled out all the stops. My mom greets me halfway up the lawn. "Nonna finished the potato salad for you."

"Best news ever," I say with a smile. I give my mom a hug, like I do as often as I can to make up for lost time. Sallie, my five-year-old coywolf, is jumping up to greet me. She is so much bigger than I ever thought she'd get, but so sweet. Much to my chagrin, Danny opted out of the coywolf offering.

"Just relax for once," my mom says.

"I think I'll do that, right after I fix myself an offensive amount of food." I dash into the kitchen to find Dr. Braun chatting with Nonna. He beats me to the buffet, laughing.

"Hello, dear. How are you feeling?" He asks. "Names yet?" He kisses me on the cheek and rubs my belly.

"If it's a boy, definitely after you." I wink. "Girl, I think after my mom, Angela. But we'd call her Angel."

"That's beautiful."

Out of the kitchen window, I see Jackie holding her daughter steady on a Shetland pony. She was the first to get pregnant. Paige will be three in a few weeks. She and Dexter married a year after our initiation. She never told him any of the details, just as she promised. Behind Paige is Shane and Veronica's little one, Nick. Jack is trying to stay ahead of him with a camera in hand. It's his first grandchild, and the most documented and photographed child in town. Jessica is close by with her new boyfriend, waving and making funny faces at Nick to make him smile. Josh and Dr. Braun follow me out to a picnic table where we take in the celebration. It's a joyous one indeed.

Danny joins us, leaving Fabrizio in charge of Celestino. Veronica and Jackie take a break to join us as well.

I look around. I have my Order leaders as needed. "Tell me what you know." I look at each member for an answer.

"Shane said she found the cave," Josh discloses.

"How far did she get? Did she find anything?"

"Not yet. But we have her on audio talking to Peter after services."

"Let me hear it." Danny hands me the device and I push play.

"That bitch isn't fooling anyone. She's going down," Tina says. Peter adds, "To Chinatown." They both laugh, getting a kick out of each other. I smile, remembering their playful wit. "I'll get a team together and we'll head back down to the entrance tomorrow," Tina says. "Roger that," Peter answers. I shut off the recording, having heard enough.

I look at Danny, who's ready to counsel me. "I know it's hard, but it has to be done."

"I never thought we'd have to do this." I pause and look at my Grand Masters. I loathe having to make this decision after how far we've come. How much good we've done all across the world even. "Have you considered all other options?"

"We have," Danny says.

"Very well. Is the new arena ready?" I ask, looking at Veronica.

"It is," she answers.

"The wolves?"

"They're a lively pack," Ryan replies. "I know it's hard. But now that we know everything, we know how this has to go. There's no way to alter this part of our Constitution."

"I never want something like this to happen again. Understand?"

Everyone promises to have a better handle on things from here on out.

"Midnight then?" I ask.

"What if they live, Imperator?" Jackie asks respectfully.

"They won't."

# EPILOGUE

I hope you enjoyed reading the Element Mystery Series. If so, please take a few moments to give me a great review on Amazon. Those stars mean a lot to us writers!

Like many works of fiction, historical truths, real places, and real people are interwoven to make a story believable and to allow readers to learn a few things along the way. This series is no exception. In fact, it's quite sprinkled with historical facts, some very researched and some experienced first-hand growing up in Bucks County. I wanted to give a little credit and some extra insight about some of the inspiring places mentioned in the series.

## Henry Chapman Mercer

I spent my teen years and young adulthood living in Doylestown, about a mile from Fonthill Castle. It intrigued me then, but not half as much as it does now. Henry Mercer Chapman was born in Doylestown, Pennsylvania in 1856. He was an archaeologist, anthropologist, ceramist, scholar, writer, and a huge collector. He was a well-rounded and creative soul.

Henry attended Harvard University and Law School at the University of Pennsylvania. He passed the bar but never practiced law. Thanks to his very affluent and beloved Aunt Elizabeth, Henry was able to travel the world. For ten years he studied castles but built his own in five with the help of ten loyal workers and one big reliable work horse named Lucy.

He became impassioned with the Arts and Crafts Movement and eventually opened a pottery factory right next to his castle where he created timeless works of art. One of the things I respect most about Henry was his ability to tell stories through his artwork. He was a great storyteller and didn't mind twisting the facts, especially historical facts. I like to think he'd be flattered by the twist I've created for him and the many historical elements woven throughout the series.

## Lake Nockamixon

I lived near Lake Nockamixon for many years, swimming in their epic-sized pool and picnicking with friends, even taking my horse for a swim on occasion in the lake.

It's a man-made lake, so it's true that as the dam was built, water filled in and submerged parts of Tohickon Village during its creation, taking a lot of history and heartache with it. A real Indian cave is submerged, perhaps even with relics that had not yet been discovered, along with other structures, such as a local bridge.

The depiction of the lake I wrote is nearly entirely true, including the weed area near the dam. There is no mechanical room, however, as described during Jenny's challenge in the weeds. As an aside, a guy I know named Kenny Magee, helped create the mountain bike paths surrounding the lake.

## Van Sant Historical Airfield

This is one of my favorite places in Upper Bucks County. It's tranquil and peaceful and they sponsor great events. My husband and I even went camping aside the airfield after watching a movie under the stars. Van Sant offers a variety of air rides and they host many events, like air balloon launches and antique car events.

## Lenape Indian History

The Delaware Leni Lenape Indians were first! That is a fact. Much of the area around Bucks County has Lenape names, including Lake Nockamixon, which means "place of soft soil" in their native language. The area is sacred by their terms, especially the many waterways and creeks.

It's unfortunately true that the Lenape Indians were driven out of the area by William Penn's sons through the historically deceptive "Walking Purchase."

The Lenape Indians were/are quite peaceful and, as far as I know, didn't have any formal punishment system.

## Ringing Rocks Park

It's more than a big boulder field. Ringing Rocks is fun and a bit mysterious. When hit with a hammer, many of the rocks ring, much like a bell. These are called "live" rocks. Geologic scientists say it began about 200 million years ago, during the Triassic age, when Pennsylvania was part of the supercontinent Pangea. *Try and say that three times in a row.* The rocks are made of diabase, or "formed by fire." Scientists say the intense cooling that occurred later fractured the rock and created the bedrock. Rocks such as these are scattered all across Bucks County.

Truthfully, there is a lack of wildlife surrounding the ringing rocks boulder field. A magnetic field though—*I may have made that up.*

## Rosicrucian Orders

There are many Rosicrucian Orders throughout the world. There is even one in Upper Bucks County. You can see their beautiful rose garden, lodge, and several mystical pyramids from the road. Pretty cool!

## Mount Gilead A.M.E. Church

I graduated from Central Bucks High School East, about a mile from the historic black church that sits atop Buckingham Mountain. I know a thing or two about the folklore, but until somewhat recently, I didn't know the historical significance behind the church.

Mount Gilead was more than an African American church. It became part of the Underground Railroad, the last station before fugitive slaves crossed the Delaware River into New Jersey. The surrounding landowners were white Quaker abolitionists, who built cabins on the mountain to help the slaves escape. Famous fugitive, Benjamin "Big Ben" Jones (1800-1875), was among the slaves. A great movie to watch for more historical insight, *The North Star.*

Learn more about the non-fiction aspects of this novel series through the author's blog on her website:

www.heatherslawecki.com

# ABOUT THE AUTHOR

Heather Slawecki lived in four towns in Upper and Central Bucks County, Pennsylvania. One of her favorite homes was an old farmhouse similar to her main character's. She enjoyed the best of everything: Swimming in streams, tubing down the Delaware River, and riding her horse almost every day with her best friend.

Heather is a proud graduate of Central Bucks High School East and of Widener University where she holds a Bachelor of Arts Degree in English Literature.

She began her writing career as a feature writer for the *Bucks County Courier Times* and has spent the last twenty-five years as an award-winning senior copywriter.

Heather currently lives in Delaware with her husband, daughter and two playful kittens who hop on her keyboard every time she starts to type! In her spare time, she loves gardening, cooking, and volunteering.

Learn more about the non-fiction aspects of this novel series through the author's blog on her website:

www.heatherslawecki.com

Follow Heather on social media to learn about events, read her free blog, and find out about new releases:

facebook.com/graylynpress

twitter.com/HeatherSlawecki

instagram.com/heather_slawecki

## ALSO BY HEATHER SLAWECKI

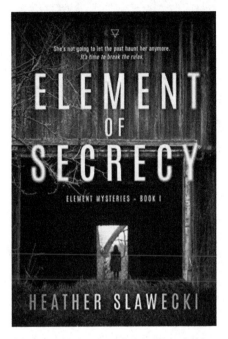

*Element of Secrecy, Book I of the Element Series*

Jenny O'Rourke has been haunted by blurred memories of the town's dark secrets for over twenty years. Brick walls and tight lips have kept her from understanding why she was torn from her home and family in the middle of the night. And why her brother's murder was brushed under the rug. To find the answers, she has to elude two powerful forces standing in her way ... an estranged but lurking father and the watchful eyes of the Witness Protection Program. She's about to break the only rule they have in common: Never go home. Jenny finds an opportunity, giving her access to everything she thought she ever wanted to know. What she discovers changes everything and leaves a small town in need of some major damage control.

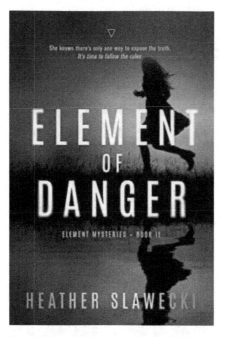

*Element of Danger, Book II of the Element Series*

A devastating murder brings Jenny O'Rourke back to her hometown. The reality is, it's not over. Not even close. This time she has a new strategy to put an end to it all—infiltrate her father's secret society. The question is, how? A chance meeting brings her face to face with a member of the inner circle, a boy she once knew. He has the intel she needs, and she has what he lustfully desires. It's a dangerous combination. Jenny finds herself swept away by the lure of adventure and the reveal of mysterious springs, sinkholes, submerged caverns, and elaborate underground dwellings. As she acquires a sliver of society knowledge, she's determined to understand the rest. But, there's only one barbaric way to get to it. Becoming one of them requires following their rules. Rules that could easily kill her. There's a lot at stake, but she's ready and willing to risk it all.